Hurt for Me

"*Hurt for Me* is a sensual, suspenseful, and sometimes terrifying walk through the secret chasms between what we tell people we want and what our hearts desire. After you turn the last page, you will be BEGGING for more from Heather Levy, the new voice of erotic thrillers."

—S. A. Cosby, bestselling author of *Razorblade Tears* and *Blacktop Wasteland*

"Visceral and authentic, *Hurt for Me* is a deliciously kinky thriller that subverts the tired, traditional power dynamics of the genre and centers the kind of women who are too often relegated to a sexy accessory."

—Christa Faust, author of *Hit Me* and the Edgar Award–nominated *Money Shot*

"*Hurt for Me* is a sizzling, expertly constructed thriller that doesn't cool down for even a second. Best of all, Levy gives us a main character, Rae, who is wholly original, richly imagined, and hugely appealing."

—Lou Berney, Edgar Award–winning author of *Dark Ride*

"Levy's latest grips you by the throat from page one and never lets up. It's a riveting, sexy, twisty mystery full of beautiful writing and characters you can't help but care about."

—Jess Lourey, Edgar Award–nominated author

"A damaged woman reclaims her power in this sharp and insightful thriller set in an original (and spicy) world. Heather Levy more than delivers on the intriguing premise of a dominatrix whose client goes missing, leading her into a shadowy world of secrets, cruelty, and corruption. A steamy page-turner."

—Robyn Harding, internationally bestselling author of
The Drowning Woman

"*Hurt for Me* is a sexy, nonstop thriller full of kink, fun, and murder. Both provocative and illuminating, Heather Levy nails it, or rather, paddles it. A must-read for anyone who likes their mysteries with a side of bondage."

—Amina Akhtar, author of *Kismet*

"A sweat-inducing dark romance wrapped in a thriller plot tight as bondage restraints, *Hurt for Me* will leave you hot for power couple Rae and Dayton, bothered by the infuriatingly realistic injustices they battle together, and begging for more from Heather Levy's brilliant mind."

—Layne Fargo, author of *Temper* and *They Never Learn*

"*Hurt for Me* is a steamy thrill ride with something for everyone: a dark, sexy romance, an exploration into the world of BDSM, a sharp, twisty thriller, and a hopeful exploration of the joy and power of chosen family. Rae Dixon is a heroine to root for!"

—Halley Sutton, author of *The Hurricane Blonde*

"Heather Levy's latest will have you gasping one minute and hollering the next thanks to whip-smart prose and a protagonist who will fight like hell to keep the past from threatening her present."

—Kelly J. Ford, Anthony-nominated author of *Real Bad Things*

"*Hurt for Me* is a raw, visceral, unforgettable novel that honestly and openly portrays the kink community while delivering a knockout of a thriller. Heather Levy's talent seems effortless as she beautifully weaves an emotional, suspenseful, hypnotizing story about a fierce, admirable heroine who has to confront her mistakes when her past and present come face-to-face. A tale of love, sex, murder, and redemption, this powerhouse of a book needs to be on everyone's must-read list."

—Samantha M. Bailey, *USA Today* and #1 international bestselling author of *Woman on the Edge* and *Watch Out for Her*

Walking Through Needles

"A spellbinding novel at the nexus of power, desire, and abuse that portends a bright future."

—*New York Times*

"*Walking Through Needles* is a challenging but worthwhile read, a standout for its frank but sensitive exploration of trauma and desire."

—*Los Angeles Times*

"A gripping, disturbing read and, perhaps for some, triggering, but I couldn't turn away."

—*Star Tribune*

"An unflinchingly brutal and beautiful journey through the darkest rivers of desire."

—S. A. Cosby, bestselling author of *Razorblade Tears* and *Blacktop Wasteland*

HURT

FOR

ME

OTHER TITLES BY HEATHER LEVY

Walking Through Needles

HURT

FOR

ME

HEATHER LEVY

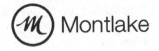 Montlake

Published by Montlake, Seattle

www.apub.com

Amazon, the Amazon logo, and Montlake are trademarks of Amazon.com, Inc., or its affiliates.

ISBN-13: 9781662516610 (paperback)
ISBN-13: 9781662516627 (digital)

Cover design by Ploy Siripant
Cover image: © indira's work / Shutterstock; © Cg_loser / Shutterstock

Printed in the United States of America

To all the kinksters, especially Christa

I suppose sooner or later in the life of everyone comes a moment of trial. We all of us have our particular devil who rides us and torments us, and we must give battle in the end.
—Daphne du Maurier, *Rebecca*

AUTHOR'S NOTE

Please note that this book covers some of the countless dangers facing sex workers today. It also includes discussions of abuse, sex trafficking and assault, kidnapping, and both consensual and nonconsensual BDSM. Care has been taken to depict these aspects in a sensitive manner.

Though this is a work of fiction, heinous crimes like this occur every day. If you or someone you know needs help or support, the National Human Trafficking Hotline is 888-373-7888. If you'd like to know how you can help fight human trafficking, visit the Polaris Project at www.polarisproject.org for more information.

CHAPTER 1

ECHO

2009

When you want something bad enough, you need to pay the consequence.
Echo could almost hear her mother's breathy voice saying the words as
she steered her cart through Ralph's grocery store, the wonky wheels
pushing her to the right as she tried to make a left into the vitamin aisle.

It was after eleven, and the only people in the store with Echo were
two workers who appeared to be around her age. She was nineteen and
had never had a job. Not a real one anyway. Clint wouldn't allow her
to apply anywhere, would call her stupid for even asking, so she never
pushed him on it because there was no point. It was always easier to do
what he said. Less painful that way.

Echo stopped in front of the wall of vitamins, her eyes roving until
she found the section she was looking for, the biggest reason for her to
be at a grocery store this late at night. She picked up a bottle and read
the back as if she would understand what any of it meant. There were
so many kinds, and she had no clue which one was the best.

She looked down at her abdomen. "What do you think?"

When you want something bad enough, you need to pay the consequence.

Her mother's words again. Echo ignored the tremor coursing through her body, making her legs as wobbly as the grocery cart's wheels. She rubbed her lower stomach, feeling the full weight of how uncertain life had been only a few hours before. How uncertain everything in her life had been for the last four years, even longer, if she was being honest with herself.

She couldn't hold it back any longer. She allowed the heavy knot in her chest to explode up into her throat, for tears to break free at last. It didn't feel freeing like she had hoped; it only made her more exhausted, so she made herself stop.

She still had so much farther to go. She threw the bottle of vitamins into her cart and rushed to collect the rest of what she needed: food that didn't require refrigeration, a refillable water bottle, hair dye, and a burner phone. She then stopped by the candy aisle to grab a family-size bag of Reese's Pieces, her favorite, because there was no one to tell her no. She already had a duffel bag she'd taken from Clint's house, which she had placed next to the ice machine near the front of the grocery store. She thought about how Clint kept his gym clothes in the bag, and she hated the thought of his sweaty residue getting onto her food and the few clothes she had taken with her.

It didn't matter. Being here, free to shop without anyone watching her every move—that's what mattered. She looked down at her abdomen again. This was all that mattered now.

Echo went to the only open checkout lane and placed her items on the conveyor belt. One of the young store employees reanimated from the corner where she was standing scrolling through her phone and slowly made her way over to Echo.

The green-haired cashier scanned every item as if she was angry she had to move. The only time she paused was when she picked up the vitamins.

"Prenatal, huh? How far along are you?" she asked Echo.

Echo tried to keep the shock from her face of being asked about the thing she'd been hiding. "Um, I think a couple of months." She wasn't sure since her period had always been unpredictable.

"You're so tiny. I bet you'll show early. That's how my sister was, like she was about to pop the whole time." The cashier scanned the vitamins and let out a hoot. "Thirty-two dollars? Shit, that's crazy."

Echo quickly calculated thirty-two dollars times maybe seven months, and the knot in her chest grew heavier.

"You'd think if the government really cared about babies, they'd make this shit cheaper, huh?"

Echo shrugged.

"I like your hair," the cashier said. "Is it real?"

"Yeah."

"If I had strawberry-blonde hair, I'd never dye it."

The first thing Echo planned to do was dye her hair, but she smiled and said nothing to the cashier. She needed to get out of there, find a motel for the night. She wished she had a car she could stay in, but she didn't own one, didn't even know how to drive, and she wasn't about to stay on the streets. They would easily find her.

As she handed the cashier the money, the young woman froze and stared at Echo's face like she was trying to work out a tricky math problem.

"Hey, you have something right here." The cashier pointed to her own lower cheek.

Ice filled Echo's head and trickled its way down her spine, making every muscle in her stiffen.

She quickly took her change and the paper bags filled with her groceries. She grabbed the duffel bag on her way out of the store. She wanted to run, but she made herself stop and turn around.

When she walked back into the store, she asked the cashier where the bathroom was.

Thankfully, the bathroom was empty. Echo looked at herself in the mirror, the dull fluorescent lights casting yellowish shadows over her pale face. She turned her head left and saw what the cashier had seen.

When you want something bad enough, you need to pay the consequence.

There, on her lower cheek, like a constellation of freckles, was dried blood.

CHAPTER 2

RAE

2024

Rae loved the smell of sweat first thing in the morning. It was better than fresh-brewed coffee, better than bacon frying in a well-seasoned iron skillet. It lit up all her senses like nothing else in the world.

There was something electric and primal about the smell of sweat, reminding her of an approaching coastal storm, of warm, gritty sand pushing up between her toes, salty wind whipping through her hair. It reminded her of endless, terrifying possibilities. She tried not to think about it so she wouldn't start shaking.

She had to focus on the sweaty, half-naked man in front of her.

Thomas Highsmith. He looked powerless kneeling on the floor at Rae's feet, which was exactly how she wanted him to feel. It's what he paid her a lot of money to do. During the day, Thomas was an executive accountant for one of the big oil and gas companies, the kind that supposedly kept Oklahoma City at the forefront of growth and opportunity even as the prisons filled with people convicted of minor drug offenses and public schools crumbled and closed from lack of funding.

Rae thought of the insane amount she'd spent on school supplies throughout the year for Lily's high school education, and she thought about giving Thomas a good kick in the ass with her black thigh-high patent leather boot.

As if he could read her mind, he looked her in the eyes for a brief second before staring back down at his hands clasped on his lap.

"We're done. Get up."

Thomas already knew they were finished because she had ended the session with the crop, as he had wanted, yet he didn't move, which sent a flicker of alarm up Rae's spine. She kept her face calm, indifferent, but she was worried about him. Not about what he might do to her. She trusted him as much as she trusted any of her clients. Without mutual trust, she wouldn't have a business. No, this worry was different. Thomas had been increasingly distracted over their last sessions, like something was preventing him from relaxing into the pain and allowing her to help him break through his mental barriers.

She swatted Thomas's back lightly—a gentle warning—with her leather crop. He finally moved a little, slowly, until he was standing. She allowed herself a moment to appreciate the red marks she'd made with the cane and crop across the fair skin of his backside and upper thighs. No matter how many clients she had or sessions she'd done over the years, seeing the marks of her handiwork always stirred pleasurable warmth between her thighs.

Thomas was standing there like a lost child waiting for his mama to tell him what to do, which wasn't like him. Rae held back a sigh. She had less than thirty minutes to prepare for her next client, but she knew she needed to address whatever it was that was bothering him.

She hadn't done much damage to warrant extended aftercare, and Thomas wasn't much for coddling anyway. She got a bottle of sparkling water, something she offered to all her clients, from the room's minifridge.

"Go ahead and get dressed."

She avoided watching Thomas tugging on his clothing, mainly because she didn't need a client getting the wrong idea, but it was hard not to look. He wasn't like her typical clients, who were mostly older, richer, and a lot less attractive. Thomas was thirty-three, a couple of years younger than her, and he was exactly her type—tall with dark, unruly hair and soft brown eyes that made him appear innocent when she knew he was anything but. She mentally slapped herself and refocused on finding out what was going on with him.

He pulled on his blue button-up, and Rae handed him the bottled water. He looked around at the large space, his eyes traveling across the room to the royal-purple accent wall and the black wooden X of the Saint Andrew's cross, which he had been tied to minutes before. He stared down at the bottle in his hand, and Rae knew the apprehension on his face wasn't from anything she had inflicted upon him over the last hour. Or maybe she had been a bit rougher with him and hadn't realized it. It'd been a difficult morning with Lily dragging ass, almost making Rae late opening the shop.

"We can remove the crop from our sessions if it's too much," she said as a way to open the conversation.

Whatever was bothering Thomas, he seemed to shake it off as he set the unopened water on the spank bench next to them and zipped up his slacks.

"No, it wasn't too much, Mistress V." He smiled a little. "I've just got an important meeting tonight at the Skirvin and—" His face dropped. "Never mind. You don't want to hear about this boring stuff."

Rae gave him no indication she cared either way, although she was used to hearing all about boring stuff. Some of her clients, especially the older guys, seemed to forget they paid her to beat them, not drone on for hours about their business dealings.

Thomas stopped buttoning his shirt when he caught Rae staring at his well-toned chest. She quickly shifted her eyes up to his face.

She played it off well and placed her hand on his shoulder, felt his muscles twitch from her touch. "Thomas, I've been sensing some . . . resistance during our last few sessions. I want to help you reach your goals, but that can only happen if we're both honest with each other." She knew he wanted to reach subspace, the blissful state of mind most masochists hope to achieve. "If we're going too fast or doing too much, I need you to let me know."

Thomas appeared surprised. "You could never do too much to me, Mistress."

Rae removed her hand from him. "In that case, we can increase the intensity, maybe add more whipping or perhaps foot torture with a misery stick. That way you can feel it all day at work as you walk around." She smiled at him, ready to see a gleam in his eye at her suggestion, but he only shrugged a little.

"Mistress," he said as if something just occurred to him, "I know I'm not supposed to ask this, but would you like to get a drink sometime?"

His question came out of nowhere, but she didn't allow it to throw her off.

She caught him staring at her breasts pushing up from her tight black corset, and the sudden confidence on his face made her feel ill.

"I don't interact with clients outside of the dungeon. You know this from our signed agreement."

"I know, Mistress V, but I've been seeing you every week for the last six months. Think of how much fun we could have outside of this room. No regulations you have to follow, no limits. You could do whatever you want to me, and then I could be in the right headspace." He paused. "I know this place that has big parties with no rules, no safe words, and I thought you could come with me and—"

"No, Thomas. No play outside of this room. And if you don't want to comply with our agreement, I can easily release you from my services." Rae motioned to the door. "It's time for you to leave now."

Thomas slipped his shoes on, his expression hurt.

Before leaving the room, he turned to Rae and said, "I apologize, Mistress. I won't bring it up again. I'll see you next week?"

Rae nodded, shut the door behind him, and blew out a long exhalation. What the hell was getting into Thomas, one of her best, most acquiescent clients? It was true that some of her past clients had expected a happy ending to their pain sessions, something beyond illegal in Oklahoma and pretty much everywhere else. There were no happy endings, no sex at all. Her clients could get fully undressed, if she allowed it, but there was no touching beyond placing them in various forms of bondage and during aftercare. Of course, erections happened, and she did her best to ignore them, although many of her clients enjoyed her making fun of their cocks.

She supposed it was an easy assumption for some of her new clients to expect sex. After all, her true work was cloaked in the guise of an exclusive spa, her dungeon space in the back of the business she ran with her best friend, Angel Paisley. If it weren't for Rae's daughter and all the unwanted attention it could place on them both, she wouldn't hide what she really did for a living. There was nothing wrong with it or any other kind of sex work, in her view, as long as it was between consenting adults. In many ways, her work saved her life.

She thought of how Thomas had looked at her, not with his normal respect but with covetous eyes as if he could own her, and her hands curled into tight fists.

Next time she saw him, she'd have her favorite purple whip ready. And this time, he'd find subspace, and the marks she made would last for weeks.

◆ ◆ ◆

"About time," Lily huffed out, her backpack slung over her right shoulder.

"I'm actually earlier than what I texted you," Rae said. Her last client was late, and she'd almost had him reschedule, but she also had Lily's braces to pay off, so she'd seen him anyway.

Lily plopped into the passenger seat. Like Rae, she was petite and fair skinned, but Lily had brown eyes that blazed like warm brandy in the sun and hair the color of burnt sugar. Rae's hair had grown darker over the years, but in the sunlight, it was still a rose blonde.

"You know Gabby can drive me home," Lily said as she buckled her seat belt. "You don't have to get me every day."

"Gabby's only had her license for a month."

"So? She's a good driver."

Rae doubted that. From the time she had first met Gabby, when Lily started high school the year before, she hadn't been a fan. The girl was rich and liked to throw her privilege around, talking down to adults and her friends like she owned the world. She tolerated Gabby because she knew outright hating her in front of Lily would only drive her daughter to hang out with the girl more than she already did.

"I'm sure she is, honey, but she's also a new driver." Rae glanced at Lily next to her. "Plus, if I didn't take you and pick you up from school, I doubt I'd ever see you."

"That's so not true, Mom. Besides, what will you do when I get my license in the fall?"

"Lock you in your room until you're thirty?"

They both laughed, and Rae almost felt relief. Her daughter was still hers. For now.

They pulled into their neighborhood, which was a few miles away from the high school. It was an older neighborhood, most of the houses single-story Cape Cods or in the two-story Tudor revival style like Rae's. The homes were old enough to be desirable to investors but not too old to deter young families looking to get into the magnet schools nearby. Rae loved it. She loved how people babied their lawns and checked on their elderly neighbors. Her house was the first she had ever owned, and she hoped it would be the last.

She had moved too much as a kid—even more as an adult—never in a place long enough to establish roots. Rae used to lie and say her dad was in the military to explain their constant moves to people. If there was one thing her dad wasn't, it was a military man. She never had an explanation ready for why her mother wasn't around.

Rae watched Lily lower the car window to wave at Klo, the neighborhood kid who lived across the street. They were the same age as Lily, had gone through elementary and middle school with her until Klo had come out as nonbinary in eighth grade and changed their pronouns. The schoolkids were relentless, and Klo's family moved them to homeschooling to avoid the bullying. Rae missed Lily hanging with Klo as much as they did when they were younger and hearing their easy banter and laughter, although Klo did sometimes come over for dinner.

"I'm making tacos tonight, Klo," Rae said as she exited her car. "You're welcome to join us."

Lily and Klo exchanged a look Rae couldn't decipher, like a secret language of smirks only they understood.

"No, thank you, Miss Dixon. My grandma's eating with us tonight."

"Maybe next time, then."

Lily followed Rae inside, petting their black cat, Iris, and dumping her bag by the door before racing upstairs to her room.

"Hey, Missy! There are hooks in the entryway for a reason!" Rae yelled as she hung up the backpack.

While she browned some ground beef, Iris rubbing against her legs, Rae checked for any messages on the kink-community sites she was a part of. One discussion thread immediately stood out to her: MISSING SUB. She pulled up the thread and learned a young woman, a submissive who was apparently new to the community, had been reported missing by her roommate, who was also a part of the kink group. The roommate had reported it to the police, but they had done nothing about it so far.

An uneasiness settled in Rae's stomach, but she shook it off. It wasn't completely unheard of for there to be bad actors within the kink community, especially after popular books and films like the laughable Fifty Shades series increased interest in BDSM. In truth, there were as many women under the delusion that they could be a submissive to a billionaire as there were asshole men who preyed on the vulnerable women obsessed with the fantasy. Rae only hoped the missing woman was off having a consensual escape into bad sex with a faux Dom before reality set in.

The unease spiked again as Rae stirred the meat in the skillet, memories trying to erupt. She knew all too well how easy it was to slip through the cracks of society, never to be heard from again.

CHAPTER 3

ECHO

2009

Echo woke up in the motel room with a horrible kink in her neck. For a moment, she forgot where she was or how she'd gotten there. She stared at the mauve-and-teal curtains pulled tight, the sun fighting to break into the tiny room, and remembered how she'd tossed and turned all night, scared someone would try to bust down the door. She held back the tears wanting to resurface. She had cried herself to sleep shortly after paying for the room in cash, and her eyes felt gummy and swollen.

The room, thank God, had a single-serve coffee maker and two mugs, so she brewed herself a cup so she could take one of the prenatal vitamins. She then ran the coffee maker again to get hot water. She mixed one of the packets of instant apple-cinnamon oatmeal she had bought at the store in the other mug and sat on the edge of the bed to eat since there was no table in the room.

Echo was afraid to turn on the TV. She didn't want to accidentally see the news, the possibility of her face splashed onto the screen, although she knew she was being paranoid. There would be nothing on the news about Clint, or Bobby, or anything that had happened. There would be nothing reported, because to the outside world, Echo Phalin was just another teen runaway, now an adult, gone for four long years with no one searching for her.

Especially not her mother. And her dad?

She swallowed a bite of oatmeal, forced it down over the swell in her throat. Thoughts of her dad always made her think of the time before her mother left them, when Echo was about to turn fourteen. He was so different then. A wide smile perpetually brightened his face, his blue eyes always sparkling with a new dad joke he was itching to tell her. *Hey, lil bunny, what kind of tree can fit in one hand?* He wouldn't even wait for her answer. *A palm tree!*

He kept Echo laughing however he could, even when things with her mother got worse, her absences from the house growing longer and longer until one day she took all her things and never came home.

Then, it was like a switch turned off in him, and everything went dark. No more jokes, no more watching B horror films on the weekend with a giant bowl of popcorn mixed with Reese's Pieces between them on the couch. No more impromptu picnics at the park or feeding the ducks and geese at the big pond close to where they lived, the same pond they once tried to skate on one winter. They had just watched *Little Women* together, the version with Winona Ryder, and Echo had wanted nothing more than to ice-skate on a pond just like in the scene with Jo and Laurie, but without falling through the ice like Amy's character. Her dad had inched out onto the ice about two feet from the pond's shoreline when they both heard the cracking. He scrambled back to her, failing to keep the disappointment from his face. She knew how he hated to let her down in any way, and she never knew how to assure him he wasn't, so she tried to lighten the mood by starting a snowball fight.

But after her mother left, her dad could no longer keep up the charade of everything being okay. Echo started noticing the pill bottles on her dad's nightstand—pain medications for ailments she didn't know he had. He didn't show signs of having an injury, yet the bottles became a constant, and then they disappeared. She thought the dark days were coming to an end and her happy dad would come back, but that was when she discovered the syringe. Echo had tried to help more with the chores to ease her dad's burden, so she had washed and folded the laundry and was putting her dad's clothes away when she found it in an empty cigarette carton her dad had hidden in his sock drawer. She hadn't even known he'd smoked.

She had wanted to confront him about it, but she was too scared he'd get mad at her for prying into his things and leave her like her mother did. So many times, she wished she had said something. If she had, she probably wouldn't be in a shitty motel room, alone and pregnant with no place to run.

Except, she did maybe have a place to go, but it would mean making the hardest call of her life.

She finished her oatmeal and coffee, both now cold, and took out the burner phone she'd bought the night before. She glanced at the clock on the nightstand: 8:19 a.m., so two hours ahead in Oklahoma. It was Saturday, and she hoped that increased the chance of someone answering.

Slowly, she pushed the ten digits she had memorized. Echo was sure it wasn't the right number after the line rang for the third time. Maybe she had a digit off, or maybe it was someone else's number now, but then a groggy, familiar voice answered.

"Hello?"

"Mom?"

A pause. "Who is this?"

"It's . . . it's me. Echo."

Another pause, so long Echo thought the line disconnected. "Why are you calling? How did you get this number?"

She had used an online white pages search to find her mother's new number and address. It was during her computer-technology class before she'd dropped out of school her sophomore year.

"Mom, I . . . I need help."

"Why don't you call your father?"

Echo closed her eyes, swallowed hard as tears wet her lips. "He d-died. Don't you remember?"

"Oh . . . of course. I remember. Your call woke me up." Her mother let out a long sigh. "So, what do you need from me?"

"I'm in trouble."

"Is it because of that drug dealer?"

Her mother had met Clint only one time, during a brief lunch, shortly after Echo's dad had died four years before. Echo somehow thought her mother would magically change after their lunch, that she'd hold her and tell her she'd take care of her now with her dad gone. But, during their meal at Braum's, her mother only stared at Clint's tattoo sleeves and low-slung jeans, the huge diamond stud in his left ear. As they were leaving the place, her mother pulled her aside and said, "You can't live with me, but if you go with him, you'll end up dead."

"Are you still with him?" her mom asked now, pulling Echo from her memory.

"I left him."

"Are you pregnant?"

Echo thought about lying, but it wouldn't matter. "Yes."

"Well then."

She waited for her mother to say more, and when she didn't, Echo's voice sounded small as she asked, "Mama? Can I stay with you? I'm in Santa Monica, but I have a little money. I can get to Sapulpa if you can send me more."

"I'm not in Sapulpa now."

"Where then? If you can't send money, I can get rides there."

"Listen, Echo, I can't. I can't take you in."

"Why not?"

"I just can't."

"But why?"

But then she heard a little girl's whining voice on the other end of the line, her mother's hushed "In a minute, honey," and she knew.

Her mother had moved on. Without her.

Echo hung up. She could still hear her mother's voice, the sudden shift from cold to warm when she spoke to the little girl, whoever she was—daughter, maybe stepdaughter. For a long time, she remained on the edge of the firm bed, completely numb.

She didn't have enough money to stay another night in the motel, so she packed up her things in the duffel bag and started walking toward the pier, the April sun warm on her face.

When she got too tired, she sat on a bench and ate a bag of Fritos, drinking some of her water as she watched tourists file on and off the boardwalk, the wild screams from the amusement park occasionally startling her.

As the sky began to fade from blinding blue into mottled pinks and purples, storm clouds in the distance inching closer, Echo walked to the shoreline. She took off her shoes and dug her feet deep into the cool sand as she searched the ocean waves for answers. Her stomach tightened with hunger, and fear reached a hand into her chest.

Whatever happens, she thought as she rubbed her abdomen, *I will never leave you.*

CHAPTER 4

RAE

2024

"How old were you when you first touched your tiny, disgusting cock?" Rae asked her client, a sixty-year-old CFO for a big local payroll company.

"Mistress V, I . . . I can't remember."

"No, you remember. Tell me the truth because I'll know if you're lying."

The client hung his head as if in shame. She enjoyed it when her older clients put on a show for her by delaying their own gratification. They were delaying hers as well. Her few younger clients were almost too eager to please her, but not as many of them enjoyed receiving the kind of pain she loved to inflict.

Rae lightly tapped the man's hairy ass with the heavy paddle she'd used on him, letting him know she was done with theatrics. It was near the end of their session, and she needed a quick way to wrap things up while still giving the client what he paid for.

"I'm sorry, Mistress. I was . . . I was eleven the first time."

"Eleven. See, was that so hard?" She lifted his head and forced him to look her in the eyes. "I'm feeling generous today. Would you prefer the paddle or the cane?"

She was already lifting the slender piece of bamboo when her client quickly said, "Cane, please, Mistress. Thank you."

Rae loved hearing the swooshing sound of the cane slicing through the air as she hit his rear end eleven times, her client loudly moaning with each strike.

She spent ten minutes on aftercare, which for this client meant wrapping him in a fluffy blanket she pulled from her towel warmer while telling him what a good boy he had been for her. Whatever kept them coming back to her, other than sex, of course, she was usually willing to do. She never judged what they enjoyed because she got as much pleasure out of inflicting what they desired. And she had been asked to do some fairly unusual play sessions over the years, like tying up a young man and popping inflated balloons next to his face and genitals. Or spitting in a woman's mouth until saliva ran down her chin (this after Rae declined to piss in the client's mouth when the woman begged her to). She wasn't into piss or scat play, but she knew plenty of fellow Dommes who were. Rae savored most of what her clients desired, especially when she got to use her favorite purple leather floggers or her black dragon-tail whip.

She only had one hard limit: no blood play. Too much cleanup involved. Plus, Oklahoma law stated that no person can consent to serious bodily injury or death, and cutting someone carried too much possibility of either for her comfort.

After her last client of the day had left her dungeon a happy camper, Rae disinfected the play space and changed into her "boring" clothes, as Angel called them. Angel was Swiffering the front lobby area, her long bright-magenta hair swaying as she moved back and forth in her cork-heeled wedges that made her towering frame that much taller. Angel had her AirPods in as she danced-cleaned, so Rae allowed herself a moment to admire her friend's green minidress gliding against her smooth brown skin, her legs the longest Rae had ever seen on a woman.

Once upon a time, they had tried the relationship thing. Rae had been lonely after so many years of being single and had never tried dating a woman, and Angel was getting out of an abusive long-term relationship, something they both had experience with. It didn't work out, but they remained friends, as they were always meant to be. Sisters, really. Angel had been her only family aside from Lily for such a long time, and Rae didn't want to mess that up.

They still needed to finish the ledgers for the month, and Rae had to make sure the booking reminders, all encrypted through a mail service, were emailed to clients before they closed for the weekend. Rae rarely worked on weekends, keeping the time free for whenever Lily decided to grace her with her presence.

Rae decided the floor was clean enough and swatted Angel's firm ass with her cupped hand.

"Girl, you fucking scared me!" Angel said as she whipped around to see Rae's smirk. She pulled out her AirPods and attempted to return the spank, but Rae dodged her.

"Come on. Let's get this shit done so we can get out of here."

"And then drinks at Ludivine?" Angel moved behind the front desk as Rae pulled up the ledgers so they could get them balanced.

"I can't tonight."

"You're no fun."

Rae bumped Angel's hip with her own. "My feet are killing me. And it's been a long week."

"What? Mr. Kick My Nuts Until They Bleed give you a hard time today? Or are your panties still twisted because your boy toy skipped this week?"

"Boy toy?"

"Hey, if I were into men, I'd be all over that white bread like hot butter."

Rae laughed. She knew Angel was referring to Thomas, who was undoubtedly her most attractive client.

"He didn't skip," Rae said, feeling the sting of disappointment again. "He just didn't show. No email, no call." And she couldn't wait until he dragged his butt back to her, asking for forgiveness. She might even have him purchase a few items off her wish list as punishment before she allowed him back.

"Maybe he found a hot girlfriend who's a sadist."

Rae snorted. "Or maybe he's the biggest pain slut and wants to see how far I'll go next time I see him."

"His funeral."

Rae smiled. "Okay, one drink. But not Ludivine. Too many clients hang out there. Let's do Oak & Ore."

"Fine."

Rae was about to get to work on the ledgers when she saw a tall, good-looking man with an olive complexion standing at the front entrance. They kept the door locked and only allowed clients inside once they were verified through their personalized code. The man, who was wearing a plaid button-up and a dark suit, wasn't a client, although she was already imagining what he would look like tied up and naked. She glanced at his left hand: no ring. He was clearly built, but she knew how to handle strong men. His face was slightly flushed from the unseasonably hot spring day, and his expression was all business.

He noticed the intercom by the door and pushed the button.

"Good afternoon, ladies," he said, his deep, authoritative voice raising alarm bells in Rae. "My name is Detective Dayton Clearwater, and I'm looking for the owner, Rae Dixon." He held up his badge.

Rae pushed the intercom button next to the front desk. "We're both owners, but I'm Rae Dixon." She could feel Angel's worried eyes on her. "What can I do for you?"

"I need to come inside and ask you a few questions about one of your clients."

Rae moved from behind the desk and cracked the front door.

"I'm not at liberty to discuss anything about my clients."

He seemed taken aback by her words, his eyes narrowing for a second. "Well, then we'll have a serious problem."

The alarm bells got louder. "What is this regarding, Detective?"

"Ms. Dixon, we have reason to believe you were the last person to see Thomas Highsmith before he was reported missing."

CHAPTER 5

ECHO

2009

Echo went into a bathroom stall and counted the cash she had left. Just under $200. Not even close to being enough for food and a bus ticket back to Oklahoma.

She moved her hand in a slow circle over her abdomen.

She had wanted to avoid hitchhiking, but it looked like her only choice now. The bus ride from Santa Monica to the Los Angeles Greyhound station had taken a big chunk of the money she'd stolen from Clint. If she'd had more time when she'd left the house, she could've searched for his big stash. But she knew they'd be coming for her. The men who scared her worse than Clint. So, she'd taken what she could find, which was still more money than she had ever held in her life.

Echo left the bathroom and sat on one of the benches. She glanced around at the crowded bus station, examined the faces of other people who looked just as desperate to get out of there. She noticed the people waiting for their bus departures tended to ignore her the same way they pretended the homeless people asking them for food or money didn't exist.

An elderly homeless man sat down next to Echo, and his entire body was shaking so much it felt like an earthquake rumbling under her thighs. She tried not to move away from him because she didn't want to be rude, but his body odor was overwhelming. For all she knew, she smelled just as bad after two days without a shower. She'd tried her best to wash up in the bus station bathroom, though.

The homeless man was mumbling to himself. He was so thin and didn't have many teeth left, and she could tell he was itching for something, maybe drugs or alcohol. He had the same tremor and wild-eyed look her dad used to get whenever he'd run out of pills.

Echo dug into her duffel bag. She had never done drugs willingly, but she knew the painful need of them, the horrible twisting in her stomach and being drenched in sweat for nights on end until Clint would give her another hit. And she'd welcomed it, the one thing that offered comfort, a way to drift off into oblivion and escape her body for a time. She couldn't help the homeless man with that problem, but she could offer him food. She picked out a package of mini blueberry muffins, something soft he could hopefully eat.

When she offered it to the man, he seemed to notice her for the first time. He grabbed the muffins without a word and shuffled off toward the back of the bus station.

All she could think about was how her dad could've ended up like the homeless man if he hadn't shot up heroin laced with something even worse—she never knew what for sure. She tried to push the image of finding her dad on the bed from her mind, the syringe still dangling from his arm, which was already bluish and cold.

"Excuse me," a woman's voice said.

Echo looked up from her lap. A curvy, raven-haired woman dressed like a 1940s pinup stood in front of her. She was the kind of woman

Echo used to see in some of the old movies her dad had loved to watch, and she guessed she was probably in her thirties.

"I don't mean to bother you, but I noticed you've been here for a long time by yourself." The woman smiled, her red lipstick bright against her straight, white teeth. "This isn't a safe place for a young woman to hang out."

Echo wasn't sure what to say. She didn't have money for a bus ticket, but she also didn't know how to approach someone for a free ride.

"Do you have someplace to go?"

Echo nodded, too nervous to speak.

When the woman leaned in closer, Echo jerked away from her. "Hon," the woman said in a quieter tone, "do you need help?"

Echo looked at the woman's face. She was beautiful, even more beautiful than Echo's mother. *Her mother.* Her mother, who'd abandoned her not once but twice.

She dropped her head into her hands, the tears bursting from her in heavy waves, her body quaking the bench beneath them. Strong arms pulled her into a sweet floral scent, a smell that reminded Echo of the wild honeysuckle she and her dad used to pick off their neighbor's fence when she was young. Pluck and suck, they'd call it, and she'd grab as many as she could, sucking the nectar from each tiny tube until the sun's heat wore her down.

"It's okay, hon," the woman said, stroking Echo's hair as she cried. "I promise I only want to help."

Echo pulled back, wiping her eyes. She paused, listening for some internal warning to go off. People don't simply help others without wanting something in return. But then she knew that wasn't exactly true since she'd tried to help the homeless man, knowing he had nothing to give her.

"My name is Vivien, but my friends call me Viv." She paused. "And you are?"

"Rae." Echo wasn't sure why she gave Viv her dad's middle name, but she didn't feel safe using her real name now. She pushed her hair behind her ears. "Why do you want to help me?"

Viv's dark eyes turned thoughtful for a moment as if she were somewhere else, far away from the bus station. She took Echo's hand in hers and smiled again. "Let's just say we gals have to watch out for each other. So, what do you say, Rae? Do you want to get out of here?"

"Where are you going?"

Viv motioned to her zebra-patterned suitcase next to the bench. "I'm heading back to my home in Albuquerque. Where are you trying to get to?"

Echo hesitated, unsure if she should tell Viv the truth, but then she didn't have any other good options. "I need to get to Oklahoma. Can you help me?"

Viv seemed to ponder it for a minute. "Well, you can stay with me until you figure things out. That sound okay?"

There were so many unknowns, like how Echo could earn money to get back to Oklahoma. She'd need to get a job. The thought of doing what she was forced to do before made her throat tighten with panic. Then there was the unknown of whether they'd follow her, the bad ones. Once they found out what she'd done, they would probably do anything to find her. Going with Viv could put the woman at risk, too, but she didn't have much choice.

She had to do whatever she needed to protect her baby. She almost told Viv about her pregnancy, but she feared the woman would change her mind about helping her if she knew.

Viv looked at the dainty silver watch on her slender wrist, a little frown playing on her lips. "The bus will be leaving soon."

"Okay. I'll go with you."

Viv popped up from the bench as if she'd been slapped with a burst of energy. She smoothed her knee-length red dress and grinned at Echo. "We better hurry our butts, then, and get you a bus ticket, Miss Rae."

CHAPTER 6

RAE

2024

Detective Dayton Clearwater was even more impressive up close, Rae decided. He was at least six feet tall, with a broad chest that strained against his button-up and dark, slightly tousled hair, as if he'd woken up, thrown some pomade on it, and called it good, which it was. He had asked to speak with her alone, so she took him to her private office, well aware that only a wall separated them from her dungeon space. The last thing she needed was for a detective to know about her business practices, especially one with intense dark eyes that seemed prepared to pierce through any bullshit and discover her secrets.

The more questions she answered, though, the more he dug, like he knew she was hiding something.

"So, Mr. Highsmith is a client at this . . . *spa*. Is that correct?" he asked Rae.

"For the last six months, like I already told you." Rae forced her hands to stay on top of her desk, although she had a sudden insatiable urge to bite her nails, something she hadn't done since she was a teenager.

Detective Clearwater wrote something down on his notepad. "And you said he missed his scheduled appointment this week. On Wednesday, is that right?"

"Yes. He's never missed before."

The detective looked up, his eyebrows raised in surprise. "Never? In six months?"

"No."

"You must give *really* good massages." He held eye contact with Rae, a slight dare in his expression.

"I do." Her voice held way more confidence than what she felt under his intimidating stare.

"You have an unusual number of male clients, Ms. Dixon."

Rae shifted in her chair. "Is that a question, Detective?"

"No."

She leaned back, her stomach filled with painful knots as she anticipated what he'd ask next.

Detective Clearwater rested his clasped hands on her desk. "I'm going to come right out and ask you, Ms. Dixon. Are you performing sex acts with your clients in exchange for money?"

"No, Detective, I don't, not that there's anything wrong with it. If cops stopped focusing on arresting sex workers and went after rapists, I'd feel a lot better about how my tax dollars are spent."

He appeared amused by her display of indignation. "I can't say I disagree, but $300 is an awful lot for one massage. Then again, I'm a government employee who can barely afford health insurance, so what do I know."

Rae offered him a tiny smirk. "People will spend a lot more than that for things that make them feel good. Especially these days."

His eyes continued to penetrate her. "Still, $300 a week for six months? That's quite a bit for an accountant to spend on self-care.

Pretty much a mortgage payment. And then he doesn't show up? Why do you think that is?"

"Like I told you before, I tried to contact him when he missed, but he hasn't responded."

"That's not what I asked."

"Detective, I have no idea why he was a no-show, but things happen. Work priorities, illnesses." She didn't enjoy being interrogated in her own office within the business she and Angel had worked for years to establish. "He simply didn't show. And you're only here questioning me because you saw my business as the last charge on his debit card? Is that normal procedure for a missing persons case?"

"It can be, Ms. Dixon."

Rae was getting tired of the questions, so she decided to lie to speed things along. "Well, I need to pick up my daughter from school soon. Are we almost done?"

Detective Clearwater's stiff demeanor abruptly shifted to being more relaxed. "How old is she?"

"Almost sixteen going on thirty-one."

He chuckled. "I hear that. Mine's fourteen, but she acts like I'm her kid sometimes. She even banned me from using TikTok after I posted a video of me doing some dance challenge."

"Well, the internet *is* forever." Rae grinned. "I once liked one of my daughter's Instagram posts, and she blocked me."

The detective returned her smile, and she felt oddly at ease with him. If they were in a much different situation, she might even enjoy getting a coffee with him. But he wasn't there to make friends with her. He was making her feel comfortable by design, waiting for her to slip up. Thankfully, everything she needed to hide from him had nothing to do with Thomas Highsmith.

The detective's face turned serious again. "Ms. Dixon, I know you're not a massage therapist."

Rae kept her face calm, the same as when one of her clients tested her patience. "My license, which you can see hanging up behind me, says otherwise. And I have it framed and posted everywhere I'm required to do so by law."

"I do see that," he said, pushing himself back into her guest chair. "But I also know two things can be true at once. I've heard rumors. About you."

Rae let loose a string of curses in her mind. She was so careful about her nondisclosure agreements, and she had plenty of ammunition if a client broke said agreement. But Detective Clearwater could be lying to trap her.

"I'd like you to show me the room where you gave Mr. Highsmith so many *massages*."

Rae's face turned numb as all the blood seemed to drain from her head. She could see the media frenzy now if the detective released information about her true livelihood. "I'm sorry, but I can't show you at the moment."

"Can't or won't?" He spoke each word like a tiny dagger aimed at her chest.

"It needs to be disinfected."

"Ms. Dixon, you can show me now, or I can get a search warrant. Whichever you prefer."

She sensed her secrets floating out from the darkest parts in her to the surface of her skin, imagined her veins spelling out everything she'd done in her past right up until this moment for the detective to see. Then she pictured Lily learning about it all through social media, the hurt on her daughter's face when she realized she'd been lied to her entire life.

"Detective, I don't have anything to do with Thomas Highsmith going missing. He had a massage with me on Wednesday of last week, and then he missed his scheduled appointment this week. Seeing my massage space won't change those facts."

He slightly nodded. "So, search warrant it is. Okay, Ms. Dixon." He stood up, his frame looming over her desk. "I was hoping you'd be more cooperative in helping us find one of your clients, but we can get information in other ways. Some ways you may not like. I'll see you again soon."

For a second, Rae wanted to yell for him to stop and turn around, that she'd show him the room and prove she had nothing to hide, but thoughts of Lily compelled her to stay quiet. After she heard the front entrance's chime go off, she let the rising panic in her chest consume her. She felt her past circle and then slam into her present like a bumper car, disorienting her, and she didn't know how to stop it.

She sensed Angel at her office doorway and looked up.

"Hey, Rae-Rae, you okay?" Angel asked.

"Of course." Rae forced a smile, her heart hammering away. "Listen, I'll do the books tomorrow. Let's go get that drink."

CHAPTER 7

RAE

2009

It was getting easier for her to answer to the name Rae. She wasn't Echo anymore. She could never be her again. And in a way, it was freeing to separate the old her from the new person she needed to become.

Viv made it easy for her to forget about Echo and everything that had happened in Santa Monica. Aside from her dad, Viv was the nicest person Rae had ever met, and not only because she allowed her to live in her home. She was kind in ways Rae had never experienced before, like when Viv offered to teach her how to drive.

As they had traveled by bus to Albuquerque, Viv mentioned that the public transportation in her city was okay but not great and how it'd be a good idea for Rae to save up for a used car. She told Rae she had a connection at a dealership and could get her a good deal, and she was shocked when Rae told her she didn't have a license and only had a little driving experience. After her dad had died, Rae had stopped obsessing over getting a car, and then Clint had swept her away to California in his old Mustang.

Now, the idea of driving meant more than fulfilling one of the many normal teenage milestones she had missed while she was with Clint. It meant better opportunities for work and maybe even getting her GED. It meant freedom.

She'd only been with Viv for three weeks, and Rae felt stronger than she had in four years. Maybe it was the good food Viv cooked for her every day, food she was teaching Rae how to make for herself. Or maybe it was taking the prenatal vitamins, something she hadn't been able to do when she was with Clint. She couldn't have let him know she was pregnant. For one, he would have assumed the baby was someone else's, even though he refused to use condoms with her. He used to demand the others wear one when they came to her room. But Clint didn't seem to know or care how the men would often remove them.

In her gut, Rae knew the baby was Clint's. It had been two months since one of the others had removed a condom with her when she realized she hadn't bled in at least four weeks.

She turned her head, watching Viv chopping carrots for the Japanese curry they were making together. Rae knew she'd start showing soon, but she was still scared to tell her new friend about the baby. Already, Rae had to use a hair band looped around her jeans button as a makeshift expander for her growing abdomen.

"Would you hand me the potatoes, hon?" Viv said, her eyes never wavering from the cutting board. Rae couldn't help noticing how adept Viv was at dicing the vegetables into perfectly even pieces.

"Did you use to work as a chef?"

Viv laughed. "Me? Heck no! But I did my fair share of shitty kitchen jobs before starting my business."

Three weeks of living in the same cozy condo together, and Rae still had no idea what Viv did at her home business while Rae worked a few day shifts during the week at a nearby Subway. She imagined Viv's work had something to do with makeup since she owned every beauty product known to mankind. But then she'd have to sell a lot of makeup to pay for her place, which looked like the after photo of an HGTV home-makeover show. When Rae had come out and asked her what she did for a living, Viv only shot her a coy smile and said, "Just a boring job that pays the bills."

They worked side by side as they listened to Viv's music, Björk's ethereal voice surrounding them as they cut, stirred, and simmered the vegetables until the entire condo smelled like the warm curry spices. While they ate at the round dining table, Rae noticed Viv glancing at her watch, the same dainty silver one she always wore. Viv once told her it was over a hundred years old.

"So, how's work been?" Viv said.

Rae swallowed her bite of curry, enjoying the subtle heat tingling her tongue. "It's not too bad. I picked up another shift for tomorrow."

"Won't be too long before we can check out my friend's dealership. Figure once you have about $5,000 saved up, we can find you a decent enough car that'll get you back to Oklahoma."

"With how little Subway pays, that'll be forever."

Viv reached across the table to pat Rae's hand. "I'll ask my friend to keep an eye out for solid cars under four thousand, but it might be a long shot." She shook her head. "Sometimes, I can't believe my first car was $700. It was a shit car, but it got me around. Everything's so expensive now."

Viv looked at her watch again.

Before Rae could ask her if she was late for something, Viv pushed away from the table. "Sorry, hon, but I've got an online business meeting I need to get ready for. Would you mind doing the dishes when you're done?"

"Sure."

A remote business meeting? On a Tuesday evening? For the first time since knowing Viv, faint alarm bells went off in Rae. She'd learned the hard way to always listen for them, but she wasn't sure why she was sensing them now. It's just that Viv had been so honest about everything else, and Rae didn't understand why she was being vague about her work.

Her first thought went straight to Clint, how she had known he dealt drugs when she'd met him in Oklahoma, but he'd assured her it was only weed, sometimes a little Adderall. But then it was so much more. And there was California, him planting all the ideas of her making it big as a singer in Los Angeles, maybe getting a recurring role on one of those Disney shows. She knew as soon as she entered the run-down apartment in Santa Monica that something wasn't right. It was the way Clint's friend, their roommate, ignored her completely while others who came over scanned her all over like she was a car they were looking to buy. Then Clint moved them to a house close to the pier, and Rae thought things would get better. That was when the girls started showing up. Young ones like her and some in their early twenties, in one day for a few weeks and then gone. She never knew where they went, except for the ones she didn't want to think about. And then the bad men came, and she knew Clint was no longer in charge.

Whatever Viv's business was, Rae knew it wasn't anything close to what Clint had been into. That was impossible.

Rae was in the middle of doing dishes when she heard knocking at the front door. She didn't want to bother Viv during her meeting, but she was also nervous about who could be at the door. She checked Viv's office, but she wasn't in there. She saw Viv's bedroom door was closed. Odd. The knocking started up again, making her heart somersault. Logically, she knew the bad men couldn't find her at Viv's house, but then the internet made everyone easy to find now. They might've found some way to track her to Albuquerque.

No. She was being stupid.

She went to the front door and looked out the peephole. It took her several seconds to figure out what she was seeing. A man wearing what looked like a dog collar stood outside the door. He had some kind of ball strapped into his mouth, and he was holding a bouquet of red roses.

What the hell?

The man knocked again, more insistent. Rae didn't have a choice; she would have to interrupt Viv's business meeting.

She softly knocked on Viv's bedroom door, but she didn't answer.

"Viv? There's someone at the door."

Nothing.

She tried to open the door, but it was locked.

"Viv?" she said louder. "There's a weird guy at the door."

Rae started knocking again, and the bedroom door cracked open. Viv's face poked out, and she was done up in full makeup, her dark hair swooped up into the 1940s style she once said was called victory rolls. She seemed fully annoyed.

"Did you say there's someone at the door? A guy?"

"Yeah," Rae said, her voice growing smaller. "He has . . . a ball thing in his mouth. Like it's strapped onto him."

Viv's face fell as she rolled her eyes. "Oh, fuck it all!"

She opened the door, revealing a mostly darkened room, except for a red light positioned to shine on her bed, which was in front of a large computer monitor. Rae could see a man's confused face on the computer screen, his nakedness apparent even from this far away.

Then she noticed how Viv was dressed: a red corset cinched her already tiny waist, and she wore thigh-high fishnet pantyhose secured with a garter belt.

Viv turned toward the computer screen and said, "Give me a minute, Shawn."

Rae felt like her tongue had enlarged by a hundred because she couldn't get any words out.

"I didn't mean for you to find out this way, hon," Viv said to Rae as she rushed past.

She watched Viv open the front door wide, apparently not caring one bit about being scantily dressed. Upon seeing her, the man fell to his knees, murmuring something Rae couldn't understand because of the ball in his mouth.

"I told you to stop coming to my home, Dean. We broke up—get over it!"

Viv slammed the door and locked it. She slowly turned around to face Rae, a sheepish smile on her face.

"And that, hon, is why you never date a client."

CHAPTER 8

RAE

2024

All weekend, Rae couldn't focus on anything. When Lily had asked if they could watch a movie together, a request so rare Rae felt like she'd seen a white owl fly past, she'd latched on to the opportunity. But as they sat hip to hip on the couch under their fluffiest throw blanket watching *You've Got Mail*, Rae could only think about Detective Clearwater's visit.

She didn't know why he was so focused on her with his investigation. And she wondered what rumors he had heard about her and who was spreading them. She thoroughly vetted all her clients, and she knew none were on the police force.

"Mom?"

Rae jumped a little, and Lily stared at her with concern.

"Did you just stroke out?" Lily said. "I asked you why the internet used to make that crazy shrieking sound like in the movie, and it was like your brain shut off."

Lily felt Rae's forehead, and she gently pushed her daughter's hand away.

"I'm not sick, silly. I'm tired."

Lily leaned into her and rested her head on Rae's shoulder. "Yeah, Angel told me you had a lot of clients this week when she took you home last night. She said that's why you were stressed out and drank too much. I mean, as much as I find drunk Mommy amusing, I don't want you to be stressing like that."

Rae draped her arm around Lily, pulling her closer. "Don't worry, honey. I didn't mean to drink that much—I'm just a lightweight. And I was only stressed because an order of essential oils didn't come in."

Lily looked dubious as she removed Rae's delicate silver watch and held it to her ear, something she often did when she was anxious, and Rae felt awful about lying to her.

She wished she could tell her daughter the truth about her work and the investigation of her missing client and about Lily's father and how Rae had no choice but to do the horrible things she had done to ensure that her baby girl lived. She couldn't. She knew Lily, knew her curious mind would make her search for her father. And when she discovered the truth? What then?

It was better to buoy her with lies than drown her in a truth that would crush her.

◆　◆　◆

By the time Tuesday rolled around, Rae's upper back was so tight with anxiety, she had trouble holding up her whip during her session with her midmorning client, a lanky CEO of an architecture firm she had tied to her Saint Andrew's cross, his back covered in lovely red welts.

She tried to rub out a sore muscle in her right shoulder as she assessed how her client was doing when she heard a banging at her dungeon door.

"Police! We have a warrant to search these premises," an officer called out. "Open this door."

Fuck, fuck, fuck.

Rae watched her client wiggle in his restraints as she heard Angel's frantic voice mixing with the yells from the police.

"What is this? A role-play thing?" her client said.

"Hold on, please!" Rae yelled as she worked to untie her client.

"Are we done already, Mistress?"

"Yes. Get dressed."

More banging on the door. Rae's rapid heart rate pounded away in her head as she helped her client gather his things, his expression a mixture of confusion and disappointment.

"Last chance! If you don't open this door right now, we'll bust it down."

"Okay, okay! I'm opening it!"

There was nothing she could do. Her stomach fell somewhere near her ass as she unlocked the door. Three officers swarmed inside, guns out and raised. Detective Dayton Clearwater entered last.

"Put your weapons down," he said to the officers, and they complied.

Her client stood there, halfway dressed, as the detective and the other officers took in the dungeon space. Rae could tell Detective Clearwater was surprised at what he was seeing, but he was trying his damnedest not to show it.

"You can finish getting dressed," he said to her client before turning to one of the officers. "Hold him in the lobby for questioning."

"But I didn't do anything illegal," the client said, sounding like he was about to cry, and Rae didn't blame him. "We didn't have sex. Tell them, Mistress."

"It's okay, James," Rae said. "I'll take care of this."

Detective Clearwater finally turned to face her, his expression back to being a mask of neutrality even as he avoided looking at her Domme outfit: thigh-high stiletto boots and a black latex bodysuit unzipped enough to show her ample cleavage.

"It seems we have a lot to discuss, Ms. Dixon."

CHAPTER 9

RAE

2009

Rae didn't know what to make of everything Viv was telling her about her work. After she had finished up with her online client, Viv poured a glass of wine for herself and a Coke for Rae, sat on the couch, and started talking a hundred miles per minute like she was afraid Rae would run out the door.

Rae didn't know anything about BDSM or what being a dominatrix involved, and she couldn't picture Viv doing the things she was describing to her.

"Listen, Rae, I know all this may be a shock for you, but it's not illegal."

Rae shook her head. "But don't your clients, I don't know . . . get off on it? How is that not illegal?"

"Please, sit down." Viv patted the couch cushion next to her, and Rae sat, arms crossed. "I don't have sex with any client, and I don't permit them to masturbate during sessions, but sometimes they come without meaning to, and I don't hold it against them." Viv seemed to weigh what she was trying to say. "Some people, and—yes, a lot of men—enjoy pain and being humiliated. Or they simply like servicing a dominant person. There are all types of submissives and masochists. And if they can't find a partner who's into it, they use my services."

Rae uncrossed her arms. "And you only see them online?"

"Now, yes. But I used to rent a space where many Dommes—that's what women Dominants are called—see clients in person. I made great money, but I was also losing a lot of it for the space rental. I learned I could make about the same amount through a website catering to people into kink, and it's less physically demanding on me."

Rae sank back into the couch, still confused.

"How did you get into it?"

Viv smiled a little. "I was young, like you, and desperate." A heaviness entered her eyes as she examined Rae's face. "My home life was . . . rough. I left home at sixteen and ended up getting into some bad things. And then I got into prostitution to pay for those bad things. It was dangerous work, and I got hurt a lot doing it, but I didn't know how to stop."

Viv exhaled as she closed her eyes. When she opened them again, Rae saw tears.

"It was the most difficult time in my life, until I met Frederick. He was a john—a customer—but he wasn't like anyone I'd had sex with before. For one, he didn't want sex. He wanted pain. And he wanted to help me get sober and off the streets because he saw something in me." Viv's expression turned reflective and faraway. "He paid for my rehab to get clean, and then he taught me how to safely cause him pain, which I did until he died eight years ago from pancreatic cancer. We were in what's called a 24/7 Dominant/sub relationship, and we loved each other completely. I don't think I'll ever know that kind of love again. Before he died, he gave me this." She caressed her vintage silver watch. "Said it'll remind me of his heart beating love for me."

Rae didn't know what to say, so she said, "I'm sorry."

Viv took Rae's hand, her palm so warm it felt like she was holding a flame. "Fred once said one person's pleasure is another person's power. And that's what he gave me—power. I was lost for so long, and he showed me how dominating someone was more than using a crop or tying someone up. It was about respect and honoring boundaries, things I didn't have much experience with until him. And he helped me shadow under a professional dominatrix, which was vital for my education."

"So, you like it?"

Viv smiled. "Yes. I love it. I look at myself as more of a therapist helping my clients through emotional roadblocks so they can live their best lives."

This fascinated Rae—the idea of finding empowerment through inflicting pain. She wondered if it was the same for the person on the receiving end.

"Would you . . . would you do it to me?" Rae said, her voice barely above a whisper, she was so nervous about the answer.

Viv's face lit up. "If that's truly what you want, I will. But I would need to know a few things first."

She asked Rae what she wanted to feel from the experience, what parts of her body made her feel sexy, what parts of her body she felt protective of, and a slew of other questions Rae would never think of being asked. After contemplating it for a few moments, she tried her best to respond, but some answers eluded her.

"I don't feel sexy at all, I guess. I've never thought about it."

"Well, Rae, I might be able to help you learn those things about yourself, but it will mean you being honest with me. I won't work with someone who's not committed to telling me exactly what they do or don't like. This is about you having control. I can help you discover things you might enjoy, but you must be vocal if you don't like something. Do you understand?"

There was a slight command to Viv's voice now, which elicited excitement in Rae.

"Yes, I understand," Rae said. "I would like to try it now."

"Okay." Viv stood up, her face stern yet kind at the same time. "Stand up and turn around."

Rae hesitated, but she complied.

"Take off your jeans, but keep your underwear on."

She did as she was told, and goose bumps rose all over her flesh.

"Now bend over the side of the couch with your hands clasped above your head."

Rae paused, worried about pressing her abdomen too hard and hurting the fetus growing in her. "Can I use a throw pillow?"

"Yes. But address me as Mistress. It's a sign of respect."

Rae positioned the pillow on the edge of the couch and leaned over, hands clasped and pressed into the cushion above her.

"I'm going to use my hand," Viv said. "I'm not going to hold back, but I want you to tell me if it's too much, okay?"

"Yes . . . Mistress."

The room was dead silent until Viv's hand met Rae's ass, the sound of the impact vibrating her body. Viv's hand made contact again. She had never been spanked before, never by her parents, but she had been hit more times than she could count when she was with Clint. And the other men . . . everything they did.

She started shaking all over, her body ice cold.

"How did that feel, Rae?"

She couldn't speak. It felt good but scary as well, like she would collapse if she allowed herself to relax too much into the pain.

"Rae?"

"I . . . I don't know."

Viv was quiet for a minute. "You can put your pants back on and sit down."

Rae obeyed, feeling embarrassed.

Viv sat on the couch next to her and took her hand. "Do you know why I stopped?"

Rae shook her head.

"Because you're not being honest with me, hon. That's how people get hurt, and I don't want to harm you." Viv paused for a beat. "And you've been hurt before. Badly. Am I right?"

Rae nodded, her eyes filling with tears.

"Tell me about it. What are you running away from?"

CHAPTER 10

RAE

2024

Rae supposed she should feel thankful Detective Clearwater allowed her to put on a robe over her black latex bodysuit before sitting her down right there in the dungeon on her long spank bench as another officer searched the space, for what she didn't know.

"Ms. Dixon, I really didn't want to resort to this," he said, his deep voice somehow sounding earnest as he moved a small cushioned stool to sit across from her.

"It sure seems like you did." Rae kept her arms tightly crossed over her chest, her eyes boring into the detective. "Like my client stated, there's nothing illegal going on here. As I'm sure you've figured out by now, I'm a dominatrix. I don't know what rumors you supposedly heard about me, but I'm sure they're wrong."

Detective Clearwater glanced around at the dungeon space again before turning back to her. "You've got me there. This," he said, motioning to the room, "is not what I expected, but it doesn't change the fact that you were most likely the last person to see Thomas Highsmith before he was reported missing."

Rae took a deep breath, willing her mouth not to drop a few f-bombs. "I don't know what to tell you. You can search my business, but you're not going to find him here."

"I don't expect to find him here, Ms. Dixon."

Rae threw up her hands. "Then what the hell do you want from me?"

"The truth." He leaned forward, resting his elbows on his thighs. "I want you to tell me anything you can remember about that last *massage* you had with Mr. Highsmith."

"Session," Rae said, her jaw set. "They're called sessions."

"Session then. I want to know how he was acting, if there was anything out of the ordinary about his behavior or anything he said to you."

Rae looked down at her hands, now clasped on her lap. She thought over that day again like she had a hundred times since the detective's first visit, but she couldn't remember anything too unusual. Except . . .

"He asked me out."

"Like on a date?" The detective began jotting down notes on a pad.

"Yes, but I reminded him I don't date clients, and he was fine with it."

"Was this before or after your session with him?"

"After." She remembered something else, but it was hard to explain to a nonkink person, and she couldn't tell if the detective was vanilla. She thought about explaining how Thomas wasn't reaching subspace during her time with him, how it was something they had been working on together and struggled with, but she didn't see how relaying the information would help the detective with the investigation. "There was something else. He . . . he was distracted. Like he was anxious about something. Not our session but something else."

This seemed to pique Detective Clearwater's interest, and he paused his note-taking. "Did he say anything about his work or what he was going to do after his session with you?"

Rae thought a moment before saying, "Yes. He said he had an important meeting at the Skirvin Hotel, but he didn't say anything else about it." Then she remembered something else she had forgotten before. "And when he asked me out, he mentioned knowing about these big play parties we could go to. I didn't ask him details about it, but I assumed he was talking about a kink party with sex involved, which, again, I made it clear to him I wasn't interested."

Only she had been. She hadn't had sex in months and hadn't dated anyone serious in years, but she knew it'd be the kiss of death to go out with a client.

The detective was furiously writing notes again, but he paused to look at her. "Have you ever heard of parties like that happening locally?"

"Of course. People have private parties all the time, including ones where there's sex involved, and there are private clubs where kinky people can play in front of others."

"But something about the parties he mentioned bothered you."

Rae disliked how perceptive and confident Detective Clearwater was, making statements when someone else would ask questions.

"What concerned you, Ms. Dixon?"

She didn't know why, but the old her, the young woman named Echo who had escaped so many years ago, hummed in her chest like a hive of bees about to be punched.

"He said there were no rules or safe words at the parties, and that's not how kink works. There are always safe words or other ways to communicate to prevent someone from getting harmed."

The detective's face turned grim. "Have you ever heard of parties like that happening in the kink community?"

"Never. Not ones I've been to anyway."

He rested his notepad on his thigh and sat up, reminding Rae of his height. "How did you get into this kind of . . . work?"

Rae crossed her arms again, this time because she felt inexplicably chilled. "I don't see the relevance of your question."

"Fair enough. That was my own curiosity," he said. "But I would like to know what you get out of this. I mean, besides money."

"I'd be lying if I said the money wasn't good, but we're also in the middle of a shitty economy, and I'm a single mom, so the money certainly helps. But what I really get out of it?" She thought of Viv, her old friend who had been so much more. "I guess some people's pleasure is another person's power."

Detective Clearwater's eyes narrowed. "That's an interesting way to put it. So, you get power from giving clients pain?"

"We both do, my clients and me. It's a power exchange." She looked him straight in the eyes. "And the endorphins you get from it can be better than the best sex."

Rae smiled to herself as the detective cleared his throat and appeared to mull that over. She tried to casually shift on the spank bench to give her lower back some relief. Her throbbing feet, still in thigh-high stiletto boots, felt like a can of biscuits left in a hot car, about to explode any second.

"We're going to need access to your client records, Ms. Dixon."

Rae shot up from the bench but quickly sat back down when pain stabbed through her feet. "Absolutely not. My clients' privacy is vital to my business. It would ruin me, not to mention what it could potentially do to my clients if their names were somehow leaked to the public."

"I understand your concern, but we need to know if we can connect any of your other clients to Thomas Highsmith. I promise we will be discreet about it."

Rae shook her head, which was starting to throb as much as her feet. "Detective Clearwater, I want to cooperate with your investigation, but not if there's even a minuscule chance of it affecting my business or family." She let out a grunt of frustration. "My daughter doesn't know what I do, and I have to keep it that way. So, no, I won't share my client records."

The detective sat for what seemed like a full minute, his eyes steadily focused on her as if he was waiting for her to change her mind. He looked around at the room and dismissed the officer who was still digging through her dungeon items.

It was just Detective Clearwater and her now, facing each other.

"Ms. Phalin, I don't think you have much choice."

His words, they punched her, and that humming, terrified girl in her chest, the hive of bees, broke free.

"What did you call me?" Her voice came out in a whisper.

"That is your real name, isn't it, before you changed it? Echo Phalin."

CHAPTER 11

RAE

2009

As she described the last four years of her life to Viv, Rae wasn't connected to her body. She was a spirit floating back in time, like in *A Christmas Carol* when Scrooge revisits his past, seeing but unable to change all the aspects of his life that plagued him.

She told Viv about her mom's affairs, the ones her mom didn't think Rae knew about, and how she had left Rae and her dad. She told her about her dad's addiction and his overdose, and she barely perceived Viv grasping her hand tight. When she told her about her mom refusing to help her leave California, Viv cursed under her breath.

But when she tried to explain why she was in California and everything that had happened with Clint and the bad men, it felt like she was conjuring evil to come find her. Yet, she told Viv everything. Well, almost everything.

She told her how Clint was the only offer of stability she had at the time, and how he had said he loved her and wanted to help her become a famous singer, something that seemed so idiotic to believe now. She was an okay singer at best, although she'd been better than anyone at her high school.

It was harder to stay disconnected from her body when she told Viv about the Santa Monica house, the one near the endless expanse of ocean that both enticed and frightened Rae the first time she saw it. It was less a house and more a prison, and she began shaking when she recalled the first time Clint had woken her from a dead sleep, his body heavy on hers as he forced himself into her. They'd had sex many times before then, but this was different. She told him she didn't want to, and he covered her mouth with his hand until he came. Then he pressed his mouth to her ear and said the thing that made her want to be dead like her dad: "This is what you're good for. Better get used to it."

She would never get used to it, not with Clint, not with the others he brought to the house. She cried so much, Clint complained about her turning off the men, said she was losing him money. That's when he held her down to inject her with a drug of some kind. She never knew what it was, but it made the world go fuzzy and dreamlike. It made her not care as much what her body did so long as her mind could wander. Eventually, she stopped fighting Clint on it and welcomed the drug hitting her system, washing away all the pain.

If it weren't for Beth, Rae might've stayed in that drug-induced stupor, not caring if she lived or died.

The first time she saw Beth at the house, she thought she must've been someone's daughter because she was so young. Unlike Rae with her rounded hips and full breasts, Beth was flat chested with a short, boyish frame. She used to ask Rae, her big blue eyes pleading, to braid her long white-blonde hair. As she braided, Rae soon learned the girl believed she was waiting for her aunt to pick her up to go live with her. When Rae asked her where her mom was, Beth said in the tiniest voice, "Mommy went to heaven." She couldn't bring herself to ask where her daddy was, but she did learn Beth's age. Nine.

"What happened to Beth, Rae?" Viv said, a quiver in her voice.

Rae kept her eyes focused on a large painting Viv had hanging next to the kiva fireplace hulking in the corner of the living room. It was of a dark-headed woman lazing on a chaise lounge, honeyed light dappling her skin, her face placid. When Rae was alone in the condo, she'd stretch her body on Viv's couch, imitating the pose and the woman's languid expression, wondering what it must feel like to have no cares in the world.

"Rae?"

Rae continued to look at the painting as she finally got the words out. "It was my fault."

"What was your fault, hon?"

She should've done something more to protect Beth, but she didn't know how. Beth had been in the house for a week, and she was getting restless. When she wasn't crying, asking when her aunt was coming for her, she was angry, throwing herself on the floor, kicking the walls, and screaming as loud as her little lungs allowed. Clint wasn't happy. The men who came in and out of the house weren't happy either.

So, Rae made the mistake of asking Clint when the aunt was going to arrive. "Never," he said as if she should already know.

"Why is she here, then?" Rae had asked, but she knew. "No, they can't. Not with her. She's only a little kid."

Clint shrugged. "Not up to me. I don't create the menu. I just pick up the ingredients."

Horror seeped in, taking over her body, and Rae shoved him hard. "No! I won't let you!"

He grabbed her shoulders and slammed her against the bedroom wall before getting right in her face, his nose touching hers. "Fucking bitch, it's not up to you! If some fuckers like tweens, it's not on me. I'm just waiting for her handler to get back to the States and get her ass out of here. But if she doesn't calm the fuck down real fast, we're going to have a big problem."

"How?" Rae said, her voice shaky with anger. "How can she ever calm down in this place?"

He released her and ran his hands through his dark hair and over his face before looking at her dead on. "You'll find out soon enough unless you can get her under control."

But how do you control a scared child? Rae once read an article about a man who'd gotten stuck climbing in a canyon. To get free, he used a dull pocketknife to slowly cut through the muscles and bones in his forearm. When Beth was in one of her rages, Rae imagined the girl rolling around on the living room floor, biting through her thin forearm like a trapped wild dog.

She tried to calm her, though. So many times by offering to play with her or doing her hair, but it didn't work. Rae was so focused on trying to keep Beth placated and quiet she realized she wasn't getting as many injections from Clint, which put her on edge and made it harder to be patient. And she needed all the patience with Beth, but the girl knew something bad was going on in the house. After two long weeks, she knew there was no aunt coming for her. And all hell broke loose.

It was a Saturday night, and Clint and some of his customers were watching a boxing match on pay-per-view. Beth had gone to the kitchen for a drink of water, and one of the men went to the fridge to grab another beer. Rae watched from the living room couch as the man began teasing Beth, blocking her from filling her glass at the sink, his hands reaching out to tickle her. She backed away from him, but he wrapped his arms around her waist and lifted her. Beth didn't waste one second. She screamed louder than Rae had ever heard a human yell and kicked, her little legs pumping up and down like pistons against the man's thighs until he dropped her on the floor.

Instead of running back to the smallest bedroom, where she had been watching a show on a little TV, Beth began picking up dishes in the kitchen sink and smashing them on the old linoleum floor.

Clint jumped up from the couch and disappeared down the hallway. When he came back to the kitchen, Beth was still smashing dishes,
Rae failing to calm her down. By the time Rae saw the syringe in Clint's
hand, it was too late. He jammed it into Beth's neck.

Rae caught Beth before she fell and gently laid her on the kitchen
floor. She did her best to push away the shards of broken glass and plates
surrounding them. She watched Beth, who was so still. Too still.

"What did you give her?" she said to Clint, who was back to sitting
on the couch.

"Same thing you all get. It's called shut-the-fuck-up juice." He
laughed, and some of the other men joined in.

Rae felt Beth's chest, which was moving slower and slower with
each shallow breath.

"You gave her too much. Look! She's not breathing right."

"Yeah, man," Bobby, Clint's partner said, "maybe you should check
on her."

Fear skipped across Clint's face, but he didn't immediately move
from the couch. When he finally came back over to the kitchen, he
knelt and touched Beth's wrist. Then he listened to her chest for a long
time and let out a succinct "Fuck."

"Oh, my God, hon," Viv said, bringing Rae back to the present.
Viv was crying with her, holding her on the couch. "You don't have to
tell me any more. It's okay . . . it's okay."

Rae was glad for it. Remembering Beth—it was like cutting her arm
off with a knife, like the climber trapped in the canyon—but she could
never escape all she should've done.

CHAPTER 12

RAE

2024

Rae poured herself more of the malbec that Angel brought over for Sunday dinner. They were quiet as they ate spaghetti across from each other, Lily oblivious to the heavy tension at the dining table.

Rae kept replaying Detective Clearwater's words in her head. Her old name had come out of his mouth, and she couldn't move her body once she heard it. She couldn't feel her swollen feet from working all day or her growing headache. She was like a ghost rising from the grave, a grave she thought she had dug so deep that no one would find her again.

The detective's expression had softened some as if he knew she was in shock. "Listen, I found out about your name change on my own, and I don't plan to share the information with anyone else. I can see you don't want that to happen. But I need your cooperation. I need your client records." When she said nothing, he added, "I promise you, no information will go beyond this investigation. Your daughter won't know. No one will know. Okay?"

And Rae had forced herself to nod.

Angel wasn't angry with Rae about releasing the client records to Detective Clearwater, but Rae knew she wasn't exactly happy about it. She was, after all, co-owner of their business, a business in jeopardy if the list of clients made it into the wrong hands. She didn't understand why Rae had given in so easily to the police, and Rae couldn't tell her. Angel knew most of Rae's past, but she didn't know about the parts that could place her in danger. Only one other person knew those parts of her life. She couldn't afford to make the same mistake again.

Rae gulped the second glass of red, welcoming the warmth down her throat and how it relaxed the tight muscles in her upper back. She rarely drank, although she did occasionally take a small dose of medical cannabis to help her sleep when her nightmares got too intense.

"Whoa, Mom, don't you have clients tomorrow?" Lily said, moving the wine bottle away from Rae, who was seriously eyeing it again.

"Last week was rough for your mom, and this week isn't looking much better." Angel lifted the wine bottle to pour herself more before offering some to Rae, who shook her head.

"Looks like Mom's not the only one who had it rough." Lily looked between them. "Did someone die or something? Y'all are acting so weird."

Rae plastered on a smile. "We're fine, honey. We've just had a lot of demanding clients lately."

"You can say that again." Angel raised her glass in a half salute and downed her wine.

"Is that why you still can't book Gabby's mom for a massage?" Lily asked.

Rae widened her eyes at Angel, who swallowed her bite of salad.

"Um, yes," Rae said. "We're booked into next year, but she should be on the wait list."

An indefinite wait list. Rae was still surprised her daughter had broken her rule about not giving out the spa's phone number. The business wasn't listed in any traditional sense. No one could easily look it up on Google, and it's not like they had it listed on Yelp. The business was advertised on kink sites only, yet Lily had given Gabby the spa's number for her mom, and now Rae and Angel had to deny the woman a booking when she called about every two months.

Sometimes, Rae wanted to give Angel the go ahead to book Gabby's mom just so she could watch the woman's face when she saw the dungeon and realized she wasn't getting a deep-tissue massage. Hell, maybe she wouldn't mind receiving the discipline she clearly never gave to her own disrespectful daughter, but Rae didn't need any more rumors floating around that could get back to Lily.

"Maybe you should open on Saturdays and hire a new massage therapist," Lily said, looking between her mom and Angel, her bite of spaghetti hovering over her plate. "Most spas are open on Saturdays, you know, and you do have a certain daughter who will be old enough to work soon. I could run the front for you."

"Absolutely not," Rae and Angel said in unison.

"Why not?"

Rae hated to see Lily's disappointment, but she had to keep those parts of her life separate. It wasn't about being ashamed of what she did. It was only to keep Lily from learning too much and asking questions Rae couldn't answer without endangering her.

"Honey, as much as I'd love for you to work at the spa, it's not possible. Our clients are rich snobs, and they would frown upon seeing a teenager at the front desk." Rae gave Lily a reassuring smile. "Besides, I thought you and Klo were going to apply at Shimmers."

Lily's face fell. "Gabby said they only pay minimum wage, and the snow cone syrup gets all over your hair and stains your clothes."

"And how would she know?"

"Her cousin worked there."

"Well, I made $5.15 per hour at my first job, and I survived," Rae said.

"Gabby said her dad might let us work at his law firm over the summer making copies and filing."

"That's the first I've heard about this. Besides, you're fifteen. You should be planning all the fun you'll have this summer, not pushing paperwork at some law firm."

Lily huffed out a dramatic sigh. "Whatever."

After dinner, Lily disappeared into her room, and Angel helped Rae clear the table.

"I don't even know this Gabby chick," Angel said, "but I kinda want to slap her."

"Right?"

Angel placed a stack of dirty plates on the kitchen counter. "So, have you heard anything from that detective?"

Rae set the sponge in her hand down and faced her best friend. "Not yet. And I know what you're going to say. That I should've waited for them to get a court order for the records, but it would've looked like we weren't cooperating. And you weren't in the room with him and his intimidation tactics."

"Exactly." Angel pushed a strand of her magenta-dyed hair behind her ear and crossed her arms. "I should've been a part of that discussion."

"You mean interrogation?"

Angel's face remained stern. "Call it whatever you want, Rae-Rae, but sometimes I think you forget we started this thing together."

Rae didn't forget. When she'd met Angel, she'd had a newborn, no job, and no rental history. But she had cash, and Angel, who was renting out her garage apartment at the time, took a chance on her. Over the course of many nights chatting on Angel's back deck, Rae slowly opened up about the life she'd had in California before coming back to Oklahoma. And Angel didn't judge her, didn't even bat her long lashes at hearing some of the most disturbing parts. But then Rae knew Angel's life had taken many dark turns too. Being a Black woman in a red state was dangerous enough. Being a Black lesbian meant always knowing your surroundings and any exits at all times.

Rae nodded. "You're right. You should've been in the room with me, but maybe it's better you weren't."

Angel raised her eyebrows.

"The detective knows I changed my name."

Angel shrugged. "It's not too hard to find out."

"I know," Rae said, "but why? How would me changing my name thirteen years ago have anything to do with his investigation?"

"Do you think he knows anything about when you were . . . you know . . ."

"Trafficked? I don't see how."

Rae had never formally reported it because reporting it meant an investigation into Clint, Bobby, and the other men, and she knew it was a rabbit hole that would never lead to justice because there never was justice for rape survivors like her. Only pity. Or worse—blame.

"Well, maybe he thinks you're cute and just wanted to find out more about your fine ass." Angel's grin spread to Rae's face.

"Oh, my God, hush!"

"Yeah, I could tell you thought he was hot shit."

"I'm serious!"

"So am I!"

Rae took the wet sponge from the countertop and aimed it at Angel, but Angel dodged it, grabbed it from the kitchen floor, and threw it back at Rae's head.

Angel held up her hands as Rae snatched up the sponge again and windmilled her arm like she was about to throw a pitch. "Truce! Truce!"

"Fine. But only if you help me with the rest of these dishes."

"Deal." Angel grinned again. "But I'm taking those leftovers with me."

Later, as Rae lay in bed reading, she couldn't stop thinking about Detective Clearwater and what else he might know of her past. Many people changed their names but not for the reasons she did.

She smiled in the soft lamplight of her room. Angel, always so damn perceptive. Rae wished she didn't find Detective Clearwater attractive, but she did. But just like with Thomas, she wouldn't allow it to distract her. She had to keep her family safe.

She was nearing the end of a juicy chapter in her book when her phone chimed. Reluctantly, she placed her bookmark and checked her phone. It was a notice from the local kink-community site she frequented the most. When she pulled up the site, she saw a post with about a hundred comments, and her stomach immediately cramped with anxiety:

ANOTHER SUB REPORTED MISSING

Two in less than three weeks.

She read a few of the comments, most complaining about the police doing the bare minimum. Another comment suggested the police were ignoring the reports because one of the missing women had an OnlyFans account and the other had a prior arrest and charge for prostitution.

Rae had a different opinion. She was sure if she dug into the histories of these young women, all under age twenty-three, she'd find vulnerable people with broken lives not dissimilar to how she used to be so long ago. She only hoped they were found before it was too late.

CHAPTER 13

RAE

2009

It had been a week since Rae had spilled a good chunk of her life history onto Viv, and instead of freaking out and kicking her out of her condo, Viv seemed even more determined to help her.

For one, her car-dealership friend let them know he'd gotten in a '95 Honda Civic with a questionable A/C and major hail damage that he would sell to Rae for a grand. Viv said it likely had more issues they didn't know about, but she'd have her mechanic friend check it out first. Then Viv told her she'd front her the money since Rae didn't have enough saved yet from her crappy fast-food job. Rae couldn't help but feel like she was doing nothing to deserve all the kindness Viv showed her. She had to contribute in some way, and she had an idea of how.

"I want you to teach me how to do what you do," Rae said to Viv as they watched an episode of *Top Chef*.

Viv paused the show with the TiVo remote and turned to face Rae. "Where is this coming from?"

Rae played with the hem of the soft cotton nightshirt Viv had given her. "I . . . I just feel like I'm not doing enough to help you. I mean, you're not even charging me rent, and you're so nice to me."

A sadness crossed Viv's face. "Hon, you do the dishes every day even when it's something we should both do, and you're constantly cleaning when there's nothing to clean. I mean, my allergies *are* definitely better since you've been here because dust doesn't stand a chance around you, but you don't need to do anything but focus on you right now."

"But I'm never going to earn enough money working at Subway to support myself. If you teach me how to do your type of work, I can do it anywhere. I can buy my own computer and earn enough money to pay you back for everything—the clothes you got me, the car, if your mechanic friend says it's good. Everything."

Viv reached out and touched Rae's cheek. "The clothes were gifts. And the car? Yes, you can pay back the portion I'm lending you, but if you can't, it's okay."

"But it's not okay." Rae felt her emotions rise to her face, knew tears would come if she didn't stop them. She found herself crying so much lately, whether at night in Viv's guest bedroom or as she walked home from work. "I don't deserve all this, and I don't understand why you'd do anything for someone you barely know."

Viv took Rae's hand. "I'm not doing any of this for only you, hon."

Rae's emotions lingered near the edge of a cliff as she waited for what Viv would say next.

"I'm doing it because you're pregnant and you need help."

And there it was. The waterworks she couldn't seem to control on full display.

"I'm so sorry," Rae said through tears. "I was going to tell you, but I was scared."

"It's okay." She squeezed Rae's hand. "I knew the first moment I saw you at the bus station."

"You did? How?"

Viv gave her a rueful smile. "Every time someone came near you, you'd cradle your stomach like this. Like you were protecting something. And you're taking prenatal vitamins."

"How—"

"I checked your duffel bag on the bus ride from California while you slept. And I'm not sorry about it. I had to make sure you weren't hiding drugs or anything else I didn't want in my home."

"Were you ever going to say anything?"

Viv pulled her throw blanket over her legs and leaned back into the couch. "I was going to if you didn't say anything this week."

"But . . . when you spanked me, weren't you worried it'd hurt the baby?"

"No, because I had no intention of doing anything else with you. I knew you weren't emotionally prepared for it anyway."

Rae brushed her tears away. "I wasn't."

"What we need to do now is get you to a Planned Parenthood."

Rae sat up straight and shook her head. "I'm going to keep it."

"Yeah, I assumed that much with the vitamins, hon. You know Planned Parenthood isn't only for abortion services, right? They can make sure you and your baby are healthy. I used them a lot before I was able to purchase my own health insurance."

This was all new to Rae. The way politicians and church leaders spoke in Oklahoma, you would think that all Planned Parenthood did was murder babies.

"Did you ever use them for an abortion?" she asked Viv.

"I did. Once. And I don't regret it." Her eyes had that faraway look she got whenever she talked about her past. "I was about your age, and I was too into drugs to even take care of myself at the time. I was lucky my aunt Cynthia helped me with it." She shook her head, smiling. "I'm sure she went to confessional a thousand times afterward."

"Didn't it make you sad to do it?"

Viv repositioned the throw blanket so it covered Rae's legs too. "No. I feel thankful I had the choice. And maybe someday I'll get the itch to have a kid but most likely not. I've never felt the desire."

"But you'd be an awesome mother." She wanted to tell Viv she was a better mom than her own had ever been.

"Thank you, hon, but being a mother is not the same as *wanting* to be a mother."

Rae's eyes filled again. She never knew if her mom desired to be a mother, but she had sure sounded like one to that unknown little girl Rae had heard during her phone call weeks prior. That day, Rae knew one truth: her mother didn't want to be a mom to her. And she would never understand why. As much as she dissected every interaction she ever had with her mother growing up, she could never pinpoint a reason why her mother didn't want her.

She looked at Viv. Beautiful Viv, with her full lips always ready to smile or laugh or sing some silly song as she taught Rae how to cook. Viv, who gave without any expectation.

"I wish you could be my mom."

"I'm too young to be your mom. But I could be your hot older sister." She playfully nudged Rae under the blanket, and they both laughed.

"I love you, Viv."

Viv's dark eyes grew misty. "I love you too."

Rae leaned over and hugged her. She couldn't get enough of feeling Viv's strong arms holding her close, and she inhaled the familiar floral sweetness of her perfume, hoping against hope the bad men would never find them.

CHAPTER 14

RAE

2024

By the time Rae dropped Lily off at school, the bright Monday morning was already hot enough to make her lower back wet with sweat, and they were barely into May. Luckily, her first client wasn't until ten, so she could freshen up before squeezing herself into her Domme outfit.

Angel was at the front desk looking over the day's schedule on the computer. Or at least that's what Rae thought she was doing until she saw her friend's face.

Angel didn't even look up from the monitor as she said, "Did you see it yet?"

"See what?" Rae dropped her purse on the counter, her stomach dropping with it.

"That motherfucker." Angel shook her head, blowing out a burst of air like she was a bull about to charge. "He leaked us to the media."

"What the fuck? Let me see." Rae rushed behind the desk and quickly read over the article Angel had pulled up, the title letting her know right away they were screwed: Investigators Question Local Dominatrix Over Missing Man.

They listed the business name, V-Love Massage, and named both her and Angel as possible suspects in the missing persons case for one Thomas Highsmith, executive accountant for Arkana Oil and Gas. It went on to state V-Love Massage was listed on popular kink sites like FetLife and The Cage for dominatrix services, but it didn't go into further details other than to say a source close to the investigation provided the information. The article was from a local news site, one of the small ones known for posting outlandish and possibly fake stories, but that didn't make it any better. Another site or the TV stations could pick it up and run with it.

"Rae-Rae, this isn't good."

"No shit." Rae read it again in case she'd missed anything.

"Kaylen sent me the link first thing this morning," Angel said. "You know I don't read that garbage site, but a ton of people do."

Rae glanced at her silver watch: almost nine. There was enough time before her first client. "I'm calling him. Care to join me in an ass-thrashing?"

"Love nothing better."

Rae pulled Detective Clearwater's business card from her wallet and dialed. Once the call was transferred to his line, Rae set the lioness free.

"Hey, asshole, thanks for leaking us to the press and probably destroying the business we took over a decade to build."

"Yeah, thanks a lot for running a woman-owned *and* person of color–owned business into the ground since there are so many in this godforsaken state," Angel added.

"Good morning to you too." Detective Clearwater sounded tired.

"So, I guess all that 'trust me' business was complete bullshit, huh?" Rae said.

"Look, I understand you're both upset, but I need you to lower your voices."

"Don't pull that patronizing shit with us," Rae said. "We'll be as loud as we want."

"Fine, but please let me explain." The detective paused as if waiting for them to interrupt. "One of the officers who attended the search of your premises did talk to a friend of his, a friend who happens to be a writer for the *Crimson Chronicle*, and the writer posted the article without permission. And, yes, before you ask, the officer is on administrative leave."

"He should be fired!" Angel said. "And you have to make the site take the article down."

"We're working on it."

"Do it faster," Rae said.

Rae and Angel looked at each other, their faces mirror images of trepidation.

The detective had the gall to audibly sigh. "Ms. Dixon, Ms. Paisley, I apologize for the breach, and I assure you both we're doing everything we can to mitigate any damage from the information that was leaked."

"Will you at least tell us if the article is correct?" Rae said. "Are we suspects?"

A few beats passed before Detective Clearwater spoke. "You're not *not* suspects, but that's the extent of what I can tell you."

Angel frowned at Rae. "I'm supposed to be drinking piña coladas in the Bahamas next month for the first vacation I've had in two years, so am I going to be arrested for leaving the country?"

"Let me put it this way, Ms. Paisley. As long as you haven't been charged, you can travel freely."

"Well, Detective," Rae said, trying to keep her voice calm, "it sure is nice to know our tax dollars are paying for such stellar investigative work. We'll just be twiddling our thumbs until you decide to harass us again."

"Ms. Dix—"

Angel smirked at her. "Rae-Rae, did you just hang up on Mr. Hot Detective?"

"Pretty certain there's no law against it."

Angel's expression turned somber again. "Are you going to say anything to Lily?"

Hearing her say it was like a jump-scare to Rae's heart. "No. I doubt anyone she knows reads that asinine site. Besides, we have enough damage control to worry about, and Mr. Diaper Pants will be here soon." She started pulling her strawberry-blonde hair back into the tight bun she usually wore for client sessions. "Will you please get his bottle warmed up?"

Angel pouted as she made her way to the small kitchen they had in the back. "I don't have enough coffee in my system for this shit."

Rae doubted there'd be enough coffee in the world to get through the hell they were certain to face.

CHAPTER 15

RAE

2009

It took two solid weeks of begging her, but Rae finally convinced Viv to teach her a little about her dominatrix work. Although she didn't outright say it, Viv seemed more open to the idea after she took Rae to her first prenatal-care visit, and they confirmed the fetus was okay.

Rae had felt like she was having an out-of-body experience watching the little blob on the ultrasound screen. She knew it was real, that she was pregnant long before the visit to Planned Parenthood, but hearing the rapid heartbeat of the fetus was a jolt of reality she didn't expect. Eleven weeks along. Dread speared through her at the thought of something taking over her body again. For so long, she hadn't had a say in what she did or did not do with her body, and now that she had the choice, she was suddenly torn. If she kept the pregnancy, everything in her life would be different. If she didn't, one of the biggest reasons for her having the strength to escape the house in California would be gone. And her chance to be a better mother than her own would be gone, too, at least for now.

All she could do was listen to her gut, the one thing she knew she could trust aside from Viv, and her gut said to keep it. So, she scheduled a follow-up visit and bought more prenatal vitamins with her meager earnings.

After Viv agreed to teach her, they both made time on a Saturday for the training, which was in the living room, the most spacious area in the condo. Viv had various instruments laid out on the coffee table, ready to go over each one with Rae.

"The first thing you need to know about BDSM is what's commonly referred to as SSC—safe, sane, and consensual," Viv said. "It's the cornerstone of what we do. Everything must be done in the safest way possible, all who participate must be of sound mind to consent, and all involved must consent before you do anything. Do you have questions about that?"

"No."

"The first aspect we'll go over is impact play. There are two basic categories of sensation with impact play." Viv held up a paddle that looked like the kind a person would play Ping-Pong with. "There's sting-y and thuddy. The bigger and wider the implement you use, like this paddle, the thuddier the sensation will be. But using something thin like this . . ." She held up a black leather whip Rae was sure could cause some major damage. "This is not only a stinging sensation. It can easily harm a person if you're not careful. And we never want to harm a person."

"But isn't that the whole point? To hurt them?" Rae said, thoroughly confused.

"Hurt, sure, if that's what they want. But never harm."

"What's the difference?"

"Hurt is temporary, but harm is long term. And harm can also go much deeper than physical pain. It can damage the psyche. Do you understand?"

Rae nodded. She knew that kind of pain.

"So, to recap, bigger, wider is a thuddy sensation, and smaller, thinner is a sting-y sensation. Some clients don't know what they like until you ask them questions first, and some will know exactly what they want and how much force they want you to use, which brings us to where you should strike on the body when doing impact play."

Viv picked out what looked like a riding crop from the coffee table. "Give me your hand."

Rae tentatively held out her hand, and Viv lightly but firmly tapped it with the crop.

"First, what sensation was that?"

"Sting-y."

"Correct," Viv said with a slight smile. "Now imagine if I would've hit your face with this."

Rae backed away from her.

"I said imagine. I would never use this on anyone's face because we never touch any part of the face or head with impact toys. We also avoid feet with certain toys, and calves, any major organs, particularly the kidneys on either side, the stomach, and the spine."

That sounded like most of the body to Rae. "Then where do you hit besides the butt?"

"Generally, the meatier the area of the body, the safer it is to hit during impact play. So, the upper back, buttocks, thighs, and you can do some light tapping of the breasts and genitals."

Genitals? She couldn't imagine using any of those tools on that area. One time when she was younger, she crashed her bike, her seat ramming hard into her pelvic bone, and she thought she would die from the pain.

Viv continued to go over each tool, and Rae saw the pleasure on her friend's face as she described her favorite implements to use on clients. But this brought up a big question.

"Viv, how do you use these when your clients are online?"

Viv cocked her hip as she drummed what looked like a slender piece of bamboo on her palm. "Most of my clients are online now, yes, but I still do play-party events and occasional in-person play for some of my old clients. As for what I do for my online clients, most of dominating someone is all in the mind."

"So, you what? Say mean things to them?"

"Sometimes, yes, I demean them. Sometimes I mother them if they're into age play. And, although I don't consider myself a findomme—meaning a Domme who demands money from their clients—I have a lot of clients who are into it."

Rae laughed. "Wait, are you serious? Men just give you money because you tell them to?"

A wicked grin spread across Viv's face. "Well, I am *very* persuasive."

Excitement fizzed throughout Rae's body when she thought of how much power she could wield once she learned how.

"Hon, I see the wheels turning in your pretty little head, but this isn't as simple as it may sound. It's the hardest but most rewarding work I've ever done, and it takes many, many hours of practice to get it right."

More than anything, Rae wanted to get it right. Before she'd dropped out of school, she'd been an honor roll student on track to go to college. Now, college seemed so far out of reach, and here she had an opportunity to earn money and make a life for herself and her child.

"I understand, Viv. I'll do the work, I promise."

Viv appraised her from head to toe. "I know you will, and I have no doubt you'll be successful. You're gorgeous, you're smart, and you listen. And listening is the most important aspect of this work I want you to learn. But it's not only about listening with your ears. It's listening with your eyes."

"You mean see how the person's reacting to what you're doing to them?"

"Exactly. Like right now I see you need to use the bathroom, so why don't we take a small break?"

Rae didn't know how Viv could tell, but she had to pee so bad. Again. She was urinating as much as her body was rapidly changing. Like everything in her life now, shifting to make room for another life to exist. For her own life to exist.

CHAPTER 16

RAE

2024

Somehow, Rae and Angel made it through the day without a single call or email from a client asking about the *Crimson Chronicle* article. Rae doubted it would stay that way, considering how fast it was spreading on the kink-community sites. Detective Clearwater may have been successful in getting the article removed from the site, but screenshots live forever.

By the time Rae drove over to Lily's school to get her, she was exhausted from putting out potential fires online in between clients. Living in a red state meant it didn't matter if BDSM practices were legal when between consenting adults. To some, it would always be considered deviant and disgusting, which meant many people had to keep their kinks private, lest their employer find a way to fire them. A lot of ultraconservatives even went so far as to suggest all members of the LGBTQ community were into BDSM and were actively grooming children. It was so ridiculous and false, but there were real ramifications to people believing those stories. Like how nearly every legislative session included a bill trying to make sodomy illegal for same-sex couples even after the Supreme Court decision on *Lawrence v. Texas*. If only legislators knew how many of their campaign donors begged Rae to peg them—something she wished she could do, but it clearly fell within the illegal realm of sex for money.

Rae forced those thoughts from her mind as she waited for Lily in the school's circle drive. When her daughter got into the passenger seat, Rae felt tension radiating from her, and she hoped against hope it was from getting a bad grade on a test or something shitty Gabby said to her.

"Hey, honey, you have a good day?"

Nothing. She glanced at Lily, saw her staring down at her cell phone.

After they drove the short distance to their neighborhood and pulled onto their street, Rae tried again. "How was your day?"

"It was . . . interesting."

Rae held in a breath until she gathered enough bravery to finally ask, "In what way?"

A long pause. "I think you know what way, Mom."

Rae's heart jackhammered in her chest.

"I guess that explains why you wouldn't book Gabby's mom."

"Lily, please let me explain—"

"So, it's true? What the article said?"

"How did you see it?" Rae said as she pulled into their driveway.

"Gabby showed me at lunch."

Of course, the teen tyrant would be the one to tell her daughter.

She parked the car in their driveway and turned toward Lily. "Honey, there's a lot of false information in that article, which is why it was removed from the site."

"Which part was false?"

The hope in Lily's eyes killed Rae. "Well . . . the part about Angel and me being suspects in the investigation, for one." Not exactly the truth, but there was no way the police could pin Thomas Highsmith's disappearance on them.

"What else?" Lily said.

Rae had spent nearly sixteen years hiding not only her work but most of her history from her daughter, and she knew the next words she said would destroy her baby girl. "There is nothing else. The rest of it . . . Lily, there's a lot I need to explain to you."

"Like what, Mom? How you lied to me this whole time? And now the whole school knows."

Rae had never seen Lily this angry before. Her sweet, mild-mannered girl's face was red, her mouth closed tight, and her eyes wide and tearful.

"Honey, please—"

"Fuck you!" Lily jumped out of the car, slamming the door as hard as she could.

Rae watched her run across the street toward Klo's house. Fine. She needed space, and Rae would give it to her, but it had hit her square in the chest to hear Lily curse at her, something she had never done.

Slowly, Rae made her way inside the house, Iris waiting for her at the front door. She stroked her black fur, and the cat circled around her legs. At least Iris wasn't angry at her.

She went to the kitchen and filled her teakettle, as if chamomile tea could possibly calm her nerves at this point. She checked her phone messages and was thankful no clients had canceled sessions. Not that it mattered too much since everything was paid in advance, but she was worried about clients stopping services altogether. Then she checked the kink-community sites again and saw a private message from one of her friends, Devon, a.k.a. Mistress Maven, a fellow Domme who worked at a local play dungeon on the weekends to pay off her student loan debt for her undergraduate degree while she worked on her master's. They never used their real names on the kink sites:

Hi V, I saw the link that was going around earlier today and read the article. I'm so sorry they
exposed you like that, but in a way I'm glad I saw
it. I need to talk with you in person if you're able.
It's important. I can meet up anytime. Tonight even.
Just let me know. XO MM

Hey M—I can meet you for a drink. Let's say
Picasso's at 6. See you soon. V

Rae sent a quick text over to Lily, doubtful she'd actually read it,
but she needed to let her know she was going out, and Lily would be
on her own for dinner unless she came home now. She was surprised
when Lily immediately texted back: Eating at Klo's.

Rae heated up a bowl of vegetable soup, but stress had killed her
appetite. She decided to down a mozzarella stick with her tea and bol-
stered herself for whatever Devon had to tell her.

CHAPTER 17

RAE

2009

Rae was so tired of hitting pillows with floggers and crops until her arms felt like overcooked noodles, but Viv said she needed more practice before moving on to an actual person. As much as Rae wanted to quit at times, a fire deep in her belly kept her determination up. And when Viv critiqued her, the fire in her grew, and she wanted nothing more than to prove her teacher wrong. She would do it until she was perfect.

"Action without intention is like a novice artist slapping clay around, making a mess of it like you are now," Viv once told her during a particularly grueling training session. "But if you put intention behind your commands, behind every impact on skin, that's when clay shapes into art. That's when you can create a masterpiece with a person's desires."

Rae tried to soak up the teachings, but it wasn't always easy with her pregnancy forcing her to acknowledge her body's and her mind's fatigue. She was fifteen weeks along now and showing much more. She didn't have any baby things yet, and she had thrown most of her money toward the prenatal visit and the used Honda Civic Viv helped her with.

Viv's mechanic friend said it would probably last another year or so without a new transmission, which was good enough for Rae. She had never had a car, and the amount of freedom it would give her made her light-headed. She still needed a license, though. She wished Viv were as patient at teaching her how to drive as she was with instructing her on dominatrix practices, but Viv's reluctance only made her work harder to get her license so she could drive the car herself.

Nearly everything in Rae's life was looking up, but she couldn't help worrying that something would come along to ruin it. Most nights, she'd wake up in Viv's guest room drenched in sweat, her heart pounding. Once, she even woke Viv up by screaming. Viv assured her she was okay, but that's because Viv didn't know what Rae did in California. She didn't know how certain people were likely still searching for Rae, which was why Rae only left the condo to go to work and to occasionally grab a few personal items at the small grocery store nearby.

Viv noticed her reluctance to leave the house, and she eventually stopped pushing Rae to come with her to meet up with friends. As much as Viv felt like a mother to Rae, she wasn't. Viv had her own life, and Rae didn't want to hold her friend back from enjoying it, even if it made her nervous on the nights Viv spent time with friends or attended play parties. During those times, Rae put her energy into her practice or reading one of the hundreds of books Viv had in her collection.

After so many weeks of the same routine, Rae felt safe, but she was also lonely. As if Viv could read her mind, she stopped eating the late Saturday lunch she had picked up for them and slapped the small kitchen island they were sitting at.

"We're going out tonight."

Rae swallowed her bite of chicken salad. "Um, I—"

"Nope, no excuses." Viv's dark eyes drilled into her. "You've been cooped up for too long, and you're coming with me to a play party tonight."

"Wait, what? Like a BDSM party?"

"You want to do this for a living, then you need to understand the lifestyle. And tonight's party is an open house, so nonmembers can attend as long as they're sponsored by a member."

Rae's anxiety sparked to life. "But I don't have anything to wear."

"We're close enough in size. You can wear something of mine—no corsets, of course. And we can disguise the baby bump if you want."

She thought about it. The party was private, and it's not like anyone there would recognize her. She told herself it was safe.

"Okay, I'm down."

"Great!"

◆ ◆ ◆

Later that July evening, Rae felt like a huge trussed turkey in the tight black latex dress Viv let her borrow along with a pair of shiny red boots and fishnet stockings. The dress had slight ruching, which helped to conceal her bump, but it didn't matter. She could've been wearing a potato sack and she'd still have felt like she was wearing a big flashing neon sign pointing to her belly. Trying to look sexy while pregnant seemed absurd, but Viv had fun making her over, hair and makeup included.

As they pulled up to the building housing the play party, Rae thought it looked like an insurance office space from the outside. The beige brick and darkened windows gave no indication of what was inside, which was vastly different from anything Rae could've imagined.

After Viv got them checked in at the reception area, the scantily dressed hostess took Viv's cell phone, then placed it in a bucket and handed her a ticket. They moved through heavy velvet curtains and entered the dungeon. The inside was filled with purple-and-red lighting, giving the open space the feel of a chic nightclub, and Depeche Mode pumped through hidden speakers, although no one was dancing.

It was overwhelming at first, seeing so many people in various stages of undress tied to cushioned benches and Saint Andrew's crosses, their Dominants spanking or flogging them. One older man was slowly being mummified in a corner by two young women gleefully dancing around him with duct tape. Another woman was standing and spread against a Saint Andrew's cross, naked, her back and rear end covered in welts from the whip a tall, bare-chested man brandished.

"Stay close to me," Viv said to her over the loud music. "And put this on." She handed Rae a purple rubber bracelet. "It lets the DM—the dungeon monitor who keeps an eye on people and makes sure everyone's safe—know you're new."

Rae slipped it on and looked around more, feeling like she had entered an alternate universe where age, race, body size, gender, and sexual orientation didn't matter; everyone there seemed to be completely in their element and not judging anyone around them. In fact, there were chairs lining the main play space and even a large room off to the side with theater-type seating and a huge window so voyeurs could enjoy the many play sessions going on.

"I'm going to be demonstrating proper caning techniques later," Viv said, "but first I want you to meet a few of my friends."

She took Rae to the back of the building where there was a full kitchen filled with people, most dressed in leather or latex clothing or sexy lingerie. Rae noticed there was no alcohol anywhere, and Viv offered her a fruit punch. She pointed out the person who made it, an older woman who vaguely reminded Rae of her first-grade teacher. And that was the thing: everyone, for the most part, looked so normal aside from their erotic attire.

Viv introduced her to a few friends, and Rae found herself relaxing a bit into a conversation about *The Wire* and a few other shows she had watched with Viv. As she was talking with a young woman around her age, a shirtless man wearing a leather mask grabbed a handful of Rae's ass and grunted out, "Fresh meat."

Quick as lightning, Viv slapped his hand away and hollered to a large bearlike man wearing a prominent "DM" patch on his leather vest. Without fanfare, the DM carted the masked man away.

"There are no second chances here," Viv whispered to her. "Break the rules, and you're out. He ignored your bracelet, which means he'd probably ignore collars too."

Rae almost forgot about the meaning of collars, and she realized how many of the partygoers, mostly women, wore one. Viv had told her Dominants sometimes gave their submissives collars to signify to others that not only did the submissive belong to them, but they were also under their protection. Other Dominants were expected to respect the collar and leave a submissive alone.

Although she belonged to no one, Rae almost wished she were wearing a collar. The masked man touching her without asking frightened her, making her wary of standing anywhere near a man.

Viv noticed her apprehension and gave her hand a squeeze. "I have a surprise for you, hon. Come with me."

She led Rae to a small room off the main play space. In the room, a young man stood next to what looked similar to a massage chair, almost like the kind masseuses use at malls.

"This cute subby is Farrow." Viv motioned to the sandy-haired man, who was undressed down to his blue bikini bottom, which left nothing to the imagination.

Rae felt a sudden, surprising desire as she admired the man's chiseled features. Her pregnancy hormones tended to elicit warmth in her pelvic area at the most awkward times, and she tried to concentrate on appearing normal and not like a panting dog in heat.

"This is Mistress Rae, the trainee I was telling you about."

"A pleasure to meet you, Mistress," Farrow said, although he didn't hold out his hand, and he didn't look Rae directly in the eyes.

"Nice to meet you too."

"Farrow here has agreed to be your first session."

Rae widened her eyes at Viv, but her friend only smiled and shifted to the corner of the room.

When Rae failed to move, Viv said, "What's the first thing you do with new clients?"

She thought about her training. "What types of sensations do you like, Farrow, and what level of intensity do you prefer?"

"I enjoy paddles, Mistress, especially wooden ones, and spanking. And I prefer not to have bruising, at least not tonight. I have a photo shoot this week."

"Okay. The safe word is red if you want me to stop."

Rae turned to Viv, who already had a number of implements laid out for her.

"How would you like him, Mistress Rae?"

Rae took the hint and directed the man to straddle the chair with his hands gripping the metal bar at the top of it, his back toward her. She ran her hands over the tools Viv had placed for her, her eyes falling on a large black paddle with metal studs. No, she thought. He wanted a wooden paddle, which she selected. She walked over to Farrow and tried to focus on where she needed to hit him. She remembered what Viv taught her—always aim for the meatiest part on the body—and she realized how much her hands were shaking, so she set the paddle down. She was nervous, of course, but she also knew it was her excitement causing her body to tremble.

Viv had warned her before to never imagine someone she hated during a session, but Rae couldn't help picturing Clint, not Farrow, on the chair, waiting for her to abuse him. She paused, shaking the image of Clint from her mind. This wasn't about him; this was about the person in front of her, and she wanted to do her best for him and to make Viv proud.

Rae mustered up her nerves and reached her hand out to stroke Farrow's backside. He shuddered in anticipation. Without warning, she cupped her hand and struck him hard on the ass. It felt good, how the vibration went up her arm and somehow between her legs. After several strikes, she felt herself go slick with the desire to do more. It was so much better than hitting pillows, so she continued to spank him as hard as she could.

She stopped when the image of Clint pushed back into her thoughts. She picked up the paddle, and the memories of the house and the men infiltrated her mind, their hands holding her down, forcing her . . . all the fear and the anger . . . and Beth with her huge empty blue eyes staring out at nothing from the kitchen floor.

She wanted to hurt this man. She wanted to make him beg her for mercy.

Her anger metamorphosed back into intense desire, which shimmered up from her pelvis to her right hand.

Rae glanced at Viv, who was leaning against the wall, her eyes carefully watching and monitoring.

"How old are you, Farrow?" Rae said.

"Twenty-one, Mistress."

Rae's lips stretched into a wide smile. "That's a good number."

And she raised the paddle and got to work on him. At first, he didn't make much sound as she struck him, but it didn't take long for him to cry out. When she got to the tenth strike, she heard him mumble something and saw his body slump a little. She almost stopped to have him repeat what he'd said, but she didn't want to break her pace when the hits felt so good pulsating throughout her body. Then Farrow turned quiet, and she smiled. Viv had told her about subspace, how submissives would sometimes become silent and more docile as their mind shifted to a blissful state. She knew this must be happening to Farrow, and she hit him even harder one more time before she needed to rest a moment.

She admired the marks on his ass that were so red she could barely distinguish the individual strikes she'd made. She touched his backside, which was as hot as a mug of tea. She wanted to do more for the last ten hits.

Rae turned back to the table of implements and reached for the metal-studded paddle, but Viv's hand stopped her.

When she looked at Viv, she didn't understand the anger on her friend's face.

"He said 'red,' Rae."

CHAPTER 18

RAE

2024

Picasso's happy hour was busier than Rae had expected for a Monday evening, so she asked to sit in the outside patio area rather than wait for a table inside. She ordered a citrusy IPA from the server and kept an eye out for Devon. The server brought her drink, which she sipped as she continued looking for her friend, who was now five minutes late.

Rae took the napkin from underneath her beer and blotted her face with it. The May evening was sweltering, the hazy sun quivering on the horizon. As much as she hated Oklahoma's heat, she could never complain about its sunsets. She was admiring the rainbowed hues, like a layered cake of purples, pinks, and golds haphazardly stacked across the sky, when Devon's shadow distracted her.

"Hey, lady," Devon said, sitting across from her, her dyed fire-red hair pulled up into a messy bun. "So sorry I'm late. I don't come out to the Paseo District often, and I got turned around."

"It's okay."

Rae flagged the server and waited for Devon to place her order before getting down to business.

"So, what did you need to discuss with me?" *And why was Devon so adamant about talking in person,* she wondered.

Without a drink in front of her yet, Devon seemed unsure of what to do with her hands. She took Rae's used napkin and began tearing it into teeny-tiny pieces.

"Well, I'm not sure where to begin. It's about Thomas Highsmith." Devon paused when the server brought her glass of red wine. "Like I wrote to you, I read the article that was going around today, and when I saw that he was one of your clients, I knew I had to say something to you."

"Do you know him?"

"Um, yes and no."

Rae had known Devon for many years. She was a tough Domme who didn't shy away from edgeplay like fire and blood cupping, but here she was looking pale and nervous. It scared Rae.

"He was a client of mine about a year back. Only did a couple of sessions with him, but he's hard to forget," Devon said. "As much as I enjoyed looking at him, I don't think I had the look he wanted. Too many tattoos, so I wasn't surprised when he moved on. Plus, he had referred someone to me, so I didn't look at it as too big of a loss."

Devon took a long drink of her wine, her green eyes shifting to the tables around them before landing back on Rae.

"So, the guy he referred to me told me about these parties. We're talking private parties for the wealthiest elites in the state. The client told me I could make a week's worth of earnings in one night of play. And you know we do private parties all the time. It's not unusual, but this one was . . . different."

Rae took a pull of her beer, waiting for her friend to continue.

Devon leaned forward, her forearms on the table as she cradled her wineglass. "Rae, I went to my first party the week before last. On a Wednesday night."

A tingle of dread tickled the back of Rae's throat. Wednesday, the same day she last saw Thomas.

"He was there. Thomas was at that party, and he didn't look happy about it."

Something else was troubling Devon, Rae could tell.

"Tell me about this party."

Devon's eyes darted around at the other tables again as if she were worried someone might overhear them. Rae had to strain to hear her when she said, "It was like *Eyes Wide Shut* on steroids. No rules whatsoever. Scenes were going on everywhere, but I didn't see a single dungeon monitor to watch over things, and a lot of the subs were clearly in distress. One submissive looked like she was completely drugged out on something, so I tried to help her to a quiet area, but some guy snatched her away from me." Devon looked down at her wineglass, but she didn't take a drink. "It wasn't a safe place for anyone there outside of the rich white assholes running it, and there were a *lot* of folks you would recognize there."

"You mean other Dommes?"

"I mean politicians, Rae. I mean big-time business owners you see on commercials trying to sell you a mattress. It was like a who's who of Oklahoma's wealthiest, and it freaked me out. What they were allowing at that party . . . if it was consensual, it didn't look like it to me. So, I left before I was supposed to do a scene with some random sub they lined up for me."

"What about Thomas? Where was he?"

"He was in a heated argument with some older man, and then I guess he left because I didn't see him again. I didn't recognize the man he was arguing with, but the guy briefly spoke with me when he offered me a drink. That was the other thing. Most of the people there were trashed or high, especially the women. When I told the man it wasn't safe to practice BDSM wasted, the motherfucker laughed and told me to lighten up." She downed the rest of her wine.

"What did this man look like?" Rae said.

Devon thought a moment. "He was really tall. Like six five. And he had super-thick white hair with dark eyebrows and the bluest eyes I've ever seen. Like they almost seemed fake, they were so blue."

"Holy shit, Devon, do you realize what this means?"

"It means you had nothing to do with whatever happened to Thomas, I know that much. But I knew that the moment I read that stupid article."

"You have to tell the police all this."

Devon's eyes widened to the size of quarters. "I can't."

"You have to. It could help with the investigation. Plus, it sounds like a lot of illegal shit was going on at that party."

Devon looked down at her empty glass. "I signed a nondisclosure agreement."

"Are you fucking kidding?"

Her eyes shot back up to Rae. "Hey, we have clients sign those all the time, so don't go judging me for it."

"This is different. Someone is missing, and this is pretty fucking important information for investigators."

Devon shook her head, her eyes filling with tears. "They will ruin me if I tell. These are powerful people."

"Then why tell me?" Rae felt anger simmering in her. "What the hell can I do with this information? If I tell investigators, it's hearsay. It won't fly."

"I don't know. I thought . . . I just wanted you to know that some-one believes you, and I'm sure the investigators will find something leading them to the party location, but it can't be from me."

"Where was the party, Devon?"

"Rae."

"Where?"

Devon sighed. "The Coulter mansion."

"Fuck."

The Coulters were an old Oklahoma family who had owned several huge oil refineries during the first half of the twentieth century until they dipped their hands into the rapidly growing technology markets, pushing their wealth into the stratosphere. The Coulter mansion sat on the farthest outskirts of north Oklahoma City, far enough from the city lights to see more than a few stars and certainly secluded enough to avoid prying eyes.

And now, somehow, Rae needed to convince Detective Clearwater to believe a story involving one of Oklahoma's elites that she heard from someone she couldn't even name.

CHAPTER 19

RAE

2009

After the play party, Rae could think of nothing else. She wanted to do it all again, despite her hand throbbing with what she'd done to Farrow. Viv, however, wasn't impressed. The first thing she said to Rae as they drove back to the condo after they left the party early made her want to shrivel up into nothing.

"What the hell was that, Rae?"

"What do you mean?"

"That wasn't how I trained you."

Rae glanced at her, but Viv was gripping the steering wheel hard, her eyes staring straight ahead. "But I did everything you said. I asked him what he liked, I used the paddle he wanted, and I—"

"No. You were not in control of your emotions. In fact, I don't think you cared what Farrow wanted at all because you never once checked on him, and you ignored him using the safe word, not to mention the fact you did zero aftercare. I did. And I stopped you from doing more damage than what you'd already done. He said he didn't want bruising, but you didn't care. You were in your own little world, hitting him without intention."

Action without intention is like slapping clay around, making a mess of it. Viv's words coming back to her, her face burning with shame.

"Viv . . . I'm sorry."

"Really, I'm upset with myself. You weren't ready, and I should've seen that. It's just I've never seen you look that . . ." She paused. "Scary."

Rae kept watching Viv as she drove, hoping she'd look at her and show her some sign of forgiveness.

"Sometimes I forget," Viv said, almost in a whisper.

"Forget what?"

Viv finally looked at her, the yellow streetlights creating a shadow mosaic across her face. "How dangerous wounded animals can be."

After Rae's shift at Subway was over the following Monday, the overused muscles in her hand were still sore but improving. Her spirits, on the other hand, were in a nosedive. There was too much awkwardness with Viv now, and she didn't know what to say or do to make it better. She knew she'd disappointed Viv, but she now realized she'd also made her friend look bad in front of a submissive and anyone else who might've watched the play session, which could've been many people since the small room had windows for easy viewing.

Viv wasn't home yet when she entered the condo, so Rae decided to make her friend's favorite dinner: pan-seared honey-soy salmon with steamed rice and salad, one of the many meals Viv had taught her how to prepare. She knew it was a weak peace offering, but it was something she knew how to do.

When Viv walked through the front door, Rae watched her hesitate in the entryway before setting her purse and keys down and heading to the kitchen.

"Smells good," Viv said, pushing a strand of her dark hair behind her ear.

"I hope I didn't overcook the salmon. I did three minutes each side, medium-high heat, like you showed me."

"I'm sure it's perfect, hon."

Hon. That was an encouraging start to their meal.

Viv took her plate and the glass of pinot grigio Rae had poured for her to the small round dining table, not to the living room couch where they'd gotten into the habit of eating while watching TV.

"Let's eat like real people tonight," she said.

"Sure."

Rae sat across from her, feeling the weight of expectation heavy in her empty stomach. After a few bites of perfectly cooked salmon, her nerves eased some. She had done something right.

Viv was about halfway done with her meal when she heavily sighed. "Okay, we need to address the elephant. And by elephant, I mean whatever you haven't told me yet about California."

Her words jarred Rae so much she started choking on a bite of lettuce. She cleared her throat and took several gulps of water, more than what she needed. She thought about saying she had to go to the bathroom, which wasn't true but likely would be any minute. She wanted to do anything else in the world but talk more about what had happened in California.

"Listen, hon, I understand a lot of horrible shit happened to you there, but what I don't know is how you escaped the situation and why you seem terrified every time someone knocks on the front door. Do you think someone followed you all the way here?"

Rae closed her eyes and tried to control the rumble of fear traveling up her back. If she told Viv, she might lose the only person still alive who loved her. When she opened her eyes, hot tears streamed down her cheeks.

"I'm scared to tell you."

Viv reached across the table and took her hand. "It's okay. You can tell me anything."

"But you may not like me once I tell you."

Viv's brow creased, her face full of concern. "You're my friend. Nothing you tell me will make me love you less."

Rae wasn't sure if she believed her, but she wanted so much for it to be the truth.

CHAPTER 20

RAE

2024

After her drink with Devon, Rae came home to an empty house and a text message from Lily saying she was staying the night with Klo. Better Klo than Gabby, but it hurt not to see her daughter, to sit her down and try to explain her lies over the last fifteen years. She wanted to hold her girl, who was on the verge of becoming a woman, to tell her she would always be her baby, her salvation. Instead, she doubled up on her edibles and fell into a troubled sleep.

The next morning, she relayed to Angel everything Devon had told her as she hurried to prepare for her first client of the day, a man who loved electrical play.

"I can't believe she won't tell the police," Angel said. "What are you going to do?"

Rae had thought about it most of the night as she tossed and turned, her edibles doing nothing but making her feel slightly paranoid. "I think I have to tell Detective Clearwater. Something about those parties feels bigger than Thomas's disappearance."

Angel stopped scrolling through the day's appointments on the computer and looked at her. "Do you think those parties have anything to do with the subs going missing?"

"I don't know." It felt like they did, but she had no proof of it, only a gut instinct. "But I'm calling him after this first appointment."

Keeping her mind on her client was a struggle, but Rae managed to get through the session with a satisfied customer. Then she called Detective Clearwater, who picked up as soon as she was transferred to his line.

"I suppose you're calling me, Ms. Dixon, to chew me out again about the article."

"As much fun as that sounds, I'm not." Rae hesitated, unsure how much she should say by phone. After what Devon had told her, she understood why her friend was afraid and wanted to speak in person. "I have some important information for the investigation, but I have to meet you in person to discuss it."

"You can meet me here at the station."

"Not there. Someplace without cops."

The detective was quiet for a moment on the other line. "I can meet you downtown at noon. Do you know where EOTE, the coffee shop, is?"

"Yes."

"Good," he said. "I'll see you then."

Rae got through her late-morning session, her last one scheduled for the day, changed into a blue, lightweight jumpsuit that brought out her eye color, and brushed her midlength hair, which was wavy from having it up in a tight bun all morning. Stupidly, her nervousness at meeting with the detective spanned beyond what she had to tell him, and she felt the need to look put together.

When she arrived at the local coffee shop, Detective Clearwater was already there, sitting at a two-top away from the more crowded main area of the café. He looked up from his cell phone, his eyes gliding over her outfit and hair.

He stood up and offered his hand to her. "Good to see you again, Ms. Dixon. Can I get you anything? A coffee or tea?"

She shook his hand, noting the warmth of his large palm against her own and how it sent flutters to her stomach. She wasn't thirsty, but she didn't mind having more time to sort out her thoughts and what she needed to tell him, so she said, "Yes, thank you. I'll take an iced latte."

He came back a few minutes later with her coffee. She took a long sip, realizing she was thirsty after all.

"So, Ms. Dixon."

"Please call me Rae."

"Not Echo?" he said, the hint of a smile on his full lips. When she glared at him, he quickly added, "I'm sorry. That was uncalled for."

"It was."

He spread his hands out on the table. "Let's start over. Rae."

"Do I get to call you Dayton?"

"If it means I'm forgiven for being a jerk, sure."

Rae smirked. She had a feeling this wasn't how he normally interacted with possible suspects in a criminal case, which brought up an obvious question.

"So, Dayton, are Angel and I still at the top of your suspect list in Thomas Highsmith's case?"

He took a sip of his hot latte, his eyes revealing that he was clearly weighing something in his mind before he finally said, "If you're asking if I think you two did something to Mr. Highsmith, then no. I don't. But you have a lot of secrets, Rae, and I can't ignore how that might play into the investigation."

Rae swallowed a sigh of relief. "My secrets have nothing to do with my clients."

"What do they have to do with then?"

He leaned back in his chair, his eyes assessing her. It made her uncomfortable, as if he could peek inside her heart and see every bad thing she'd ever done.

"Why are you so curious to know?"

"It's my job to be curious, and I don't like it when I can't figure someone out."

"Well, like I tell my daughter, disappointment is the spice of life."

He chuckled. "I'm rarely disappointed, but then again I'm *extremely* patient."

Something about his tone and intense stare made heat rise to her face, and she hoped he couldn't tell she was blushing.

"What do you want to tell me, Rae?" He had a pen and small notepad ready.

She let out a long breath and told him everything Devon had described about the party and seeing Thomas arguing with a tall man there. When she went into the details Devon had told her about the older man, the one with the white hair and piercing blue eyes, Dayton's body tensed.

"Did this friend you won't disclose know the name of the older man?"

"No, they didn't know anyone outside of the client they were with and Thomas, but they recognized a lot of community leaders there."

"And this all supposedly happened at the Coulter mansion?"

She didn't appreciate the word he'd used—supposedly. "They had no reason to lie to me about this."

"Except that it conveniently points blame away from you and Ms. Paisley."

Rae crossed her arms. "This is why I wasn't sure if I was going to tell you. You cops have no problem busting into a small legal business owned by a couple of women, but when it comes to old, rich white men, you look the other way."

"Hey, I hear what you're saying. Trust me, I know all about the shitty apples plaguing most police stations—"

"But you're not one of them?" she interrupted.

"Try not to be." He glanced around at the other tables, most of which were now empty as people's lunch hours had ended, and leaned forward, his voice low. "I'm not saying I don't believe you, but I can't do anything with hearsay. I need to speak directly with your friend."

"They won't talk. They're scared."

Frustration was all over Dayton's face.

"And there's something else," she said, already regretting what she was about to say. "There are two subs that have gone missing within the last three weeks, both women. They've been reported to the police, but it doesn't look like anyone's taking it seriously."

"Subs?"

"Submissives. People who enjoy being controlled by a dominant person."

"Like masochists?"

"Not all submissives enjoy pain."

"Do you know these women's names?" He held his pen over the notepad, ready.

"Only their handles on the kink sites. I don't know them personally." She gave him the handles and a description of the women.

"Okay, listen," he said, his voice getting even lower. "I need you to find out when the next party is, and then I can look into it. Is that something you can do for me?"

Before speaking with Devon, Rae had never heard of parties like that happening in Oklahoma, aside from what Thomas had told her before he disappeared, and her friend made it clear she never planned on attending another. She could scour the kink sites, but she doubted she'd find any information about it. If Devon didn't know when the next party was, Rae didn't like the only other option she could think of right then to get the information.

She returned his gaze. "Yeah. I can do that."

CHAPTER 21

RAE

2009

Viv sat at the dining table across from her, waiting for Rae to speak, to open her chest and spill all her secrets. She wasn't sure how to begin because there was nothing easy about what she had to tell her.

"After Beth, after what Clint did . . . I wanted to die too. I even tried to find where Clint hid the drugs he gave us so I could inject myself with everything he had. But then I heard them talking—Clint, Bobby, and the bad men."

"The bad men?" Viv said, the concerned crease between her brows deepening.

"After Beth died, these men came to the house, but they were different from the usual men who came. They looked rich and wore nice suits. There were two of them, and they weren't happy about what happened to Beth." She suppressed more tears from coming. "They talked about her like they owned her, like she was a pet, and they told Clint he had a week to get another girl, or they would take back the deposit they gave him and kill him and his partner Bobby."

Viv shifted in her chair and gently pressed Rae's hand as if to urge her to go on.

"I knew I was pregnant, or I was pretty sure I was since I didn't get my period, and I kept throwing up. And Clint was so angry about Beth. He kept blaming me for it and how he owed a lot of money to the rich men because of me, and he . . ." She sucked in a few breaths, slowly in and out, trying to calm herself. "He hit me more, and I was scared he would find out about the pregnancy and kill me. He always warned the women not to get pregnant, that they were worthless if they did. He said it like we had a choice, like we could stop it from happening." Thinking about it still made her angry.

"Do you know who the father is?" Viv asked.

"Clint."

Viv covered her mouth with her hand.

Rae told her about how Clint said he couldn't get another young girl so fast, and he and Bobby were making plans to leave California, although he didn't indicate where they'd go. At first, he didn't say what he was going to do with Rae or Maria, the other woman still in the house. She was older than Rae by a couple of years, but she looked a lot older. Then Clint changed his plan. He made Maria clean up, gave her a nice outfit to wear, and made her do her hair and makeup. Then he sent her out to the Santa Monica Pier with one goal: find a girl, lure her with ice cream or whatever worked, and bring her back to the house. If she failed, he would kill Rae. Rae had never prayed so hard for someone to fail at something, but Maria came back with a child younger than Beth. The little girl had springy caramel curls, and she couldn't have been older than five. After some prompting, Rae learned her name was Katelyn.

The day after she brought Katelyn to the house, Maria died from what Rae hoped was an accidental overdose. As much as Rae wanted to join her, she couldn't. She needed to help the girl escape and somehow get her back to her family. She'd failed to protect Beth, but she wouldn't fail again. She also thought about the child possibly growing in her, and it gave her strength. So, she waited until Clint left the house. Bobby never left unless Clint was there to keep watch. Rae couldn't find Clint's stash of hard drugs, but she did find nine sleeping pills hidden between the mattresses in Maria's old room. She tried not to think about why Maria had been hoarding pills as she crushed them up into a fine dust and carefully funneled them into a bottle of beer she offered to Bobby. Fifteen minutes later, he was passed out on the couch.

She searched again through Clint's room, more thoroughly this time since Bobby was knocked out. There was an odd, heavy smell in the room, sickeningly sweet, and she wondered if it was from how dirty the space was, the scent of body odor hanging in the air as well. She grabbed Clint's gym bag, quickly emptying it out. She found a roll of cash hidden in his sock drawer. She didn't have time to count it, so she shoved it into the duffel bag. She didn't know when Clint would be back, so she hurried to her room to collect what clothes she could and stuffed them into the gym bag.

Katelyn was scared and reluctant to move from Beth's old room, the one with a little TV and a few stuffed animals, but Rae told her she knew where her mommy and daddy were, and they had to leave now to see them. Her words worked because Katelyn jumped off the bed, but not before grabbing one of the stuffed animals, a purple teddy bear.

That's when Rae heard the front door open, and her stomach bottomed out. She told Katelyn to stay in the room with the duffel bag. Quietly, she inched down the hallway until she saw Clint attempting to wake up Bobby.

"Get up," Clint said, smacking Bobby's head. "You get into my shit again, you motherfucker? Fuck."

He turned around to see Rae watching him.

"What the fuck you looking at, Echo?"

The longer she stood there, fully dressed with tennis shoes on, the quicker he appeared to realize what was happening, that she was going to escape.

She stood for what seemed like a lifetime, not sure what to do with the fear and anger rolling inside her, but her body screamed *CHARGE*, so she did. Clint probably had about eighty pounds on her, but she slammed into his body with the force of a linebacker. She shoved him enough to make him fall backward onto Bobby's slumped form on the couch. Frantic, she searched around the living room for something she could use as a weapon. There was nothing heavy, so she grabbed Bobby's empty beer bottle from the side table and smashed it over Clint's head. It dazed him for a second but didn't knock him out, so she ran to the kitchen.

"You fucking bitch! I'm going to kill you!"

Her heart was pounding in her ears as she quickly found a paring knife in the sink. Clint was coming up behind her as she turned around and jabbed at him, missing. He tried to grab her hand holding the knife, but she dodged him and landed a blow to his thigh. She didn't have enough strength to pull the knife out to strike him again, so she backed up fast as Clint looked down at his injured leg. He yanked the knife out with a howl and went after her, pulling out the handgun he had tucked in the back of his jeans.

She ran toward the front door, away from where Katelyn was waiting for her in the back bedroom, but she knew she wouldn't make it without getting shot, so she hit the floor, her bare knees burning as she crawled on the rough carpet to Bobby's passed out body. She ran her hands along his jeans until she found the semiautomatic she knew he had on him. She had never shot a gun, but she held it in her hands like she had and aimed it at Clint. He stopped dead.

"Put the fucking gun down, Echo," he said, his voice strangely calm.

She had to use her whole palm to pull back the slide, but she heard the satisfying click and knew the gun was ready to shoot. "I'm leaving, and I'm taking Katelyn with me."

"The fuck you are. Put the gun down, and we'll forget any of this happened."

She shook her head, the gun unsteady in her hands.

"I'm serious. We can forget about all of this. I love you, Echo, you know that."

Laughter burst from her; she couldn't help it. Clint loving anyone but himself was the biggest joke.

"You had nothing before you met me. An addict father, a mother who didn't give a shit about you. But I didn't leave you like they did. I took you in and fed you, kept a roof over your head. I took care of you."

She steadied her hand. "Just let us leave. I won't say anything to the police if you just let us leave."

"You know I can't do that." Clint's face turned hard as granite, and he smiled. "You know, you never were bright. Bet you didn't know how often your dad came running to me for his shit. It's too bad he got a dirty batch. And now you get to join him."

He raised his gun, aiming for her head, and she didn't think. She pulled the trigger. She heard a bullet whiz by her head, missing Bobby's body and blasting the plastered wall behind her. Then she saw bright red spreading across Clint's upper right shoulder. He dropped his gun, pressing his left hand to the bullet hole, his face bone white as he slid down the opposite wall to the floor.

She stood up and went over to him, kicked his gun out of his reach.

He looked up at her, sweat dripping from his face. "You stupid bitch, you don't know what you just did. They're going to find you and kill you. That girl's worth a hundred grand to them."

She took the butt of the gun and slammed it against the side of his head, and he was out. He was going to die anyway, she was sure, and she hoped it was slow, especially after she was able to process what he had told her. Her father got drugs from Clint, drugs laced with something bad, something that instantly killed him.

She looked around the living room. Her fingerprints and Katelyn's were all over the house. The police would come here and find a dead body and Bobby, who would then be awake and tell them it was Rae, that she was the one who had done everything. There was no Maria still alive to corroborate what had really happened in the house. She didn't even know where they'd put her body after she'd overdosed. She didn't know where any of the women had gone when they'd left the house, but her gut told her they were all dead. Used and drugged and killed. Her rage boiled up again.

She wanted to burn it down. All of it.

Rae went to the back bedroom and found Katelyn gripping her purple bear, her eyes glued to the TV screen as if she hadn't heard all the commotion down the hallway.

"Katelyn, I need you to come with me now."

She slung the duffel bag over her shoulder and took Katelyn's tiny hand. She quietly led her outside and told her to wait next to the darkened house next door. Then she went to the detached garage, searching around in near darkness until she found a plastic gasoline container, the one she saw when Clint or Bobby would mow the lawn. There wasn't much fuel in the container, so she poured it all over the recliner in the living room, hoping it would spread to the rest of the house. Then she took a Bic lighter from Clint's pocket, lit a paper receipt she found on the coffee table, and threw it on the chair, which exploded into flames.

She left the house, using her shirt to wipe down the doorknobs, same as she had done to the garage handle, doing her best to remove any trace of her prints, praying the fire would burn any inside.

Once outside, she stood a moment and watched the fire glow orange through the living room window, the curtains starting to catch.

Rae found Katelyn waiting where she'd told her to stay.

"Are we going to find Mommy and Daddy now?" she said, her voice so small.

"Yes, honey. We're going to find them."

It wasn't exactly a lie. She wasn't sure how to find Katelyn's parents, but she remembered how people back in Oklahoma would leave newborn babies at fire stations with no questions asked. She didn't know if California was the same, but she had no choice. She knew there was a fire station near them since she'd hear the sirens going off down the street several times per week. So, they walked in the direction she'd heard the sirens before. It felt like an hour passed before they came up to the station. There were lights on inside.

"Okay, Katelyn, I need you to go inside that building and tell the nice people your name. If you know your mommy's or daddy's name, tell them that, too, okay?"

Katelyn looked confused, but she nodded.

"And, Katelyn, don't tell them my name."

She watched as Katelyn's stubby legs walked across the lawn past a towering palm tree. Once she was inside the glassed entrance, Rae waited until she saw a firefighter approach the girl.

Viv's face processed everything Rae had told her. "Then I found a way to the bus station and met you." Now that Rae had told her friend everything, she felt completely drained.

Viv had kept a hold of Rae's hand the entire time she spoke. She let her hand go and downed her white wine.

"Are you sure they're dead?" she asked.

If there was one thing Rae was sure of, it was that Clint and Bobby were dead, and it was because of her. As soon as she'd moved in with Viv, she had searched about the fire to see what the police knew. They had found two unidentified bodies in the house that was reportedly owned by a company called Felton Holdings LLC; the fire was deemed to be arson.

She nodded at Viv.

"And you think these bad men, the rich ones, are going to track you here?"

"Yeah."

Viv was quiet for a long time, her eyes staring at her plate of half-eaten salmon and rice. She looked up at her, and Rae couldn't tell what she was thinking. She hoped she wasn't about to tell her to get the hell out of her home.

"Hon, you did what you had to do. You saved that little girl, and you prevented those men from hurting more people. And the bad men." She paused. "I think if they were coming after you, they would've found you by now."

Rae didn't think that was true, but she said nothing.

"But now," Viv said, "you have to make a decision. Are you going to do the work to heal from this trauma, or are you going to let this turn you into the kind of monsters you escaped from?"

As much as she hated it, she knew Viv was right. She thought of Farrow and how blissfully out of control she had felt as she hit him. She had wanted her hate to consume her, but she couldn't afford to allow it again. Soon, she would be a mother. A mother with secrets, like her own. Maybe all mothers had secrets. The thought gave her an uneasy comfort.

CHAPTER 22

RAE

2024

After her meeting with Dayton Clearwater, Rae came home to find Lily and Gabby in the living room, huge Starbucks drinks sweating condensation all over the live-edge wood coffee table a friend had made for her, no coasters, with some annoying YouTube video blasting on the TV. When Lily finally noticed her standing there, she quickly looked back to the TV screen as if she had never seen her but not before subtly nudging her friend.

Gabby turned around on the couch, the smattering of freckles across her nose scrunching as she grinned at Rae.

"Oh, hey, Ms. Dixon."

"Hi, Gabby."

Gabby stood up, the venti drink in her hand the size of her forearm. She took a long suck of what looked like pink milk and smiled again. "How are you doing with, like, everything? That's got to be so hard having people trash you all over the internet like that. I know it's been crazy hard for Lil. Isn't that right?"

Lily didn't look at her friend as she turned down the TV.

"We're doing fine, Gabby, but I think it's time for you to go home."

"You don't have to leave," Lily said to her friend, her face suddenly apprehensive, like she was being left to the wolves.

"Sorry, Lil, gotta meet up with Zayden at the mall," Gabby said as she slinked past Rae to get her Prada purse hanging in the entryway. "My mom said it's probably not a good idea for me to be seen here anyway."

"Gab, wait."

But Gabby was already out the door. Lily jumped up from the couch, arms crossed tight.

"God, Mom, it's not enough for you to ruin your own life, but now you've got to ruin mine too?"

"Please, sit back down, Lily. We need to talk about this."

"I don't want to hear anything you have to say," she yelled and ran upstairs to her bedroom.

Rae rushed up the stairs to follow her and was greeted with a door slammed in her face.

She almost broke her own rule about privacy, but she stopped herself from busting through the door and knocked instead. She got radio silence.

"Lily, honey, please." Her voice cracked with emotion. "I didn't mean for any of this to happen, and the article was taken down, so people can't share it anymore."

Still silence.

"You can't keep ignoring me." But she knew firsthand how stubborn her daughter could be at times, something Lily had inherited from her. The only tactic that usually worked to bring Lily out of her room when she was upset was her favorite food. "I'm going to order a pizza from Hideaway. Extra bacon."

The pizza arrived and still no Lily, although Rae heard her slip downstairs to grab some slices as she was finishing her own while watching an episode of *Big Mouth*, something they usually watched together.

After dinner and a glass of wine she normally reserved for the weekend, Rae texted Devon a coded message to find out when the next party at the Coulter mansion would be: Hey, girl, just need to know when the next get together is going to happen. Really enjoyed hanging out at the last one. XO V

A few minutes passed before her phone dinged: Sorry, I'm not sure when the next one will be, but I hope to see you soon! X MM

So, Devon, whether she was lying or not, wasn't going to be any help. Rae had already searched through every kink site she could think of, scrolling through pages and pages of event notifications, but none pointed to the Coulter mansion. They had to spread the word somehow, and her only guess was that it was by word of mouth. Surely, others within the community knew something about the parties, but she couldn't simply create posts asking about it online. She'd need to be stealthy about it.

She went through the events calendar again on her favorite local kink site and saw there was going to be a play party on Saturday night. It was at a local dungeon where she had taught BDSM workshops several times over the years, and she knew it would be packed with both Dominants and subs.

Rae submitted her RSVP and paid her door entrance fee through Venmo. Normally, she looked forward to play parties, but not this one. This time, she'd have to somehow get information without placing herself on the radar, and she wasn't sure why she should have to do anything at all when Dayton admitted he didn't think she or Angel had anything to do with Thomas Highsmith's disappearance. But the fact that they were still on the suspect list at all was enough for her to at least try to get the information the detective asked for. More than that, she hoped her help would lead the investigators to find not only Thomas but the missing submissives, the women the police didn't seem to care anything about. Or at least they didn't care enough to throw resources behind searching for them.

If she succeeded, she and Angel would be cleared and perhaps their business could survive. And maybe Lily would eventually allow her to explain why she'd lied, and she could rebuild trust with her daughter. She had to succeed because she didn't want to think about what could happen if she didn't.

CHAPTER 23

RAE

2009

Rae held up her new driver's license again, her cheeks hurting from smiling so much. It displayed her old name, Echo Phalin, because she had no choice unless she legally changed it, which she promised herself she would do someday. It took much longer than she'd expected because she had to obtain proof of identity from Oklahoma first, which meant doing something she had wanted to avoid for the rest of her life, if possible.

A man with a highish voice had answered the phone when she'd made the call. "Hi, um, is Jill there?" she said.

"Who, may I ask, is calling?"

"Uh, I'm her daughter. Echo." She sucked in a deep breath and held it, afraid he would immediately hang up.

"Oh. Oh, wow," he said. "Let me get her for you."

Several moments passed before her mother got on the line. "Echo? Are you okay?"

The concerned tone in her mother's voice stunned Rae. She steeled her rabbit-quick heart leaping away in her chest. "Yes, I'm okay."

"Where are you?"

"Albuquerque."

"Did you go back to that drug dealer?"

"No, I'm with a friend I met in California. I'm living with her, and she's helped me a lot. Even helped me get a car. She's really nice, and she doesn't expect anything from me."

Her mother seemed to read between the lines because her voice turned cooler. "I had no way to reach you."

Rae ignored the implication because she knew her mother hadn't planned on doing anything for her, but she could now. "I need my birth certificate and my social security card so I can get my driver's license. Will you mail them to me?"

Her mother was dead silent for a full minute. "You're not coming back here?"

"I don't know. Maybe, but not until the baby's born."

"You're keeping it?" She sounded surprised.

"Yeah. My friend's been taking me to prenatal appointments, but I need ID so I can get my own place and get on Medicaid here before the baby's born. So, will you mail them to me?"

"Why don't you come back to Oklahoma?"

"Because there's nothing there for me."

The line went quiet, but Rae swore she heard her mother suck in a trembling breath. "Where do you need me to mail them?"

And a week later, a plain manila envelope arrived with her documents. Nothing else. No letter from her mother begging her to come home and live with her and her new family, the man with the high voice and the little girl. Not that Rae would've dropped everything to go back, but it would've been nice to know her mother felt something for her aside from disappointment for not being whatever it was she apparently needed.

She didn't allow it to hurt her for too long. She had her driver's license now. She had freedom. And the first thing she did was drive her Honda Civic along Central Avenue, windows down in the August heat since her A/C was junk, past the many restaurants and eclectic shops she wanted to visit as soon as she made more money. Most of everything she made now went toward her prenatal visits, car insurance, and thrifting for baby clothes, but she wanted to get Viv something to show her how much she appreciated everything she'd done for her. She took twenty dollars she'd saved and went to one of Viv's favorite thrift stores, where she bought a jade-colored bangle she'd recently seen her friend eyeing. She had an ulterior motive with the gift, too; she wanted Viv to help her start up a camgirl account on MyFreeCams, a site she learned of when she heard some of her male coworkers at Subway talking about it.

After Viv got done with her last online client for the day, she helped Rae prepare a pasta dish and Caesar salad, which they ate at the dining table. They were almost done eating and chatting about their days when Rae pulled the bangle from her hoodie's pocket. The thrift store had wrapped it in pink tissue paper, which made her feel better about not getting a box for it.

"What's this?" Viv said when Rae pushed it across the table to her.

"A little present to say thank you."

Viv unwrapped it and gasped in delight. "Oh, I love it! How did you know I wanted this?"

Rae shrugged and smiled.

Viv didn't remove the silver watch she always wore and slid on the bangle next to it, her expression full of admiration as she waved her hand.

"Thank you, hon. That's so sweet of you."

"It feels small compared to what you've done for me."

Viv removed the bangle and wrapped it back up in the tissue. "Don't discount all the work you've done to help yourself and that little one growing in you."

"Speaking of work," Rae said, "I heard about a website from my coworkers called MyFreeCams, where people can make money online streaming videos. I've been thinking about doing it, but I'm not sure how to get started."

Viv paused in taking a bite of pasta. "You do realize most people make money on that site by performing sex acts like getting naked and masturbating for viewers, right?"

Rae had guessed as much by how the guys at her work were talking, but she knew the site was open to other types of live video streaming after researching it. "I do, but I was hoping to eventually use it for dominating people like you do. Since I don't have my own site like you, and no one would even go to a site if I made one since I'm new, I thought it would be a good idea to start out by using an existing platform where a lot of customers could find me."

Viv seemed to contemplate the idea as she took her time chewing and swallowing her food. "It appears you've already made up your mind about it."

"I have."

"Well, it's not a bad idea, but you have to be super careful with sites like that. I've heard about customers harassing camgirls and not much being done about it. And if you're not doing nudity with it, it could be harder to get money. Are you going to show your baby bump? I've heard it's a big draw on those sites. Even some of my Domme friends made a ton of money topping people when they were pregnant."

"No, I wasn't planning on showing much of my body. I'm not ready to be seen like that yet."

"You'll definitely make less money then. As long as you know that going in."

This was something Rae thought about a lot, but she wasn't sure what Viv would think. "Um, I know a lot of customers like feet. So, I was thinking I would only film my feet stepping on things like dolls or food. But in a dominating way?"

Viv's face brightened with excitement. "Okay, I'm liking this idea. We could get you some Ken dolls, and you could tie them up in your live streams. Let your viewers request what they want done."

"Yes, that's exactly what I imagined." Seeing Viv's enthusiasm about her idea made her plan feel real.

"And you're right—you'd be building a clientele until you have the baby." Viv squealed and slapped the table with her palm, making Rae jump. "Let's go celebrate your brilliant idea."

"Okay."

"How about some I Scream Ice Cream?"

"Hell yes!"

Rae couldn't think of a better way to celebrate than playing arcade games and eating the best damn ice cream in all of Albuquerque.

CHAPTER 24

RAE

2024

The week went by fast, which Rae normally would've been happy about, but each day meant another day closer to Saturday and the play party. She had called Dayton to let him know her plan, and he was understandably frustrated with having to wait. She wanted to tell him tough shit and to do his own legwork, but she also knew she was likely his best chance at acquiring the information he needed, and that gave her at least some advantage in the situation.

Meanwhile, Lily barely crossed her path all week, choosing to get rides home with friends rather than have Rae pick her up. She didn't see Gabby's black Lexus during drop-offs, a bittersweet triumph. Like their sometimes-elusive cat, Lily would magically show up for mealtimes, grab her food, and skitter back to her bedroom to eat. When Rae got done with clients early enough, she'd stop by the house before running errands, entering her daughter's lair to retrieve the stacks of dirty dishes she refused to bring down. Rae told herself she'd allow Lily the rest of the week to get her aggression out before she'd try to talk with her again and reestablish the family ground rules, which included doing the damn dishes.

By the time Saturday arrived, Rae's nerves were a mess, but at least she wasn't alone. Once Angel knew of her plan, she decided to go with her to the play party. She even came over to Rae's house to get ready, like they were two teenagers about to sneak into a club. Angel was a kinky person, no doubt, but she wasn't so much into BDSM aspects of kink. Her kink ran more along the lines of three-ways with beautiful women she picked up at gay bars like Alibis. Yet, like Rae, she baby-powdered herself and shimmied into her tightest latex outfit for the play party. She even wore a cute, studded pink collar.

"You can own me for the night," Angel said, casually swinging the long metal chain attached to the collar, "but only because I don't want guys grab-assing me."

"Uh, I don't know how I feel about walking around with a leash on my Black friend."

"So, no leash?"

"No leash."

Angel mock pouted. "Guess I'll have to live out my furry fantasy another time."

Rae rolled her eyes. "Let's do this."

They pulled up to the nondescript building that gave off abandoned-warehouse vibes, and Rae pushed down the nerves attempting to resurface. At the entrance, they showed their confirmation emails for the event to the bouncer and checked in their phones with the hostess, and they were in. One thing Rae loved about Subspace's dungeon was it looked like anything but. It felt more like a farmers' market but with various play scenes scattered throughout the large interior, which glowed with black lights mixed with LEDs that rotated through every color in the rainbow. The entire back wall of the building was devoted to a bar serving only creative nonalcoholic cocktails and a lounge area filled with plush seating perfect for people into sensory play.

"Let's get a drink," Viv said.

Angel nodded, and they made their way toward the back, passing quite a few sexy scenes, including one where a woman was having neon candle wax dripped all over her naked breasts.

"Damn, I might have to try that," Angel said, barely loud enough for Rae to hear over the thumping music.

Once they were in line for a drink, Rae pulled Angel close enough to whisper-yell in her ear, "Remember, follow my lead and don't say anything about Devon or give any indication you know any details about the parties."

"Got it."

They both ordered a blackberry-ginger mocktail and started making rounds until they found a group of people Rae knew well. One was a fellow professional Domme like her.

"Hey, gorgeous, I didn't know you were coming out tonight," Bessie, a short redheaded Domme, said as she side-hugged Rae.

"It was sort of last minute. We were needing to get out and have some fun."

"I haven't seen you out in a while," another Domme said. She was a tall brunette, and Rae had to dig deep to remember her name: Sadie.

Rae smiled. "We've just been busy. You know how it goes."

"That's good that you're still getting business after . . . you know," Sadie said with a smirk, and Rae remembered why she never cared for her.

"That whole thing was bullshit," Bessie said and took a sip of her drink, which glowed green under the shifting lights. "I mean, I hope they find your client and everything, but to try to put that on you? So typical. Those assholes are always trying to push around anyone in the sex work industry. Well, fuck them."

"Hear! Hear!" Angel said, raising her glass high before remembering she was supposed to be submissive, something impossible for her friend. A few submissives standing around stared at her, so Rae decided to give her an out.

"She's not mine." Rae indicated Angel, who widened her eyes at her. "I suggested she collar-up to avoid unwanted attention."

"Good idea," said a petite blonde with the biggest breasts Rae had ever seen on a person that size. Rae didn't know her, but she gave off come-hither vibes. "I know I wouldn't be able to keep my hands off you."

Angel and the woman exchanged a look that could scorch the sun, and Rae had a feeling she'd be leaving the party alone.

They spent the next few minutes chatting and catching up with the group. When Bessie excused herself to get another drink, Rae joined her. She didn't think Angel would mind since she appeared enthralled with the blonde.

"These drinks are good, but they would be a hell of a lot better with a little Tito's," Bessie said, playfully nudging Rae's side with her elbow as they waited in line.

"For real." Rae glanced around them before asking, "So, I have an odd question for you, Bess."

"What's that?"

"Well, I had a client recently tell me about play parties he knows of where things get pretty . . . wild. Like no-holds-barred, off-the-radar kind of shit where professional Dommes can make a lot of money. Have you heard of anything like that?"

Bessie's face dropped. "That's so strange that you ask. I had a client invite me to something like that last week. Said I could do anything I wanted there. No rules or safe words. And it was at a mansion or something."

"Did he say when the party was going to be?"

"Yeah. It was last Wednesday."

"Did you go to it?" Rae said.

"I couldn't that night, but they're having another one next Wednesday at nine."

Rae did a happy dance in her head.

"I don't think I'm going to it, though," Bessie said, pulling cash from her corseted top.

"Why's that?" Rae got her own money ready as they were next in line.

Bessie turned to her. "Something about it doesn't feel right, you know?"

"Yeah. Seems like it'd be a big liability for everyone involved to have no safe words."

"A lot of money to be had from what my client said, but he could've been lying. He's always trying to proposition me. You know the type."

"Yeah, I sure do." Rae grinned. "You should tweezer his balls. Get him back in line."

"Ooh, that's evil! I love it."

They paid for their drinks and met back up with the rest of the group, who were being regaled with a story by a huge older man in head-to-toe leather, his surprisingly toned cheeks hanging out of his assless chaps.

Angel materialized beside Rae, hissing in her ear, "You look happy. Did you get it?"

Rae gave the slightest nod.

"Thank fuck. Can we please go now?"

"We just got here. And I thought you and Miss Big Tits were hitting it off."

"Oh, my God," Angel said, exasperation dripping from her voice. "She is all over my cooch, saying how she wants me to be her little Black slave girl, and I'm like bitch, I don't know you, and even if I did, I'm not into that plantation slave-master bullshit."

Rae, as Angel knew, wasn't into that kind of play either. Or the whole Nazi role-play some people got into. She'd heard of some Black submissives finding empowerment from it by topping white Dominants from the bottom, something she still had trouble wrapping her mind around. Then again, she found agency by beating the shit out of powerful men, which probably equated to thousands of dollars saved in therapy costs.

Speaking of powerful men, Rae spotted a decent-looking guy appreciating her from across the lounge area. He wasn't wearing a collar, and his slim-fitting dark suit, a bit out of place for the party, told her he wasn't there to dominate anyone. Too restrictive for movement. She wasn't sure he was a bottom until he winked at her and removed his tie, making sure she saw him as he snaked it around his wrists, a not-so-subtle move letting her know he was into bondage.

Her heart rate picked up as she imagined him tied up, his naked body a blank canvas for the pretty marks she could make.

"Okay, we can leave," she said to Angel, "but let me get one tiny play in first. After all, I deserve a prize."

She couldn't wait to wipe the cocky smile off the man's face, to watch his eyes glaze over with pleasure.

CHAPTER 25

RAE

2009

Sometimes, Rae felt like a little kid again when she set up her various dolls for scenes. She mostly used male figures, but sometimes she used female, and occasionally androgynous, dolls that reminded her of David Bowie, her dad's favorite singer. During her live streams, she'd dress the dolls in lingerie or underwear, sometimes full outfits, but in the end, they always ended up nude.

Viv, who was way craftier than Rae expected, helped her make miniature crops and floggers with some fabric they bought. She even found shops on Etsy where people made doll-size BDSM outfits and toys. Rae's new prized possession was a tiny strap-on dildo she'd use to punish her dolls, a.k.a. her clients on MyFreeCams. It astonished her how much they enjoyed watching her step on the dolls or dig her freshly pedicured feet into a piece of cake. The more aggressive, the better. She rarely spoke, but when she did, she'd lower her voice and inject as much sternness behind her words as possible, emulating Viv.

One of her most popular types of streams, she learned, was the one where she used dental floss or embroidery thread to tie up her dolls. Viv was teaching her about Shibari, the Japanese form of decorative rope bondage, and Rae loved creating intricate patterns with her always-willing Kens and Barbies. She found she was good at it. Plus, it didn't matter if she imagined the dolls as Clint or any number of the other men who'd hurt her. She could lose control without harming someone like she had with Farrow. She never wanted to hurt anyone like that again. She had attended more play parties with Viv, where she practiced on actual people, and she was learning how to compartmentalize the angry part of herself, the hurt girl who wanted to hit until she saw blood. It was hard work, though, and she felt safer working on inanimate objects. With the dolls, she could do whatever she wanted, not only what her audience desired to see.

Rae wasn't earning top dollar yet, but she was easily making enough to quit her job at Subway. And now that she was set up on Medicaid, she didn't have to pay as much for her prenatal visits, which allowed her to buy the bigger necessities for her baby.

"Have you thought of a name for her yet?" Viv asked while they looked for a crib at a nice secondhand store. They were taking advantage of the mild September afternoon to walk around and shop.

It hadn't taken Rae long to think of a name as soon as she'd found out she was having a girl a few weeks prior at her twenty-week visit. She remembered learning about Claude Monet her freshman year of high school, the year before her dad died. Her dad had once told her about the one and only time he'd left the country, when he was in his last year of high school. His small town's church raised enough money for him to go on his senior trip, a week in France exploring the culture and the endless museums. He said Monet's *Water Lilies* series mesmerized him with how the soft colors danced across the canvas, as peaceful as any warm, lazy Sunday afternoon in Oklahoma. It reminded him of days spent with a tall glass of sweet tea and a good book on the front porch, haint-blue paint overhead to ward off bad spirits.

"Lily," Rae said with a smile.

"That's a pretty name, hon." Viv walked over to a crib. "Lilies symbolize rebirth. I'm not religious, as you know, but my parents forced me to attend Vacation Bible School, and we always made lilies out of tissue paper to represent the resurrection."

Rebirth. Rae loved the idea of her child being her rebirth, her resurrection from the hell of California.

"What do you think of this one?" Viv asked, leaning on a white crib with elegantly painted green scrolls of sage.

"I love it, but I don't know where I'll put any of these things." Viv had already bought a crib mattress, a white changing table, and some weird contraption that allegedly stored dirty diapers without stinking up a room.

Viv sucked in her lips, thinking. "Well, I figured we'd set up everything in your room for now. But at the rate you're going with your streaming, I thought you'd want to move back to Oklahoma and be closer to family."

Rae knew she couldn't live with Viv forever, but she didn't have a solid plan yet, aside from earning as much money as she could before the baby came at the end of November, a little over two months away. When she thought about it for too long, fear paralyzed her entire body, and she began to doubt her ability to handle a child alone. She obviously understood that a newborn wouldn't be good for Viv's home business, so she had no choice but to figure out a new living situation as soon as possible.

"I'm not going back to Oklahoma. At least not yet."

Viv stopped searching through a row of strollers and looked at her. "I will never understand your mother. But, don't you have other family, like grandparents? Or aunts or uncles?"

Her mother was an only child, but her dad had a brother who was serving a long sentence for assaulting a police officer. She wasn't sure, but she thought he was still at Joseph Harp Correctional Center in Lexington. Her grandparents on her mother's side had died in a car crash when Rae was young, but her grandmother on her dad's side was alive. She lived at the top edge of Washington, where her dad said the coastal forests grew so thick no light touched the ground, and the only time Rac had ever really spoken with her was at her dad's funeral. Her grandmother was so distraught, having lost one son to the prison system and then another to an overdose, that Rae never dreamed of reaching out to her. She was in her early seventies when Rae's dad died, and at the time Clint had seemed like a better option. At least an option she was familiar with.

"No, I don't have anyone, but don't worry. I've got a lot saved for my own place." Not a total lie, but she had no idea how much she'd need to get her own apartment. She needed her own place because she and Viv had already fudged their household income so Rae could get on Medicaid. "I promise I'll start looking for an apartment as soon as I have enough."

Viv came over to her, pulling her into a side embrace to avoid Rae's baby bump. "I didn't bring it up as a way to push you out the door. Listen." She gave Rae a little squeeze. "You and Lily can stay with me for as long as you want. We can make it work. I use headphones for my sessions anyway, so a little background noise won't disrupt much. And when she's six or eight weeks old, she can start day care."

Rae hadn't even thought about day care, but the idea of leaving Lily with strangers terrified her. There was too much she needed to prepare for, and panic crept up her spine, making her nauseous. Her mouth watered uncontrollably, and she swallowed and swallowed, but she knew she couldn't stop it. She leaned over and threw up all over a white bassinet.

A young worker nearby gasped at the mess Rae made, and Viv called out, "We'll take this one. Thanks!"

Rae let out a weak laugh, which quickly turned into sobs. She wasn't a child anymore. No matter how much she felt like one sometimes when she played with her dolls during her live streams, she would never be a child again. And for the first time in a long time, she missed her mother.

CHAPTER 26

RAE

2024

Rae wrapped up with her last client for the day, her body aching from how much she'd tossed and turned in bed the night before. Her Monday wasn't as busy as she'd expected because two more clients either dropped her services or were so deathly ill, they couldn't find the strength to call and cancel. That damn article. It could've done way more damage, so she tried not to let it bother her too much. At least the clients she'd had the longest were loyal.

She changed into jeans and a breezy tunic top and redid her hair into a messy bun before going to the front.

Angel's face was screwed up in concentration as she stared at her computer screen. Rae saw she had their ledgers up. She knew what the numbers looked like, but she hadn't had time to digest what it could mean. Angel tore her eyes away from the screen and gave Rae a once-over. "You look nice."

"Nicer than those numbers?"

Angel scowled. "Morton dropped out."

"Seriously?" Charles Morton, a hedge fund manager, had been one of her oldest clients. "Fuck. Did he say why?"

"New wife, new rules."

"Bullshit. His first and second wives never knew where he spent his play money, so why would he tell the third?"

"Because the article strikes again."

Rae wanted to sit on the floor and cry. Not because of losing Morton, although it did hurt her feelings he didn't tell her in person. Coward. It was everything, and the stress kept piling on until she wanted to shut down. Lily was still avoiding her at every turn, and seeing how much pressure Angel was under with their shrinking budget was all too much. It didn't matter if clients paid in advance if they didn't schedule future sessions with her. She couldn't take much more, and she had always thought she could take on anything. She was a survivor, but sometimes she wondered at what point a person stops surviving and starts imploding.

Angel sighed. "Rae-Rae, if we keep hemorrhaging clients like this, our rainy-day fund is going to be gone in less than a month."

"I know." Rae pinched the bridge of her nose in a failed attempt to stave off a headache. "I'm going to see about booking more private events for the weekends. Something until I can get new clients on board."

Angel nodded. "So, is Mr. Hot Detective still coming here to chat?"

Rae had called him that morning and simply stated, "The thing you asked about is this Wednesday night." She knew he'd know what she meant, and she didn't want the information about the party to be connected to her. He then asked to speak with her in person, not at the station. She wasn't sure if it was because of the article and the fact that every officer there probably knew about her and her business now, and he wanted to avoid restirring the pot.

"Yeah, he should be here soon. You sure you don't want to stick around for it?"

"Can't," Angel said. "I have my dental appointment at three, and I still need to run by the vet to get Regé's meds."

"Okay. I'll call you later and let you know how it goes." She looked at her friend—her family—and it killed her to see her so worried. She went behind the front desk and hugged Angel hard from behind. "We're going to be okay. All right?"

Angel didn't say anything, but Rae felt the motion of her nodding.

Fifteen minutes later, Rae heard the intercom buzz when Dayton arrived. She placed a bookmark in the book she was reading and let him in. She saw he was dressed almost as casually as she was with a plaid button-down and jeans.

"Any good?" Dayton said when he saw her holding the book.

"I think so. I'm only on the third chapter."

"I usually know within the first paragraph."

"I try to reserve judgment until I've read the first quarter," she said. "But I have high standards."

Dayton feigned being offended by her insinuation. "Maybe I can tell right away if something's good because I have better judgment than you."

"I doubt that."

"Who's your favorite author?"

"Daphne du Maurier," Rae said without pause.

"Ah, *My Cousin Rachel.*"

Rae smiled, surprised he knew the author's work. "One of her best."

"It's my favorite."

She moved from behind the front desk, feeling every bit of her five foot two next to his tall frame. "So, you're off duty?"

"What makes you say that?" he said, looking taken aback.

She motioned to his clothing. "I thought your kind were required to wear a suit at all times, even to bed."

"You're mostly right. We had a training session this morning on a new system we're switching to soon. Hence, business casual."

"I guess it's nice they allow you to feel human every now and again," Rae said. "Where would you like to talk?"

"Doesn't matter."

She had him follow her down the hallway to the back. When they reached her small office, Dayton walked past her toward her dungeon space.

He turned around, his expression unreadable. "Actually, can we talk in here?"

Rae cocked her hip, not amused. "I'd rather not."

"I have a negotiation for you, Rae. You negotiate with your clients in there, right?"

"Yes."

"Then let's talk in there."

She had no clue what his intentions were in going inside her dungeon. "Are you trying to proposition me?"

He smiled. "I wouldn't dream of it."

She stopped herself from rolling her eyes and unlocked her dungeon room. Instead of the moody LED lighting she usually turned on, she flipped on the bright overhead recessed lights. She didn't need him getting any ideas, but if he did, she wouldn't hesitate to use her defense skills.

She sat on a white furry stool, forcing him to choose between a spank table or the cushioned bench that doubled as a cage. He chose the cage and glanced around the room almost like he was studying it.

"So, what is it you want to negotiate with me?" she said.

He pulled his eyes away from her Shibari rope collection to look at her. "I want you to come with me to that party this Wednesday."

"And why in the hell would I do that?"

"You may not care so much about what happened to Thomas Highsmith," he said, "but I know you care about the missing women in your community who might be tied to all this. Am I wrong?"

"No, but what makes you think I would have access to that party? By all accounts, it's invite only, and I don't have an invitation."

He leaned forward, resting his palms on his thighs. "They invited your friend, so I'm thinking you show up dressed in one of your dominatrix outfits. You could wear a mask of some sort to help disguise your identity and tell them your friend invited you to help her with the, uh . . . subs. I'm sure you can be persuasive, and I doubt they'd turn away a beautiful woman."

Rae couldn't hide the incredulity from her face. "This is your negotiation? Crash a party? And what would be your role? My submissive?"

He bit his bottom lip before answering. "Precisely."

"What exactly is the negotiation then? Because this isn't feeling like a choice."

"It's completely your choice, and the trade-off for doing it is that you and Angel could get removed from the suspect list."

"You could do that now without my help," she said.

"I wish I could, Rae, but even I answer to a higher-up, and my higher-up says your friend's story doesn't hold a drop of water. It's all hearsay, like I warned you before. Unless we get evidence of wrongdoing at that party."

Rae shook her head. "I can't believe this."

"I'm trying to help you and Angel, but you know I don't have access to your world."

"Let's be very clear," she said, not hiding the disdain in her voice. "That is *not* my world. We're talking about a party for rich people who by all reports don't give a shit about people's safety. And you want to waltz in there and do what? Record what happens and bring it back to your boss as proof?"

"In a nutshell, yes," he said. "And if that means dressing up in a gimp suit and pretending to be your submissive to find out what happened to your client and those missing women, I'll do it."

What he was asking her to do was insane. She thought about how much Lily and her business had already suffered because of the leak Dayton allowed to happen. She had no desire to put herself in an even worse position than she was already in.

"Well, I'll make this easy for you." Rae stood up. "It's a big hell no. You can go now."

For several moments, Dayton didn't move. He locked eyes with her with that intense stare of his. "And what happens if more women disappear? And you could've done something to prevent it?"

She wasn't about to let him guilt-trip her. She had survived in life because of herself. Not the police. And she almost said as much to him before she realized he didn't know her history.

"Dayton, my job is not to do yours for you. Please leave."

Without another word, he left.

CHAPTER 27

RAE

2009

Rae repositioned her webcam to get a full view of her hog-tied Ken doll she'd nicknamed Bruiser; then she poured chocolate syrup all over him. She moved her camera again, this time up, making sure her midsection wasn't in the shot. She wasn't comfortable yet showing her full face online, the thought of someone recognizing her in the back of her mind, so she wore a cheap cat mask on the upper half of her face. She took the syrup-covered doll and got a perfect shot of her shoving him into her mouth as far as possible without gagging, ensuring she showed a lot of teeth as she ripped the doll's head from its body. She got quite a few customer tips with that move.

Although Rae avoided doing anything too overtly sexual during her live streams, thinking it would lessen her credibility as the Domme-in-training she was trying to be, she realized she earned more if she at least showed her face at times, especially her mouth. She used to hate her pouty lips, which reminded her of her mother's, but now she loved them. She loved gliding red lipstick across them and seeing them pop against her fair skin. She loved how they looked as she blew kisses goodbye to her audience after a scene. And she loved that they helped her make money for a better life. She only wished she could kiss herself with them.

As soon as her live stream was over, she cleaned up the chocolate-syrup mess, which was made easier by having wet wipes nearby and a waterproof mat on the floor. Then she got into comfortable clothing, locked her bedroom door, and pulled her laptop onto her bed.

Whenever Viv was out of the condo like she was now, Rae got into the habit of watching BDSM porn on her laptop and masturbating to the images of people being restrained and dominated. She especially loved seeing strong men tied up and helpless and being denied release as a beautiful woman edged them ever closer to coming. It was the middle of the afternoon, but she didn't care. In some ways, the thought of Viv coming home earlier than expected heightened the experience for her.

Clint had watched porn all the time when she'd first met him. He told her it was normal for guys to watch porn during sex, that it wasn't as fulfilling for men without it playing in the background, but she knew it was a lie, even when she was fifteen. She'd seen movies, and when people made love, they weren't watching TV; they were completely enraptured with each other. She knew what romance was supposed to look like. Tom Hanks and Meg Ryan in *You've Got Mail*, chatting online for hours, building a trusting friendship that naturally turned into romance. To love. What she wanted someday. To be held and listened to, to touch and be touched. But her seven-month-pregnant body didn't care about love. It was horny all the time, and porn and a small vibrator fast-tracked her to orgasmville.

She was about to reach climax when the doorbell rang. *Shit.*

Rae closed her laptop, pulled up her lounge pants, and hesitantly made her way to the front door. She looked out the peephole and saw a man in a nice suit. Her first thought was of the bad men, but this man didn't look like any of the men she had seen in California. Still, she didn't know him and didn't feel comfortable opening the door. Just as she was about to turn away and get back to her personal time, she saw Viv walking up the sidewalk to the condo. She greeted the man, her face wary. Rae could tell she didn't know him either.

She watched Viv and the man speak for a few minutes, her friend's face appearing concerned; then the man handed her a card and made his way back to his vehicle, which Rae saw was a black Dodge Charger. She quickly moved away from the door when she heard Viv's key opening the lock.

When Viv saw Rae standing in the entryway, she quickly glanced behind herself toward the man, who was now in his vehicle.

"Get behind the door," Viv said to her, urgency in her voice, which scared Rae.

Viv shut and locked the door, looking relieved.

"I don't think he saw you," she said.

"Who was that?"

"A detective."

Rae's heart rate picked up, and she felt nauseous. "He was looking for me?"

Viv tossed her keys and purse on the entryway table and let out a huge sigh. "Yes, but I told him you no longer live here."

"What did he want?"

"Let's sit down," Viv said, moving toward the couch.

Rae joined her, her nausea getting worse by the second.

Viv knitted her brows. "He's helping the California police because your first name was given to them by the little girl you saved. She only knew your first name, your real name, but it's unusual, and the police figured you might've been missing as well. They ran your first name for any missing people within the United States, and 'Echo Phalin' pulled up a recent missing persons case. Then they searched for credit applications and driver's licenses under your name, and it pointed them straight here."

Rae couldn't believe it. Had her mother reported her missing? Maybe after her first call to her when she was still in California? Or perhaps it was her mother's new spouse who reported her. She was so confused.

"Hon, they want to speak with you about what happened with the girl. They know you didn't hurt her and that you saved her, but the girl is too young to say much else."

Rae was too stunned to speak at first, but she calmed herself enough to whisper, "They didn't ask about the fire or Clint and Bobby?"

"No, but I didn't want to take any chances, so I lied about you living here." Viv shook her head. "Shit, maybe I just made things worse."

Rae took Viv's hand. "I don't want you to get in trouble." She paused. "I think . . . I think I should talk to him, find out what he knows."

"I'm not sure if that's a—"

"No," she said, feeling more and more adamant about her decision. "I'll talk to him, tell him I told you to lie because I was frightened the people who hurt me would find me. I'll tell him what I can without saying what I did."

"But what if they do know, and they connect you to the fire and their deaths?"

"I'll take the chance. They need to know about Beth and Maria, so their families will know what happened to them. And if they arrest me for that, then . . . then . . ." Her tears cut off her words.

They clutched onto each other hard on the couch, and Rae felt like all her dreams were about to crash around her.

CHAPTER 28

RAE

2024

The Monday evening after her meeting with Dayton, Rae couldn't help feeling like she'd made the wrong decision by telling him no on the party. It was that damn pleading look he gave her. He was invested in this case—that was easy to see—but something told her he had more at stake. Stupidly, for a second, she wondered if he was worried about something happening to her if the case wasn't solved. Sometimes, she wanted someone to worry about her, someone who could hold and kiss her and say everything would be okay. It made her long even more to have someone greet her when she came home, someone who wasn't an angry teenager or a hungry black cat.

Not for the first time, she thought of Viv and the deep connection she'd had with Frederick, the man who introduced her to kink. Rae had tried to share that part of herself with people she'd dated in the past, but finding a man who wasn't intimidated by a dominant woman in bed was tricky. The only person who understood was Angel. Even then, she knew what she and Angel had wasn't a romantic love, the kind they both deserved. And sometimes she wasn't sure if love like the kind Viv and Frederick shared was possible for her. It wasn't like she needed to give a partner pain, however much she enjoyed it. She scratched that itch during her work, after all. But she wanted someone she didn't have to lie to about her past, about what she'd done to survive.

Without a single reservation, she knew she'd have to hold certain secrets until the day she died. For the most part, it didn't bother her too much, but she missed intimacy. Not sex but true intimacy, where you share those dark, hidden parts and feel acceptance. Since she could never tell a partner, "Hey, I once killed two men in a fire I started," what she wanted would never be in the cards for her.

Rae's thoughts were interrupted when she heard Lily's footsteps coming down the stairs. She was so tired, she almost stayed put on the couch with her apple-cinnamon tea warm between her hands, but she couldn't allow Lily's ghosting of her to continue. She padded to the kitchen and saw Lily searching through the pantry.

"I got you more of those Tate's oatmeal raisin cookies you like," Rae said.

Lily pulled the bag of cookies from a shelf as she offered Rae the tiniest of acknowledgments by glancing at her.

"Lily, we can't keep on like this." She tried and failed to keep the quiver from her voice. "I miss you, honey, and I'm sorry this whole thing embarrassed you with your friends. I truly am, and I'll do whatever you need me to do to rebuild trust. Just please talk to me."

Her daughter stared at the white quartz countertop as if it held all the answers to her problems. Then she looked up at Rae, her eyes red from crying. "I don't feel like I know you anymore. Like maybe I never knew you."

"You do, honey. I'm still the same person." Rae rushed to Lily, wrapping her arms around her. She felt a slight thrill when her daughter didn't push her away. "I'm the same, but there are some things I need to tell you about my life before you were born. And it's so hard for me to tell you because I don't want you to hurt or feel sad about it."

Lily pulled back a little, tears coming down her pretty face. "I want you to tell me everything, Mom. No more lies."

"No more lies. I promise."

Rae prepared Lily some hot tea to go with her cookies, and they settled on the living room couch. She didn't know how to start, so she started from the beginning, with her parents divorcing and her dad's overdose. Then Clint sweeping her off to California for a new life when her mother wouldn't take her in.

"Wait," Lily said, "your mom wouldn't let you live with her? Why?"

The confusion on Lily's face pained Rae. She had no good way to explain it to her because she never understood it herself.

"My mother wasn't a happy person, and she tried to have a different life with someone else. She got married to the last man she was cheating on my dad with."

"Did she have kids with him?" Lily said.

After all these years, her chest tightened to think of it. "Yes, she had a daughter."

"Have you ever met her?"

"Not in person," Rae said. "We messaged a few times through Facebook a year ago when she moved to Texas. She's a hard-core conservative like her dad and stopped messaging me after I posted about us going to the Pride parade last summer."

Rae braced herself and continued with her story, knowing her daughter would have more tough questions for her. She told her about her time in California in the house near the ocean, but she tried not to go into the details of her abuse. She'd had many discussions with Lily about consent and what it looked like, and it was easier to tell her she was raped than to tell her all the other horrible things they did to her for their entertainment.

"So, that Clint person, he trafficked you and those other women in the house?" Lily's eyes were wide, her oatmeal cookies and tea untouched.

"At the time, I didn't know what it was called, but yes."

She knew she needed to tell her about Beth and Katelyn, too—the hardest parts for her to talk about. Lily seemed to sense she was struggling to say more because she took her hand and said, "It's okay, Mom."

Rae took a few deep breaths and told Lily the rest. All of it, about how Clint accidentally killed Beth with an overdose, about Maria getting Katelyn before she died—whether an accidental overdose or not—and how Rae escaped with Katelyn after drugging Bobby, shooting Clint, and starting the fire.

Lily was quiet for a long time, and she knew her daughter was calculating the years. Then she asked the question Rae dreaded the most. "Were you pregnant with me when you escaped?"

Rae nodded.

"So, my biological dad wasn't a one-night stand thing, like you told me?"

"No, honey."

"Do you know who got you pregnant?"

Rae wanted to disappear into the couch. She'd promised no more lies, but she couldn't bring herself to tell her daughter the truth. "I don't, and maybe that's a good thing."

Lily's mouth dropped open like she had more questions, but she said nothing.

"I know this is a lot to take in," Rae said, which had to be the biggest understatement ever. "And I don't want you to think for one second that you weren't wanted because, honey, you saved me, and in a way, you also saved that little girl because I wouldn't have had the strength to do what I did if it weren't for wanting you to be safe."

Lily's eyes filled with anger, and Rae was afraid of what she was thinking.

"If your mom would've helped you, you wouldn't have gone through all that." Lily's jaw tightened. "I hate her for it."

Rae pulled her in close and held her. "If she had taken me in, you wouldn't exist. I would go through it all again if it meant having you."

"But what if the police ever find out about what you did? They'll arrest you."

Someday, Rae would tell her more, but she recognized Lily was reaching maximum capacity for revelations. "They won't. I promise you."

Her daughter looked unconvinced. "How did you become a . . . dominatrix?" Lily said the word like it was wrapped in filth, which stung.

"First off, I want you to know how I feel about my work. There's nothing wrong with any kind of sex work, even prostitution, as long as it's consensual and between adults, no matter what the current laws may say. What happened to me when I was younger was obviously the furthest thing from consensual." She briefly told her about Viv and how she'd come to live with her and about how she'd gotten started in her career. "The work I do now gave me back control of my life, and it allows me to give you the kind of life I wish I had growing up. It also allows me to help other people who sometimes feel shame in who they are and what they like because some people in society think it's wrong and are vocal about it."

"Like how the kids in middle school bullied Klo for being nonbinary?"

"Sort of. Like LGBTQ folks, people into what's called BDSM can face a lot of prejudice for coming out about it. I've known people who've lost their jobs for being open about doing the sorts of things I do for my clients." Rae glanced at her watch. It was late and a school night. "There's so much more I want to tell you about Viv and when I lived in Albuquerque, but you need to get ready for bed, and I have an early session tomorrow."

They both stood up, Lily looking dazed. Rae hugged her long and hard and kissed her head, which was tricky since Lily was now taller than her. "I love you more than anything in this world."

"I love you, too, Mom."

Lily didn't seem to want to let go, and Rae didn't mind one bit. They stood like that for a good while before Lily broke free and headed back to her room, abandoning her cookies and now-cold tea on the coffee table.

Rae cleaned up the table, taking their mugs to the kitchen. She grabbed her phone off the counter and did one last check of her social media, and her heart stopped when she came across a friend's Facebook post:

> Hey, everyone, this is to let you know that Devon Mayes has been missing since last Friday. She was last seen by her sister when they ate lunch. Devon said she was going to run errands before meeting with friends, but she never made it to the happy hour meetup. If you have any information, please contact local authorities. Her family and friends are so worried about her, and we pray for her safe return home.

Under the post was a selfie of Devon she recognized as her friend's Facebook profile pic, Devon's vibrant red hair blowing against her smiling face, the orange sunset forming a glowing halo around her head.

Those rich, elite motherfuckers. They got to her; Rae knew it in her bones.

She didn't think as she pulled up the number saved in her phone. She dialed, not caring that it was after eleven. Dayton picked up on the second ring.

"Rae?" He sounded wide awake. "What is it? Are you okay?"

"I'll do it. I'll go to the party with you."

CHAPTER 29

RAE

2009

It was freezing inside the waiting area at the police station, and goose bumps rose all over Rae's body. Normally, she was so hot from her pregnancy she would've been happy walking around naked everywhere, but the station felt like a walk-in freezer.

Another half hour passed before the detective came out to greet her. He was of average height with graying brown hair and kind eyes.

"Echo Phalin," he said, his hand outstretched to shake her own. "I'm Detective McHugh. Sorry for the long wait."

"Nice to meet you."

"Follow me. I have a quiet space for us to talk."

She followed Detective McHugh toward the back of the station through a series of hallways to a small room. It looked like the kind of interrogation room she'd seen on TV shows, and she felt her armpits and palms get wet.

"Have a seat." He directed her to take the plastic chair opposite him, a scratched-up table between them. She wondered how many people had sat in this room before, their nerves so bad they dug their fingernails across the table's surface. "I'm glad you decided to speak with us, Echo. I know it must've been hard coming forward to talk about what happened to you."

"Um, sir," she said, hating how timid her voice came out. "I go by Rae Phalin now."

"Okay, Rae." He then told her he was going to record their discussion to make sure he got everything she said correct. "I want you to tell me in your own words how you came to meet Katelyn Reid."

It was strange hearing Katelyn's full name. Her reunion with her parents had been all over the news in California, but the media had left out her first name since she was so young.

"Uh, two men held me in a house in Santa Monica. I'm not sure where the house was, but it was near the ocean," Rae lied. She knew exactly where the house was before she set fire to it, but the detective didn't need to know it. "Another woman was there too. Her name was Maria."

"Do you know Maria's last name?"

"No, but she had dark, wavy hair, and I think she might've been Hispanic because she spoke Spanish a lot." Rae recalled how Maria would curse at Clint and Bobby in Spanish because she knew they wouldn't understand her, and Rae caught a few words because of her two years of Spanish in school.

"And what were the men's names?"

"Clint and Bobby."

"And why were they holding you and Maria?"

Rae stared down at the erratic gouges in the table. "For the other men who came to the house. They . . . they kept us for them."

"For sex?"

This was so much harder to talk about with a stranger, and she wished Viv were sitting next to her. She sucked in a breath and nodded.

"I need you to please say it aloud, Rae."

"Yes, for sex."

"And how did you meet Katelyn?"

"One of the men, the one named Clint, forced Maria to get a little girl from the pier, so she brought back Katelyn."

"And what did Maria do with Katelyn when she brought her to the house?"

"Maria didn't do anything to her. She only got her and then she . . . she died the next day." Her vision blurred with tears, but she forced her emotions down. "She didn't want to get Katelyn, but Clint threatened her, so she did it. I think she overdosed on purpose because she knew what would happen to Katelyn, and she felt responsible."

Detective McHugh was taking notes. "What was going to happen to Katelyn?"

"These rich men were going to buy her from Clint and Bobby. I'm not sure what they were going to do with her, but I think the same thing they did with us. The rich men were upset because the first girl, Beth, died when Clint accidentally killed her."

The detective's expression grew grimmer. "I know this is difficult to talk about, Rae, and you're doing a really good job." He paused. "Now, I need you to tell me everything you know about Beth. What she looked like, her last name if you know it, her age—anything that could be helpful for us to identify her so we can inform her family."

Rae told him everything she could remember, including how Beth died.

"It sounds like she was a fighter, like you," Detective McHugh said. "I have another difficult question for you, Rae. Katelyn's family wants to get her the best possible help for what she's gone through, so they need to know if anyone ever touched Katelyn sexually."

"No, never. I was always with her so they wouldn't touch her."

"Okay, that's good. She was lucky to have you watching out for her." The detective offered her a small smile and wrote down more on his notepad. "So, now, we need to know how you and Katelyn left the house."

This was where Rae knew she had to stay strong. Say the lie and mean it. "Clint left the house, so it was just Katelyn, me, and Bobby. Then Bobby took some drugs and passed out on the couch, so I got Katelyn, and we left."

"And that's when you took her to the fire station?"

"Yes."

"Do you know if Clint or Bobby tried to search for you and Katelyn?"

"I don't know. I just tried to get far away from where they kept us."

"And when you escaped, why didn't you go back home to your family?" he said. "Why did you come here with a woman you didn't know?"

Rae dug her thumbnail into her palm as hard as she could and imagined she was hurting one of her dolls during a live stream. "I didn't have anywhere else to go. My mother and I . . . we don't talk, and my dad's dead."

He nodded, writing more down. "Is there anything else you can tell us about Clint, Bobby, or the other people they were working with, the rich men, that might help us find them?"

Rae knew Clint's last name—Clarkson—but she didn't want the police to know and find some way to identify the bodies in the house and connect them to her. She knew Clint didn't own the house since a company called Felton Holdings LLC did, and she couldn't find information on it, no matter how much she searched online.

"All I can do is describe them."

She gave the detective a full description of both Clint and Bobby, how Clint was lanky with dark hair and Bobby was shorter and more muscular with thick, mousy-brown hair.

"Thank you, Rae. You've been very helpful." Detective McHugh handed her his card, which she already had from Viv, but she took it anyway. "If you think of anything else, please call me. And we have your contact information in case we have further questions."

That was it. No more questions. Nothing about a fire. No questions about Rae's pregnancy and whether it was tied to her being trafficked. No gotchas before she left the interrogation room at all. He simply shook her hand and walked her back to the front.

It wasn't until she was sitting in her Civic, the September sun shining bright into her hot car, that she realized why she felt so hollow inside.

Not once did the detective offer her help after the hell she'd experienced for nearly four long years.

CHAPTER 30
RAE

2024

Rae had hardly slept the night before, after learning about Devon, and her body was wound tighter than the rope she'd used to bind her last client of the day. She felt responsible for her friend's disappearance, although she knew it was stupid to think that way. After all, she'd done what Devon had asked her to do by keeping her name out of the investigation, but now it didn't matter because Rae had no choice but to reveal it.

When she'd called Dayton last night, he was confused at first about her one-eighty decision, until she told him about Devon. And now they had little time to prepare for the party the next night, so Rae had asked him to come to her space after she was done with work.

As if she weren't already feeling enough guilt about Devon, she'd lied to Angel. She'd never told her about Dayton's proposal, and she said nothing about agreeing to go to the party. Angel had been so busy handling their struggling business budget while trying to prepare for her Bahamas trip, she hadn't seen the social media posts about Devon yet, and Rae didn't tell her. Instead, she suggested Angel take the afternoon off to de-stress. Then she arranged for Lily to stay over at Klo's house the next night so she wouldn't be home alone while Rae was out.

Rae's phone buzzed. A text from Dayton: I'm here.

She'd asked him to park in the back of the building so their meeting could be as covert as possible. Maybe she was being paranoid, but she imagined someone watching her business, seeing who came in and out.

She let Dayton in through the back door, and he immediately took off his suit jacket and loosened his tie.

"Fuck, it's hot out there," he said, wiping sweat from his forehead.

"I don't want to know how June's going to feel." Rae was a cool-weather person, through and through. "I need it to be October, like, yesterday."

"Same."

He followed her down the hallway to the dungeon space. Before she opened the door, she turned to him and said, "Are you ready for a crash course in BDSM practices?"

"I think so." He didn't sound like he was ready at all, but Rae wasn't about to walk into the party with Dayton looking like a scared, lost puppy.

"Just pretend you're back in college, and you have a final the next day you haven't studied for yet." She opened the dungeon door and flipped on her low lights, keeping the brighter recessed lights off to avoid spurring a headache from her lack of sleep.

Dayton draped his suit jacket and tie across her spank bench and rolled up his shirtsleeves. She noticed he had a tattoo of an intricate feather stretching the inside length of his right forearm. The feather was so detailed it looked real.

"That's a beautiful tattoo," she said. She had wondered if he was indigenous due to his deep olive complexion, but it felt rude to ask.

He looked down at his arm like he'd forgotten he had it. "Thanks. Got it a long time ago. Do you have any?"

"No. I've never been able to decide on a design, but maybe someday."

He smirked. "Sure you're not afraid of the pain?"

"Pain is the last thing I'm afraid of."

Dayton sat down on her furry stool and whipped out a little notepad. He looked like an overly eager student.

Rae went over to him and snatched the notepad from his hands, tossing it to the floor. She thought it best to go ahead and throw him into the deep end. "You won't need that. You only need your eyes and ears. When we're at the party, you will not speak unless I ask you a direct question. And when you answer me, you will include the phrase 'Yes, Mistress.' You will not interact with anyone else. If someone touches you, I will take care of it. You'll need to take all the tough man, patriarchy shit you have and tuck it away for the night because you will be mine for the evening."

Dayton opened his mouth as if he was about to argue with her, but he kept quiet.

"Good. I'm glad you understand." She began by going over general safety protocols for BDSM and basic types of play he might see at the party. Then she described the types of impact implements used in BDSM play. She walked over to her wall of toys and picked up one of her favorite impact tools. "This beauty is a studded paddle. You can stop looking scared because I'm not going to hit you with it."

"I'm not scared."

Rae glared at him. "Come here." She could tell he'd never had a woman speak to him like this. His face was a mixture of curiosity and confusion about what to do. "Dayton, I need you to get used to me speaking to you like this because you will likely see a lot of people commanding others at the party. As a submissive, you don't have to worry about anything except for what I want you to do. So, come here."

He got up and slowly walked over to her. She almost wished they were having a real session, where she could have him strip down to nothing, but she had to stay focused.

"Hold out your hand." He did as he was told, and she ran the paddle across his palm. He shuddered a little, but she couldn't tell if he liked it. She motioned to her wall of toys. "You might see many items like this being used at the party, and from what I've heard, not all the submissives there will look like they're enjoying what's being done to them. But, no matter what we see, we cannot intervene or this whole thing will go to shit. Do you understand?"

"Uh, if I see someone getting seriously hurt, I have a duty—"

"You have no duty but to do as you're told while we're there. Do. You. Understand?" she said, punching each word so he'd know she was serious.

"Yes." He added a spiteful "Mistress," and she wanted so badly to tie him up and whip him.

"One big rule while we're there is to never drink anything with alcohol. Really, don't drink anything they offer us unless you know for sure it's water."

"You think they'd try to drug us?" Dayton said, already breaking her rules about not speaking.

"I don't know what they'd do, but I don't want to take a chance. And I didn't give you permission to speak."

He let out a frustrated sigh. "Okay, Rae, I'm all about learning what I need to know, but I am not submitting to you right now. Tomorrow night, I'm all yours, and I'll be the best damn submissive you've ever seen, but right now, I don't want to pretend. So, let's talk as ourselves."

Rae crossed her arms. "Fine. We'll talk as ourselves, then, but it won't change how I'll be treating you tomorrow night because it'll be expected."

"I know." Dayton stood next to her Shibari ropes. He reached out and touched one of the silky coils hung up on the wall, and she remembered how he'd stared at them the other day. "Huh. Softer than I thought it'd be."

Rae moved past him and pulled the rope from the wall. "You know, BDSM and dominating isn't all about pain. Some people are into sensory play, like feathers and furry mittens. Or being tied up in soft rope like this." She uncoiled part of the rope and placed the end of it in his hand.

He looked at her with what she interpreted as anticipation, and she suddenly felt nervous.

"Aren't you going to show off your skills?" he said, his lips curling up ever so slightly.

"If you consent, sure."

"I do."

"Place your hands behind your back."

Dayton let out a hearty laugh. "I know you got a kick out of saying that, but I like to keep my hands where I can see them."

"Suit yourself." She unraveled the rest of the purple rope and quickly got to work securing his wrists together, explaining the knots she was making as she went along. Then she created an elaborate pattern as she bound his forearms as well. It all took her less than five minutes. When she was done, Dayton tested her work by trying to wiggle free. She enjoyed seeing him tied up, more so because he seemed so open to trying it.

"Shit," he said, a big grin on his face. "You're really good."

His praise stirred butterflies in her again. She knew she was in danger of pushing the line too far with him, but she tugged his bound hands down anyway, pulling him closer to her, only a whisper's distance from her face. "And now I can do practically anything I want with you."

She felt it again. His anticipation. It was the same electric current she noticed in her clients the moment before she'd strike them, when their desires reached out to greet her as they welcomed the pain she joyfully bestowed. She knew if she tugged him any closer, she'd be making a big mistake, so she released her hold on him.

She avoided the puzzled expression in his eyes as she unbound him as fast as she had tied him, and she thought she sensed the spell breaking between them until he softly said, "Rae?"

She never knew a name could contain so much unspoken, but she made herself ignore it.

"I hate to disappoint you," she said as she coiled the rope back into a tight circle, "but I don't have a gimp suit. My clients usually bring their own outfits. I do have a mask that should fit you, though. We don't need anyone recognizing you."

Dayton rubbed his wrists. "What should I wear? It has to be something I can put my bodycam on."

Rae dug out the gimp mask. "Hmm, would you be comfortable with your shirt off? We could maybe have the bodycam on a leather chest harness."

"It'd be too noticeable. It's smaller than the bodycams street officers wear, but it's still the size of a button."

"Okay, so I'd go with your nicest suit. If you have a tux, even better." She handed the mask to him, and he gently took a hold of her wrist.

"You don't have to do this if you don't want to," he said, his eyes saying the opposite of his words.

She placed her hand over his. "We're going to do this, but we can't fuck it up. I want to come home to my kid, and I know you want to come home safe to yours too."

He nodded.

CHAPTER 31

RAE

2009

Since Rae's meeting with Detective McHugh, she couldn't sleep. She told herself it was due to Lily's near-constant movements inside her belly throughout the night, but she knew it was really because she'd opened up herself and Viv to possible danger by talking with the detective. They'd gotten what they wanted and dusted their hands of her. She didn't trust the police. She didn't trust anyone aside from Viv.

When Rae had told Viv about the meeting, Viv was enraged with the New Mexico police. "The least they could've done was offer you counseling services," she'd said to Rae. "The lazy bastards."

Rae thought it was more than laziness. It was apathy. Like her mother, unconcerned about anything that didn't directly affect her. She only hoped the police would be able to use the information she'd given them to find Beth's and Maria's families, but she didn't like exposing herself after being comfortably hidden for so many months.

She didn't want to seem paranoid, but she found herself staying inside more and more, afraid to leave the house. She used to go to the store to help with grocery shopping, but now she gave Viv money to get her what she needed. Viv noticed Rae reverting to her hermit existence, but she didn't say anything.

They went on for a week like that, pretending everything was fine, until Rae had no choice but to leave the house since she had a prenatal visit at Planned Parenthood.

"Wow, twenty-seven weeks now," the nurse said as she removed the lubricant gel from Rae's abdomen with a paper towel. "Getting closer. How have you been feeling, Rae?"

"Fine. Just a little tired."

Rae normally enjoyed watching Lily doing acrobatics on the ultrasound screen, but now she wanted to get back to the safety of the condo.

"I don't want to worry you, but your baby has tachycardia."

Rae sat up on the exam table, sudden anxiety making her face go numb. "What does that mean?"

"It's an abnormally high heart rate. Normal is between one hundred ten and one hundred sixty beats per minute, and your baby's is at one hundred ninety," the nurse said. "Have you had a lot of stressors lately?"

Rae paused. "Yes."

"That could be the cause, but just to be safe, I'm referring you to a prenatal cardiologist." She placed a hand on Rae's shoulder. "In the meantime, try to find ways to eliminate as much stress as possible. Take gentle walks and meditate. Yoga's good too."

After she made it back to her car, Rae held her belly and cried. "I'm so sorry," she whispered to her baby. It was her fault for focusing so much on all the bad things that could possibly happen, storing up apprehension in her body with no release, instead of worrying about being healthy for her child. As she drove home, she vowed to start walking along the trails near Viv's condo.

Really, she wished she could de-stress by topping an actual person, not a plastic doll for online viewers, but it was too physically demanding for her now with how big her belly was getting and how swollen her feet were all the time. She was never so relaxed in her life as she was after she dominated someone, though. She fed off their energy, the thrilling exchange of the power dynamic she shared with them, which could never be replicated online.

As she pulled up to the condo, she saw Viv talking to a man outside their door. She didn't recognize him, but something about the way he looked at Viv bothered her. Like he owned her. She knew that look.

Viv didn't seem to notice Rae as she parked and watched them from afar. They were arguing about something, and then the man yanked on Viv's arm like he was trying to get her to go with him. She slapped him, and he pushed her hard against the front door.

Rae jumped out of her car and ran up to them. "Get your hands off her!"

The man turned around and glanced at Rae. "Mind your own business, preggo."

"She is my business."

"Rae, let me handle this," Viv said, her voice trembling.

The man looked at Viv. "Who the fuck is this girl?"

"Who the fuck are you?" Rae said, and Viv shot her a wide-eyed warning.

The man turned back to Rae, a nasty grin on his face. "I'm the messenger."

She didn't know what he meant, but she wasn't about to let him hurt Viv. "Well, messenger, you have a second before I call the cops."

He leered at her before he whipped around and held Viv against the door by her neck. "One week," he yelled in her ear and stormed off to his car.

Rae quickly opened the door and pulled a stunned Viv inside, locking the dead bolt behind them. She sat her friend on the couch and went to the front window.

"He's gone now."

Viv kept touching her throat, her face drained of any color.

"Who was that?"

Viv looked at her and closed her eyes, shaking her head.

Rae sat down next to Viv and put her arm around her. "Did he hurt you? Do you want me to call the cops?"

Viv opened her eyes. "No, don't call them. I'm okay."

"Who is he?" Rae asked again.

"My ex-husband."

CHAPTER 32

RAE

2024

Dayton picked up Rae from her house at nine in a vehicle she didn't recognize as his. When she got into the car, he explained how it was an undercover police vehicle with fake tags in case anyone at the party tried to track them, which didn't help her to get her nerves under control. No matter how hard she tried, she couldn't get her mind in Domme mode, but she needed to, fast.

"You look nice," she said to him because he did. His dark suit was more formal than his detective clothing, and it looked good against his olive complexion.

"Thank you." Dayton glanced over at her as he drove. "You look nice, too, but . . ."

"Don't worry, I've got a party-appropriate outfit under this." She hated showing up to events in a skimpy Domme outfit, much preferring to reveal her attire when she chose to, so she typically wore a long belted silk dressing gown that reminded her of the 1940s film sirens she used to watch with her dad. She even had her hair done up in a pinup-girl style. She smiled to herself, thinking of Viv and her love of 1940s fashion.

"When we get there," Dayton said, "I want to hang back for a bit, let the place get busy so I can get footage of as many people as possible."

"Got it. And I'll keep them distracted so they don't suspect you're recording."

With how fast Dayton was driving, it only took them twenty minutes to reach the outer limits of the city. Then they were on a bunch of side roads that seemed to stretch on for miles into the darkness since there were no streetlights in the area. Rae counted the signs warning of deer crossings, hoping they wouldn't slam into one.

Eventually, they slowed until they found the turnoff for the mansion, which was at the end of a long tree-lined drive. There was a massive closed gate at the end of the path, and Dayton cussed under his breath. They stopped and saw a brick post containing an intercom. Dayton pushed the button, and a man with a gruff voice spoke.

"What is the password for the evening?"

Rae and Dayton looked at each other, their mouths miming "Fuck."

Rae leaned across Dayton. "My name is Mistress V. I'm a friend of Mistress Bessie, who invited me to help her with scenes. She must've forgotten to tell me about the password."

"Hold, please."

For several horrible minutes, they waited in silence. She knew Bessie wasn't there, and she hated throwing her name out like that. Rae was about to tell Dayton it was over and to turn around when the man's voice came back on the intercom.

"You may enter. Pull into the east parking lot and check in with the hostess. They're waiting for you."

The gate rolled open, and Dayton pulled forward. After they parked, Dayton surprised her by holding her hand. His palm was slightly clammy, and she was positive hers was as well. He didn't say anything, just squeezed her palm, which made her feel somewhat better about walking into a wasp's nest.

Rae slipped on her leather cat mask, which covered the top half of her face, while Dayton put on the latex mask she'd let him borrow, which was shaped like a dog's head. She placed a studded collar on his neck and connected it to a long metal leash.

"Ready?" she said.

"Woof."

They walked into a dimly lit side entrance to the mansion where two hostesses checked them for weapons and cell phones. They went through Rae's toy bag thoroughly as well. Then they were asked to stay there. For what, they didn't know, but Rae's heart rate was going nuts until she saw Bessie coming toward them, wearing a stunning blue corset covered in rhinestones. She couldn't believe her friend had come to the party, but she couldn't fault her when these bastards apparently offered a ton of money to Dommes.

"Mistress V!" Bessie said with delight, as if she'd been expecting Rae all along. She looked over at Dayton. "And you brought a pet. What's this fine creature's name?"

"Fido." Rae tugged on Dayton's leash, and he lowered his head in deference like she'd taught him.

Bessie pulled in close to Rae, hugging her as she whispered in her ear, "I don't know why you're here, but please don't lie to them again."

"Mistress," one of the hostesses said to Rae. "You may leave your bag and robe here. The floor has many fine implements for you to use."

Rae wasn't keen on leaving hundreds of dollars' worth of toys with strangers, but she complied. When she removed her silk dressing gown, she heard Dayton gasp. She tried not to smile, but she knew she looked good in her retro-inspired, high-waisted purple latex booty shorts and her mostly sheer, black lace halter top. She wore her favorite thigh-high black boots, with no stockings on.

Bessie took Rae's arm. "Let me show you around."

Rae gently pulled on the leash, and Dayton followed behind them.

They entered a huge hall that reminded Rae of a ballroom. It felt like something out of *Downton Abbey*, with heavy antique chairs and chaise lounges throughout the massive space, ornate crystal chandeliers dimly lit overhead, lush velvet draperies, and carved wood accents everywhere. There were play scenes going on throughout, with small audiences surrounding each. She saw most of the people in attendance were men, and all the men were white, some younger but mostly older. She only saw one other male sub.

She didn't turn around to look at Dayton, but she hoped he was getting good footage of the people there because she was already seeing a lot wrong with the party. One woman submissive was tied to a large Saint Andrew's cross, but she was clearly unconscious from the way her head and body lay limp and unresponsive to the hits being administered by a male Dominant. Another woman, who was being held by two large men, was hysterically crying as a younger man finished carving the word "whore" above her right breast. Rae looked across the room and saw three men having brutal sex with a woman who appeared so out of it there was no way she could've consented.

Rae could tell Bessie was as uncomfortable as she was with the scenes going on, but they were both good at hiding their shock. She could only imagine what Dayton was thinking.

Bessie brought them over to a group of impeccably dressed older men. "They want you to do a scene for them," she said in Rae's ear. "Do whatever they ask you to do."

Rae had expected as much, which was why she'd brought her bag of toys, but she didn't like being thrown into it like this.

"Good evening, Mistress V," a striking man said to her, and she knew he had to be the tall, blue-eyed, white-haired man Devon had described to her. She recalled how Dayton had tensed up after she'd mentioned him when they were at the coffee shop, and she saw him stiffen again. "What a beautiful pussy." The man motioned to her cat mask. "Are you declawed?"

"It's inhumane to declaw a cat," Rae said.

"I'm glad we agree." The man snapped at a woman who was completely naked. She brought him a pair of black gloves fitted with sharp metal claws on each finger, which he handed to Rae. "Make her bleed for us."

Rae handed him back the gloves. "I only use my claws in defense."

The white-haired man smirked. "Bold. But you're new, so we'll give you a pass this time. And only because Mistress Bessie's been such a pleasure." He glanced at Dayton behind her. "Perhaps you'd have more fun with your puppy."

"No," Rae said too fast. "He's being punished, so no playtime for him." Not that Rae didn't want to dominate Dayton, but she wasn't going to do it without his consent and in front of dozens of rich assholes. "I'd love to play with your pet, though, if she's willing."

"She's always willing." He snapped his fingers, and the sub came back over to them. She knelt before Rae, her head down. "Use a whip."

Rae didn't like being told what to do with a submissive, but she remembered Bessie's warning, so she had the sub stand up and move to the wall where there was a metal hard point. She placed the sub in restraints and secured her to the hard point, so her arms were raised above her, leaving her bare back toward the audience forming around them. Rae saw Dayton in the small crowd, his eyes visible through the mask, his body frozen at seeing what Rae saw. The sub's back was already covered in angry red welts that looked ready to split open.

She spent the next ten minutes trying not to make the sub bleed with her strikes. Luckily, she knew how to be gentle with a whip, but every hit caused the sub to flinch. She felt no pleasure in hitting the woman. It was impossible when she didn't feel either of them were in control of the situation.

"Make her bleed," another older man in the audience said, his voice filled with boredom.

"Yes," the white-haired man said. "Be a good pussy and give us blood."

Rae turned toward the sub and closed her eyes. She hated this so much. She lightly stroked the sub's back as she whispered to her, "This one will hurt the most, but it'll be the last. I'm so sorry."

She raised the whip and brought it down hard on the sub's back, and a long streak of red formed. The sub cried out, not in pleasure, as blood dripped down the woman's backside, and Rae's stomach turned. The audience behind her clapped, something so deeply wrong and bizarre to her. She looked around for a blanket, bottled water, anything at all for aftercare, but there was nothing.

A man wearing a gimp mask swooped in and took the sub away, but Rae didn't know where he was taking her.

"Good kitty," the white-haired man said. Another sub brought over shot-size drinks on a large tray. "Let's have a toast." He saw Rae's hesitation. "No need to worry. It's all natural—just a blend of fruit juices and vitamins. Got to keep up your strength."

Everyone in the circle of people, including Bessie, took the offering. Rae reluctantly accepted one. The sub handed one to Dayton without asking Rae if he could have one first, which she found odd since it went against normal protocols and no other sub was offered a drink. She stared at Dayton, hoping her eyes were telling him they had no choice but to take the shot. If they didn't, they would look out of place. She told herself it was probably safe since they were all drinking it.

"Bottoms up!" the man said, and they all downed their shots. It tasted too sweet and tangy, and she wanted to throw it up.

Rae needed to get away from the group before she went into a full panic attack, so she pushed through the crowd to Dayton, grabbed his leash, and directed him to follow her. He tried to whisper something to her as they walked, but she stopped him. She was too nauseous to speak yet.

She found an obscenely lavish bathroom, leaving Dayton outside while she ran cold water over a thick hand towel and pressed it to the back of her neck, which didn't do much to calm her. She'd been in the bathroom for too long, and she didn't want Dayton to worry. After leaving the bathroom, they wandered around forever, searching until they eventually found an exit leading to an outside courtyard surrounded by a beautiful garden. It looked like something out of a fairy tale, with tall hedges and pathways leading in various directions.

As soon as she found them a quiet, secluded spot, she pulled off her cat mask. Dayton yanked his off his head as fast as he could and removed the collar and leash from his neck. His face was as pale as if he'd walked through a thousand ghosts at once.

"Are you okay?" she asked him.

"No. You?"

"Not even close. Let's sit down and cool off." She saw he was overheated from wearing the mask. At least the evening was pleasantly mild.

There was no bench in the hidden spot she'd found, so they sat on the thick grass. Dayton loosened his black tie and collapsed back onto the ground like he was exhausted. Rae removed her boots and stretched out on the grass next to him. They stayed silent for a long time.

"That was . . . I don't even know what the fuck I just witnessed in there," he said, looking up at the sky. "That one woman being cut up and the other woman with the three men . . . you have no idea how hard it was for me not to do something."

"I know."

Dayton turned his head to look at her. "I could tell you were trying not to hurt the woman when you were whipping her. I'm sorry I got you into this."

"I got myself into this," Rae said. "Did you get the footage?"

"Yeah." He sat up and removed his jacket and tie. "God, it's so hot."

Now that he said it, Rae found she was hot, too, but the night air had felt so cool and inviting before.

"There were too many people I recognized in there," he said. "Politicians, business leaders. I even saw the former police chief. This is so much worse than I imagined."

"I want to know who that white-haired man is. He seems to be a leader of . . . whatever this is."

"He has to be. How he treated those women, like they were animals. I wanted to kill him."

Dayton turned quiet next to her. She noticed he was running his hands along the grass, up and down, his eyes closed, and she wondered if he was doing it to self-soothe after witnessing so much horrible shit. But then she found herself doing it too. The grass was so cool, and her skin felt fevered. She wanted to remove the sweaty lace clinging to her breasts, but her brain kicked in and stopped her from pulling off her halter top.

"This is the fluffiest grass I've ever felt," Dayton said, his eyes open again and staring at her. "It feels so good."

"It does feel good." She wanted to roll around on it like a dog, to feel each blade poking her skin. A question popped into her head, and she paused her grass-stroking. "Can I ask you something?"

"Of course."

"Why did you look up information on me? I mean, outside of your investigation."

He didn't appear surprised by her question. "I wanted to see if my instincts were right about you."

"What did your instincts tell you?"

"That you've been through a lot." He smiled a little. "And that you would be someone important in my life."

Rae couldn't fully process the candor of his words, her mind concentrated on both the overwhelming sensations around her—the cool grass, the heavy, sweet scent of the garden's flowers, the hum of insects—and how what he said pooled in her chest, warm and fuzzy.

She turned onto her side, facing him, and he did the same. "And were your instincts correct?"

He reached out and cupped her cheek, and she couldn't breathe. She wanted to feel his lips on hers, and then he was there, inches from her face, his woodsy-spiced cologne drawing her closer until there was no space between them, only urgency as he held the back of her head and their lips met. His hand pressed low on her back, pushing her into him, his hardness against her as their kisses grew deeper and more needful.

She felt strange, like it was all a dream, and she wanted to be everywhere at once but also inside him, to be in his lungs breathing his air, to feel what he felt touching her and her, him. She knew this feeling, and the realization pulled her from the moment. She needed to say something to him, but she didn't want it to stop.

"Dayton," she breathed into his ear between kisses. "I think they drugged us."

He didn't stop kissing her, so she said it louder. He pulled back from her.

"Shit." He seemed to assess how he was feeling. "I think you're right. I feel weird." He looked confused. "But I . . . I've thought of you . . . and this."

"I've thought of it too," she admitted without a second thought. "I think they gave us ecstasy or something like it." It was one of the many things Clint used to give her to make her more compliant for his customers. "It can take a few hours to pass. We won't be safe to drive until it does."

"We should stay here until it wears off." His hands were still on her, his fingers gripping at her hip hard like he wanted to open up her skin and crawl inside. He moved his hand over her stomach and up to the center of her chest, the heat from his palm seeming to go through her.

"You're right. We should stay here." She unbuttoned his shirt and lowered her hand, gripping him through his pants; the soft groan he made she swallowed with a kiss.

He pushed up her lacy top and kissed her breasts before running his teeth along one of her nipples, lightly biting her and sending a ripple of pleasure straight between her thighs. "You're so fucking beautiful."

She wanted to tell him he was, too, but she was beyond words now. She could feel everything passing through her, his warm breath against her neck as he kissed her, his hands tugging her latex shorts down, over her knees, her legs opening to the balmy evening air, his fingers finding her tender, wet ache for him. It was all so dreamlike, the way she didn't see him removing his clothes, yet she was running her hands over his broad chest, stroking his hardness, their bodies pressing tighter as a breeze danced over their nakedness. She found herself straddling him, closing her eyes as he slid into her, and it felt like he was reaching, spreading into every part of her.

The night sounds surrounded them—the soft hoot of an owl in the distant woods, a zephyr rustling the leaves in the trees, the sharp chirp of crickets—joining their ragged breath as fast as the blood pumping through their veins with the bright golden moon overhead.

CHAPTER 33

RAE

2009

Viv stopped shaking on the couch, but her face remained pale, so Rae wrapped her in a throw blanket. She didn't know Viv had ever been married, and she didn't understand why her friend had never mentioned it.

"I should've told you about him," Viv said. "I thought I was done with that part of my life."

"What did he want, and what did he mean by 'one week'?"

Viv let the blanket fall off her shoulders. "He means I have one week to give him the money I made on the sale of the house I owned in California. That's why I was there and how I met you. I was completing everything for the sale after my divorce from Mark."

"Was it his house too?"

"No," Viv said. "It belonged to my great-aunt who left it to me after she died, which was after the divorce was finalized, but Mark believes everything I own belongs to him. He found out about it somehow and thought I hid it from him. I was already renting here in Albuquerque to get away from him, and I had a realtor friend help me sell the house in California so I could put money down on this place."

Viv rocked herself on the couch. Rae had never seen her so scared.

"He's a dangerous person, Rae. And now he knows I'm here. I don't know how, but he found me." Viv took Rae's hand. "I don't think he realizes you're living here with me, but he'll find out soon enough. And I'm worried he'll do something like hurt you to get at me."

Rae instinctively cradled her baby bump. "Can't you file a restraining order or something?"

"I will, and I have before," Viv said, "but he's violated them so many times in the past."

"What do the police do when he violates them?"

A sour expression crossed Viv's face. "Not a goddamn thing."

Here Rae had been agonizing over the bad men possibly finding her and killing her for helping Katelyn escape, and now she had to worry about Viv's ex. She wasn't sure if there were any good men left in the world. Except for her dad, she reminded herself, but even he hurt her by leaving her alone with nowhere to go after he died.

"Still, you need to report it so there's a record of what he did to you," Rae said, standing up to get her purse. "And I'm a witness. Let me drive you to the police station."

Viv didn't move. "He has everything of mine. He already took all the furniture, my old clothes I had to leave behind. The '78 Chevy Nova I loved. It'll never be enough for him." Rae saw a fierceness in her eyes. "I'm not giving him one more thing. Not one goddamn thing."

Rae nodded. "Let's make the report then. And they can take pictures of your neck where he grabbed you."

Viv finally got up. "Okay."

Rae stopped by a taco truck for dinner on their drive back from the police station. Filing the report took way longer than she'd expected, and it was now early evening, the setting sun casting a pink glow over the Sandia Mountains. "*Sandía* means 'watermelon' in Spanish," Viv had once told her, and Rae was transfixed every time she saw the rose-tinted peaks. But not this evening.

Her mind was too filled with frustration at the police. The officer who took Rae's witness statement seemed to be going through the motions with no real concern about Viv's safety. When she described how Mark held Viv against the door by her throat, his facial expression never changed. Like it was something normal to him. But then Rae used to think it was normal for her, when Clint, Bobby, or some of the other men hurt her. It was easier to pretend everyone experienced the same thing so she wouldn't feel alone.

She needed a plan in case Mark came back around, and from what Viv had told her, she fully expected him to get violent again. If he did, she wanted to be ready.

Rae poured Viv some red wine and ran her a bath after they ate, hopeful it'd make her friend relaxed enough to get some sleep. She didn't tell Viv what she had learned at her prenatal visit. It would only give Viv more stress. The strain of the day made Rae want to collapse into bed with all her clothes on and sleep for days. Not exactly how she would've chosen to cure her insomnia, but she would take it.

Once Viv was comfortable in her bath, Rae decided to skip her evening live stream. She couldn't handle seeing the vulgar comments from her male viewers right then. She took a quick shower in the guest bathroom and made herself some tea while she checked her email. She had ordered two pairs of maternity jeans online since she'd had trouble finding any at the local thrift stores, and the site hadn't sent her the shipping notification yet after ten days.

No email from the site, but she had an email from someone named Marilyn Reid. She was afraid to open it. The email was from Katelyn's mother, and Rae didn't think she could handle anything else, good or bad. She almost closed her laptop without reading it, but her curiosity was a bitch. She quickly read it and then read it again, more slowly:

Dear Echo,

We're sorry to email you like this, and we're not even sure if this is the correct email for you since the California police refused to give us your contact information. However, we were able to convince a nice receptionist at the New Mexico police station to give us the email address you gave to detectives. If this is you, we want to thank you for saving our little girl. She still talks about you and calls you her angel lady.

We can only imagine what you went through to save her. Thank you will never be adequate, but we are so thankful for you and hope you're doing well given all you've experienced. You are a true blessing to us. If you ever need anything, please never hesitate to reach out.

Eternally grateful to you and God,

Marilyn and Ben Reid

Rae stared at the phone number they included, the numbers blurring as she rubbed tears from her eyes. She knew she should write them back, but she didn't know how to respond. She wondered if they would still be thankful for her if they knew she had failed to save Beth or Maria. Or if they knew she killed two men in the process of saving their daughter.

Lily thrashed inside her, her tiny fist stretching Rae's stomach out at a grotesque angle. She circled her hand across her belly, over and over until Lily's kicking subsided.

Yes, she thought. If it meant killing a hundred men to save Katelyn Reid, Rae was sure the girl's parents would be thankful.

CHAPTER 34

RAE

2024

Everything was bloodred and bright in every direction. Rae heard birds chirping nearby, but she couldn't see them, and she tried to speak, but her mouth felt like it was stuffed with cotton balls. She was thirstier than she'd ever been in her life, but she was also cold, and her entire body felt bruised.

Open your eyes, she ordered herself. *Open them, damn it.*

Her right eye cracked open, then her left, and for several moments she had no idea where she was or how she'd gotten there. She turned her head and saw Dayton, his eyes closed and his mouth slightly parted. Her head was resting on his outstretched arm, his other arm draped over her waist. She saw they were both completely naked and out in the open in a garden, the sun creeping up over the tall hedges surrounding them, casting an eerie rosy glow on their skin.

Then she remembered: last night and being drugged, the things Dayton said to her and how they'd been unable to stop themselves.

She carefully slid his left arm off her and sat up. Her head was pounding, but she forced herself to stand up and put on her halter top and high-waisted booty shorts. Then she sat back down, a wooziness overwhelming her.

She watched Dayton as he slept, her eyes soaking up the contours of his body until she landed on a bite mark on his upper left arm. Then she recalled the last thought she had before completely succumbing to the compulsions of the drug: she wanted to taste Dayton, to feel his flesh taut between her teeth as she ran her tongue over him, so she bit him. Hard. The memory of it, of how intense he came in her after she did it, ignited flames in her hips, and she had to stop herself from pressing the mark.

A sudden rush of guilt blazed through her chest, the same feeling she had when she'd been caught cheating on a spelling test in second grade. There had been no consent the prior night, and, logically, she knew it wasn't possible with being drugged, but it still nagged at her.

She couldn't wrap her mind around what they'd done. He had wanted to have sex, but a piercing anxiety went through her that it was only the drug talking. She knew he'd wake up and realize it had been a mistake. It didn't feel like a mistake to her, though she never would've chosen those circumstances to have sex with him. Even before they were drugged, she knew she had sensed a connection with him from the moment they'd met, but she also knew attraction could be a flighty creature, especially in men.

She studied the feather tattoo on his right inner forearm. She hadn't noticed before, but she saw the vanes of the feather contained two words cleverly disguised within the design: "For Tula." She ran her finger across the tattoo, wondering who Tula was, and Dayton stirred awake.

He looked as confused as she likely had minutes before. His face turned red when he saw he was naked, and she turned her head away from him as she handed him his clothes.

"Thank you," he said before he got dressed.

When she was sure he was clothed, she turned to see him checking that his bodycam was still on his suit jacket, bewilderment remaining on his face. He looked at her, and his face reddened again.

"It wasn't a dream," he said. "What we . . ."

"No." She found one boot next to her, the other several feet away by a rosebush. She wasn't too steady on her feet yet, and stiletto boots didn't seem like a great idea, so she kept them off.

Dayton still looked lost in his thoughts. "Did you bite me last night?"

"Uh, yes," she said. "Sorry. I can help you clean it." She felt the guilt rise in her again, burning her face. "It's not something I normally would've done without asking first, but . . . you know."

He searched her face, a thousand emotions playing out in his eyes. "If I hurt you last night, I—I'm sorry. I would never . . ." He ran his hands over his face a few times like it would erase what happened. "This is so fucked up."

She had been in so many compromising situations in her past where consent was nonexistent. Hell, most women have, but she could see this was a new experience for him. "We were drugged, so we can't blame ourselves for what happened. We can talk about it more later if you want, but first we need to get my toy bag and get out of here before they find us."

Dayton's expression turned all business then. Good. She needed him to be in alert-detective mode.

They half stumbled around the maze of the massive garden, trying to find their way back to the mansion, but they kept coming to more dead ends in the high hedges. Rae didn't know how she'd found the secluded spot the night before, but now she wished she could remember the path they'd taken.

She stopped walking when panic crept up on her. "What if we get caught? Will your team know to come find us if you don't show up at work this morning?"

One look at Dayton's face and her heart sank.

"They don't know we're here, do they?"

"Rae."

She threw her boots down. "Are you fucking kidding me?"

"Please, let me explain," he said as he tried to hold her shoulders.

She pushed him away. "I can't believe you. What if something happened to us? Those crazy fucks could've done anything after they drugged us!"

He held his hands out in front of him like he was trying to calm a wild animal, which was exactly how she felt. She wanted to punch him.

"I know, I'm sorry."

"Tell me why right fucking now," she said quieter. She was worried someone would hear her screaming at him.

"Okay." He pinched the bridge of his nose, his eyes closed tight for a moment. He looked at her, and she saw pain in his eyes. "I was going to tell you, but I didn't know how yet. I needed to come here, but the chief wouldn't approve it, so I had to get here through you."

"I don't understand. Don't they care about Thomas Highsmith's case? Why wouldn't they investigate a lead like that? And the missing women?"

"Because they're not interested in messing with the Coulter family," he said.

"Then why did you want to come here, Dayton?"

He walked over to a concrete bench and sat down, his face drawn. "I came here to find the man who murdered my cousin thirteen years ago."

It was the last thing Rae had expected him to say, and she waited for him to say more.

"When I met you," he said, "I knew you were hiding something. So, yes, I looked into you, and when I saw you had changed your name, I looked further, and I read the statement you made to the New Mexico police on the Katelyn Reid case."

He knew about her being trafficked then. He knew about Beth and Maria, too, and what she had reported on Clint and Bobby.

"They let you slip through the cracks. It wasn't right, Rae, what the police did. You deserved justice for what happened to you."

"What does that have to do with your cousin?" she said.

"Her name was Tula, and she was so smart and talented. She used to win for her dancing at all the Red Earth Festival competitions. We grew up around each other, and then her mother passed when she was twelve, and she came to live with us. We were more like close siblings than cousins." He paused, a heaviness entering his eyes. "We're both Choctaw, but I never lived on the reservation like she did. My father's half Choctaw and my mother's a quarter, and they chose to live in the city where they thought I'd have more opportunities."

This explained the eagle-feather tattoo. She knew different types of feathers were held sacred to the tribes.

"Tula had trouble acclimating when she moved in with us. She wasn't used to being in a big city and not being surrounded by her people. I was three years older, and I tried to watch out for her, but she kept distancing herself from me and the rest of our family. Then she got pregnant at seventeen and became addicted to pills and then harder drugs. And she eventually turned to sex work."

Rae had the urge to sit next to him and take his hand, but she was still angry at him for lying to her.

"The last time she was seen was when a wealthy-looking, white-haired man with unusually blue eyes drove over to where she was working the streets. Witnesses said they saw him invite her to a party. A fancy party at a mansion with every drug she could want. She went with him after some of her sex worker friends warned her not to, and police found her body dumped in a ditch five days later. She'd been tortured. Caned and burned, but she also had a lot of drugs in her system."

"I'm sorry," Rae said. She saw his grief was still raw. "But you really think he's the same man?"

"I know he is, just like I knew you would be the one to lead me to him after you told me what your friend witnessed at the party."

That's what he'd meant then about her being someone important in his life. It wasn't because he was interested in her; it was what she could do for him.

"So, you used me?" she said. "And last night . . ."

Dayton stood up and came over to her. He squeezed her upper arms, and she didn't pull away from him this time. "I meant what I said last night, Rae. But I did use you, and I'm sorry for it. I didn't see another way to get to the party and confirm what I knew in my gut. I had to see him. And this is the only lead I've had in over a decade. The police stopped investigating Tula's death the moment they learned she was a sex worker and a drug addict. And there's never justice for indigenous people, anyway." His face contorted with repressed anger for a moment. "After that, I changed my major in college from secondary education to criminal justice because I thought it would help me find her killer."

She processed his words, disappointment and confusion burrowing deep in her chest. He had wanted to be a teacher, and he upended his life to find his cousin's murderer. Now, he was upending hers in the process. "Where do we go from here?"

"I don't know yet." He lifted his hand like he was going to touch her, before lowering it just as fast. "But I'll do whatever I need to make sure you're safe. I didn't mean for things to go like this."

She turned away from him, annoyed with the tears forming in her eyes. "Just get us out of here."

"All right."

With their minds finally clearing, they were able to find their way back to the large stairs leading into the rear of the mansion. Dayton told her to follow the perimeter of the building to where the side parking was located while he sneaked inside to find her things. Quietly, she made her way to the parking lot area, her mind distracted by everything Dayton had told her.

More and more, her anger at him lessened, but it was simmering under the surface. In any other circumstance, if someone betrayed her, she was done with them. She'd learned that skill the hard way with her mother. But she also knew vengeance could make a person do things they'd never dream of doing, like burning down a house. She couldn't fault Dayton for wanting to avenge his cousin, but it didn't mean she needed to be a part of it.

Several minutes passed before Dayton finally met up with her at his car. Thankfully, he held her toy bag.

"I couldn't find where they put your robe," he said. "Sorry."

At this point, she was glad to get out of there. Strangely, the large gate they had entered through last night was left open. Almost like they knew Rae and Dayton were still there.

As he drove her back to her place, she tried to prepare herself to walk into work like a normal person. She didn't know how she was going to tell Angel any of this.

"When will you be able to get the bodycam footage?" she said to break the silence.

"I'll try to go through it later today, but I've got a lot I need to do at work first."

"I want to see it."

He glanced over at her, surprise on his face. "I'll let you know when I have it ready."

"Good."

The more she thought about what had happened to Tula, the more she hated the idea of the same happening to Devon or the other women. If she could help, she would, especially since the police weren't interested in doing their jobs. And she couldn't shake the feeling of having a target on her back now.

CHAPTER 35

RAE

2009

Viv wasn't herself—not since the day Mark had come to the condo. And Rae hated him for it. She wanted the strong, vivacious Viv back, not the anxious person who seemed on the verge of crumbling. But she didn't know what else she could do besides what she'd already done with the police statement.

It didn't help that she had to focus on working, doing as many live streams as she could to save money for when Lily was born, and she'd be forced to take a few weeks off. Stomping on Barbie heads with high heels was the last thing she wanted to do, but she gave her viewers the show they'd come to expect. How Viv was able to do client sessions at all in her state of mind was a wonder to Rae.

"What can Mark actually do if you don't give him the money from the house sale?" Rae said as they ate lunch in front of the TV. According to Mark, Viv had four more days to come up with the funds.

Viv glanced at her. "Legally? Nothing. Physically, emotionally?" She looked down at her sandwich. "He can do a lot of damage. And he's desperate because he made a bad business deal and owes a ton of money to a loan shark."

"Doesn't he know what you do for a living? You can just beat his ass."

A bitter smile spread across Viv's face. "It's actually how we met. At a play party. He thinks of himself as this alpha-Dom, and he wanted to collar me and control everything I did and said."

Rae had never heard of a Dom trying to own another Dominant. She knew about switches, people who enjoyed both ends of the power-exchange dynamic, but she didn't understand how two Dominants could work in a relationship, at least not from a kink standpoint.

"He never took my work seriously. He doesn't believe women should dominate men at all, and he still thinks I'm secretly submissive."

Rae chuckled. "He obviously doesn't know you then."

"That's the funny thing, hon," Viv said. "If you're told something often enough by someone you love, you start to believe it. I had just lost Frederick, and Mark was charming and handsome. He said all the right things, and I ignored all the wrong things."

"If he comes back, I'm going to whip his eyeballs out of his head." Rae was only half joking, but Viv's face turned serious.

"I don't want you to be anywhere near him when he comes back. Promise me you won't answer the door if he comes by when I'm not here."

If it meant getting the old Viv back, Rae would do a lot more than blind Mark, but she said, "I promise."

They were in serious need of groceries, and Viv was too ill to leave the house. Or that's what she said, but Rae knew she was fine. Viv had barely left her room in four days, but Rae heard her doing client sessions every day. It was like Viv was lying low until the deadline Mark had given her was up.

As much as she hated going to the store alone, Rae grabbed their reusable canvas bags and drove over to Trader Joe's to get them some necessities. She was trying to find the almond milk Viv liked when she sensed someone staring at her in her peripheral vision.

She casually peered to her right and saw Mark. Now that she had a better look at him, she didn't see what attracted Viv, who seemed way out of his league. He was of average height, with a forgettable face except for his hazel eyes, but he appeared more muscular than she remembered. For some reason, she wasn't scared of him and turned to face him head on.

"Do you think following me intimidates me?" Rae said to him.

His eyes penetrated her. "You would know if I was trying to intimidate you."

"You're wasting your time being here, so you should go back to whatever rock you crawled out from under."

He moved close enough to Rae that she smelled his cloying cologne.

"I know you're leeching off her, preggo. Bet she's got you set up real nice, buying you things and cooking for you like you're her pet. She always had a soft spot for losers."

She sneered at him. "I can see that."

"You stupid cunt."

Rae ignored him and went back to searching for the almond milk.

He gripped her shopping cart, preventing her from moving it. "Tell Vivien I still have the thing she wants. And if she ever hopes to get it back, she'll have the money ready."

"I'm not telling her anything." Rae pushed her cart hard to remove his hand. "She doesn't owe you a penny, and if you come around again, you'll be violating a protection order, and the cops will be all over your ass."

The sudden change in his eyes after she mentioned the protection order made Rae wish she'd said nothing about it. He looked ready to strangle her until an older male worker asked them if they needed help with anything. She could tell the store worker was trying to see if she was okay without making a scene.

"No," Mark said. "I was just leaving." He gave Rae one last blazing glare. "See you soon, preggo."

CHAPTER 36

RAE

2024

Rae dragged her ass into work less than an hour after Dayton had dropped her off at her house. She'd taken a quick shower to get the funk off her, the hot water helping to ease her sore muscles. As she ran her pouf over her skin, she saw fingertip-size bruises on her body, mainly over her hips and thighs, and the memory of Dayton's hands digging into her flesh as he thrust inside her, his throaty moan as he came hard, pulsed heat between her legs so powerful she felt like a newborn foal trying to stand upright for the first time.

When she gave Angel the rundown of the night before, she wasn't as mad at Rae for lying to her as she'd expected her to be. Her best friend was more worried than anything. And intrigued by what had happened with Dayton.

"Well, that sure complicates things, doesn't it?" Angel said. "I never thought you'd be crazy enough to screw a cop."

"Detective."

"A detective is just a cop with a suit and a college degree, Rae-Rae." Angel ran her big brown eyes up and down Rae's body. "You do have a happily fucked glow about you. Guessing y'all didn't use protection."

"Kinda hard when you're drugged out of your mind."

"Girl, tell me you got Plan B."

"Got it on my way here." Rae had to stop traditional birth control years before due to the horrible side effects, and she needed to get a new IUD.

"So, do you like him?" Angel said, her expression thoughtful.

"I don't know," Rae lied. If anything, she was afraid of how much she did like Dayton. Liking him didn't mean she trusted him after he'd lied to her. And besides, they didn't know much about each other. "All I can think about right now is how tired I am."

"At least you only have two clients today," Angel said as if it was a consolation, although Rae knew the two sessions would be a struggle given her exhaustion. "Mr. Nipple Clamps is up first."

Rae sighed. "I need more coffee than exists in the world."

"You and me both, sis."

◆ ◆ ◆

Rae came home to find Lily and Klo chilling in the living room. She hadn't seen Lily since the prior morning, and she hated that she hadn't been home right after dumping her life story on her daughter three nights before. Seeing her laughing with Klo eased her concerns some.

"Y'all have fun last night?" Rae asked them.

"Yeah," Lily said. "Klo's parents were gone, so we had a wild party with cocaine and strippers. You know, Mom, just live, laugh, loving."

Rae shot Lily a playful glare. "Well, I hope you didn't stay up too late since it was a school night."

"Lil crashed out at ten, Ms. Dixon," Klo said, a sly smile on their face. "And my parents were home."

"Want to stay for dinner, Klo?"

"Sure. Let me call my mom."

She loved that kid. Rae only hoped Lily appreciated the friendship as much as she did.

She grabbed her phone from her purse in the entryway and saw a missed call from Dayton's work phone. The stupid butterflies were back, like she was a teenager about to call her school crush.

"Do you have the footage ready?" she said as soon as he answered.

"Yeah, I've got it on a flash drive. Can we meet at your office?"

"I can't. I'm making dinner for my daughter and her friend." She paused. "But, if you'd like, you can come to my place, have some honey-soy salmon, get interrogated by some teens. Then we can go through the footage in my office here." She added, "Unless you need to be home with your daughter."

Dayton was quiet for a few beats. "Uh, yeah, I can do that. Carli's at my mom's house this week."

Interesting. Rae figured he shared custody of his daughter, but he hadn't talked about it.

"Okay. Dinner's at six."

She hung up, in disbelief she'd invited him for dinner. With her kid at home no less. Luckily, she had an additional salmon filet since she usually made extra for her lunch the next day.

An hour later, she was sitting next to Dayton at her dining table, Lily and Klo looking devious across from them. She didn't think it could get any more awkward, but then the teens started whispering to each other as they stared at Dayton.

Lily grinned at her friend. "He does. Tell him."

"You look like the Darkling," Klo said to Dayton. "If he had a tan."

"What is that?" Dayton said.

"It's a character from a show," Lily said.

"Based on the books," Klo added.

"Hopefully that's not a bad thing." He turned to Rae as if she would be able to confirm, but she shrugged.

188

The teens giggled, and Rae wanted to yell at them to eat faster. She needed to see the bodycam footage. She knew it was a near impossibility, but she hoped against hope she'd see Devon in the background of the party somewhere.

"This is delicious," Dayton said to Rae, and she saw he was almost done with his plate. "It's the first home-cooked meal I've had in two weeks."

"Glad you like it."

"So, why are you here again?" Lily asked him.

"He's a part of an investigation I'm helping with." Rae felt Dayton's eyes on her.

"But, Mom, I thought *you* were the one being investigated." Rae could tell by Lily's lopsided smile she was being facetious, but she didn't need the reminder. "Aren't there, like, rules against having dinner with a suspect?"

Dayton cleared his throat. "Uh, your mom is helping me with a different matter."

The teens peeked at each other, a knowing look passing between them.

After they were done eating, Rae cleared the plates, declining Dayton's offer to help, before they settled in her office. She dragged over her extra chair they could sit side by side at her desk. He pulled out a flash drive and plugged it into her laptop.

"Sorry about the dinner interrogation," Rae said. "I did warn you."

Dayton looked at her, and she couldn't tell what he was thinking. "You know, Lily's not wrong. About there being rules. I could get into serious trouble being here with you."

"Then don't be here."

He appeared hurt by her words. "That's kind of the problem, Rae. I can't seem to not be around you, and it's distracting me from my work." He paused as if he was carefully picking his words. "I think you'd agree we skipped a few steps last night. And as much as I'd like to know what it'd be like to kiss you without being drugged by nutcases, I . . . I don't think it's a good idea right now. I think they wanted to distract us, and we can't let them."

There it was. She knew he was right, but hearing it felt like a hundred wasps stinging her chest at the same time.

She forced herself to say, "I completely agree."

He seemed like he wanted to say more, but he shifted to face the laptop.

"So, your daughter—Carli—spends a lot of time at your mom's?" Rae said, trying to shift to a less uneasy topic. "Not with your ex?"

"There is no ex." He turned back to her. "I didn't think to tell you this before, but Carli is my cousin's daughter. My parents took care of her after Tula was murdered, but then my father passed, and my mom started having health issues and couldn't care for her full time. So, Carli's been with me since she was about three."

"But you call her your daughter."

"To her, I'm the only father she's known. And I look at her as my daughter."

She wished she hadn't pried because it only made her yearn to know more about him, and for the first time in years, she wanted someone to know her.

"I didn't mean to be nosy. I was just curious," she said, not wanting to make things more complex than they already were between them.

"She's a lot like Lily. Witty and bright and full of Gen Z jokes I'll never understand." He smiled.

"Lily's definitely got the witty thing down."

"What about Lily's father?" he said. "Does she get to see him often?"

Clint's face flashed in Rae's mind. "No, he's never been in the picture."

Dayton nodded, probably assuming Lily's father was simply a deadbeat dad, and turned back to the computer. "Okay, let's take a look at this thing." He pulled up the biggest file on the flash drive and hit play. "If you see any of the missing women, let me know. I've seen their photos, but you would probably spot them better than I can."

Rae got as close as she could to the screen without blocking Dayton's view. Many minutes passed as they watched the footage, and she didn't catch sight of Devon or the other women. Then the footage showed Rae whipping the sub, and she wanted to look away. She wished she could reverse time and tell that white-haired bastard to fuck off instead of complying with his demands.

The bodycam moved away from the crowd surrounding her whipping scene. This must've been when Dayton took advantage of people's distraction to get more shots of the room. The camera slowly panned across the huge ballroom, and Rae did a double take.

"Wait, back up, back up!" she said. "Can you get the prior frame up and freeze it?"

"Sure."

He did, and Rae felt like the air had been punched out of her. She didn't understand.

"It's not possible," she whispered, feeling light-headed.

"What is it? Do you recognize this person?"

"Yeah, but . . ." She was going to be sick. She looked around for her little office trash can but moving only made her more nauseous. Her head felt like it was filled with ice cubes, and her lips went numb from breathing too fast. She knew the signs well. She was having a panic attack, and she couldn't stop it.

"Rae, are you okay?" He glanced back at the frozen image on the screen. "Shit. Is Robert Coulter one of your clients?"

Robert Coulter? His last name is Coulter?

"Let's lean you forward," Dayton said, his words sounding assured but faraway. "Like that, head between your legs. Breathe in slowly, counting to ten, then out slowly."

She knew what to do, but she couldn't make her body do it, so she let him move her like she was a puppet. All she could do was chant to herself: *But he's dead, he's dead, he's dead. Bobby's dead.*

"What did you just say?"

Fuck.

CHAPTER 37

RAE

2009

On her drive home from the store, Rae ran through everything that had happened with Mark and what he'd said to her. No doubt, he'd threatened her, but instead of being afraid of him, she was angry. She was done with men making her and other women feel unsafe in the world.

After she put away the groceries, she knocked on Viv's bedroom door. She didn't hear a client session going on, so she entered. Viv was on her bed scrolling through her phone, totally zoned out from what Rae could tell.

"I got us groceries. I can make us some baked chicken tonight."

Viv started and put down her phone. "Sorry, hon, I didn't hear you come in."

"Um, I have to tell you something," Rae said. "I saw Mark at the store."

Viv sat up, her eyes wide. "What did he do? Did he try to hurt you?"

"No, but he wanted to scare me." She sat on the edge of Viv's bed. "And he wanted me to tell you something. He said he has the thing you want, and he'll give it to you if you give him the money."

Viv shut her eyes, her mouth a hard line.

"What does he have that you want?"

In answer, Viv showed Rae her left wrist, which was bare.

"He took the watch Frederick gave you?"

"Yes," Viv said. "He took it when he was here. When he grabbed my arm, I didn't even feel him undo the latch because I just wanted to get away from him. He knows how much it means to me."

"That asshole!"

"There's nothing I can do." Viv's eyes teared up. "But hopefully once he figures out I'm not trading money to get it back, he'll give up and go back to California."

Rae hated Mark even more now. Viv never took off her watch unless she was bathing. She remembered when Viv had told her the watch was like Frederick's heart; to hear it ticking was like he was still alive and with her. Rae wished she had something of her dad's she could keep close to her, but all she had were memories.

"What if he doesn't give up?" Rae said.

Viv stood up from the bed, a fire in her eyes. "Then he'll see what a real Domme looks like."

Rae wanted to jump up and dance. Her friend was being herself again.

"Forget the chicken. We should go out," Viv said. "The state fair is still going on. You down for some deep-fried food and people watching?"

"Absolutely."

Rae hadn't been to a state fair since her parents took her to the Oklahoma fair when she was ten. She'd eaten two corn dogs, followed by an entire bag of cotton candy and two large lemonades, then promptly threw up after riding the Zipper. To make her feel better, her parents sang "Islands in the Stream" at the karaoke tiki hut where all the drunk people gathered in the shade to escape the sun. Her parents weren't drunk, but they sounded like it as they sang their hearts out, pointing to her like she was the only one in the crowd. Her chest tightened as she thought about it.

The New Mexico State Fair looked pretty much the same as Oklahoma's, with Native American dances, livestock shows, rickety carnival rides, and anything you could possibly think of to deep-fry, including butter. Viv had grown up in Albuquerque, and she knew all the best places for food.

She steered Rae away from a food truck. "Not that one, hon. Now this one has the best Navajo tacos you'll ever eat. Not that greasy, white-people fry bread."

And Viv was right; it was one of the best things she'd ever eaten. One thing she loved about being pregnant was how much she could eat. She was always hungry, but she never worried about gaining too much weight because it was all for the health of Lily. So, she scarfed down every bit of the light fry bread slathered in a meat-and-bean sauce with cheese, lettuce, and jalapeños.

"I could eat five of those," Rae said as they found a spot to rest. "I would have sex with that taco if I could."

Viv laughed. "Pregnancy still got you all horny?"

Rae blushed. "Yeah. It's weird because I've never been like this before."

"It's the hormones," Viv said. "Your testosterone increases, and your blood flow goes nuts, especially in your sex organs."

Sometimes Rae forgot Viv had been pregnant before she got an abortion. "Did your nipples get all funky when you were, you know, pregnant?"

"You mean did they double in size, get dark, and stay erect 24/7?" Viv smiled. "Yeah, they got funky, but it goes away."

Everything about Rae's body felt foreign to her. Her breasts were huge, she had to brush her teeth at strategic times so as not to throw up, and she couldn't sleep unless she had three pillows placed around her and in between her legs.

Viv suddenly bounced up from her seat, her face beaming. "I want to hear you sing."

"No!"

"Come on! I hear the karaoke tent, and I've heard you singing around the house. Go show them how it's done."

"Oh, my God. Fine."

They made their way over to the large karaoke tent. Rae selected a song and let the deejay know which key. They had to wait thirty minutes for her song to come up, and as soon as Rae heard the opening to "Islands in the Stream," her nerves almost got the better of her, but she took the mic and focused on Viv's grinning face in the crowd. The deejay got her attention, and she okayed him to join her in the duet.

And for a time, it was like Mark didn't exist, and Rae was so happy she thought her face would split from smiling so much.

◆　◆　◆

It was late by the time they got back to the condo. They were still laughing about the big old cowboy they'd watched sing Prince's "Kiss," falsetto voice and all, as he gyrated on the small stage. The crowd ate it up, and the man had an unexpectedly nice voice.

Viv had planned to have a few beers while they were out, so Rae had driven them to the fair in her Civic. It felt good to be useful so Viv could relax. And Viv definitely needed a driver because she was a lightweight. In Rae's experience, there were two types of drunk people: angry or happy. Viv was the latter, thankfully.

They were walking down the sidewalk, almost to the front door of the condo, when Rae stopped dead. Viv gasped when she saw what Rae was staring at.

Viv's car. It looked like someone had dumped acid all over the hood from the way the paint bubbled up.

They didn't have to say it; they knew it was Mark. And they didn't have to work hard to interpret his meaning. It was a warning as loud as the thunderous screams they'd heard at the fair's midway.

CHAPTER 38

RAE

2024

One slip of the tongue, and now Rae had Dayton staring her down as she came out of her panic attack, woozy and drained.

"I'm going to pretend for a second I didn't hear what you just said." He sat back down on the office chair, running his hands through his dark hair. "How do you know Robert Coulter?"

Rae's lungs burned from dry heaving moments before, but she made herself speak. "I never knew his last name. He went by Bobby when I knew him . . . in California."

She knew Dayton put the pieces together when his face dropped. "Bobby, as in the Bobby you talked about to the New Mexico police?"

She nodded.

"Oh, shit." Then he straightened his posture. He was back in detective mode again. "Why did you think he was dead?"

She couldn't tell him. There was no way to tell him without revealing everything else.

"Rae, I need you to tell me why."

Don't cry, she screamed at herself. *Don't fucking do it.*

Dayton's expression softened. "Did you hurt him in self-defense when you escaped with that little girl?"

A realization hit her. In the frozen image of Bobby still up on her laptop, he was looking straight toward Dayton. Straight toward her, presumably watching her as she whipped the sub. The knowing look on Bobby's face. She had her cat mask on, but the lower half of her face was exposed, and her skimpy outfit displayed most of her body. But no. There's no way he could've recognized her.

"Rae, you need to talk to me."

"Okay," she said. "I drugged him. To get away with Katelyn."

"Why did you think he was dead?"

God, nothing went past him. "I didn't know how much to give him to knock him out."

Dayton went quiet. He didn't believe her, not fully. She may not know him well, but she knew him enough to name the look on his face.

"You did what you had to do," he said like he was attempting to convince himself. "And he's obviously alive. This could bolster the case against what they're doing at those parties, if you would be willing to testify about what happened in California. We can tie him to the trafficking. You gave the police a good description of him."

"No. I can't."

He looked perplexed. "I understand it would be difficult to relive—"

"No, Dayton. You don't understand how difficult it would be because you didn't experience it. I'm not going to put my family through that."

He nodded, but he looked frustrated at her decision. "You're right. I'm sorry. I'm just trying to figure out a way to make him pay for what he did."

If only he knew Bobby had been the one person who didn't rape her in the Santa Monica house. Not that he was a saint. His thing was hitting them, sometimes restraining them for hours. She thought of Clint, and her blood went cold.

She didn't know how Bobby had made it out of the fire alive. The articles she'd read years ago mentioned two unidentified people had died in the fire she'd started. She didn't understand. If one of those bodies wasn't Bobby's, then whose was it? Nothing made sense.

Bobby certainly knew Rae was the one who had killed Clint. He wasn't an idiot, and he would've figured out she'd drugged his beer and started the fire. He didn't say anything to the police, though, or they would've arrested her in New Mexico. But, of course, he couldn't say anything without placing himself in the middle of an arson investigation with two dead people.

Her only guess was that Bobby had woken up and escaped as Clint's body burned. Perhaps the rich bastards who wanted to buy Katelyn helped him clean things up, and Bobby came back to Oklahoma to lie low.

"What do you know about him?" Rae said. "About Robert Coulter."

Dayton rubbed his face like he was trying to stay awake. She knew he must be as tired as she felt. "Um . . . I actually went to college with him. He was a couple years ahead of me. Typical rich kid. He threw his money around, went to all the frat parties, got in trouble with the campus police a lot." He looked Rae in the eyes. "A student accused him of rape, but he wasn't charged, and she dropped out. His parents made a sizable donation to the school that year." His voice dripped with causticity. "Then he left soon after. Last I heard he was traveling the world."

Rae ran through all the possibilities in her head about how she could tie Bobby to the trafficking another way without having to testify.

"If I told you the address of the Santa Monica house where he kept me, would you be able to look into something for me?" she said.

"Possibly." He paused. "But you told the New Mexico police you didn't know the exact location of the house."

"I lied." She knew everything about that house, every dirty corner of it, except for one important thing. "It was owned by Felton Holdings LLC. I've never been able to find any solid information about the company, though."

Dayton had his phone out to enter the information into his Notes app. "Why didn't you tell the police this before?"

"I was too scared at the time," she said, which was partially true.

"I'll see what I can find out." He closed out the footage file and removed the flash drive from her computer. His face was troubled. "I fucked this whole thing up, and I still don't have any real information on that white-haired guy. Since I didn't legally obtain this footage, it can't be submitted for evidence of wrongdoing at those parties. I can use it for leads to track down possible victims, but that's about it. Besides, proving there wasn't consent in something like this is going to be hard as hell."

Rae figured as much. They had both gone to the party with their own agenda, and they'd both failed. "I know. But it's something. And I'm sure it's more than what your colleagues have."

As much as she wanted to know what other leads his department had, she knew Dayton would never tell her.

He placed his hand on her knee, and she started from being so tired. "I promise we'll find your friend." He stood up, and she dragged her butt up too. "But we both need sleep now. I should go."

Rae walked him to the front door, where they awkwardly hovered, not knowing how to say goodbye. She decided for them and hugged him. He hugged her back, and they stood like that for a good while. She pressed her face into his shirt and breathed in his scent—warm and earthy with a hint of spice. She didn't want him to be the first to pull away, so she did.

"Good night," she said, her chest aching to touch him again.

"Good night."

And then he was gone.

CHAPTER 39

RAE

2009

It wasn't much of a silver lining, but at least Viv's car was still drivable. The acid Mark had tossed on her car ate through most of the paint on the hood but didn't leak onto the engine underneath.

They reported it to the police the next morning, but they said without proof that Mark did it, they couldn't do anything. Rae was tired of the police doing nothing and said as much to Viv as she drove them home.

"I swear, you could have a knife in your chest, and they would still say there's nothing they can do."

Viv stayed quiet. Rae could tell she was frustrated, too, but she was also weirdly calm.

"We have to do something," Rae said, wanting to see Viv fired up again.

"I will." Then she smiled at Rae.

It was the strained kind Viv flashed when she didn't want Rae to know she was troubled. She was trying to protect Rae when Rae wanted

Viv to protect herself. Mark's deadline was fast approaching, and Viv didn't seem as worried as Rae wanted her to be.

"Let's get some breakfast tacos," Rae said to brighten Viv's mood. Viv loved tacos of any variety, especially if a place had good green sauce. One of the first things Viv had taught her when she came to Albuquerque was the importance of picking your chili sauce: red or green.

"Sounds good, hon."

◆ ◆ ◆

Rae wanted to stick around at the house the next day, but she had her appointment for the prenatal cardiologist. The doctor was a nice woman who was quick and to the point. Lily's heart rate was back to a normal level, and Rae felt a huge wave of relief. Her evening walks had worked. She'd also been drinking more water and avoiding caffeine, which was way harder than she'd expected.

She'd reluctantly told Viv about Lily's tachycardia the night before, and Viv had insisted Rae take a break from doing so many live streams.

"I still have plenty of money from the house sale," Viv had said as she rubbed Rae's head while they watched TV. Rae remembered how her mother used to rub her head, and her chest constricted into a painful knot. "Let me help you."

Rae didn't say yes or no. She'd been too relaxed with her head on Viv's lap, feeling loved and wishing she could stay in the moment forever.

Now, she looked forward to getting home so she could tell Viv the good news about Lily.

But as soon as she got to the condo, she knew something wasn't right. The door was slightly ajar. Viv's car was in her normal parking spot, though, so Rae ignored the caution rising in her and entered.

"Viv?" Nothing looked out of place in the living room when Rae glanced around. "Viv, I'm back."

No answer.

The kitchen light was on, so she checked there first. A full cup of tea sat on the countertop, a carton of almond milk sitting next to it. Rae felt the cup, and it was cold.

Fear crawled up her spine. "Viv?"

She went to Viv's office, but she wasn't in there. She didn't want to go to Viv's bedroom, but she made herself. The door was cracked.

She pushed the door open, and she immediately wanted to shut it. *I don't want to see this. I don't want to see this.*

"Viv?" she cried.

On her bed, Viv lay half-naked, her hands tied with her own ropes. Bruising circled her neck, her dark eyes open and so bloodshot they looked like they were bleeding.

Rae ran to the bedside and worked to untie Viv, but it was no use. Viv's skin was cold and bluish. She threw her body across Viv's, holding her, wanting to breathe life back into her lungs.

"No, no, no, Viv, please, please! You can't be gone, you can't!"

This isn't happening, this isn't happening.

She thought she heard a rustling in the other room, and she froze. *Oh, God, Mark.* She looked up, scanning the room, her heart hammering against her ribs. Was he still here?

She pulled out her cell phone and dialed 911. She whispered for them to come fast, her crying making it hard to get words out.

This couldn't be real; it couldn't. It was a nightmare, and she tried to wake herself up. It's just a nightmare.

She looked at Viv's face, her mouth open like she had desperately fought for air, and Rae moaned. She didn't recognize the animal sounds coming from her as she stroked Viv's raven hair.

Even as the paramedics arrived and pulled her away from Viv's body, Rae kept the insane hope that her friend would sit up in the bed and laugh like it was all a joke.

CHAPTER 40

RAE

2024

It was amazing what a good night's sleep could do, although it took Rae two edibles to get there. Totally worth the slight hangover she had as she spanked her client's ass with a zeal she hadn't felt since before Thomas went missing. The image of Bobby's face flashed in her head every other minute, and she couldn't help imagining him as she hit her client.

She thought of Viv's training, how she had told Rae to never take out her anger on a client, but she figured Viv would forgive her this once. For those seconds she saw Bobby's face on her laptop, it was like she was a teenager again, lost and hopeless to escape the dumbest decision she'd ever made by leaving Oklahoma to go with Clint. The worst thing was she'd probably make the same decision if it meant having Lily. And if it meant knowing Viv.

Rae wrapped up with her last client for the week and came to the front where Angel was scrolling through photos of the Bahamas resort she was staying at in two weeks.

"You're obsessed." She playfully nudged Angel's side. "And I'm jealous."

"You could still come with me," Angel said. "But I will be having lots of hot sex with beautiful women, so . . ."

"You know I have to be here. School year's not over yet."

Angel's face dropped a little. "I just hope your crush doesn't ruin my *nonrefundable* plans. I mean, how the hell are we still suspects? Or are we?"

That was a good question. "I'll check with him. And he's not my crush unless you count him crushing my heart the other night." She tried to be flippant as she said the words, but Angel saw right through her.

"You told me he said it wasn't a good idea to start something right now."

"Yeah?" Rae said.

"So, not right now doesn't mean never." Angel flashed her bright smile, and Rae couldn't help but return it.

"You're too optimistic for me *right now.*"

"What do you prefer, Rae-Rae? Some of that goth music you're always listening to and a vial of tears around your neck?"

Rae laughed. "Maybe."

Angel held her shoulders. "Listen, you had sex with a hot man, and you survived some fucked-up shit with a bunch of privileged white people. Trade out the man for a woman, and that's a typical night for me."

"One-night stands are your thing, sis," Rae said. "I just . . . I don't know. With Lily getting older, I guess I realized how alone I'll be once she goes to college in two years."

Angel hugged her. "I love you. We'll find someone for your crazy butt. Okay?"

"I love you too."

Rae didn't tell Angel what she was really thinking, which was that she didn't know how to trust her gut now when it came to potential relationships. So many times, she'd thought an attraction was going one way, only to find herself alone. Dayton was no different. She had thought there was a strong current between them, and it hurt to know she'd been wrong again. But anything with him would've been impossible anyway. A dominatrix with a detective? It'd never happen.

They closed for the day, and Rae checked her phone as soon as she got in her car. She had a few missed calls and a text from Dayton: Call me as soon as you get this.

Ominous. She called him back.

"I've tried calling you all afternoon," he said.

"I've had clients all day."

"We found a body matching the description for one of the missing women."

Rae heard herself gasp.

"Is it . . . is it Devon?"

"No," he said. "From the tattoos on the body, we're fairly sure it's Cierra Martin."

Cierra. She'd forgotten that was the sub's real name. She had golden-blonde hair and was tiny. And so young. Only twenty. God, when her family finds out.

"How did she die?"

He sighed. "I shouldn't even be telling you any of this, but it looks like a possible overdose. She was badly beaten as well, so we don't know yet if her injuries contributed to her death."

She suppressed the emotions rising in her when all she wanted to do was scream. Devon could be next. The other missing woman could already be dead. Thomas Highsmith too. "Have you found out anything on Felton Holdings?"

"I've been too busy with this new development to check yet, but I will." He paused. "I'm worried about how close you are to what's going on."

"I know how to take care of myself," she said, not meaning for her tone to sound so harsh.

"I don't doubt it, but we both saw what kind of people were at that party. Just be careful and stay vigilant."

"You too. And let me know if you find out anything."

She ended the call and allowed herself a good cry in her car before she had to go home to Lily and pretend that people within her circles weren't showing up dead.

◆   ◆   ◆

Rae doubled up on her medical cannabis again that evening before crawling into bed. She kept scrolling through images on Cierra's Facebook page on her phone, knowing it would only make her insomnia worse. Cierra had been an intelligent, beautiful young woman attending her junior year in college. She had every possibility ahead of her. She'd also been new to kink and only wanted to explore her sexuality, and someone powerful had used it against her.

Rae finally closed out the Facebook page and was about to read a book when her phone buzzed. It was a texted link from an unknown number. *Nope.* She went to delete it when another message popped up: Have a good night, Pussy.

What the fuck? Everything in her told her not to click on the link, but she did.

A video came up, and she immediately knew what it was going to show her when she saw the tall hedges surrounding the small garden enclave. There was no sound on the video, but the bastards had recorded everything between her and Dayton. She watched as the effects of the drug took them over, remembering how it had made the grass feel like heaven beneath them, and she knew what was coming next.

The sex was rougher than how she remembered it. In the moment, it had felt like they were in their own two-person orchestra, each an instrument they knew how to play together in perfect accord. Watching now, it was much more primal, like two animals wanting to devour each other. She couldn't look away, not until the video abruptly ended while she and Dayton were still going at it nearly two hours later.

She checked the time. It was almost midnight. She didn't know how she could fall asleep after what she'd just watched, her body incongruently needful when she knew she should be scared. She knew the white-haired fucker had sent the video as a threat, but she didn't want to think about it yet. Her edibles were kicking in hard, but her mind, however, was wide awake.

Just as she thought about calling Dayton, her cell phone rang, startling the crap out of her. It was him.

"Did you get the link too?" he asked.

"Yeah." He was so quiet she could hear an ambulance's siren in the background. When the siren passed by her neighborhood, she heard it on his end too. "Where are you?"

"Outside your house."

Rae sat up, her head swimming in the edible fog. "I'm coming to the door," she said and hung up her phone.

Dayton was standing on her porch wearing a T-shirt and jeans, his face full of wonder as if he didn't know how he'd arrived there on his own.

"Come in."

They stood in her entryway, a pregnant silence heavy between them as they stared at each other. She realized she was wearing her old, oversize Betty Boop nightshirt, possibly the most unattractive piece of clothing she owned, and she cringed internally.

"I just wanted to make sure you were okay," he finally said, his voice low. "I'm sorry. I shouldn't have come over like this."

An image from the video flashed through her mind, his hands roughly squeezing her breasts as he took her from behind on the grass, and her stomach tightened. "No, I'm glad you did."

His eyes wandered down past her collarbone to where Betty Boop's Cupid's bow lips blew a kiss to him. "The video they took, it's a warning." He looked back up. "I don't want you to be alone."

"I know I should be freaking out about it, but right now . . ." She wanted him. She wanted to know what it would be like with him, to breathe in the woodsy scent of his skin without being drugged against her will. He seemed to be thinking the same because he wouldn't stop charting the lines of her breasts with his gaze. "How much of it did you watch?"

He didn't answer her; he didn't have to. She knew he'd watched all of it, too, when he held her face and kissed her lips like he was hungry for them. He pressed her against her coat closet, his hands cupping her breasts as she grabbed a handful of his ass.

It was crazy—she knew it—but it felt too good to question the timing of what they were doing. She was tired of feeling untethered, like she'd float away if she allowed the what ifs to take over. She wanted to escape into the pleasure she knew he could give her, and she wanted him to find escape with her too.

He slid his hand up her nightshirt and groaned when he discovered she didn't have underwear on, his fingers finding her slick and ready. Her mind and body were too overwhelmed by the sensations of his fingers on and inside her, mixed with the effects of the cannabis, and she stopped him before her light-headedness could make her pass out.

"You okay?" he whispered. "Do you want to do this?"

"Yes." She paused, her heart racing. "Just give me a minute. I'm really high from my edibles."

"Seriously?"

She grinned. "I've got a card."

"Lucky." He caressed her face, his thumb grazing her lower lip, and began kissing her again, slower and more deliberately. He paused, seeing if she was okay, and she nodded.

Then she thought of Lily upstairs. "Let's go to my bedroom."

Quietly, they crept to her room on the first floor. As soon as she shut and locked her door, Dayton pulled off her nightshirt and stood a moment taking in her nakedness in the lamplight.

"I could look at you forever," he said and paused. "This is a bad idea, what we're doing, isn't it?"

"Probably."

She helped him remove his clothes, running her hands over his well-toned body and pausing at the bite mark she had made on his upper arm. She pressed her fingers into the bruising it had caused, gently at first and then harder, and Dayton sucked in a sharp breath, one of her favorite sounds. He captured her hand in his, surprise in his expression.

Then he smirked. "You really do like it, don't you? Giving pain."

"You have no idea how much."

He moved her hand back to the bite mark. "You didn't ask first. Do you want to hurt me?"

There was no point in lying. "Yes."

He pushed her fingers into the mark, wincing. "You can do this. But only this."

It was more than she'd ever expected of him, and she pressed as hard as she could as they found each other's lips again. Soon they were entwined on her soft rug, her cat in the corner silently judging them as Dayton rained kisses down her stomach, his arm hitching her left thigh up so he could taste her, his tongue circling and teasing until she was desperate for release.

She ran her fingers through his hair, fisting the thickness tight. As she got closer, she found the bite mark again and drove her thumb deep into the muscle. The sound Dayton made, the slight whimper coming from such a strong man, was enough to explode pleasure throughout her body as contracting waves passed over her.

After her muscles relaxed again, the intensity of the orgasm clearing the cannabis fog, all she could think was that Dayton was right; this was a bad idea.

Dayton pressed his lips to hers as he slowly sank into her, her body still vibrating with the aftershocks of the earthquake he had left in her.

Yes, it was a bad idea. And she couldn't have cared less.

CHAPTER 41

RAE

2009

Nothing seemed real to Rae. Not how the paramedics pulled her away from Viv's body, or how the medics looked her over for possible injuries, or how their faces subtly shifted from being concerned about her well-being to guarded once the cops arrived and took her away in a police cruiser. Not even as she sat in a smelly, cold interrogation room did it feel real.

They didn't arrest her, but they didn't go out of their way to be kind to her. They didn't know what Rae knew about Mark. And they didn't know Rae had lost the most important person in her life.

Grief washed over her again, made worse when Lily began punching around in her belly, and Rae couldn't catch her breath from crying. *Viv, why did you let him in? Why?*

Rae overheard an officer say there were no signs of forced entry. It didn't make sense. Viv should've called the police when Mark showed up.

Viv's blue face flashed in Rae's head again, and she moaned. She couldn't take the pain twisting her stomach, clutching her throat tight until she choked on her tears. It was too much to handle.

She sat like that, sobbing off and on, for what seemed like an eternity before someone finally came into the room. She looked up from her tear-soaked arm to see a woman dressed in an oversize pantsuit with a white blouse.

"Rae Phalin?" the woman said. "I'm Detective Kennedy. Can I get you anything to drink or eat? Or a blanket? They keep it like a meat locker in here. Supposedly, it's to keep people alert." She smiled a little at Rae.

"A blanket, please."

The detective left and came back with a thin, scratchy blanket. She sat across from Rae and let her know they were going to record her statement.

"Okay, Rae, I know this is hard, but I need you to tell me everything that happened today up until you found Vivien Dixon."

"Viv. She went by Viv."

Rae went over the entire day, detailing her trip to the prenatal cardiologist up until she came home to find the front door ajar.

"It was Mark. Her ex-husband. I don't know his last name, but I know it's not Dixon."

Detective Kennedy jotted down notes on a scratch pad. "We did see Viv had a recent protection order against him."

"And it didn't stop him from killing her!" Rae couldn't help yelling. "Y'all did nothing!"

"Rae, I understand you're angry," the detective said, using a calm voice that only made Rae more pissed. "And we will do everything we can to find out who killed her."

"I just told you who killed her!"

"We have to collect more information before we can determine that, which I'm sure you understand. We want to put away the right person, which may be her ex-husband. But we won't know unless you cooperate."

Rae wanted to scream until her lungs shriveled up. They were only wasting time, allowing Mark to get away.

"What do you need, then?" she asked the detective. "I can describe him. And I know what kind of car he drives and the color. It's a red Corvette, a newer one. Just please get him before he escapes back to California."

"Okay, Rae, go ahead and give me his description."

Rae told her everything she could remember about Mark and what Viv had told her about him owing money to a loan shark. She told the detective about his deadline for the house-sale money and how he had stolen Viv's precious watch to manipulate her into complying with his demands. Rae even told them about his not-so-subtle threat to her at Trader Joe's.

"There was an older store worker there who witnessed it too. I can describe him, and you can ask him yourself."

"This is all good information, Rae, and we will get people on it. In the meantime, I need the name of the prenatal cardiologist you saw today."

"Why?" But then she realized. She was a possible suspect, and she didn't want them wasting any more time looking at the wrong people. "Fine. It's Dr. Preethi Kumar."

"Thank you." Detective Kennedy took down the information. "Now, I need to ask what exactly was your relationship to Viv? We understand you live with her."

"She's my best friend." A sharp pain hit her in the chest when she said the words. "She helped me when I had no one."

"Was it only a friendship? Nothing . . . romantic?"

Rae couldn't believe they were asking her this. "No, she was like my mom."

The detective's face looked uncomfortable as she said, "We found some items in Viv's room that point to BDSM practices and possible sex work. Do you know anything about that?"

She didn't understand why they were focusing so much on all the wrong things. "She's a professional dominatrix. She does it online, and it's completely legal."

"As far as you know, has she ever had any issues with anyone who used her services?"

Rae replayed all the conversations she'd had with Viv. "No."

"Besides her ex-husband, do you know if she ever had any issues with other exes?"

She was about to say no until she remembered the fateful night she'd learned about Viv's work. "Sort of. His name was Dean. I don't know his last name. And I don't think she really had a problem with him. He once came to the condo with flowers after they broke up, but she sent him away. He used to be her client, and she said they dated for a few weeks until he got too needy."

"That's good. Will you please describe him for me?"

Rae gave as much detail of Dean as she could, although she thought it was pointless.

"This is all helpful. Thank you for your cooperation." She smiled at Rae. "Now we're going to need to keep you here for a little bit while we check on some things."

A little bit turned into several hours. Rae didn't know what time it was, but it had to be late evening. Apparently, they were able to confirm Rae's whereabouts when Viv was murdered because they said she was free to go.

"But where do I stay?" she asked the officer who was checking her out.

"You can't stay at the crime scene until it's been cleared, which might be tomorrow."

Rae wasn't sure if she could ever stay at the condo again after seeing Viv's lifeless form on her bed. She wasn't sure if she could stay there anyway since she wasn't the owner. She wasn't even a renter.

Panic tried to grip her throat again, but she wouldn't allow it. She had to be strong and find a safe place for tonight. For Lily. She had her debit card since Viv had talked her into opening a free checking account. She could get a motel room.

She drove to a Motel 6 and checked in. She was so tired, she didn't stop for food, although she was starving. So, she took the few dollars she had on her and went to the vending machine. It was slim pickings, but she was going to make a meal out of a bag of potato chips, Reese's Pieces, and a Coke.

The night air was humid as she headed back toward her room on the second floor. She glanced over to the parking lot to check on her car, which was still where she'd parked it. Then she saw it. A red Corvette.

It couldn't be Mark's, but maybe it was. It sure looked like his car.

Rae climbed the stairs to the second story, wondering if she was going to pass by his room on the way to her own. She decided she would eat her food at the window and keep watch.

If he was staying there, she would find out. And then she'd make him pay.

CHAPTER 42

RAE

2024

When Rae woke up, the Saturday-morning sun filled her bedroom with a warm peachy glow. She felt her thick mattress beneath her and vividly recalled crawling into the bed with Dayton sometime during the night when they'd had sex again. Afterward, they had talked for what seemed like hours until they fell asleep in each other's arms. She turned onto her side, ready to kiss him awake, but the sheets were cold and empty next to her. Then she heard someone moving around in her kitchen and knew it had to be him. Lily never got up before noon on weekends.

Rae used the bathroom and threw on a robe. As she left her bedroom, she heard her coffee bean grinder, and she hurried to the kitchen to stop the racket before it woke up her daughter. But Lily was already up, standing next to Dayton and showing him how to use their fancy espresso machine. They both turned to her at the same time as if they had choreographed it to creep her out.

"Good morning, Mother Dear," Lily said with a sly grin. "Your *friend* woke me up banging around."

"Morning." Rae wanted to evaporate. Lily would never let her live this moment down.

Dayton looked thoroughly sheepish. "Sorry, I didn't mean to wake you all up. I was going to make us coffee, but I've never used a professional machine like this. I'm used to a Keurig."

"K-cups are horrible for the environment, you know?" Lily said to him.

"Oh, I know," he said, smiling at her. "My daughter said the same thing, so I switched to the reusable kind."

Lily made a humph sound like she didn't believe him. "So, you stayed the night? Working on whatever it is you all are working on?" Her daughter dragged out the last words.

Dayton looked at Rae like she was the life jacket to his drowning man. He had a teenager, too, so she didn't feel the need to school him on how to respond. There were no secrets with Lily now, so she would know the truth eventually either way.

"Uh, yeah," Dayton said. "We, uh, were up pretty late . . . doing work."

"Is that what adults call sex now? 'Doing work'?" Lily said without a hint of sarcasm. Rae was in awe and a bit terrified of her.

Dayton looked like he was about to melt into a puddle of embarrassment.

"I think we can take it from here, honey." Rae shot her daughter her best mom glare, and Lily scurried off to her room upstairs.

Dayton appeared relieved. "Glad I handled that well."

Rae smiled. "With Lily, the truth is always the best way to handle things."

"And we've been so good at that?"

"I don't know about you, but I'm trying to be better at it," she said as she came up to him, feeling a bit unsure of how to be around him yet. The first morning after sex was always awkward. Do you hug without asking? Kiss? Technically, this wasn't their first time, but it felt like it since they weren't high out of their minds on ecstasy.

Unlike Rae, Dayton didn't seem to have any reservations about what to do, and he kissed her lightly on the lips while his hands found her ass.

"Here," Rae said, "let me show you how this thing works. Lily begged me for it and never uses it."

After she made them both lattes, they went to the living room. She knew they had a lot to discuss, and she needed all the caffeine to process it.

They talked about how they'd received the link and opened it when they realized who'd likely sent it.

"I was about to delete it," Dayton said, "but the next text read 'woof,' and I knew it was from them."

"Can you trace the texts? Find out exactly who sent it?"

"We can try, but my guess is it was sent from a burner phone. That will make it more difficult. But I'm more concerned about them knowing our real identities."

Rae had thought of that, too, the idea making her queasy. She took a sip of her coffee, trying to clear her head. She caught Dayton staring at her.

"They're warning us to stop digging," she said. "They can use this as leverage, especially if they know you're a detective, and here we are having postsex coffee."

He set his mug down on the coffee table. "Do you regret last night?"

She glanced down at the mug in her hands. "No." She looked up again, seeing the relief on his face. "Do you?"

"I was thinking a hundred things at once when I saw the video. One, that they would send this to everyone at my precinct, and I'd be fired and how that would affect Carli. And that I would never be able to get justice for her mom or Cierra Martin. Or find Thomas Highsmith and the other missing women. But mostly, in the moment, I thought of you. So, no, I don't regret it at all."

"What do we do now?"

"Well, they know I recorded the party. The video they took showed me checking the bodycam on my jacket, but they also probably know I can't do much with it, so I think their warning was just that. A warning."

Rae didn't agree. If there was one thing she knew about powerful men, it was that they enjoyed swinging their dicks around, displaying their authority however they could.

"But I'm going to look into Felton Holdings and see what I can find," he said. Then he paused. "I did find out something interesting about the Santa Monica address you gave me. It suffered a large fire in 2009, and two people died, neither with active dental records to identify them. The owners filed an insurance claim, said the house was supposed to be unoccupied at the time of the fire and blamed squatters, but it was denied because authorities deemed it arson." His eyes probed hers. "Would you know anything about that?"

Rae closed her eyes. She didn't want to lie to Dayton any more than she needed, so she opened her eyes and nodded.

"That's why you thought Robert Coulter—Bobby—was dead. Did you start that fire?"

She was positive he could hear how fast her heart was pounding, but she had no choice but to lie about this part. Dayton was an open person, but even he wouldn't be cool with her murdering someone, even someone as horrible as Clint. "No. And I don't know who could've been in the house besides Bobby."

Dayton had the peculiar ability to make his face go completely blank, so she had no clue how he felt about something.

He sighed. "Okay," he said to himself. Then he gazed at her. "Are there any other skeletons I should know about?"

"Before what? You decide to cut your losses?"

"That's not what I'm saying." He rubbed the stubble on his chin. "I'm just trying to figure out how you got into such a desperate situation when you were so young. Why didn't your family help you?"

It was nearly impossible to explain to others, so Rae never did. But she tried with Dayton. She told him about how her mother had abandoned her and her dad, remarried someone else, and had another kid. She almost broke down talking about finding her dad after his overdose.

"No offense, but your mom sounds like an awful bitch."

"No offense taken," Rae said. "You know, after she left my dad and me, I asked her why. And she told me, 'When you want something bad enough, you need to pay the consequence.' So, I guess a new life was what she wanted, and leaving me behind was the consequence."

It was the worst thing her mother had ever said to her. The pain of abandonment was no longer the same, but she was sure it would hit her again when her mother died. But it wouldn't even come close to when she'd found Viv—who would always be her true mom—strangled to death, and she wasn't ready to tell Dayton about it yet. That kind of pain was evergreen.

"I will never understand how a parent could do that to their child," he said. He held her hand. "I'm sorry you went through that."

In the past, Rae had a sneaking suspicion her relationships hadn't worked out because of the imbalance of trauma, not that she normally spoke about her own. It was hard to pretend she'd grown up in a normal family situation with an average teenage life only so she could feel equal in a relationship. Most of her past partners didn't understand why she didn't enjoy certain sex positions or dirty talk, but it was because it reminded her too much of what had happened in California. With Dayton, she didn't have to worry about those aspects as much for some reason. Maybe it was because he had his own demons. Or maybe he shared her innate ability to read body language, something she did every day in her work, and he knew when she was uncomfortable.

"As much as I love talking about my fun past, I need to ask you something," she said with a bitter smile. "Not so much for me but for Angel."

He leaned into the couch. "You mean the whole are-you-two-still-suspects thing?"

"Uh, yeah."

"You can tell Angel she can take her trip without worries."

Rae released a huge sigh.

"Guess I should've told you sooner."

She slapped his leg hard. "Asshole!"

"Hold on, feisty, I have a call." He pulled his phone from his pants. "I have to take this."

He stood up and moved over to her front windows, to where she couldn't catch what he was saying. After he ended the call, he came back over to the couch but didn't sit back down. His face was tense.

"I need to go. They just found Thomas Highsmith's body."

CHAPTER 43

RAE

2009

Rae dozed off sometime around midnight, the vigil at her motel-room window proving uneventful until the sound of someone slamming their car door woke her. She rubbed her burning eyes and searched the parking lot below. She had been right about the red Corvette. There Mark was, carrying a small paper bag she was certain contained a bottle of liquor and climbing the stairs to the second story, the same floor she was on. He must've left at some point after she'd fallen asleep.

She ducked when he passed by her room. She quickly cracked her door open to see if she could tell which room was his. He was only four doors down from her, and she felt sick. Her head told her to call the police and let them know where Mark was staying, but her heart told her to hurt him.

She rubbed her belly. Lily must've been asleep since she wasn't moving.

No, she couldn't simply stomp over to Mark's room and bash him in the head, as much as she wanted to. But if he still had Viv's watch, she would find it and take it back. Viv once told her she wanted Rae to have it if something ever happened to her, but Rae didn't know how she could ever accept something so precious. If anything, she wanted to bring it to Viv, to place it on her wrist before her funeral.

God, the funeral. Rae knew Viv had many friends and some extended family she spoke with in New Mexico, and Detective Kennedy had told Rae they were contacting her next of kin. Rae was thankful she didn't have to figure out those arrangements because she didn't know what Viv would've wanted. Cremation? Burial? Her chest hurt thinking about it.

She rubbed her eyes again. She had to stay awake this time so she could see when Mark left his room. Her can of Coke was empty, and she had one dollar in change left in her purse. She decided to risk leaving her room for another can. She needed every bit of caffeine to stay awake, and she said a silent apology to Lily.

The vending machines were in the opposite direction of Mark's room, and she walked as quietly as she could to them, the dimes and nickels sweating in her fist even as the October evening cooled her skin.

She slid the coins one at a time into the machine.

"Can you hurry it up?" a man's voice said behind her.

She knew the voice, and her body tensed up. *Shit.* She had nowhere to go. She punched in the code for a Coke, lowered her head, and turned around, hoping to walk on past him.

"Preggo? What the fuck are you doing here?"

Scared as hell, Rae threw the can of Coke at his head and ran. But instead of running to her own room, she kept going until she got to Mark's. The door was cracked, and she rushed inside and shut it. She locked him out just as he came up to the door, banging it with his fists.

"You fucking cunt! Open the fucking door!"

"Fuck you, you murdering piece of shit!" Rae said.

"What the hell are you talking about?"

"I'm calling the cops!"

All she could hear was her heart pounding in her ears, her lungs burning from running, as she called 911 from the room's phone. She relayed where she was to the dispatcher as calmly as she could with Mark still pounding away at the door.

When she hung up the phone, she searched the room for the watch. She looked in his small suitcase but didn't see it. She checked all the drawers and the bathroom, but it wasn't there.

"Where's her watch?" she yelled at the door.

"Tell her if she wants it, she can fucking get it herself. She knows what I want."

He was lying, pretending like Viv was still alive; she knew it. The cops would arrive any minute. It was now or never.

"Where is it?"

He kicked the door so hard, the frame cracked. Rae scanned the room and saw something poking out from under the bed's pillows. The butt of a gun. She grabbed it just as the door flew open. Mark stopped charging forward as soon as he saw the gun in her hands.

"Hey, now," he said, his hands out in front of him. "Put the gun down. We can talk about this."

Tears streaked down Rae's face, and she blinked hard and fast to clear her eyes. "There's nothing to talk about. You killed her, and I'm getting her watch back, you motherfucker."

Mark's hazel eyes were wide, and she saw the left side of his forehead had a goose egg where the Coke can had hit him. "Look, I didn't do anything to Vivien, but I'll get you the watch, okay? Just put the gun down."

"Get it now." She kept the gun aimed at his head, but her hands were shaking bad.

He noticed. "Listen, girl, you're going to hurt yourself with that. Just put it down."

"No. *You're* going to hurt if you don't give me the watch right fucking now!"

Mark moved his hand to his jeans pocket, but instead of pulling out the watch, he lunged for Rae. She pulled the trigger, but she missed him, and then he was straddling her on the bed, working to get the gun from her hand. He dug his fingers into her wrist hard, and she had no choice but to let go. He didn't aim the gun at her, but he didn't need to since she was now terrified to move.

"You are one crazy bitch, preggo." He pulled the watch from his pocket and dangled it in front of her. "All for this?"

Just then she heard the sirens. Mark turned his head toward the busted-in door, and Rae took the chance. She snatched the watch from his hand, and he hit her hard across the face, making her fall backward onto the bed.

Cops swarmed the room and pushed Mark to the floor, hands pressed into his back.

"I didn't fucking do anything!" he said to them as they cuffed him.

"Are you okay, Miss?" one officer said to Rae, helping her sit up on the bed.

The side of her face was on fire. "I think so."

"We have paramedics on the way, and we'll have them look you over. Make sure your baby's okay."

Rae held her belly as if Lily would fall out of her at any second. She'd been reckless, and she didn't know how she would forgive herself for putting her baby in danger. But she had the watch clutched in her hand. She told herself it was worth it.

The cops hauled Mark from the room, and Rae's lips curled. *We got him, Viv. And now he'll pay for what he did to you.*

CHAPTER 44

RAE

2024

Her client was dead. Rae thought about the six months she'd spent with Thomas Highsmith in her dungeon, his weekly sessions something she'd come to look forward to not only because he had been nice to look at, but because he was a good, respectful client. And she couldn't stop wondering what happened at the meeting he was going to at the Skirvin after he'd left their last session and what happened to him later at the Coulters' party.

Thomas's death was all over the news the next two days, mainly because he was an executive for Arkana Oil and Gas, one of the premier oil producers in the state, and, predictably, the news loved to feature the deaths of attractive, young white people. She watched the morning news and saw a story confirming Thomas died from a fentanyl over-dose by injection, which immediately rang as bullshit to Rae. She'd been around drug users, and Thomas hadn't been one. She'd seen every inch of his body, and he never had any signs of track marks. She called Dayton right after watching the report.

"Hey," she said when he picked up. "I just saw Channel 4's story on Thomas. He never did drugs. Not that kind, anyway."

"You don't know that for sure, Rae."

"Well, don't you think it's awfully strange how people keep showing up dead from overdoses? What about Cierra?"

Dayton turned quiet on the line.

"It was fentanyl, too, wasn't it?" she said. "Her supposed overdose, even though by all accounts she wasn't into drugs and was a year away from graduating with her college degree."

"I agree the coincidence is hard to ignore, but we need a clear way to connect her and Thomas to the parties. And I'm working on it."

"How? How are you working on it?" Rae felt like she was reliving everything that had happened with Viv, the police saying they would handle it but dragging their asses.

"Hey, I'm frustrated too." He lowered his voice. "I got a lot of heat trying to push the information from your missing friend about the Coulters' parties, and now I'm on a different lead. That's all I can tell you."

"What about Felton Holdings?" she said.

"I have a friend who owes me a favor looking into it. I might hear back today. And, yes, I'll call you as soon as I hear back from them." He sounded tired and stressed.

"Did you all ever find out who Thomas was meeting with at the Skirvin before he went to the party?"

He sighed. "Working on it."

"And you're not going to tell me anything else about it."

"Rae."

"Fine."

She hung up on him and then felt bad about it. She didn't want him to get in trouble by divulging information about the investigation, but she also hated being in the dark when those crazy assholes had one of her good friends and might come for her next. It was all uncomfortably familiar. She knew it wasn't uncommon for people to overdose from fentanyl, but it reminded her too much of the Santa Monica house, how Clint and Bobby would keep her and the other women under control with small doses of something similar unless they proved themselves no longer profitable or manageable.

She had to find a way to connect everything. Bobby obviously had his hands all over what was happening, and she needed his connection to the Santa Monica house. She knew in her gut he was helping to provide women for the parties the same way he and Clint had collected women and children for men in California and who knew where else.

For now, though, she had to concentrate on keeping her business afloat, so she got ready for work. As she drove Lily to school, her daughter was unusually quiet.

"You okay, honey?" Rae said, glancing at her.

"Mom, I heard about what happened with your client. The one who was missing. And someone made this horrible TikTok about you." Lily paused. "They made it sound like you killed him."

"Oh, baby, I'm so sorry this is affecting you." She reached over the car's console to squeeze Lily's hand. "But Angel and I aren't suspects, and detectives are investigating it."

"Like that Dayton guy?"

Rae peeked at her, and Lily's face appeared confused.

"Are you, like, dating him now?"

"No. We're just . . ."

"Having sex?" Lily said.

Rae clutched the steering wheel so hard her knuckles turned white. She hadn't had a chance to explain what had happened over the weekend to Lily. "Yes, we had sex. But it wasn't something we planned. It just happened, and we haven't really discussed what that means yet."

"Did you use protection?"

Rae had drilled into Lily's head since she was twelve about consent and safe sex practices, and she wasn't about to tell her they didn't use protection the first time. They had the second, so she said, "Yes, of course."

"He seems nice. And he doesn't seem like a crazy person. So, I guess it's okay if you go out with him as long as he's good to you."

"Thank you for the permission, Your Highness." Rae looked at Lily, but she was now scrolling through her phone.

After she dropped off Lily, Rae stopped by for coffee and walked into work feeling apprehension she couldn't shake. She had a busy day ahead of her, thank goodness, and she had to stay focused.

"Morning," Angel said when Rae handed her one of the to-go coffees she'd picked up for them. "Thanks, Rae-Rae." She had concern in her eyes, making Rae wary. "Um, so you're trending on TikTok."

"Oh, fuck this day."

"Guess who created the post?"

"The *Crimson Chronicle*?" Rae guessed.

"Nope. Begins with Gabby, ends with little bitch."

She should've known Lily's friend would try to milk attention from the situation. Since Lily had failed to mention that tiny detail, she guessed the girls were no longer speaking. One piece of positive news.

"Have you seen it?" Angel said.

"No, and I have no interest in anything that privileged twat has to say."

Angel took a sip of her coffee. "It may sound crazy, but I think the news on Thomas's overdose actually helped us. You have two new inquiries for services. Guess now that people know you're not a murderer, they're cool with you beating them."

Rae had no doubt some people still thought she could've been responsible for Thomas's death, regardless of what the media now reported.

"I just hope you survive while I'm gone. One more week, baby, and my ass is lounging on a white sand beach surrounded by a sea of thong bikinis."

Rae didn't know what she'd do without Angel the following week, but her friend deserved a vacation more than anyone she knew. It would be tricky, but she could handle scheduling sessions and sanitizing the dungeon room on her own while checking clients in and out.

After she got through the four clients she had, she was ready for a hot shower and a meal she didn't have to make. She was towel-drying her hair after her shower when her cell phone rang. It was Dayton, and the apprehension Rae had felt earlier in the day was back.

"I found him," he said. "I found the white-haired bastard."

CHAPTER 45

RAE

2009

Rae couldn't stop touching Viv's watch as an older male detective sat across from her in the interrogation room. Before the paramedics had checked her over, ensuring she and Lily were okay, Rae had slipped the watch onto her slender wrist, surprisingly comforted by its slight weight, like it contained a miniature version of Viv's heart, beating and still alive.

After the paramedics had cleared her, the police had taken Rae to the station to give a statement. She was so tired she had fallen asleep on the way over, and she could barely keep her eyes open as the detective had her go over everything that had happened in the motel room with Mark. She couldn't remember the detective's name, but he had a monotone voice, making it even harder for her to stay alert.

"So, you had no prior knowledge of Mark Pendergrass staying at the same motel as you? Not before you saw him outside of your room?" the detective said.

"No."

"Then why did you go to his motel room after the confrontation by the vending machine?"

Rae dug her nails into the palm of her hand, forcing herself to be awake and say the right thing. "I thought it was my room. I didn't stop to look at the room number. I was too scared because I knew he just killed my friend, and the police were going to investigate him. I was afraid he'd try to kill me too."

The detective squinted as he read over his own notes, the wrinkles around his eyes deepening. "We're checking out his alibi and holding him. For now, you're free to go back to your motel room."

She was relieved, but she tried not to show it. "Will someone let me know if he's released? And when I can go back to the condo?"

"Yes, someone will contact you."

An officer drove her back to the Motel 6. As much as she tried, she didn't get much sleep, not even after she took a long shower. She waited for a call that never came in the morning, and she didn't want to check in for another day at the motel, so she drove over to a Panera for something to eat until she heard from the police. When noon rolled around, she still hadn't heard from anyone, so she called them, and an officer told her the crime scene had been cleared. They didn't have any updates on Mark yet.

It took every bit of her strength to drive back to the condo and walk through the door. There was dirt tracked all over the wood floors from the people who had been in and out of the home, and Rae had an urge to clean the entire place. She went to the kitchen, her heart aching when she saw Viv's almond milk still sitting on the counter next to her untouched tea. She dumped the milk and cleaned the mug, and an emptiness in her chest threatened to swallow her whole.

Some pragmatic part of her brain told her she needed to get herself ready and do a live stream. She knew she needed the money, but she had no desire to do anything. The thought of tying up dolls for viewers online seemed absurd to her now. What did anything matter with Viv dead? Another logical part of her reminded her the condo belonged to Viv. She would need to find a new place to stay, and she didn't have nearly enough to put down a deposit for an apartment. Not in Albuquerque, where rent was so high. She didn't have the energy to think about it.

She avoided looking at Viv's bedroom as she walked down the short hallway to her own. She looked at the crib Viv had helped her set up in her room, and she felt like someone poured lead inside the center of her, in between each rib and over her heart, weighing her down. She curled up on her bed, too tired to cry. Somehow, she closed her eyes and fell asleep.

The next two days passed in a blur. She only left her bedroom to use the bathroom and occasionally grab a drink or something small to eat from the kitchen. The remaining time she slept. It was as if she hadn't closed her eyes in weeks, and she welcomed the times when she could escape into the dreamless black of sleep. Other times, she'd wake up hyperventilating, the memories of Viv's bloodshot eyes or Beth's small lifeless form in her arms haunting her.

It was the end of another listless day when her cell phone vibrated next to her head. The police station. Finally.

"Rae Phalin?" a vaguely familiar woman's voice asked.

"Yes." She felt drugged as she tried to sit up in the bed. The waning, flushed light of dusk splashed across her bedroom walls.

"It's Detective Kennedy. I'm calling about Vivien Dixon's case." There was a moment's pause. "I wanted to let you know that we're charging Mark Pendergrass but not for murder."

"What?" Rae's stomach suddenly hurt. "Why not?"

"I know this may be difficult to hear given everything you told us, but he didn't kill your friend. We do have someone in custody for her murder."

Rae was wide awake now. "I don't understand. If it wasn't Mark, who killed her?"

"We were able to pull clear footage from a neighbor's security camera of a man entering the home, and we matched the person to Dean Berryhill, the ex-boyfriend you had described. He confessed this afternoon."

The ball-gag guy? "That can't be right."

"It is, Rae," Detective Kennedy said. "We found some pretty explicit messages he sent to her. He'd been harassing her for some time, although it appears she didn't engage with him. And then he turned violent, which is often how these cases go."

Rae didn't want to believe it even as she remembered how poorly Viv had been tied up when she was strangled. Like it had been done by someone not skillful at using ropes.

"What about Viv's car? And Mark's threats?"

"The neighbor's security camera did show Mark damaging Viv's car, which he admitted to doing after she filed a PO against him. And he's been charged for that as well as for his aggravated assault of you. It's a felony charge."

The detective said it as if it would make Rae feel any better, but it didn't.

"I know this information doesn't help the pain of your loss, but I hope it gives you some comfort to know the person who did this will be prosecuted. I spoke with Viv's parents, and they should be in town within the next day or so to handle the funeral arrangements."

Viv's parents? The parents Viv hadn't spoken to in almost two decades because they had abused her throughout her childhood. The last people Viv would want making decisions on her behalf.

The detective ended the call with a promise to let Rae know if they needed her to testify beyond the statements she'd already given. The feeling of lead filled her chest again as it had the last three days, and Rae closed her eyes and wished for the sweet nothingness of sleep to take her.

CHAPTER 46

RAE

2024

Alexander Pearson—the white-haired man's name. Dayton told her his friend came through and found the owner of Felton Holdings LLC, a company with funds held at an offshore bank and no presence online. The company barely existed on paper and was clearly being used to funnel money not intended for government scrutiny.

Dayton's friend dealt with investigations involving online activity and found the Felton Holdings name referenced on a particularly disturbing site on the dark web, which was associated with a cultlike group into the torture and rape of women. The group was run by mostly wealthy white men who held parties all over the country and distributed videos of BDSM-type torture and sexual abuse for high dollar amounts. If people had enough money, they could attend the parties in person.

Felton Holdings was one of several subsidiaries owned by Alexander Pearson, doing business in Oklahoma and California. But when Dayton tried to find any information about him on social media, he came up empty. After scrolling through hundreds of pics and posts, he finally came across an old photo in which one of Pearson's extended family members had tagged his son, Felton Pearson. And there he was, the white-haired man, much younger but with the same tall, imposing figure.

"And guess who one of his companies is associated with?" Dayton said over the phone.

"The Coulters?"

"Bingo. The subsidiary reported a million dollars last year in gross earnings from the Coulters as a consultant, and I can guarantee that offshore account is where he keeps the money he collects from these parties and the videos they sell."

Rae was excited. This could be it; they could actually tie this bastard to the parties and Bobby along with him. "Can you, I don't know, get a subpoena or something to find out where the funds are coming from to the offshore account?"

She could tell he was driving from the whooshing sound of the highway in the background. "I would if I had a direct reason to obtain one. Remember, my higher-ups don't want to touch anything to do with the Coulters. The family has more influence than I realized."

"Then what the hell is the point of knowing this information if we can't do anything with it?"

"I have an idea, but I'm not sure if you'll like it. Can you meet with me now?"

She looked at the time. Almost five. Lily had texted Rae earlier about meeting up with friends after school, which made Rae feel better about the viral TikTok Gabby had posted. At least some kids weren't complete assholes about it.

"Yeah, but I'll need to be home by six thirty for Lily."

"Perfect. I have to get Carli from soccer practice at seven. Want to get a drink at Frida? I'm near Paseo and can head that way."

"Sounds good."

Rae wondered if a drink qualified as a date if the date involved trying to take down a possible sex cult. She got dressed in sandals and a strappy-but-casual blue cotton dress and threw her not-quite-dry hair into a simple topknot. She didn't have time for much makeup, so she dabbed a little pink gloss on her lips and brushed bronzer across her pale face.

Dayton was already at Frida's bar when she arrived. He chose the smaller, discreet bar in the back of the restaurant, the one with a little library where she and Angel once discovered several nude photography books. They had giggled like schoolgirls looking through the black-and-white photos.

When Dayton saw Rae, he gave her a long once-over before he stood up from the tucked away two-top he'd picked out. He touched her lower back and spoke into her ear. "You're going to distract me with that dress."

She blushed and sat down across from him. "You're doing a fine job of that yourself." He looked good with his slim-fitting jeans and button-up, the sleeves rolled up enough to show his strong forearms.

"Maybe we should've met at your place instead."

She got his intimation. "We can always hold this meeting in the back seat of your car."

"You obviously haven't seen it," he said. "It's a graveyard of Carli's extra soccer equipment and forgotten hair scrunchies."

"Mine's clean."

He grinned. "God, I wish we were here for a different reason."

"Me too." She usually kept her cards close to her chest, afraid of being rejected if she came on too strong with someone she was interested in, but she couldn't help flirting with Dayton when he seemed to enjoy it as much as she did.

A server came by to take their drink orders, and Rae used the moment to shift her mind away from the lust trying to sidetrack them both.

"So, what's this idea you have that you're not sure I'll like?" she said.

"Well, considering my superiors have no interest in airing the Coulters' dirty laundry, I thought maybe we could let the media do it for us." He saw Rae's confusion and continued. "We send the major outlets the footage I took at the party and some other key information about Felton Holdings and Pearson's association with the Coulters. Anonymously, of course. It could pressure my chief to look into it further and get the subpoena for the offshore account."

Rae crossed her arms, feeling abruptly chilled. "You're right. I don't like it."

"I get it," he said. "It's a big risk. The media could do nothing with it. Same with my superiors."

"And meanwhile, the Coulters and that Pearson guy could send people after us in retaliation and make sure we mysteriously OD. Besides, I'm in the video."

"We could edit you out."

The server dropped off their cocktails. Rae took a sip of her jalapeño-laced drink as she thought over his idea more. "I think it's too much of a risk. Don't you know any hackers who can tap into Pearson's offshore account? Avoid the subpoena altogether?"

"I hate to say it, but for it to be used in court, the information has to be obtained legally."

Instead of loudly cussing, Rae downed more of her drink. "So, basically use the illegally obtained footage to get legal evidence? No wonder the police never get shit done. Too worried about stepping on rich people's toes."

Dayton looked down at the twisted orange zest floating in his old-fashioned. "Trust me, I wouldn't suggest this if I had a better idea."

"I need to think about it."

"Okay. I know it's not an easy thing to agree to, but we can't sit on it for too long." He looked at the bookshelves next to them and pulled out a thick volume Rae recognized as one of the nude photography books she and Angel had ogled during their visit. "What do we have here?" He opened it and landed on a page displaying a muscular man who was stupid-level hung. "Goddamn. This book might give me a complex."

Rae laughed. "As if you have anything to worry about."

He gawked at the photo some more. "At least I don't have to worry about finding pants that fit."

"As long as you fit me, what does it matter?" she said, feeling every bit of her drink. She couldn't believe she had just said that cheesy-ass line to him.

He ran his fingers over his smiling lips. "You certainly have a way with words."

They finished their cocktails, and Dayton paid the server. He walked her to her car, the slight breeze feeling good against her skin.

"I'm curious," he said as they took their time getting to where she parked. "Has anyone ever tried to dominate you?"

"Some have tried."

"God rest their souls?"

She smiled. "Have you? Dominated someone, I mean."

He thought about it for a second. "Does choking count? I once dated someone who was into that."

Rae tried to picture him choking her, and the idea wasn't completely unappealing. She'd had fun with breath play countless times, although she was usually on the giving end. "Yeah, it counts."

When they made it to her car, Dayton turned to her. "Can I ask you something else?"

"Sure."

"Did you choose your work because it gives you control with men after what you went through?"

Rae fiddled with the silver watch on her wrist. There was so much she hadn't told Dayton yet, including about Viv and how she was murdered, and she knew she would eventually, but for now, she simply said, "In a way, yes. But I don't do it as a form of revenge or anything against my male clients. I do it because I enjoy it, and I love giving my clients pleasure in being themselves. A lot of people feel shame about enjoying pain or even giving it, and it shouldn't be that way if it's between consenting adults."

Dayton almost appeared diffident as he said, "I don't want you to think I'm not open to new things, but I'd be lying if I said I wasn't uneasy about what you do. About what you like. But it also intrigues me. The idea of giving up control to someone else."

"It takes a lot of trust on both sides."

He took her hand. "I hope you know you can trust me."

She wanted to so much. "Maybe we could start by going on a real date sometime when things are less . . . unpredictable."

He pulled her close. "I kind of don't mind being unpredictable with you."

Then he kissed her, one of his hands holding her face, his other hand tracing the outline of her breast with his thumb. It was a strange juxtaposition of wanting him to take her right there in the parking lot while feeling the weight of what he'd proposed to her about the footage. She didn't want to think about what her answer would be. She only wanted to enjoy the feel of his hands on her and was as reluctant to pull away as he was.

CHAPTER 47

RAE

2009

Tricia and Anthony De Luca were not exactly what Rae envisioned for Viv's parents. They were far worse. As soon as they stepped into Viv's condo, they were making plans like Rae didn't exist.

If their plans had involved the funeral, Rae wouldn't have felt so disgusted by their intrusive behavior, but they didn't seem to care about organizing anything except for putting the condo up for sale and taking the money back to where they now lived in Chicago. Cynthia, Viv's aunt who seemed the total opposite of Tricia, was the only person helping Rae with decisions: the funeral home, the type of flowers— yellow gerbera daisies, Viv's favorite —the music choices, which were as eclectic as her friend had been. It was too much, and Rae was thankful for Cynthia.

No one said anything about the watch Rae wore, Viv's watch. She had wanted to place it on Viv's wrist, but Viv's parents had already had her body cremated. "No reason to spend a bunch of money for a wooden box in the ground," Viv's father had said. So, Rae decided she would keep the watch, to honor her friend and feel her close, the way Viv had kept it to feel close to Frederick. And once Cynthia told her Viv had legally changed her last name to Dixon after Willie Dixon, the famous blues musician Viv loved, Rae knew someday she'd legally take the last name as well. She soaked up as many stories as she could from Cynthia, stories that showed Viv in her kindness and effortless glamour.

"She told me about you, you know," Cynthia said to Rae as they prepped a traditional Italian meal together for the family and friends who were coming for the funeral the next day. "You were very important to her. I think she saw herself as a big sister to you."

Rae stopped pressing the edges of ravioli Cynthia was teaching her how to make, quashing tears from coming again. "It doesn't seem real that she's gone."

Cynthia sucked in a deep breath like she was holding in tears, too, and side-hugged Rae. "She was one of a kind, my Vee."

That night, Rae had trouble falling asleep with Viv's parents in the house with her. Hearing their loud movements in the home kept startling her awake as soon as she'd drifted off. She wished Cynthia were at the condo, too, but she was staying at a nearby hotel.

The next day was a blur Rae remembered in bits and pieces. More family and friends showed up at the funeral home and paid their respects. There was crying, then laughter, as people gave eulogies, stories Rae wanted to hear and burn into her memory, these other sides of Viv she didn't know, but she couldn't seem to grasp on to any words for long before her mind went numb.

After the funeral, people filled the reception room, where Cynthia and Rae served the food they had prepared, the food Viv's parents had watched them make the day before without offering to help. Rae felt like a machine, ladling food onto paper plates, Lily's movements in her the only thing making her feel real.

She was dead tired by the time they got back to the condo. Cynthia helped her clean the serving spoons they had used, and Rae was glad they'd had the foresight to use foil serving trays they could toss. Tricia and Anthony drank the leftover wine they had served at the funeral, giving Rae a taste of their alcoholism Viv had once mentioned to her. They were sloppy drunks, loud and obnoxious, and she couldn't handle it after the long day.

"Could y'all please keep it down?" she said to them.

Tricia stopped her chatter and sneered at Rae. "*Y'all*. You're from one of those hick states, huh? *Southern*." She overexaggerated the word, drew it out as if Rae spoke like a caricature.

"I'll finish up," Cynthia said to Rae in a lowered voice. "You go rest, and I'll take care of them."

"This isn't your place, girlie," Tricia slurred from the couch. "Your free ride is over. You've got one week to get you and your shit out of here."

Cynthia touched Rae's shoulder, which was trembling with a rage she had nowhere to put. "It's okay. It's just the wine talking. Go take a shower and try to get some sleep."

Rae shot a hateful glance at Tricia and Anthony and went to her room. She was too tired to shower, and her mind was heavy with Tricia's words. She knew Viv's parents meant it; Rae had a week to find a new place to live, and here she was seven months pregnant. Without enough for a rental deposit, she didn't know what she was going to do.

Lily kicked her hard in the ribs, and Rae thought about Beth, how she had kicked and kicked when Clint's friend lifted her up from behind, before Clint came running with the syringe. Beth had fought so hard, and Rae needed to find the fight in herself again too. She needed to be the person who had helped Katelyn, the strong person who set a fire and left her abusers to die.

Katelyn.

Rae took out her cell phone and pulled up her emails. She scrolled until she found the one from Katelyn's parents, Marilyn and Ben Reid.

243

She reread their message over and over: If you ever need anything, please never hesitate to reach out.

She stared at the phone number they had given to her. An Oklahoma number.

They had been on vacation in California when Katelyn was taken from them. That's what the news articles had stated. Katelyn was there one moment, gone the next from the crowded Santa Monica Pier.

Rae had looked them up before. They lived in Yukon, a suburb not far from Oklahoma City, far from where Rae's mother now lived in Tulsa.

She looked at the time. It was a little after nine, so after ten in Oklahoma. Too late to call. But then she heard Tricia's and Anthony's raucous laughter in the living room, and she dialed the number. She held her breath until a woman's soft voice answered.

CHAPTER 48

RAE

2024

Thursday brought another hellacious heat wave, something that used to be uncommon for May in Oklahoma, but now it seemed like the norm. Rae finished her long day of clients and sat in her car blasting the A/C, happy she'd been too busy before to think much about the decision she'd made.

After thinking it over, Rae had called Dayton that morning to tell him no on his idea. It was too risky, and she'd already gambled a lot when she went to the party with him. She had to think about Lily and Angel and how everything could affect them. All she could do was trust Dayton to abide by her decision and not send the footage to the media.

Lily got a ride after school with a friend, so she was already home eating a snack in front of the TV when Rae arrived.

"Hey, Mom." Lily's face appeared worried.

"Hi, honey. Everything okay?" God, she hoped it wasn't another viral TikTok about her.

"I don't know. Something weird happened today at school during lunch."

Rae set her things down in the entryway and sat next to Lily on the couch. "What happened?"

"Well, my friends and I were all outside eating in the courtyard, the one by the student parking, and this lady came up to us and said I could make a lot of money by modeling at some fancy party."

Rae's blood turned cold. She tried to keep her voice level because she didn't want to freak out her daughter. "So, she wasn't a student?"

"No. She was young, though, and really pretty, and my friends thought she maybe worked for a modeling agency, but something about her was . . . off."

"In what way?" Rae said, uneasiness worming into her stomach.

"I don't really know how to describe it. She just kept staring at me all creepy and said I was exactly who they were looking for. Then she gave me this." Lily handed Rae a card with a phone number handwritten across it. "She said to call if I was interested. I was the only one she gave a card to."

"You didn't call, right?"

"No," Lily said, her eyes wide.

"Good. Can you describe what she looked like?"

"I took a pic of her when she wasn't looking. I was pretending to check my phone."

She handed Rae her cell phone, and Rae had to fight to stay calm. The woman in the photo looked like the submissive Rae had whipped at the Coulter mansion's party. She felt a bit of relief that the woman wasn't dead.

"Will you send this photo to me, honey?"

"Yeah."

"And if you see her again, don't talk to her and call me right away."

"Okay, but you're scaring me," Lily said, her chin doing the trembling thing she did when she was upset.

"No, it's okay. You did the right thing by telling me. I only want you to stay aware. Not everyone has good intentions, even if they're a young, pretty woman." Rae hugged her tight. "Now no more snacks. I'm making dinner in a bit."

Rae went to her office and shut the door. With shaking hands, she looked at the photo Lily had texted to her. Petite brunette with a dancer's figure. Yes, it was definitely the sub. She had no doubts. She looked at the card in her hand. There was no way it was a coincidence the woman gave the number to Lily.

Before she could think it through too much, she called it.

The dial tone was odd, and she thought about hanging up, but someone answered.

"Hello, Echo."

Hearing his good ole boy drawl made her want to vomit.

"Or should I call you Rae now? Or maybe Mistress V?"

"What do you want, Bobby?" she said through clenched teeth. "Besides fucking with my kid."

"You have a lovely daughter. Smart too. We knew she would get the message across to you."

"What message is that? That you're a pathetic piece of shit? Tell me, how did you escape the fire?"

"When a person's skin is melting, they have a tendency to wake up."

"And did you drag Clint out with you? Did you save him?"

"I was a bit preoccupied with saving myself."

"Such a great friend." Her body relaxed a little in knowing Clint wasn't going to creep back like Bobby had, like the Terminator coming out of the flames. "What did you do? Have Mommy and Daddy pay off the investigators to lie and say there were two bodies so you could slip away and start a new life?"

He huffed out a laugh. "There were two bodies, Nancy Drew. That used-up Hispanic chick was in Clint's closet, waiting to be disposed of. Just another poor Jane Doe with no dental records."

Maria. Rae was too stunned to catch her breath.

"You know, we had a lot of fun watching you and that detective fuck in the garden. Like two cats in heat. So raw and unlike the shy, scared girl I remember. Not so scared now, huh? You should be."

She swallowed hard and made herself speak. "I should've poured the gasoline on you instead of that recliner."

"Oh, but you didn't," he said, the coolness of his voice making her nauseous. "If it makes you feel any better, I have third-degree burns on my legs. Do you have any idea how painful skin grafts are?"

"For you? Not painful enough."

He made a low growling sound, like an animal hungry for an attack. "This is what you're going to do, *Rae*, so listen because I'm only going to say it once. We know the detective has the video he took on a flash drive somewhere on him. You will get it from him without him knowing. Then you will record yourself destroying it. You will then send the recording to a number that will be texted to you tomorrow. If you haven't sent the recording two days from today, you and everyone you care about will suffer immeasurably. Do you understand?"

The room seemed to be spinning around Rae for a second, and she couldn't find her voice.

"Do you understand, Rae?" he repeated.

She swallowed over the thick lump seizing her throat. "What if I can't get it from him?"

"You will."

Then he hung up.

For several minutes, she couldn't move, her eyes glued to a photo on her desk, one of Lily when she was about five. She had wanted to try ballet, so Rae had spent the money getting her signed up, but then Lily quit soon after she took the dance studio's photos in her little pink tutu. When Rae asked her why she didn't want to dance anymore, Lily had told her a boy kept trying to kiss her, and the teacher ignored her pleas to make him stop.

Rae let out an odd, guttural laugh. A crazy person's laugh. No girl was safe in this world, not even a little girl trying to learn ballet. And now she knew, no matter what, she couldn't escape her past, and it would drag down Lily too. The laugh turned into her sobbing into her arm. She didn't know how long she stayed like that, but she eventually stopped herself. She had to stay strong and do what she needed to do to keep her family safe.

Rae thought about Dayton. She didn't know if he'd try to stop her from taking the flash drive, so she decided it would be better not to tell him about the call. But he had the footage, presumably on him or at his house. Why didn't those crazy fucks break into his home and get it themselves? Not that she'd wish it on him. Maybe they didn't want to risk it. Dayton probably had security cameras at his place. Seemed like everyone did now since the self-monitored kind were a lot cheaper. Most people in her neighborhood had those doorbell cameras, same as her, ready to catch porch pirates in action.

She let off a scream in her head and dialed Dayton's number.

"Hey," he said. "I was just thinking of you."

"I was thinking of you too." She bit her bottom lip hard, hating herself for what she had to do. "I know Carli's back home with you now from your mom's, but I'd really like to see you. Do you think I could maybe swing by later this evening? I could bring some wine."

He was silent on the line for a moment. "Uh, yeah, that sounds nice. Is nine too late?"

"No."

"I'll send you my address. Just text when you get here."

She pressed the palms of her hands to her eyes, willing herself not to cry again. Then she got up, went to the kitchen, and started dinner as if the world wasn't crashing around her.

CHAPTER 49

RAE

2009

This is only temporary. Rae repeated it to herself as she pulled into Ben and Marilyn Reid's neighborhood in Yukon. The Oklahoma sky was robin's-egg blue and painfully cheerful even as the October day had chilled her enough to throw on a coat when she had stopped for gas.

Leaving the condo in Albuquerque had been one of the hardest tasks of her life, but she had nowhere else to go. For an agonizing second, she almost called her mother, ready to beg for help again. She couldn't handle any more cracks in her heart, which felt ready to shatter beyond repair after Viv. She only wanted a safe place to give birth to Lily, and Marilyn sounded so nice over the phone, her voice buttery and warm when she told Rae they had a large guest bedroom she could use as long as she needed.

So, Rae had packed her meager belongings into her Civic, including her computer setup for live streams and the baby items Viv had helped her buy. Cynthia helped her break down the crib before she had to go back to where she lived in Santa Fe, Rae weeping in her arms as they hugged goodbye. Cynthia reminded her so much of Viv; it was like losing her friend all over again.

Rae sucked in a few deep breaths as she slowed down, scanning the house numbers for the correct address in the Reids' neighborhood. All the houses looked the same—large brick new builds with no established trees, only saplings and unimaginative landscaping without color. She pictured Marilyn and Ben's home decorated not with original paintings like Viv's but with signs from Hobby Lobby saying "LIVE, LAUGH, LOVE" or "BLESSED."

She found their home after driving past it and having to turn around. They opened the front door before she was fully out of her car with her purse.

A wisp of a woman with ash-blonde hair came up to her car. "Echo? I'm sorry, I mean Rae. I'm Marilyn." Her smile was eager, maybe nervous, which somehow put Rae at ease. Marilyn pointed to the man following behind her. "This is my husband, Ben." He had soft brown eyes and dark curly hair.

"I'm so happy to meet you both," Rae said, and she meant it.

Marilyn went to hug her and stopped. "I'm sorry, I'm a hugger. Are you okay with that?"

"Of course." It was surprising how strong Marilyn was as she held her.

Rae caught Ben's eye, and he looked away from her. He moved toward her trunk. "I'll help you with your things."

"Katelyn's still at school, but we'll be getting her soon," Marilyn said as she grabbed one of Rae's bags. "She's so excited to see you again. Isn't that right, honey?"

Ben said nothing, and Rae assumed he didn't hear his wife since he beelined for the house with her large suitcase. She carried as much as she could and followed them inside.

Their home was larger than any house she'd ever been in. It was an open concept with hardwood floors and heavy leather furniture, the walls painted the color of a stormy sea. She spotted a faux wood sign in the kitchen reading "WINE O' CLOCK." Everything was spotless with no signs of a child living there. Like a museum.

Once all Rae's belongings were inside the house, Marilyn made them some herbal tea and asked her a million questions, namely about the baby and how her pregnancy was going.

"We did IVF with Katelyn. She's our miracle baby." Marilyn smiled so much, Rae's face hurt watching her. "We've been trying again for a few years, but no luck."

Rae noticed how silent Ben was as he watched them talking. She didn't know if he was shy or if it was his personality to be standoffish, but she felt self-conscious around him.

"We'll have to help you get set up for prenatal care here," Marilyn said. "Anything you need, we'll help you with it. I mean, we owe you so much. It's the least we can do. Right, honey?"

Ben stared at Rae, his face unreadable. "Right."

Marilyn stayed behind at the house when Ben left to get Katelyn from school. Rae had hoped Marilyn would go, too, so she could have a moment without questions, but she had a feeling one of them would always stick around until they trusted her to be alone in their house. She didn't blame them. They didn't know it, but she had lied to them about why she needed a new place to stay. She said the friend she was living with was moving up north, and Rae needed a way to reestablish herself in her home state before Lily was born. Telling them about Viv's murder would only scare them, and they had already been through a lot with Katelyn.

It was exhausting being vague in answering Marilyn's questions, and Rae was thankful when the front door opened, and she heard little footsteps running throughout the house looking for them. Rae's throat tightened when Katelyn ran into the guest bedroom where Marilyn was sitting on the floor helping to reassemble the crib for Lily. It had been over six months, and the girl already looked different. Taller, maybe, and her caramel curls were a little longer.

She was sure she looked different to Katelyn, too, now heavily pregnant with her hair dyed a darker shade. But, no, Katelyn smiled at her and whispered, "Angel lady."

"Hello, Katelyn." Rae didn't want to cry and frighten the girl, but she couldn't help it. She was so happy to see her alive and thriving. "I love your pink dress."

Katelyn did a spin in her frilly dress, which looked way too fancy to wear to school. "Mommy said I could wear it today because you were coming."

"It's very pretty, like you. Is it okay if I give you a hug?"

Katelyn nodded and ran up to her, arms wide. So trusting. She pictured Katelyn on the Santa Monica Pier, Maria luring her away with promises of ice cream, and Rae hugged her tighter.

Ben suddenly filled the doorway to the bedroom, watching Rae hug his daughter. Something in his expression made her uneasy, and she let go of Katelyn.

Marilyn's smile stayed plastered on. "Ben, honey. Would you mind helping with this? I can't get this weird screw thing to work."

"Oh, no, I can do it," Rae said, trying to lower herself to the carpeted bedroom floor without losing her balance.

"No." Ben took the screwdriver from Rae's hands. "I'll do it."

"I figured we could order a pizza tonight." Marilyn's smile never wavered.

"Pizza!" Katelyn jumped up and down, grinning.

Rae mirrored Marilyn and smiled. "Sounds great."

After a semiuncomfortable dinner, Rae was ready to bathe and be alone in her room.

"You can use the guest bathroom in the hallway," Marilyn said. "There are extra towels in the linen closet."

Rae took the longest hot shower, her tense muscles finally relaxing some after driving for over eight hours straight from Albuquerque. She wrapped a thick towel around herself and was about to quietly head back to her room when she heard hushed arguing coming from the living area. She moved farther down the hallway, staying close to the wall to hear better without being seen.

"How can you trust her, Mare? We know nothing about her."

"She saved our daughter. What else is there to know?"

"That's what the police said because that's what she told them." Rae heard Ben blow out a sigh. "She could've been involved in it."

"Oh, so now you don't believe our own daughter, everything she told the therapist?"

"That's not what I'm saying."

"Then what are you saying?"

A pause. "She could be a grifter. She could be one of those people who takes over your house and never leaves."

"If you keep acting rude to her, you're going to ruin this for us." Marilyn spat out each word.

"Ruin this for you, you mean."

"Fuck you."

Another pause and a loud exhalation. "Okay. I'll be nicer to her."

"You better. You owe me this."

Rae heard movement, and she darted down the hallway to her bedroom and shut the door. She swallowed over the anxiety balled up in her throat. She wasn't sure what she had just walked into by coming to live with the Reids. She repeated to herself, *This is only temporary.*

CHAPTER 50

RAE

2024

Dayton's house wasn't too far from Rae's. It was tucked away in an older neighborhood close to the Paseo Arts District, where Rae and Lily would go to the First Friday Art Walk most months. She liked to imagine them going with Dayton and his daughter sometime, assuming whatever she had with him wasn't just a fling, but the idea dissolved when she considered what she was about to do. She didn't know if he would trust her again after she stole the flash drive.

She texted him when she arrived like he had asked. He opened the door and quietly said, "Glad you found it okay."

He took the wine she'd brought from her hands, and she glanced around at his place as he ushered her toward the back of his house. His home was tidy, something she didn't expect for a single dad, and tastefully decorated in a rustic farmhouse style mixed with Native American artwork. They stopped by the kitchen, which had French doors leading to a back deck.

"Let me open this really quick," he said, grabbing a wine opener and two juice glasses.

Rae thought of Viv, how she'd drink her wine in juice glasses too. She used to say it was the Italian way, but she said the same about many things that probably had nothing to do with being Italian.

He poured the malbec and handed her a glass. "Let's go out back."

She wasn't sure why he didn't want to be inside the house. She wondered if his daughter was already asleep when it was only nine, which would be a bit strange for a teenager. Maybe she was ill, and that's why he was being so quiet. They settled on two cushioned chairs he had on the deck. He turned on some string lights in the backyard, dimming them.

"Is Carli asleep?" she said and sipped the wine to control her nerves. "Not that it's not nice being outside."

"No." He gazed at her for a few beats. "Uh, I'm not ready to tell her about us yet."

Rae looked down at her wine, a pearl of insecurity forming in her chest. "Because of what I do?"

"Not at all," he said, his voice too emphatic, which made her think there was truth to what she'd asked. "I just haven't dated in quite a while, and Carli had a hard time when my last relationship ended. So, I'd like to wait a bit before I introduce you to her. I hope you understand."

She did, but it also made her think about the awkwardness of Lily meeting him. She wondered if Dayton thought she was a bad mother for allowing it to happen. Parenting for her was often like being trapped in a pitch-black room, and she didn't always know how to find a lamp to shed light on situations, but then she reminded herself she didn't have the best example to follow.

"Of course, I understand." She fiddled with her watch, felt the soft thrum of its ticking against her fingers, before drinking more of her wine, hoping the alcohol would somehow help her get into a seductive mood, which was the furthest thing from her mind. She needed to distract him so she could find the flash drive. She watched him sip from his glass. "Do you like it?"

"I know nothing about wine," he said, "but it tastes good to me." He paused, examining her with his dark eyes like she was a slide under a microscope. "Are you okay?"

"Yeah. Why do you ask?"

The space between his brows creased as he scrutinized her more. "You seem nervous. You have a pretty obvious tell when you're anxious."

"A tell?"

"Everyone has one. Like a tic when they're nervous or being deceptive. Yours is playing with your watch. It's pretty. Is it a family heirloom?"

"You could say that. And I'm not nervous," she said, but her voice shook.

"You know, I didn't have any expectations with you coming over tonight, if that's what's bothering you."

She held his gaze and tried to tap into a confidence she didn't feel as her mouth quirked. "Really? No expectations?"

"Okay, maybe I did. But I don't want you to think this is only about sex for me, and I don't want you to feel pressured."

"Maybe I like pressure, especially if it's done right."

Dayton fixed her with his eyes again, almost like he was trying to decode her words and see if she was serious. Then he set his glass down on the little table between them and stood up. He placed his hands on either side of her chair and leaned in, gently kissing her before kneeling down in front of her chair. He looked up at her, the string lights dancing tiny fires in his dark irises.

"Tell me what you want, Rae."

She had imagined this scenario many times, him on his knees in supplication, begging her to allow him to touch her. He wasn't exactly begging, but his eyes were. It was a subtle shift in power, one she knew he was offering to her like a tentative gift. She took it from him, and the swell of control made her forget about why she was at his home to begin with.

"I want you to kiss me." She motioned to her lap. "Right here."

He moved his long fingers along her thighs, pushing up her flouncy skirt until her panties were exposed. Without a word, she let him slide her thong down and watched as he parted her legs. When he ran his tongue inside her, she closed her eyes tight and allowed herself to sink into the pleasure he was giving her. Just like before in her bedroom, he knew what he was doing, and a moan escaped her lips as her fingers tugged his thick hair, pressing him harder against her.

She wanted to suspend time, to allow herself to swim in the growing tickle and feel it spread warmth throughout her body, to explode pure, blind bliss from the center of her. But then Bobby's threat flashed in her mind, and she involuntarily shut her thighs, forcing Dayton to stop.

"I'm sorry, I can't do this," she said. She felt disgusting for trying to manipulate Dayton, like she was Bobby's puppet. She'd been manipulated enough in her life to know how that kind of betrayal felt.

He pulled back from her, and she had to look away from the intensity in his eyes. "What's wrong?"

She reached for her wine. She downed it in a few gulps, then smoothed her skirt back down over her thighs.

Confusion was all over his face. "If this is going too fast, then tell me." He paused. "Or did you change your mind?"

"No, it's not that." She took several deep inhalations to stifle the panic in her. She had to say it. "I . . . I need the flash drive with the footage."

"What?" He stood up and stared at her. "Why?"

Rae froze for several moments, thinking over what she should tell him. If she told him the truth, he could still refuse to help her, but she also didn't feel right lying to him. There was only one way to find out.

She told him about the sub giving the card to Lily and the call with Bobby and his demands.

"I sent Lily over to her friend's house so I could come here. I was too afraid to leave her there alone. I told her I forgot something important at work."

"Why didn't you just tell me this before?" He sounded hurt. "Why did you go through all this fucking pretense?"

"I—I wasn't sure if I could trust you."

"Seriously, Rae? You talk about mutual trust with your clients, and you won't even give me a chance to earn it with you. Why?"

"Because my clients don't have the power to hurt me like you can!" She immediately wanted to pluck the words from the air, to tuck them back deep inside. It was a truth she'd never spoken aloud, and hearing it made her feel like one of her Shibari ropes slowly fraying. All these years, all the progress she thought she had made to heal from her past, but she still held her trust of men in a cage she was scared to fully open.

Dayton crouched next to her chair and ran his thumb across her cheek, wiping away her tears. "Both of us have that power. And the risk is worth it to me to see where this goes, but if it's not to you, then say so."

She searched his face. The closer she got to him, the more the tenderest parts of her seemed to split and ooze, exposing her like an old wound reopened. She didn't know if he would run when he saw those repugnant parts of her, and she had never allowed anyone close enough to find out. Not even Angel.

She took his hand. "Look, I'm sorry I lied. I was scared for Lily." She paused, more words on her tongue, but she didn't say them because it'd be like cutting open her chest and handing him her heart. *You're worth the risk to me too.*

Dayton studied her face as if he was waiting for her to say more. He finally looked away. "Okay . . . so the flash drive . . ." He sat back down and rubbed his face with his hands. "First off, I'd love to know how they're so sure I have the footage saved on one. They could've tapped into our phones, but I don't remember us mentioning the drive. And what's the point of destroying it when we can save endless copies? They have to know that."

She'd thought of that too. "I don't know. Maybe it's symbolic for them. To feel like they have control over us and scare us at the same time."

"Something about it doesn't feel right." He looked out into his yard for several moments and turned back to her. "Think about it. They knew we didn't belong at the party, but they let us in anyway. I don't think they would've done it if they knew who I was, and I'm not sure if Bobby recognized you until they saw the recording of us. Maybe they thought they were only catching a couple of party crashers and wanted to fuck with us, or they might've known you were associated with Thomas Highsmith. But I feel like I'm missing something important."

"Either way, you have something they want," Rae said. "And I can't risk my family by not doing what Bobby asked."

A muscle along Dayton's jaw twitched. "You're right." He got up and went inside the house. When he came back, he handed her the flash drive.

"You already saved a copy, didn't you?"

"What do you think?"

She stood up and sighed, relief washing over her. "Thank you."

Dayton held her arms, pulling her into an embrace. "Can we be done with lies now?"

She nodded into his chest, the sound of his steady heartbeat comforting to her.

"Good." He stroked her hair. "Now go destroy it."

CHAPTER 51

RAE

2009

Living with the Reids was like dressing up for Halloween every day, everyone pretending to be something they weren't. The masks never came off around Rae, and she wasn't sure if she wanted to see Marilyn and Ben without them. Since overhearing their argument her first night in their home, she knew she could never relax too much with them. She had to be a perfect guest, keeping everything clean at all times and attending church with them on Sundays, so they wouldn't throw her out.

Everything was for Lily. She'd only been with the Reids for three weeks, but it felt like so much longer. A little over a month before Lily was due, and then she'd find the cheapest place she could afford with the money she was saving.

After her first week with them, the Reids went back to work during the day, leaving Rae on her own until she'd pick up Katelyn for them in the afternoons. That was her trade-off for living with them—being a babysitter. It was the one good thing about living there, being able to play with Katelyn. She was such a sweet girl, always singing and dancing around the house like a fairy child, sprinkling joy everywhere she went. It was the only time Rae could be herself.

She was sitting on the floor in Katelyn's bedroom playing Barbies with the girl, unsure if she would be able to get back up on her own, when Katelyn dug out a baby doll from her toy box.

"This one is you," Katelyn said, holding up a Barbie with blondish hair. Rae had stopped dyeing her hair, so her strawberry-blonde was growing out. "And this one is my baby sister."

Rae smiled. "Oh, is your mommy pregnant?" Marilyn hadn't said anything about being pregnant, but she knew they had experienced a failed IVF attempt again shortly before Rae arrived.

"Um . . . no." Katelyn kept playing with her dolls, her expression confused. "Mommy told Daddy Jesus brought you here. She said you came to give them a miracle baby. Like me!"

What in the hell? Rae kept her voice level, but she was thoroughly freaked out. "Did they tell you that?"

Katelyn stopped dancing her dolls around on the floor. "I heard Mommy when she was making dinner."

"Does your daddy think the same thing as your mommy?"

Katelyn looked up at her and frowned. "Daddy was being mean. He said you should go away, but I want you to stay forever."

Rae didn't know what to say. Katelyn was so young—she could've easily misinterpreted what her parents had said—but then Rae couldn't ignore the uneasiness stirring in her gut. If she brought it up with Marilyn and Ben, they might get mad and tell her to leave. She had nowhere to go and was only weeks away from giving birth. She had no choice; she'd have to wait it out.

The next day, she went over her finances. She had withdrawn all the money she had earned while she was in Albuquerque and started up a new bank account in Oklahoma. She missed doing a lot of live streams after Viv died, and a good chunk of her money went to her prenatal care. If she did at least two live streams a day every weekday when the Reids weren't around, she could have enough for an apartment she was looking at in Oklahoma City.

It was a little after noon, and she had time to do another live stream. She shut her bedroom door, which didn't have a lock, got out the dolls she kept hidden in her suitcase, and slipped on one of her half-faced masks and her sheer stockings. As she got into her session, she found a good rhythm with her audience, something she hadn't felt since Viv's death, and she bloomed with the power of being back in control. It had been so long since she felt the desire to masturbate, but the need rushed over her as she gave her viewers a good show.

Rae was biting one of her Ken dolls, then slowly running her tongue along the doll's plastic torso and between its legs, where smoothness replaced the real thing, when she heard a quick intake of breath behind her. She turned and saw Ben watching her from her doorway. She hadn't heard him open her door, and she definitely hadn't heard him knock first.

Shit. She cut her live stream and grabbed a blanket from her bed to shield her half-naked body.

"What in the hell are you doing?" Ben said, and Rae couldn't tell if he was shocked, angry, or both.

She removed her mask. "I . . . I'm sorry. I was just . . . it's my work, but it's not what you think."

He entered her room but stayed back from her bed where she was sitting. "I knew you were hiding something."

"You're hiding something too." The words left her mouth before she could stop them.

He moved farther into the room, his eyes glued to her. "And what exactly is that?"

The shame of getting caught moments ago turned into a heady mix of fear and anger. "I know about what Marilyn said. About you all wanting my baby, but you can't have her."

Ben's eyes widened. "Where did you hear that from?"

She didn't want to get Katelyn in trouble, so she said, "I overheard you two arguing."

He clenched his jaw. "I don't want your baby."

"But your wife does, doesn't she?" Rae felt like a caged animal. "Is that why you're letting me stay here? Because you think you can just take my baby once she's born?"

"I never wanted you here," he said. "But since you are, I think it's time you face the reality of your situation. You're what—nineteen? Barely an adult. You have no money, no family you can reach out to, and now I see what you've been doing during the day. This . . . whatever this is." He waved his hand at the dolls she had splayed out, tied up with embroidery thread. "You have nothing to offer a child."

Rae hated him so much right then. She didn't want to hear her own insecurities thrown back at her.

"But that doesn't mean I want to take your baby." Ben sat on the other end of her bed, which was still too close for her. "I want my wife to be happy, but a baby isn't going to make that happen. She's not capable of being happy."

She stared at him, uneasy with how frank he was being. "Why?"

He looked down at her stockinged feet. "Because she wants perfection in everything."

"Is that why you hate me? Because I'm messing up your perfect life?"

His eyes shifted to her face. "I don't hate you, but I don't trust you."

"But I didn't do anything to make you not trust me. I would never hurt Katelyn or you and Marilyn."

"I don't know what you're capable of, Rae."

She didn't know what she was capable of either after everything that had happened in California and New Mexico. "Then help me, and I'll move out."

"So, you want to leave?" He said it like he didn't believe her.

"I want a place of my own. For my baby. And this is what I can do right now to make money." She pointed to the dolls. She didn't tell him how she actually loved what she did, how it seemed to draw out a hidden strength within her. "I don't really know how to do anything else, and I don't have a high school diploma, and I'm not sure how to get one."

He stared at her for a long time. "If you're serious, I can help you study for your GED. But you can't tell Mare. And she can't know you're doing this kind of . . . work. She may try to come across as a progressive Christian, but trust me—she's not."

More secrets. Rae didn't know how many secrets a person could hold inside before they'd explode.

She looked Ben in the eyes. "I'm serious. I want to do it." And she did. She knew whatever she did in life, having a GED was important.

Ben gave her the first real smile she'd seen from him. "Then let's put your time to better use."

CHAPTER 52

RAE

2024

As much as she tried to avoid it, Rae kept checking her cell phone in between clients. It was Monday afternoon, and she had received the text Bobby promised the Friday before. The text only included a different number, likely from another burner phone, which Dayton told her he would look into. She had sent the recording of her smashing the flash drive into tiny bits with a hammer. So far, she'd had no response, but she wasn't sure if she was supposed to get one.

Dayton was right. There was no point in destroying it if he had the video saved elsewhere, and she started to believe her initial instincts were incorrect. Maybe they weren't only trying to scare them into compliance. It was almost like they had toyed with them by pitting her against Dayton, trying to get her to break the tenuous trust she was attempting to build with him. Like they wanted them to feel isolated, which would make them more vulnerable.

Rae felt vulnerable enough without their help. She thought about the weekend, how she had met up with Angel Saturday night for drinks and dancing at their favorite queer club. Angel encouraged her to invite Dayton so she could "check his intentions" before her trip, which Rae grudgingly did, fully expecting him to politely decline. To her surprise, he showed. And the way he was slamming shot after shot, it was like he wanted to escape himself. She didn't question it too much because she was doing the same. In some ways, she liked seeing the looser side of him. He had even tucked a dollar into a male go-go dancer's neon-green G-string, she and Angel hooting the entire time.

Afterward, she and Dayton shared a Lyft back to her place, both of them too tipsy to drive. Lily had stayed the night with a friend, so they didn't have to be quiet when Dayton bent Rae over the side of her couch, yanked off her thong, and drove into her from behind with a fierceness that made her sore the next day.

Rae shuddered at the memory and pushed it to the back of her mind. She had to get ready for her last client of the day, who was new, and then Angel would be off the rest of the week for her Bahamas trip.

She looked over the information for the new client again on her office computer: Troy Farris, age forty, into canes and bondage. From his submitted photo, he was built like a truck. Figured. Seemed like the bigger the man, the more they enjoyed being broken by a small woman.

Angel was looking over her trip itinerary again when Rae walked to the front desk.

"When the newbie arrives, will you go ahead and send him on back?" Rae said.

Angel pulled her eyes away from the computer monitor. "Sure thing. Oh, and you mind if I skip out early after I get him checked in?"

"Don't tell me you haven't packed. You freaking leave tomorrow."

Angel shot her an incredulous look. "Sis, I've been packed for a week. I just found another cute bikini I need to get."

Rae smiled and rolled her eyes. "Fine. I can handle closing up."

"And when I get back, maybe you and your eye candy can come out to the Copa again," Angel said. "You know, so I can do a little more interrogation for ya."

"In case you forgot, I'm not a masochist."

"You loved it," Angel teased. "I asked all the questions you're too chickenshit to ask."

"Like when you asked him if he'd let that go-go dancer blow him?"

Angel flashed a huge grin. "You know you kinda wanted to see it happen."

"Oh, my God, hush." They both chuckled, and Rae hugged Angel since she wouldn't see her later. "Call me before you leave tomorrow morning, okay?"

"You got it."

Rae went back to her dungeon room.

About fifteen minutes later, the new client entered the space, a cloud of horrible body spray following him inside. Troy was even larger in person, with muscles bulging all over his body. A roid head. Wouldn't be her first, but it felt like a workout tying up hulking men like him, and her energy was waning.

Rae stood legs apart, arms crossed, her face calm and friendly with a dash of sternness. "Hello, Troy. Before we begin, do you have any questions or concerns outside of what we covered in your new client paperwork?"

"No."

A talker. "Okay. I can step out while you undress to your comfort level."

"I'm not undressing for you." His tone struck her as disrespectful, something she wasn't fond of with clients, especially new ones.

"As I said, it's to your comfort level. And while you're in this space, you will address me as either Mistress or Mistress V. Do you understand?"

He glared at her. What kind of game was he into? He'd been vetted, his background check cleared, but there was no way to background-check a personality.

"If you choose not to play by my rules," she said, putting plenty of authority behind her voice, "then you can leave. But there are no refunds."

He must've realized she meant it because he held his wrists in front of him like he was ready to be bound. Good. Once she had him restrained, she'd cane the asshole right out of him.

When she turned to her wall of toys and reached for her large leather restraints, she sensed movement behind her. Before she could turn around, Troy was on her, grabbing her from behind and lifting her up. She drove her spiky heel down hard into his kneecap, and he threw her to the ground, knocking the wind out of her. She screamed out for help as she scrambled to her feet. Rae lunged for one of her whips on her toy wall, but the man was on her again before she could reach it, squeezing her so tight she thought she'd pop like an overfilled balloon.

"Your friend already left," he growled into her ear. "And if you want to live, you'll stop struggling." That's when she realized he had a knife pressed to her throat.

She stopped kicking her legs, and he set her down. She touched her neck. No blood. Adrenaline raced through her veins, her body fighting the need to go back into fight mode again. "What do you want from me?"

"We want you to make a call to Detective Clearwater."

Rae's stomach dropped. He wasn't a psycho client trying to rape her. He was with Bobby and the Pearson guy.

"Get your cell phone," Troy said, if that was even his name, which it probably wasn't. Likely a stolen identity to get through her vetting.

"It's in my office."

"Get it."

He followed her closely as she got her phone from her office. As soon as she had it in her hand, he said, "Call him on FaceTime. Do not point the phone in my direction, or I will slit your throat."

She dialed Dayton's number, but he didn't answer.

"Call again," he said.

Just as she was about to try again, Dayton called her back.

"Dayton, listen," she said, keeping her voice level and clear, "I need you to switch the call to FaceTime."

He detected the anxiety in her words. "What's going on, Rae?"

"Please, just do it."

His face pulled up on her screen, and she could see her own strained expression minimized in the corner of her phone. Troy came up beside her, pressing the knife to her throat while staying out of view of the phone's camera.

"What the fuck?" Dayton's eyes got huge.

"Detective Clearwater," Troy said, his voice suddenly dropping a full octave. "We need you to uphold your end of things, or there will be consequences."

What was he talking about? What end of things?

"I told them already. I don't have access to it." Dayton was using his stiff detective voice, but there was an edge of panic, which drove Rae's heart into her throat.

"Yes, you do." Troy pressed the knife deeper into her skin, her pulse beating against the blade.

"Goddamn it, I don't. Please, don't hurt her."

"It shouldn't be this one you're worried about, Detective."

Dayton's face lost all color, his eyes turned to steel. "If you touch my daughter, I will fucking kill every one of you."

"You have until Thursday to figure it out." Then Troy told Rae to hang up. Dayton immediately tried to call back, but Troy took her phone from her hand and threw it on the ground. He released her and leered at her tight Domme outfit. "Pull up the information you have on me on your computer."

Reluctantly, she sat at her desk and pulled up his client information. The photo of him came up, along with what she now knew was his fake background information.

"Delete it all. Now." Once she did, he said, "Thank you for your cooperation. I really don't like destroying pretty faces if I can help it. I'll let myself out."

CHAPTER 53

RAE

2009

Ben wasn't kidding when he said she'd be doing a lot of work to earn her GED. He had bought her a thick prep book and showed her where she could go online to take free practice tests. After failing the first one, she knew it wasn't going to be as easy as she'd imagined. All the good grades she'd earned her freshman and sophomore years in high school meant nothing because she didn't know enough to pass. Not yet anyway.

For the most part, she had been alone in her studies over the last two weeks, but Ben's work as a graphic designer meant he could work from home some days. During those times, he'd help her study by quizzing her and checking her progress with the practice tests. The more time she spent with him, the less she understood why he was with Marilyn. They were total opposites. Where Marilyn was extroverted and overly talkative, almost bordering on manic at times, Ben was laid back and quiet.

If there was one thing they did have in common, it was their desire to uphold appearances in public. At the house, Rae rarely saw them show each other affection. But when they went to their church, which was one of those megachurches that preached more about politics than anything in the Bible, Ben and Marilyn held hands and gave every impression of being a loving couple.

"How did you and Marilyn meet?" Rae asked Ben after he quizzed her over some math problems in his office.

He rested the prep book on his desk. "Why do you want to know?"

"Just curious. You're both so different."

"Haven't you heard the phrase opposites attract?"

"Yeah," she said, although she thought couples needed to have at least some things in common. "But . . . never mind."

"No, what were you going to say?" He fixed his brown eyes on her.

"It's just . . . you don't really talk to each other."

Ben looked away from her, glancing at the design work he had pulled up on his computer. "Talking's not our thing."

"What is your thing, then?"

He turned back to her. "You shouldn't be asking me personal questions like this." He sucked in a breath. "I think we're good for today. You've got this section down."

Rae didn't mean to overstep a boundary, but she wanted to understand the weird dynamic between Ben and Marilyn and why they kept secrets from each other.

"What would happen if Marilyn knew about you helping me with the GED stuff?" she said.

He stared at her. "She would think I had an ulterior motive."

"Why would she think that when you're just helping me?"

"You're not this naive, Rae." He leaned forward in his office chair. "You're young and pretty, and most men would have a motive in helping you. And after what you've experienced, I'm sure you know what that motive is."

Rae shrank back from him, and he noticed.

"I'm not one of those men."

She had no way to know for sure if he was telling the truth. "Why do so many men want to hurt women?" She didn't say it because she expected an answer. It was only a question she had asked herself many times, and it fell easily from her lips.

"Because it's easier for men to take something than to earn it," he said after a moment. "Men are taught to take things because it shows they're powerful. And a man without power is nothing in our society."

"Do you believe that?"

Ben turned quiet. "It doesn't matter if I believe it. It's just reality."

Rae wondered what would happen if all the women in the world collectively decided to rise up against men, killing all the ones who had molested, raped, or beat them. She imagined there wouldn't be many men left.

"Do you still think I'm a grifter?" she asked him, and his mouth opened a little in surprise.

"You shouldn't eavesdrop. But, no, I was wrong to think that about you. However, I do think you're more capable than you want other people to believe because you think it will protect you to appear innocent. I see how you act around the people at church. But what I saw you doing with those dolls that day . . . you know plenty about how things work."

The way he was looking at her, shame wrapped its claws around her heart. It quickly turned to rage. "What does that mean? That because I was forced to do things I didn't want to do by men who wanted to feel powerful, I don't get to have power myself? I don't get to take back what they stole from me by enjoying anything to do with sex, especially if I make money from it?" She swiped her hand across her eyes, brushing away tears.

Ben shook his head like he was disappointed. "Is that what you think you're worth then? An object for men to look at? How is that empowerment?"

"Because I choose it!" she yelled. "And I don't need your help anymore." She started to leave his office.

"Rae, wait."

She turned around.

"We met in college. Mare and me. And we don't talk now because we both know if we did, we'd have nothing to say to each other. So, it's easier this way. For Katelyn."

Rae thought about her own mother and father, the lonely silence stretched between them for so many years. And they had probably believed she didn't notice, but it had eaten a hole in her chest to feel her mother's indifference toward her dad because she saw it bleeding over to her.

She watched Ben slumped in his chair, and she saw her own dad, always pretending things were fine, doing everything possible to avoid conflict. "You talk crap about how I found empowerment for myself, but where's the power in playing pretend happy family with your wife?"

Ben's mouth tightened. Rae didn't wait for a response and left the office.

That night during dinner, Marilyn kept watching Rae, her smile blinking on and off like a toy whose battery was dying.

"I got a call today," Marilyn said as Rae took a bite of the pork chops she'd made for the family. "From the manager of an apartment complex in Oklahoma City."

Rae swallowed her bite, feeling her throat tighten until she thought she'd start choking. She had submitted her application for a cheap apartment, and it required three references. The only people she knew of to put down were Ben, Marilyn, and Viv's aunt Cynthia. The rest of the application had been stressful to complete, with questions she didn't have easy answers to, like her work history and education.

"I thought you were going to stay with us until after you give birth." Marilyn's body tensed up as if she was afraid of Rae's answer.

"Um . . . I think it would be better for me to have my own place before Lily comes."

Katelyn's little face scrunched up into a frown. "I don't want Rae to go. Daddy, don't make her go away."

It was fast, but Rae caught Marilyn's glare at Ben.

"I'm not making her go away, pumpkin." Ben glanced at Rae. "You heard her. She wants to have her own home for when her baby comes."

Marilyn's smile blinked back on. "Rae, don't you think it's irresponsible to move so close to your due date? What if something happens, and you're not prepared for it?"

"That's her choice to make, Mare."

This time Marilyn's glare was full force on Ben before she turned it on Rae. "Well, if you leave before the baby comes, we're not going to be able to help you financially. And I don't know how you'll pay for rent *and* cover the cost of the birth."

Rae looked at Ben, but his eyes were on his plate of food. All his talk about men taking power made her want to get right up in his face and hysterically laugh until her voice went hoarse. He had no power in his relationship, and he was going to let Marilyn manipulate her into staying. Fuck that. She would find a way, but she needed time to figure out Medicaid in Oklahoma to cover her pregnancy costs. Viv had helped her with those things before, but now Rae had to learn it on her own, and all the forms were overly complicated.

Rae forced a smile. "You're right. It's not a smart idea to move right now."

A satisfied grin spread across Marilyn's face. "I'm glad you're seeing reason. Really, Rae, what were you thinking? You don't even have a job."

Ben caught Rae's eye. They had their own shared secret.

CHAPTER 54

RAE

2024

Rae's first thought after Troy left was to call Angel and make sure she was okay. She didn't trust herself not to break down and didn't want to freak out her friend right before her trip, so she texted her instead, without mentioning what had happened.

She couldn't stop shaking, not even when Dayton showed up less than ten minutes after she'd called him when Troy left. Rae had checked the front and back doors, making sure they were locked, and her pulse skyrocketed when she heard Dayton pushing the intercom buzzer over and over to be let in through the front.

He rushed inside and held her tight against his chest like she was going to vanish. He pulled back from her and examined her neck. "Are you okay?"

"I think so."

He paced the lobby, raking his hand through his hair, and slammed his fist down hard on the front desk, making her jump. "Those motherfuckers!"

She felt light-headed and sat down on the love seat in the lobby. "What did he mean about you holding up your end, Dayton? What do they want from you?"

He stopped pacing and stared at her, his eyes wild. "They want me to destroy evidence."

"What evidence?"

"For a recent high-profile rape case involving one of their little cult members, Stephen Andersson." Dayton sat down in a chair kitty-corner from her. "He's a Swedish businessman who has ties to the Coulters, and his former assistant accused him of rape and battery. They want me to tamper with the rape kit, make it unusable."

Rae breathed through the pressure in her head portending a migraine. "When did they contact you?"

"Last Friday." He let out a sardonic laugh. "They left a greeting card shaped like a dog on my windshield. I knew it was them. It had a number written inside, and I called it. They threatened to hurt Carli, my mom, you—anyone I care about unless I come through."

So that's why he drank so much when they went out Saturday with Angel. He didn't seem to care how trashed he was getting, like he wanted to be outside himself. He was escaping an impossible decision.

"Do you really not have access to the evidence?" she asked.

"Of course, I have access. But if I get caught, it means I go to prison. Besides, I'm not a dirty cop."

"Why you, though? You said you saw the former police chief at the party. They probably have other cops in their pocket who could do it for them."

"You're right. They might have some inside guys, but I don't know. I figure if they do, they don't want them to get caught and have it lead back to them. And they made it very clear I'm disposable. They just want it done. And I pretty much fell into their lap when we went to the Coulters' party."

"Why didn't you tell me about this before now?"

"I should've, but it involved an active case. But now?" He shook his head. "It doesn't matter if I tell you. They're forcing my hand, which is why I sent Carli back to my mom's house, at least until I can find something to pin the fuckers." He paused, blowing out a sigh. "There's something else. They hacked into my computer last Friday and erased the file, even the backup I saved to the cloud."

"Fuck." The migraine was definitely coming now. "Why the hell did they have me destroy the flash drive then? They could've just broken into your house."

"It doesn't make a lot of sense to me either. But I think they knew I wouldn't leave it at my house during the day, and it was too risky for them to break in with me there, so they used you to do it because you could get close to me. They needed the hard evidence gone." He leaned forward, cradling his face in his hands for a second. "And now we have nothing to threaten them with."

Rae rubbed her temples. "At least we have video of the guy who attacked me. We have security cameras."

"How did he get in?"

Rae stood up and walked over to the front desk to pull up the security footage. "He posed as a new client under the name of Troy Farris. Sound familiar at all?"

"No." Dayton came up beside her at the computer.

"He got through our vetting, probably using a stolen identity. He had me destroy the client file with his photo, but I got the motherfucker on . . ." The security footage was black. "Shit. I don't know why nothing's showing."

Dayton stepped over to where a camera was set up in the corner of the ceiling. "He didn't cut the feed here. Do you have more cameras set up somewhere else?"

"Just the one pointed at the back exit," she said.

She followed Dayton down the hallway, past her dungeon. Sure enough, the box containing the wires for the camera feeds was cut.

Rae felt like screaming. "He must've done it before he came inside the dungeon space."

"Besides you, did he touch anything?"

"The doorknob of my space and I assume the front entrance when Angel let him in."

Dayton looked frustrated. "I can try to pull prints. I'm going to use the back exit to grab my kit. Avoid touching anything and stay close by."

He came back a few moments later, and she let him in. He used some sort of black powder and what looked like a tiny duster on both her dungeon doorknob and the front door handle.

"Damn it," he said under his breath after he was done carefully dusting the front entrance. "I can't get a clear print." He sat back down in the front lobby next to her on the couch. "Okay, give me your best description of this guy."

Rae pictured Troy's leering face and huge muscled body, describing everything she could remember in as much detail as possible. "And he had about a pound of Axe body spray on."

Dayton's face turned to stone. "I'm not sure, but your description sounds a lot like Benson, a hothead in my department. He douses himself in some cheap shit everyone complains about. Used to be chummy with the former police chief too." He pulled out his phone, searched for a moment, and showed Rae a Facebook photo. The profile pic was dark, a sunset in the background. "This the guy?"

"I don't know. Maybe . . . shit."

"All right. It's something to look into at least." He gazed at her. "This is all my fault, dragging you into this mess to find Pearson."

"Yes, it is." She attempted a smile, but her head hurt too much.

"That's one of the things I appreciate about you. You don't sugarcoat." He placed his hand on her upper thigh, and she realized she still had on her Domme outfit. "Whoever it was, I'm going to make him pay for touching you."

"Just make sure I get to join you. I'd love to cane his ass into nonexistence."

He nodded. "We're going to get them."

She hoped he was right.

CHAPTER 55

RAE

2009

After Marilyn had cornered Rae during dinner about the apartment application, they finished the meal in uncomfortable silence. Then Rae took a shower and went back to her bedroom, reading a book until the house went quiet.

It was close to midnight, and she couldn't sleep from Lily endlessly kicking her. She got up to get a drink of water from the kitchen and saw a small glowing red dot in the backyard as she walked past the sliding glass doors. She moved closer to the glass and saw the shadow of Ben. She didn't know he smoked.

She quietly slid the door open and stepped out into the yard. The November night was frigid, and she longed for California's mild weather, one of the few things she missed about the state.

She coughed, and the shadow turned around. "Rae? What are you doing up?"

"Lily's being active." She shivered and ran her hands up and down her arms.

"Go back inside. It's too cold."

"I will when I'm ready. Does Marilyn know you smoke?"

Ben snubbed out his cigarette. The solar lights in the backyard provided weak illumination, but she saw enough of his face to know he looked tired.

"I don't really care if she does," he said. "It wouldn't stop me."

"Then why hide it?"

He took off his jacket and handed it to Rae before sitting down on one of the patio chairs. "Haven't you ever kept a secret just so you have something of your own?"

"Yes." Rae had too many. She put on his jacket and sat down on a chair near him, the metal seat freezing through the fabric of her pajama pants. "I think everyone has a few secrets."

"Do you want to know one of mine?"

She wasn't sure if she did, but she said, "Um . . . sure."

Ben turned his head toward her, but she couldn't make out his eyes. "The day Katelyn was taken, I was relieved."

Rae didn't know how to respond. She didn't know if he was about to confess something horrifying, and she now regretted coming outside.

"I was terrified, too, of course," he continued. "But it meant I didn't have to make a decision I had dreaded for a long time."

Then he told Rae the rest of his secret. The day Katelyn was taken was the day he was going to drop the D-word on Marilyn. He told Rae he had fallen in love with the former youth pastor at their church. Former because when Mare discovered Ben was having an affair with a man, she threatened to lie and say the pastor had molested Katelyn. The pastor ended up resigning and moving to the East Coast to avoid an inevitable controversy.

That was almost a year before, and the trip to California was supposed to be a last-ditch effort to bond as a family and rebuild the marriage that had never been built to begin with, according to Ben. He told Rae he'd always known he was attracted to both men and women, but he grew up in the church and believed he was an abomination because it was what he was taught. So, he only dated women. He met Marilyn in college, and they became good friends and were part of the same denomination, so it made sense to get married. It was expected, and he loved her enough.

But then their communication began to suffer, and their sex life slowed down to almost nothing, and the IVF treatments started when Marilyn became obsessed with getting pregnant. He started to see Marilyn for who she truly was—insecure and manipulative—and he lost his love for her. He fell into a depression until he started helping the youth pastor with Sunday services, their easy conversations turning into much more.

"After Katelyn was kidnapped, Mare fell apart," Ben said. "I couldn't leave her like that. But then you happened, and we had Katelyn back. And nothing has changed. Mare and I are basically roommates."

Rae bounced her legs to keep warm. "Why are you telling me all this?"

"I honestly don't know." He let out a small laugh. "I guess because you seem like an open person, and I've never told anyone. Feels kind of good to say it."

"Why don't you just divorce her now?"

"What kind of father would I be to put my daughter through more trauma after what she's been through? I don't know if I can do that to my little girl."

Rae thought of her mother. "Getting divorced doesn't mean you're abandoning Katelyn. She probably won't understand now, but when she sees you happier, she'll know it was the right thing to do." A shiver passed through her body. "I wish my parents would've gotten divorced before they got so messed up." She was glad it was dark out and Ben couldn't see her tears forming. "They kinda messed me up, too, you know."

Ben was quiet for several moments. "Rae, I'm going to give you money for the deposit on the apartment. I can't help you with the birth costs, but I have a friend who works at DHS who can help you get set up with SoonerCare."

"Why would you do that for me?"

"Because of Mare. If you stay here until after Lily's born, she'll find a way to have her taken from you and placed in her care as a foster parent. It's what she wanted to do as soon as you contacted us. She got it into her head it was God's way of giving her another child." He paused. "And I think I'm finally done playing pretend with her."

CHAPTER 56

RAE

2024

Ever since Rae's attacker had found a way to bypass her client vetting, she was even more hypervigilant, especially with Angel gone on her Bahamas trip. And now she had no security system until the company came out to fix the cut wires later on in the week. All she could do was double-check the entrances, making sure the doors were locked whenever she was with a client.

She'd thought about canceling her sessions for the rest of the week, but she couldn't afford the loss in income. She told herself they wouldn't come for her again since it was Dayton they wanted, but then she'd perseverate on what could happen to him and his family.

"Mistress? Do you want me to get dressed now?"

Rae pulled herself back into the moment. She blinked and looked down at Nancy Cress, an HR executive for Arkana Oil and Gas, the same company Thomas Highsmith had worked for. She avoided having clients who worked for the same place, and it typically wasn't an issue she had to worry about, but she had made an exception with Thomas.

They had no way to know they were both her clients unless they spoke with each other about it, which she doubted would happen. Nancy was an attractive middle-aged woman married to a deeply religious man who thought doggie-style was a perversion. She was a sporadic client, scheduling sessions every two months or so, and she loved rope suspension, something Rae enjoyed doing for her, although only a few of her clients were into it. She scanned the woman's body, how the impressions of the rope crisscrossed her fair skin, and she wondered why Nancy stayed married to someone who didn't allow her to be herself. In some ways, she reminded Rae of Ben.

"Yes, Nancy. You can get dressed now," she said, trying to keep her focus.

After Nancy got dressed in her tailored suit and silk blouse, she seemed hesitant to leave the dungeon space.

"Mistress, I . . . I need to discuss something with you before I leave."

Rae hoped she wasn't about to drop out as a client. The business had hemorrhaged enough money after the article. "What is it?"

Nancy's expression turned serious as she pushed her dark auburn hair behind her ear. "I knew Thomas Highsmith before he died—not well but in passing since we worked in the same building. You know, small talk at the coffee station. And . . . well, I saw the article in the *Crimson Chronicle* before his body was found."

Rae crossed her arms. "Then you know he was a client and that I had nothing to do with his death."

"Oh, I know." Nancy flashed a nervous smile. "I felt weird not addressing it with you since I learned he was also a client of yours." A sadness crossed Nancy's face. "Sometimes I worry I helped contribute to his overdose."

Rae's heart did a little jump. "Why would you think that?"

"Because as the HR manager, I was tasked with firing him on the day he went missing." She looked down at her designer pumps. "He took it hard, but there was nothing I could do about it. I'm just the messenger."

"Why was he fired?" Rae felt like she was on the verge of learning something vital.

"Uh, I'm not at liberty to tell you." Nancy shook her head. "I'm sorry, I shouldn't have brought this up with you. I hope you won't drop me from your services."

Shit. "No, I'm glad you told me. I was sad to hear about Thomas's death."

"Me too. He was a kind person," Nancy said. "And, in a way, it's nice to know we had a secret in common. Well, his was a secret before that stupid article."

"At least the police got them to take it down, and you and my other clients are protected. I promise you that."

Nancy smiled. "Maybe the article wasn't the worst thing to happen. It opened up some conversations at work with a few of my coworkers. I can't be open myself, but now I know I'm definitely not the only one in my office who's into this sort of thing."

As soon as Nancy left, Rae texted Dayton to call her and began sanitizing the dungeon space and closing up shop for the day. He called her back as she was starting her car.

"What's going on?" he said in a lowered voice after she'd answered. "Your text seemed urgent."

She told him about what Nancy had said, although she didn't give away her name. "So, did you know he was fired the same day he went missing?"

"Yeah. I did." He paused, and she heard the sound of girlish laughter in the background. "Supposedly, he was fired for making a serious accounting error."

"But you don't think that's the reason?"

"No, I don't think that's the whole story. I think he was being used as a pawn the same way they're trying to use me, and he got caught."

Rae heard the high squeal of girls laughing again. "Where are you?"

"Outside of Roxy's with Carli and her friend. I promised I'd take them for ice cream after school today since I haven't seen her in a few days—not since I sent her back to my mom's until I get this shit figured out."

The deadline for him to destroy the evidence in the rape case he told her about was the next day. "You don't have much time. What are you going to do?"

Dayton let out a long sigh. "What would you do, Rae, if you were in my position?"

Clint and the fire burned across her mind for a second. "To protect my family? I'd do anything and everything, but this is different. If you do this, you're taking away possible justice for a rape survivor."

He was quiet for a moment. "It would change the core of who I am as a person. How do I move forward from something like that?"

She didn't have an easy answer for him. She knew the things she'd done in her life had fundamentally changed her, not always for the good. But she kept Viv's words in her head whenever she questioned those gray areas of herself: *Are you going to let this turn you into the kind of monsters you escaped from?*

"You learn how to live with the new version of yourself."

CHAPTER 57

RAE

2009

Over the next two weeks, Ben followed through on his promise to help Rae. His friend at DHS was nice in explaining the process of Medicaid in Oklahoma, but the woman couldn't do anything beyond giving information. Rae didn't qualify since the state looked at total household income, and Ben and Marilyn earned well over the threshold. As for the apartment deposit Ben said he'd give her, he told her he needed to move some things around first so Marilyn wouldn't notice.

Rae was as restless as Lily squirming around in her belly. She didn't like waiting on someone else to make something happen, and it was getting harder for her to do live streams to earn more money. Her body no longer felt like her own, her feet so swollen she worried something was wrong with her. Maybe there was, but she couldn't afford to check.

She was thankful to have an ally in Ben, but it didn't stop her from sinking into dark thoughts at night when she couldn't sleep. Sometimes, she'd get up, feigning that she needed a drink of water only to see if Ben was outside having a secret smoke so she could talk with him. But most of the time, the dark thoughts kept her glued to her bed, unable to shake the ghosts of Viv, Beth, and Maria.

The one positive was that she'd passed her practice GED test and was ready for the real deal. The test was over a hundred dollars, which seemed like a lot to her, but she was glad to pay it if it meant opening up opportunities for her.

"Math fucking sucks," she said to Ben during one of his teleworking days. They had gone over the arithmetic portion again, and she had made several simple mistakes she should've caught. "Maybe I'm not ready yet."

Ben swiveled in his computer chair to face her. "You *are* ready, and you *will* pass. It usually takes people two to three months to prepare if they work full time, but you've been lucky to have time to study during the day, and you're smarter than you give yourself credit for. Better to take it tomorrow like you planned than wait until you have a screaming baby. Trust me."

The online test was almost eight hours long, and she hoped the website was right in saying she could get the results the same day. Ben was going to pick up Katelyn for her since she couldn't pause the test once she started it.

"Thanks," she said. "I need to get out of my head."

"Give your brain a break for tomorrow."

Rae rested the remainder of the day, only leaving her bedroom to play with Katelyn for a bit after Ben got her from school and to help Marilyn with dinner. Marilyn was unusually quiet as they chopped vegetables for a soup, and Rae didn't mind. Conversations with Marilyn were one sided, like she was interrogating her to find out any small detail to latch on to and criticize. Rae noticed she did it to everyone, including Katelyn. If the girl came home with a scraped knee, Marilyn wouldn't ask her if she was okay and then tend to it; she'd reprimand her for being careless. In many ways, Marilyn reminded Rae of her own mother.

"I noticed you've been studying for your GED," Marilyn said after she seasoned the soup.

Rae tried not to look surprised. The only way Marilyn would know about her studying was if she'd gone into Rae's bedroom and snooped around until she found the study guide or if Ben had told her. Either option put her on edge.

"Uh, yeah. I thought it would be a good idea to do it before Lily's born and I won't have time to study."

"Well, don't be surprised if you fail it the first time." Marilyn leaned against the kitchen counter. "Besides, I'm planning on taking some leave after you give birth. You know, to help out. You can study then."

Rae fought to keep the anger from her face. She knew exactly why Marilyn was taking leave. "You don't have to do that but thank you. I appreciate it."

"It takes a village, right?"

"Right."

◆ ◆ ◆

The GED test the next day was the hardest, longest form of self-torture of Rae's life, but it was done. She finished the last module right before Ben came home with Katelyn in tow, and all she wanted to do was sleep.

"How'd it go?" Ben asked after he knocked on her door.

"I'm never taking another test again in my entire life."

He chuckled. "That good, huh? Well, I'm sure you passed."

"I'm going to be obsessively checking my email until I get the notice."

"I'll handle Katelyn so you can decompress."

"Thanks."

Rae ended up napping until Marilyn woke her for dinner. She was so drained, she scarfed down her food and went back to her bedroom to crash again.

When she awoke, it was morning, the light filtering through the sheer curtains making everything appear as if it were covered in gauze. But, no, this wasn't her bedroom. It was Viv's, and she was lying on Viv's bed, the same bed she had once crawled into after one of her nightmares. Viv had held her all night, stroking her hair. The familiar ache for her friend was like a pile of large stones resting on her chest, crushing her. She turned onto her side, and Viv calmly stared back, her milky skin ethereal against her black hair. Rae couldn't get her mouth to form words, so she reached out to touch her, to see if she was real, but Viv's face turned somber.

"You need to wake up, hon."

"I don't want to. I want to stay with you."

"I wish you could, but you have to wake up."

"No. Please let me stay with you."

"You can't. Get up, Rae. Now!"

She gasped awake. She swore she smelled Viv's sweet, floral perfume surrounding her, and she started crying. Then she felt wetness underneath her and immediately thought she'd peed the bed. But when she flipped on the nightstand lamp and pulled back the sheets, she saw a great plume of red.

CHAPTER 58

RAE

2024

Dusk blazed orange and fuchsia across the sky as Rae and Lily ate some Big Truck Tacos takeout on their back patio. She was admiring her daughter, how the setting sun made her face glow, and she thought about Dayton and how he must've felt spending time with Carli, knowing she was in danger if he didn't follow through and tamper with the evidence. She wanted to help him, but she didn't know how.

She knew what it was like to be cornered, to make a quick decision and change the course of your life in an instant. Sometimes it worked out, like when she'd met Viv, and sometimes it was like crawling on your hands and knees through broken glass. It had been that way with Marilyn and Ben, and she avoided thinking about them.

"Do you still talk to Cynthia?" Lily asked.

As they ate, Lily had asked Rae more about Viv and everything that had happened in New Mexico, and Rae tried to tell her as much as she could about how she got started in her work without going into too many details. It hurt too much to remember some parts, like

Viv's death, but she knew Lily was trying to put together the pieces of how her mother had come to be the person sitting in front of her. She couldn't fault her for wanting to know when she had never had the courage to ask those questions of her own mother.

"Yes, we still talk on occasion," Rae said. "She's actually planning to visit sometime next year." She didn't say how Cynthia was dealing with the tail end of breast cancer treatments, so the visit was up in the air.

Lily's face turned contemplative. "Mom? All these things you went through, is it why you haven't really dated anyone?"

"I've dated, honey."

"Not really. Not anyone you've brought around me." Lily bit her bottom lip. "I just want you to be happy, so if that Dayton guy makes you feel that way . . . well, you should see what happens and don't worry about me."

"I'll always worry about you because that's what parents do."

"Not all parents," Lily said, and Rae knew she was alluding to the grandmother she'd never met.

Before Rae could respond, she heard the doorbell chime. She wasn't expecting anyone, and she pushed down the sudden anxiety bubbling up.

Lily checked the doorbell camera app on her phone since Rae had left her own phone inside the house. "Huh. That's funny." She showed Rae her screen, and there was Dayton on their front porch.

"You finish up dinner while I see what he needs."

Lily smirked. "Okey dokey."

When Rae opened the front door, Dayton looked like a glass vase perched on the edge of a table, waiting for the slightest brush to knock him over.

"I'm sorry to come over here like this," he said. "I tried calling you."

"I was out back with Lily having dinner. Come inside." She shut the door, noting the thick folder in his hands. "What's going on?"

"I need your help with something. If you're willing."

"Of course."

Dayton looked past her toward the back of the house, and his expression shifted from urgent to friendly. "Hi, Lily. Sorry to interrupt your meal."

"It's okay. We're done anyway." Lily held the trash from the takeout as she slowly walked into the kitchen, her eyes on them. "Never mind me. Just throwing this away."

"Uh, we need to go over some things in my office, honey," Rae said.

After she and Dayton settled in her office, he plopped the folder on her desk. "Thomas Highsmith's bank records. The real ones."

"What do you mean, 'the real ones'?"

"So, that meeting Thomas had at the Skirvin Hotel bar before the Coulters' party was with Bobby Coulter. A witness confirmed it, but I just learned there was another man at the meeting with Thomas. Unfortunately, the bartender didn't have a good description of him, but he didn't recognize Pearson when I showed him a photo, and the hotel doesn't have any video footage."

"That's good, though. It ties Bobby to Thomas."

"Yes, but get this." Dayton ran his hand through his hair. "Benson, the guy who might've attacked you, was in charge of obtaining Thomas's bank statements, which is what led us to you to begin with. Once I combed through the statements myself, the numbers weren't adding up. Benson doctored them and did a shit job at it too. It took a minute, but the bank sent new copies directly to me as I was finishing up ice cream with Carli and her friend."

Rae leaned forward in her office chair. "Okay, so what do you need me to help with?"

"This is a lot to go through." He opened the folder that was about two inches thick. "I don't trust most people at my work right now. I need help going through every statement and highlighting anything that seems off or unusual. Any large amounts of funds deposited or withdrawn, any odd-sounding names."

Rae looked at the time; it was nearing eight. "All right. Let's do this."

He handed her a highlighter, and they got to work. It was grueling going through so many statements without a clear needle in the haystack, but she eventually found patterns in some of the transactions other than normal charges for gas, meals, and utility bills. They kept at it for two hours, Rae only pausing to say good night to Lily and grab a couple of beers.

Rae stared at her half of the stack. "Okay, so I saw recurring transfers into Thomas's account from someplace called Uroboros Inc., with regular transfers from his account two to three days after he'd receive the funds."

Dayton glanced at his own stack. "Same. Now's the fun part. We need to add up all those funds going in and out."

"Your idea of fun sucks."

He reached out and placed his hand on her thigh. "I know. Thank you for doing this."

"You owe me cunnilingus," she half joked.

He laughed. "It's a promise. Whatever you want."

What she wanted was to pin the bastards and protect Dayton and his family from being harmed. And she wanted Devon and the other missing woman to be found alive, but after Thomas and Cierra, her hope was fading.

They combined their stacks and went through them again, Dayton adding everything up with a growing smile like it was enjoyable for him. Rae always felt insecure about her math skills, one of the reasons why Angel handled their ledgers most of the time. She knew it probably stemmed from her lack of a formal high school education, and she made a vow to herself right then to finally listen to Angel and pursue an associate's degree in business management.

Dayton looked over the numbers, a big grin on his face. "They're almost the same amounts. Nearly a quarter million dollars in and out over the last six months."

"What does it mean, though?"

"My guess? Money laundering. The individual amounts are under what banks are required by law to report."

Rae fondled her empty beer bottle. "But where was all this money going to?"

"That's what I'm going to look into tomorrow. But for now . . ." He stood up and held out his hand to her, pulling her up from her chair. "I'd like to make good on my promise." He kissed her deeply, and she melted into his embrace.

She knew he was probably feeling the same high she was experiencing. They were on the cusp of taking the bastards down, and the thrill of it made her restless, needful. She pulled back from Dayton, wondering how far she could push him. He'd been so open before, allowing her to hurt him.

They went downstairs to her bedroom, and she moved to the corner of the room, pointing out one of her favorite pieces of furniture she rarely got to use.

"It looks like a low chaise lounge but curvier and more cushioned, right?" she said.

"Let me guess. It's for sex?"

"Good guess."

"The purple velvet gave it away."

"Come here."

Dayton cocked his head at her commanding tone as he moved over to her. "Oh, so is this what we're doing?"

"Only if you consent." She was already unbuttoning his shirt.

"I do . . . *Mistress.*"

Rae grinned, excitement whirring electric through her. She went to her closet and came back with a coil of black Shibari rope.

Dayton's eyes lit up. "You a mind reader?"

"It's my job."

She directed him to hold out his wrists after she had him remove his clothes, and when she had him bound, she made him recline back onto the chaise face up. Then she secured his tied hands above him to a hard point at the top of the chair, keeping his legs free on either side.

"Are you comfortable?" she asked him as she lightly ran her fingernails down his chest and over his abs, causing his breath to catch.

"Surprisingly so."

"Good."

"And . . . a little nervous."

"We'll take it slow. Just say 'red' if you want me to stop."

She undressed for him, savoring the sight of him getting aroused. Then she straddled the chair, Dayton's body underneath her. She kissed his lips, his chest, and along his collarbone, pinching his nipples as she did it, and he held in his reaction. Most people did at first, but that was part of the fun, easing someone into the pain and watching them relax into it before they gave themselves fully to her. After a few minutes of pinching, she felt his muscles loosen, and she knew he was ready for more. She stood up and pulled out a leather crop she had placed beside the chaise. When Dayton saw it in her hand, he tensed.

"I'll be gentle."

"I trust you."

She tapped his inner thighs lightly several times before giving him a stronger strike with the crop, and he finally cried out. She stopped and studied his breathing, waiting for him to relax again before she began tap-tapping ever so gently before popping him harder. She repeated the rhythm several times: tap-tap-tap pop, making the last hit increasingly harder. He was taking more than she expected for his first time, but she didn't want to push him too much too fast. She decided he deserved some edging as a distraction from the pain she had given him.

She knelt at the foot end of the chaise, running her nails over the tender pink marks she'd made on his thighs before taking him fully into her mouth. She heard him moan as she brought him close to climax only to stop. She started again, bringing him even closer before stopping again.

She did this several times before he called out, "Fuck—yellow—whatever pause is!"

Rae smiled at him. "Too much?"

Dayton's breathing was rapid, his eyes glazed with need. "I want to be inside you."

"You mean you want to come?"

"Yes," he groaned. "Please."

"Don't worry, I'll let you. Eventually. But ladies first."

She straddled him and positioned herself directly over his face.

"Bon appétit."

CHAPTER 59

RAE

2009

Placenta previa wasn't a term Rae had ever heard of before the ER doctor looked over her ultrasound results and explained it to her. He said her case was mild since her placenta was positioned near her cervix and not actually covering the opening where Lily would come out.

"It's not that uncommon in women under twenty," the doctor said. "Your placenta is a little over two centimeters away from your cervix right now. Normally, at your late stage in pregnancy, most OBs will go ahead and encourage a C-section to avoid the possibility of increased bleeding. We'll see what the OB says when they look you over."

Rae looked over at Ben, who had brought her to the hospital in Yukon. Marilyn fought to be the one to take her, but Katelyn started crying for her mom with all the commotion going on in the house. While Marilyn was distracted with Katelyn, Rae told Ben she wanted him to be the one with her and begged him to leave. So, he had.

The ER doctor left the triage room, and Ben pulled out his phone. "I'm going to step outside and call Mare to update her, but I'll be back soon."

Rae knew he was really going outside to smoke, but she wasn't upset with him for stepping away. She was too nervous to care what he was doing when she was facing the possibility of having Lily early.

A while later, the OB doctor came to her room.

"So, as you know, we do see placenta previa on your ultrasound, but I'm actually more concerned about your labs, which show strong signs of preeclampsia. I'm going to check your feet and hands, okay?" The doctor pulled back the blanket and gently pressed Rae's feet and then her hands. "See how you have edema—that's swelling. And your blood pressure is elevated. Have you been having any headaches or changes in your vision lately?"

"Um, yes. Sometimes." But she had thought it was caused from all the studying for the GED test.

"All right. At this point, I'm confident you can still have a normal vaginal delivery, but we'll need to induce you before your preeclampsia becomes a more serious issue."

She went over the process with Rae, how they'd use something called prostaglandins to thin her cervix and then give her a hormone called Pitocin to cause contractions and start labor.

"We'll be monitoring your baby's heart rate the entire time. And we'll have the operating room ready in case we need to get you moved for a C-section," the doctor said. "Do you have any questions?"

"No." Her mind was too scared to think of any.

The doctor touched Rae's shoulder and smiled. "It shouldn't be too long before we can get you moved, so hang tight."

It took another two hours to get Rae moved up to the labor-and-delivery unit. By the time it was evening, Ben still wasn't back, and she assumed he had gone home to rest or get something to eat and would come later on. The next day was a blur of discomfort at first and then hours of excruciating pain once they started the inducement process.

Ben never came back, and Rae realized she'd have no one familiar with her as she gave birth. So many things could go wrong. She could start hemorrhaging and die, and then what would happen to Lily? Would Ben and Marilyn take her, or would the hospital call Rae's mother? She didn't want either option. The horrible possibilities kept piling up in her mind until she broke into sobs.

A kind older nurse noticed Rae crying alone in the hospital room, and she parked herself by the bed with a cup of crushed ice for Rae and murmured soothing words. The nurse stayed by her side during the entire labor process. Just as Rae thought there was no way she would survive the pain, she felt a rush of fluids from her body, and the doctor placed Lily on her chest.

A nurse swooped in and took Lily to check her over and get her lungs cleared out. The first time Rae heard Lily's lusty cry was the most surreal, beautiful moment she'd ever experienced. All she could think of as she felt the weight of Lily's body against her chest and tried to get her baby to latch on to her breast was one of the words on the GED test: *kismet*. All the hell she'd been through leading to this moment of fate. Her Lily. Her rebirth.

At some point, she fell asleep with Lily in a hospital crib next to her bed. She woke up to the sounds of a woman cooing. As her eyes focused in the dim light of the hospital room, Rae saw Marilyn holding Lily, rocking her. Ben wasn't in the room. Rae reached for the red nurse's call button and pushed it.

"Put my baby down," Rae said, punctuating each word with loathing.

Marilyn looked over at Rae and smiled, but her eyes were like ice. She placed Lily back in the crib and came over to the side of Rae's bed. "I came to drop off your things." She motioned to the recliner in the room, which was covered in Rae's belongings—her luggage and a couple of garbage bags filled with items. Even the crib Viv had bought had been broken down and was leaning against a wall. "I know what you've been doing with Ben. Manipulating him, trying to seduce him into leaving me. It didn't work, and now you have nowhere to go, and no one to support you. I hope it was worth it."

It couldn't be true. Ben wouldn't do this to her. But then she looked at the heavy suitcases and the crib and knew Marilyn didn't bring them up to the room on her own.

An older nurse responded to the call button. "What do you need, sweetie?"

"I woke up and saw this woman holding my baby," Rae said. "She threatened to take her."

"I know her," Marilyn said to the nurse.

The nurse turned to Marilyn. "Ma'am, you need to come with me. I'm calling security to have you escorted out."

Before leaving with the nurse, Marilyn looked down at Lily. "I'm so sorry you have a sick pervert for a mother."

The two days following Lily's birth, Rae couldn't rest and recover. There was no time. Instead, she called the apartment complex about the available unit, only to find out they'd already rented it. She couldn't afford the deposit on any of the other available apartments she'd found online, so she started scouring Craigslist, which she knew was a gamble. So many creeps used the site.

She lucked out and found a listing for a garage apartment in an older neighborhood near the Plaza District. She called the number and left a message on the voice mail with her cell phone number.

If there was one piece of positive news, it was seeing the email confirming she had passed the GED test. She wanted to feel proud of her achievement, but the truth was she was too tired. She felt like she'd been on a journey, and every time she thought she was done, that she could finally live her life, something else happened, and she'd have to start over. All she really wanted to do was to rest.

Rae had finished breastfeeding Lily when she had a call on the hospital phone in her room. She answered it, sure it was some hospital administrator calling to tell her the crazy amount she would surely owe for the birthing costs.

"Rae?"

It was Ben, one of the last people she wanted to speak with.

"Please don't hang up," he said. "I . . . I need you to know it wasn't my idea to kick you out. Mare found the GED guide I got for you and saw the notes I'd made in it for you. I told her I was just helping you study, but she didn't believe me. She also found your dolls when she went through your things, thinking I was cheating on her, and I tried to explain to her what they were for, that it was for your work, and it only made things worse."

"You said you would help me, but you're just a coward. And now Lily and I have nowhere to go."

Ben was quiet on the line before he said, "You're right, I am. Mare threatened to use the emails I'd written to Scott—the ones she found during the affair—against me if I proceeded with a divorce and if I didn't help her move your things out of the house. You know how this state is. No court is going to give custody, even shared custody, to a queer man."

Rae hadn't thought about that possibility, but it didn't mean she forgave him. "I'm sorry she did that to you." She wasn't sure what else to say to him. "Well, you said what you wanted to say, and I understand why you did it, so . . ."

"Wait. Mare doesn't know about the funds I was going to get for you. I've been depositing small amounts into a secret account I've had for the last three years, in case I ever left her. I need your PayPal account, and I'll send it over."

"You don't have to do that."

"I want to do it."

As angry as she was with him, she couldn't afford to reject the money, so she gave him the information.

"I'm sorry, Rae. I wish I could do more."

He'd already done way more than her own mother ever had. "Thank you, Ben." She paused. "I hope you find a way to leave her."

She checked her PayPal account a while later and saw Ben had transferred over $1,800. Much more than she'd expected, but she knew it wouldn't cover the cost of the birth. Before she could worry about it too much, a short, heavyset woman entered the room. She held a folder in her hands and didn't look like a nurse.

"Hi, are you Rae Phalin?"

"Yes."

"My name is Cora, and I'm a patient advocate. I just need to go over some things about your stay with us before you're discharged tomorrow morning."

This was news to Rae. She had thought she and Lily would get to stay for at least another day.

"I see here you don't currently have insurance," Cora said. "Are you employed at present?"

"Um . . . no." She wasn't about to let this woman know about her live stream income, which wasn't taxed because she didn't report it.

"And have you applied for Medicaid?"

"I tried, but the Medicaid people said my household income was too much." Rae looked over at Lily sleeping in the crib. "That was when I was living with some people, but they kicked me out."

Cora glanced at the suitcases and the pieces of the crib that'd been broken down. "I see. So, you have no place to go?"

"I'm waiting to hear back on a place I called on. I have a little money, but not much." She'd keep the money in the PayPal account secret for now.

"Well, you might qualify for what's called retroactive Medicaid. I can help you with the process, and if you meet the requirements, your birth will be covered, and you can get on WIC, which will cover supplemental food costs and formula if you need it. You can even get a breast pump under Medicaid and might qualify for childcare assistance. And we can get you connected with the Catholic charity group about housing if you don't hear back on the place you're looking at."

Finally, something good. "That would be great. Thank you so much."

Cora took down some information and said she'd get the process started.

Later on, as Rae watched the sunset bathe the trees in gold outside her window, she got a call on her cell phone.

"Hi, is this Rae Phalin?" a perky voice asked.

"Yes."

"I'm Angel Paisley. You called about the garage apartment on Craigslist?"

Rae sat up in the hospital bed. "Oh, my God, yes. I'd love to rent it. I have cash and can move in tomorrow."

"Whoa, there! We haven't even met, and I'm not about to rent to some crazy lady."

"I promise I'm not," Rae said, sounding every bit the crazy person. "I . . . I really need a place to stay by tomorrow. I have nowhere to go for me and . . . and my baby."

"Oh, hell no. You have a kid? I posted for a young, single woman only. No kids. No pets."

"Please, I just gave birth, and I'm being discharged tomorrow. I'm nineteen, and . . . and I don't have anyone to help me." She hated crying on the phone with a stranger, but she couldn't hold back her emotions. "I'll be a good renter. And I don't do drugs, and I'm good at cleaning. I could even clean your place if you want. Please, just give me a chance."

"Shit." Angel let out a heavy sigh. "You know this is a garage apartment. A sublet. It's barely five hundred square feet."

"I don't care; I'll take it."

Angel went quiet, and Rae thought she'd hung up for a second. "I really hope I'm not making a big-ass mistake by renting to you."

"For real? You're going to rent it to me?"

"You're lucky I'm desperate. My college buddy decided to skip out with my girlfriend—sorry, *ex*-girlfriend—and I need to make rent. I can't afford to live on campus."

"Oh, thank you so much! You have no idea what this means."

"Please don't make me regret this," Angel said.

"You won't. I promise."

When they ended the call, Rae was floating. She went over to Lily and lifted her from her crib. She nuzzled her baby's head, breathing in her sweet, powdery newness.

Holding Lily felt like holding a dream made tangible. Like she had accomplished the most important thing she'd ever do in life, and it was exhilarating but also terrifying. She thought of her mother, of whether she'd felt the same way holding her after she was born, so full of love. A love that wasn't enough. She kissed Lily's head, and she couldn't imagine ever abandoning her.

She held Lily close and walked over to the huge window to enjoy the last of the November sunset, the gold-and-russet leaves mesmerizing.

"This is the beginning of good things for us," she whispered to her sleeping baby. "Just you wait."

CHAPTER 60

RAE

2024

Concentrating the next day was impossible, in part because Rae kept replaying the night before, when Dayton submitted to her, giving her the best orgasm she'd ever experienced. And from the intensity of Dayton's, she knew he'd be open to playing with her again. Flutters stirred in her chest when she thought about being in an actual relationship with him and getting to play out her fantasies with someone she cared about, not simply someone paying her.

In between clients, Rae checked her phone, wishing Dayton would call to update her on what he'd found out. She was nervous as hell for him. Even if he did discover where Thomas had been transferring the funds he received, she didn't know how the information would protect him or his family from the Coulters when he hadn't destroyed the rape evidence like they'd demanded.

It was close to three when he finally called her.

"Please tell me you have good news," she said.

"I don't know if I'd call it good, but it's news." Dayton paused a beat. "That company depositing funds to Thomas's account, Uroboros Inc., is one of Pearson's businesses. Supposedly an accounting firm, one with an offshore account. They transferred funds to Thomas, and then Thomas transferred the funds to an investment account run through the Coulters."

"So, you found the tie to them." Rae sank back into her office chair, the smallest bit of relief relaxing her body somewhat. "Do you think the funds from the Uroboros place were from the parties?"

"Yes. And I don't think Thomas was the only one cleaning the funds."

There was something that bothered her about what Dayton said. "Why isn't this good news?"

"It is, but . . ." Dayton went quiet. "I learned the real reason why Thomas was fired from Arkana Oil and Gas. He skimmed $4,800 from their accounts over the course of four months before he stopped, but they caught on. I looked over Thomas's bank account information again, and it looks like he also started skimming on the amounts he was transferring to the Coulters' account two months before he went missing. The amounts totaled $2,400. So, $7,200 total that he skimmed."

Rae didn't need Dayton to tell her what it meant. The total added up to six months' worth of weekly sessions with her at $300 a visit, the length of time she had him as a client. "They killed him because he was taking money from them to pay me?"

"We don't know that, Rae."

But she did.

"I believe he went to the party that night at the Coulters to beg his way back into their good graces," Dayton said. "He knew he fucked up, but I don't think he realized how deep he was in. After they knew he was fired from Arkana, they didn't have a safe way to launder the money through him, and Thomas was in heavy debt. A man without a job can't very well be transferring money to an investment account. He was no longer valuable to them, *and* he stole from them. Basically, he was screwed either way."

Rae's stomach twisted with the idea of Thomas taking such a risk for her services. He made good money. She knew that from her vetting, but she didn't check people's credit, only their criminal history. "What if Bobby and the other guy who was with him met with Thomas at the Skirvin to encourage him to go to the party that night and beg Pearson for forgiveness? Then they had him where they wanted him and killed him. Makes sense to me."

"I agree," Dayton said. "It seems the most plausible. And at this point, I'm almost positive the other guy was Benson."

"When are you taking this to your chief?"

"I'm meeting with him here in about ten minutes. I'll call you later and let you know how it goes."

They ended the call, and Rae was ready to go home. She had the strongest desire to see Lily and hold her. She'd been doing too much running around with the investigation and work, and she needed some mother-daughter time. She cleaned up the dungeon and front lobby and drove home, stopping by Starbucks to get Lily her favorite drink as a treat. When she got home, she expected to see Lily in the kitchen, grazing for snacks after school. She called out for her, but Lily didn't answer.

She texted her. No response, so she called Lily's cell phone, and it went to voice mail. She knew Lily never checked her voice mail, but she left a message anyway. "Hey, honey, I just got home. Where are you? You said you were getting a ride home with Ella. Call me. I got you a drink." She waited a few minutes and still no response. She called Ella's number. "Hi, Ella, it's Lily's mom. Is she with you? She said you were taking her home today."

"I dropped her off like twenty minutes ago."

"Okay, thank you. If you hear from her, please tell her to call me."

She called Klo next to see if Lily had gone to their place, but Klo hadn't seen her.

"Where the fuck are you?" Rae said under her breath, panic inching up her back. She called Lily's cell again and left another message. "Lily, call me right now. I'm worried."

She checked the Find My app and saw Lily's phone was close to their neighborhood. She hopped in her car and drove to the location where it pinged, but it was only a side road with overgrown grass choking a drainage ditch. Rae parked and searched the area, and her ears began ringing when she saw the sparkly purple case of Lily's phone. She picked it up, and the screen was cracked as if it had been thrown. It was password protected, and she didn't know Lily's code to open it.

She started hyperventilating, her head going cold when she imagined Lily hurt and crying out for her. *No.* She didn't have time for a panic attack. She got out her phone and called Dayton.

"They have her. Bobby and those fuckers." She barely got the words out through her rapid breathing. "They took Lily."

"Okay, Rae," he said. "I need you to take some deep breaths and tell me everything you know."

She did her best to explain it to him, but she knew her instincts were right. They took her.

"Have you checked your doorbell camera footage? If she was dropped off, the camera should've caught something."

Rae couldn't believe she hadn't thought of that. "I'm going to check it now." She paused to take another deep breath. "I didn't know who else to call." She felt herself breaking down. "I don't know who's involved at the police station, if there are other officers, so I didn't call 911. I don't understand. If Bobby wants revenge, why not come for me?"

"Just go back to the house. I'm heading there now."

When she got back to the house, she pulled up the doorbell camera footage. She didn't see anyone, including Lily, except for a mail carrier earlier in the day. The camera didn't show much beyond their front porch. Someone could've taken her before she made it to the pathway leading to the front door, and the camera wouldn't have caught it. Most people were still at work, and the younger kids who lived in the neighborhood hadn't been released from school yet. She didn't see anyone outside their homes. No witnesses.

She was a mess waiting for Dayton to arrive, her mind frantic with the possibilities. She couldn't stay still, but pacing her living room only made her dizzier from hyperventilation. She went to the kitchen and downed one of her emergency Xanax. Slowly, her panic attack subsided.

Dayton arrived, and she told him about the camera footage.

"I'm so sorry, Rae." He ran his hands over his face. "This has to be retribution for me going to the chief with the information we got and not following through with destroying the evidence. Maybe Benson caught wind of my meeting this afternoon, and he let Pearson and the Coulters know, but I was careful about keeping it all private. I don't get it, though. Why target you and not me? Carli and my mom are okay; I already checked. I sent them to stay at a hotel last night to be safe."

Rae didn't know if this was Bobby's way of paying her back for trying to kill him in Santa Monica, but he was about to find out how far she'd go to protect her child.

"I'm going to the mansion. I'm taking my gun, and I'm leaving now." She hated owning a gun, something she'd bought years ago just in case, but she was glad she had it now.

Dayton's eyes got wide. "No. You could be walking into a trap. Besides, we don't know if they're keeping her there."

"What the fuck am I supposed to do then, huh?" She felt like pulling her hair out. She didn't trust the police to do anything. They'd never come through for her in the past. "I can't wait around until she shows up dead."

Dayton's jaw tensed, and he seemed to be in thought for a few moments. "Okay . . . fuck." He sucked in a breath. "I'm going with you then."

"Are you sure? You know they could kill us, Dayton."

"I know," he said. "I'll let my chief know where we're going before we go inside the mansion. I trust him more than anyone else at my precinct, but doing this means I'll probably get fired. It doesn't matter now. He has everything he needs to formally charge Bobby Coulter and Pearson. If something happens to us or Lily, they'll know who's responsible and have no choice but to get off their asses."

"You don't have to do this."

Dayton wrapped his arms around her. "Yes, I do. I won't let them hurt you or Lily."

Rae's eyes hardened. "If they touch her in any way, they will hurt for me in ways they've never dreamed."

CHAPTER 61

RAE

2024

Dayton wanted to wait until it was darker before they drove over to the Coulters' mansion in his Subaru SUV, but Rae said she would leave without him if they didn't go earlier. Besides, she didn't want to walk through the woods surrounding the mansion in the dark, and they would have to enter the grounds from the back, hiking through about a half mile of heavy foliage to the garden and through the hedge maze. It was the only way they could try to stay undetected.

He parked his vehicle along a shoulder bordering the woods and turned to Rae. "You remember the plan?"

Rae nodded. Before they left, Dayton had found the old blueprints to the mansion online and pointed out the basement located at the southwest corner. They agreed the basement was the most likely place to start their search, in case Lily or Devon was being held there.

"There's no way to know where their cameras are located," he said. "We have to stay low and stick to the sides of the hedges and then run for it through the open garden area to where the basement is. I texted my chief our location and why we're here, but he hasn't responded, so I don't know what he's going to do, if anything." He sighed. "Are you ready?"

"Yes." Her Xanax from earlier was wearing off, and panic poked its fingers at her brain again, but she had to believe she'd find Lily. "Let's get these fuckers."

Dayton leaned over and kissed her hard on the lips. "We stick together at all times."

Walking through the thick woods as the sun descended was nowhere near as frightening as all the thoughts going through Rae's head. She couldn't stop thinking about what had happened to Cierra Martin, how she was raped, her body beaten before being tossed like trash. Rae barely registered the small brush and tree limbs scraping against her jeans as they carefully headed in the direction of the mansion.

Rae realized how nervous Dayton was by how much he was whisper-chatting as they walked. He kept talking about his family like he wasn't going to see them again and wanted the woods to hold on to his memories. He told her about his *pokni*, his grandmother who had passed away the year before, and how he used to cook with her and his mother when he was younger, making fry bread and *tanchi labona*, which he said was a traditional Choctaw dish made with hominy and pork. He talked about how hard it was to get the indigenous youth, including Carli, to learn about the traditions and carry them on.

"I was only twenty-three when Carli came to live with me," he said as they moved closer, toward the tall hedges of the garden. "I had no idea what I was doing, but at least I had my mom and my *pokni*. I don't know how you did it at nineteen on your own."

"It was hard, but Angel tried to help as much as she could after Lily was born." Rae recalled how much she'd looked forward to getting Lily down at night so she and Angel could relax and talk while sipping warm apple cider during the winter months when Lily was tiny. "She was a busy college student at the time, so I found my own place as soon as I could. And then I had the idea about the dominatrix business, and Angel had the brains to make it happen."

"You're lucky to have her as a friend," he said. "You know what she told me when we were all at the club?"

"No."

"'If you hurt her, I'll cut your cock off.' Then she handed me a dollar for the go-go dancer."

Rae grinned. "She's always had my back." And she hoped she would get to see her best friend—her sister—again and hug her.

Dayton took her hand and stopped walking as they saw the lights of the mansion above the tall garden hedges. He turned to her, and she pushed up on the balls of her feet to kiss him, hopeful this wasn't the last time she'd feel his lips on hers.

"Okay," he said. "We stay close to the edges and make our way that direction." He pointed toward the east side of the massive estate.

It started to feel real, the danger they were walking into. Goose bumps rose on her body, although it was warm out. They pressed themselves against the hedges, moving to the southeast corner of the mansion. It took forever since they had to constantly pause, listening for any signs of people. Finally, they came to the end of the hedges and faced the wide-open area of the garden, which was as beautiful as Rae remembered it. Beautiful, but terrifying since they'd have to cross it without being seen.

Dayton took her hand again and squeezed it. They looked around, making sure they were in the clear, and he gave the go ahead to run. Rae's lungs burned as she pounded across the manicured lawn to the side of the mansion, Lily's face in her mind. *I'm coming, honey.*

They made it to the other side, and Rae saw the entrance to the basement. It wasn't like the typical exterior basement entrance a normal home would have with a bulkhead and a metal latch. This door was thick metal with a dead bolt, definitely not original to the old mansion. She didn't know how they'd get inside.

Rae tugged on Dayton's arm, silently pointing to a high window nearby. It was the kind that could be pushed out to allow air in, and it was slightly ajar. He frowned at her. It was too tall for them to reach. She made a motion for him to lift her up onto his shoulders so she could get inside, but she could tell by his face he didn't like the option. She had to get in, though, and she could find a way to let him inside once she got her bearings. She made the motion again, and Dayton shook his head, but then he held out his hands to lift her up.

Once she got onto his shoulders, she listened for any sounds coming from the window and heard nothing. It was difficult to keep her balance while trying to yank the window open enough to let her through, but she managed. She had a better look now and saw the window opened to a storage room of some sort. If she were careful, she could lower herself onto what looked like cases of canned goods.

She gave Dayton the go ahead to push her up more, and he struggled to keep a hold of her feet as she shimmied her way through the tight space. As she turned her body to get through, her handgun fell from the back of her jeans to the ground outside.

She heard Dayton grunt below. She stopped herself from cussing and kept inching herself inside because it was too late for her to get back down for her gun. She'd have to get it from Dayton once she found a way to let him in. She tore her T-shirt as she slid through the other side, but she made it.

Rae scanned the storage room and saw two doors, one larger and another smaller and narrower with a padlock. Something told her to go to the smaller one, which was wooden and appeared as old as the estate. She pressed her ear to the door and heard hushed mutters. The voices sounded feminine, and Rae's blood rushed to her head.

"Lily? Are you in there?" Rae whispered, but the murmurs stopped.

She had to get inside, and she searched the space for anything she could use to break the lock. There was nothing but the stored food. She took a large can of tomato sauce and slammed it against the padlock. Panicked sounds came from the other side of the door.

"Stop it, Rae!" a voice hissed. "She's not in here, and they'll hear you."

"Devon?" She was so happy to hear her friend's voice she wanted to cry. "I'm going to get you out of here, but I have to find Lily first. Do you know where they took her?"

"I don't, but I heard they were having a special party tonight when they took her from here earlier." She heard someone crying. "There are three other women in here with me. Please, get us out. One woman's badly injured, and she's been unconscious for a while."

"I will."

Rae texted Dayton's phone to say what she'd found, but the service was crap, and the message failed. She re-sent it and hoped it would get through. She had to find a way to get him inside, which meant going through the other door and facing the unknown.

She cracked the door and saw it opened to a long hallway stretching on either side. She thought about where she was in relation to where the party had been held when she was there before, and she went right. She found a marble staircase at the end of the hall and listened for any footsteps before climbing them to the next floor. She tried to remember which floor the party had been on, but she wasn't sure, so she decided to keep moving, staying close to the wall as she searched for some kind of exit she could use to let Dayton inside. But she didn't find one, so she went back in the other direction. Nothing. Her anxiety began to cloud her thoughts as her breathing increased. She was lost, and she didn't know which way to go.

She checked her phone, and her text message showed as failed again. She'd have to do this alone and hope Dayton would find a way inside. *Okay, you got this,* she chanted to herself. She moved away from the wall and went deeper into the mansion until she came to a huge library with floor-to-ceiling windows, the lights from the garden twinkling outside.

She now knew she was on the right floor because she remembered seeing the edge of the garden from the ballroom area where the party had been held.

She steeled herself and forced her feet to move, to carry her to the great hall, where she hoped to hell she'd find Lily.

"Where you running off to, Echo?"

Rae's heart stopped at hearing that familiar voice coming from behind her, her old name out of a phantom's mouth. Shaking so much she could barely move, she slowly turned around, and every drop of blood seemed to drain from her body.

Clint stood up from a leather club chair in a shadowy corner of the library, his dark hair longer and pulled back into a low ponytail, the pure, evil joy in his eyes holding her hostage. She saw the skin on his right arm was red and shiny, like cherry taffy tossed on the ground and left to melt under the blistering sun.

He grinned. "You got here just in time. We're about to have a lot of fun."

CHAPTER 62

RAE

2024

Rae couldn't process what was happening. There was no way Clint was alive and well, standing only feet from her. He was supposed to be dead, burned to a crisp fifteen years ago. This couldn't be real, but the cold sweat running down her back said otherwise.

"How?" The word caught in her throat, choking her.

"Bet you feel like you're seeing a ghost, huh?" Clint said with a sneer. "Here's the thing, Echo. If you really want someone dead, you don't shoot them in the shoulder. Might've helped if you tossed a little of that gasoline on me too. Lucky me, Bobby coughed himself awake in time to save my ass. And here we are. Reunited at last."

Her mind raced, replaying what Bobby had told her and the news articles she'd read about the fire. There were two unidentified bodies in the house. Maria's and . . . "Who—who was the other person? The body the police found at the Santa Monica house." The one Bobby made her believe was Clint.

The corner of Clint's mouth quirked. "Can't you guess?"

She searched her memories. The putrid, sweet smell in Clint's bedroom as she had searched for his stash of money, the scent she thought was rotting food. Maria had only been dead for a day. But Beth . . . "No."

"That day we had to move her from the shed to the house before the neighbors could complain about the smell. Pearson didn't want us burying her in the yard, so we had to improvise until we could get rid of her another way. But that was your fault, wasn't it, Echo? And you let her little body burn when she could've been buried."

Rae's insides felt like a hundred eels slithering, making her want to double over. She had burned any evidence of what had truly happened to Beth and Maria, and there was nothing she could do to change that.

He stepped forward, and she instinctively moved back from him.

The old her wanted to shrink into her skin, to protect herself however she could. But she wasn't that timid, broken girl anymore. He wouldn't get into her head by blaming her for Beth's death. Her hands balled into fists. "Where the fuck is my daughter?"

Clint flashed his shark teeth. "Lily. She's a pretty thing, like you."

Hearing Clint say Lily's name, seeing his salacious smile as he called her a pretty thing, nearly paralyzed her again, but she forced herself to refocus. She had to get to her daughter.

"Where is she?" she repeated.

"You were always pretty, Echo. You might've been shy and dumb as hell, but you made up for it in looks."

Rae saw slight movement behind where Clint stood. It was Dayton, his head badly bleeding as he looked unsteady on his feet. He had his gun in one hand, his other raised and pressing a finger to his lips. She pretended she didn't see him and stared Clint down.

"It always did make you feel like a big man to put women down," she said, her eyes keeping watch on Clint's hands, which were twitching at his sides. "And yet here you are still playing lapdog to men more powerful than you'll ever be. Just doing what you're told, right? Like when you and Bobby met Thomas Highsmith at the Skirvin and convinced him to walk into a trap. That was you, wasn't it?"

He smirked but not before his eyes widened, giving him away.

"So dumb I'm right, aren't I?"

"I would love to kill you right now so I don't have to listen to your stupid fucking mouth anymore, but that would ruin the surprise, and I've waited too long for this not to enjoy every second."

"What surprise? That it took you and Bobby this long to find me?"

The humor left Clint's face. "We always knew where you were, Echo. If it had been our call, you would've been hunted down a long time ago like the sad, pathetic animal you are. But then you and that detective started sniffing around where you didn't belong, and all bets were off."

She believed him. For over fifteen years, she couldn't explain why she never felt safe, even when she was positive Clint and Bobby were dead, and this was why.

"Why wasn't it your call, Clint? Why didn't you and Bobby come after me if you knew where I was this whole time?"

He grinned. "It doesn't matter. I have you now, and you'll finally get to know what real pain feels like."

Rae saw his muscles tense, the angry, scarred skin of his right arm stretching, reaching for his gun. He was about to make a move. She saw Dayton at the other end of the library, his gun aimed at Clint.

"Get down, Rae!"

She threw herself to the ground and heard several gunshots. Then everything went quiet until she heard a pained grunt and ragged breathing. *Please,* she prayed, *let it be Clint.* She lifted her head enough to see Dayton on the marble floor, blood starting to pool beneath him as his eyes rolled back in his head. "No!"

Clint came over to her, his left shoulder bleeding. He looked down at her, the butt of his gun raised to strike. "Like I said, don't aim for the shoulder."

Lights flashed behind her eyes, and she felt a split second of intense pain, and then nothing.

When Rae opened her eyes, her head was heavy like a blood-engorged tick about to burst. She was sitting in a chair, her hands tied behind her back. She raised her head a little and saw about a dozen people, most she didn't recognize. She was in the great hall, Pearson and Bobby standing in front of her, Clint off to the side, his left shoulder bandaged. She didn't know how long she'd been out.

She heard whimpering. It hurt to move her head too much, but she turned to her left, and her heart felt like shattering when she saw Lily gagged and tied to a chair next to her, tears running down her cheeks.

"It's okay, honey, I'm here." Rae tried to keep her voice calm, but it wasn't possible.

"Hello again, Mistress V," Pearson said, his perfectly tailored suit as immaculate as his snow-white hair. "I must say I'm sad to see you in this position. Poor Thomas told me how skilled you are before we unfortunately had to end our partnership with him. He did try, however, to pay off his debt by bringing you into our fold. And, honestly, I was inclined to let you go. I admire your resilience. You remind me a lot of myself, how you reinvented your life after your time in Santa Monica." He walked over to her, his eyes examining her with sadness like she was a disappointment. "I forgave you for the mess you made of my investments there, much to the dismay of Bobby and Clint, but I don't forgive twice. Business is business, and I don't appreciate your interfering with mine. I think it's time for retribution. You got your revenge back then, and now we deserve ours. Don't you agree?"

"Fuck you!"

Pearson's impassive expression made her want to claw his eyes out. "The other unfortunate business involves a certain detective I'm sure you're familiar with. He helped us with a matter and then got . . ." He waved his hand. "Distracted. I had hoped to maybe use him again, to let him *reinvent* himself, but it's not possible."

Dayton. Rae's chest tightened so much she couldn't breathe for a second. She didn't even get to hold him, and she didn't know where they'd taken him or if he was already dead. Then Pearson's words fully hit her. They thought Dayton had destroyed the rape-kit evidence. Maybe they didn't know about Dayton's meeting with the police chief that afternoon after all. Or if they did, they weren't giving anything away to her. She felt the rope binding her hands. It was silky like Shibari rope, but she could tell whoever had tied her didn't do a good job, and she started stretching her wrists out, over and over, thankful no one was standing behind her to see.

"I guess the fortunate thing is he's still alive to watch the consequences of trying to help you and your daughter."

Before Rae had a chance to feel any joy in knowing Dayton was alive, everyone in the room turned to see his semilimp body being dragged by two hulking men, his hands bound in front of him. She immediately recognized one of the men as the one who had attacked her in her dungeon. He had to be Benson.

Dayton had a gunshot wound to his right thigh and a head wound bleeding down the left side of his face. The men slammed him into a chair and held him there by his shoulders. Dayton's eyes fluttered open long enough to lock on to Rae, and she saw an apology lodged in his expression.

"He got a nasty head injury killing one of my best men outside in the garden, but I must say Clint did a number on our *brave* detective," Pearson said. "So, now he gets to bleed out watching us play with you and your lovely daughter." He moved over to Lily and knelt on the floor in front of her. He caressed her cheek, a sickening paternal look spreading across his face. "You get to go first, my dear."

"Don't you fucking touch her!" Rae screamed, her insides burning with the desire to cut off Pearson's hands so he could never touch Lily again.

Pearson snapped his fingers, and a large man with a gut untied Lily from the chair and yanked her up, Rae yelling the whole time as she fought to loosen her bindings. She heard Dayton's voice yelling too.

"Remove her clothes and get her on the cross," Pearson said, and the large man fought to pull off Lily's T-shirt as she thrashed in his arms. He was sweating with the effort, but he got her shirt off, exposing her sports bra, before hauling her over to a large Saint Andrew's cross. Pearson turned to Clint and pointed to a table full of various implements—paddles, canes, whips. "You have the first go. Do whatever you like. Beat her, fuck her. I don't care."

"Don't do it, Clint!" But he moved over to Lily, who was kicking the large man as he attempted to get her jeans off. Rae didn't want to do it, but she had no choice. She closed her eyes tight and let out an animal howl. "She's your fucking child!" She cried with the words. "She's yours, you bastard!"

Clint froze and stared at Lily, and she saw his uncertainty.

"It's true, Clint. For God's sake, she has your fucking eyes!"

Lily had stopped fighting the large man and was looking at Clint, at this man partially responsible for her existence. Rae saw the shock on her daughter's face, and her chest felt like it was caving in. She couldn't make herself look at Dayton to see his reaction.

"I'm so sorry, honey. I should've told you. Please, Lily, please look at me." But Lily continued to stare wide eyed at Clint, her mouth open in horror.

"You are just full of delightful surprises, Mistress V," Pearson cooed, his eyes lit up like blue flames. "Go ahead, Clint."

Clint didn't move. Rae saw the recognition on his face. He knew she was telling the truth, but she didn't trust what he'd do with it.

She almost had her hands free from the bindings as Pearson turned to Bobby. "Maybe we made a mistake in giving your friend a second chance. Perhaps he needs to go back to the streets, selling pills to high school kids and stay-at-home moms. He doesn't have the stomach for the revenge he's begged for all these years, the thing I'm being generous enough to give you both when I could have saved all the fun for myself." He motioned to the small audience. "Such ungratefulness when our esteemed guests are patiently waiting."

Clint's face was pale and sweaty as he looked at Lily's crying face. Rae kept her eyes on him while she got one hand free from the ropes, then the other. He turned toward Pearson and Bobby, acquiescence in his eyes, and she knew he was going to do it. He was going to hurt Lily. She jumped up from the chair and snatched a long whip from the implement table, quickly pulling her arm back and striking Clint's face right on his eyes. He screamed, clutching his face as blood poured down his cheeks.

The large man let go of Lily's arms and came at Rae. She positioned the whip again and struck him above his eyes, and red streaked his forehead, giving her the opportunity to aim lower. It didn't stop him, and she grabbed a large metal-studded wooden paddle from the table. She threw all her weight into her arm as she slammed it against the side of the man's head with a sickening crunch. He went down hard, blood dripping from the paddle in her hands.

Her breath came fast and harsh, her body and mind seeing nothing but red. She wanted to destroy them all. She glanced over at Clint and saw him pressing his T-shirt to his eyes, the white cotton soaked through with red. When she turned to face Bobby and Pearson, whatever Bobby saw in her eyes made him turn and run. A few members of the small audience started to leave the great hall as well. Pearson's once impassive expression was now angry, his lips curled back in a snarl.

"Come on, Pearson, I thought you saw yourself in me," she taunted him. "Too much of a chickenshit to get your hands dirty?"

He motioned to the two men holding Dayton down. "Take care of her."

As soon as the men started coming for Rae, Dayton threw his bound arms around one man's neck, using whatever strength he had left to choke him. Benson, the other man, didn't turn around and kept coming for Rae.

She held the studded paddle up, ready to strike, but her adrenaline was waning, the paddle feeling heavier in her hands. When she barely made contact with Benson, she didn't pull back fast enough, and he latched on to the other end of the paddle. She was in a tug-of-war with him and was losing. Her head was pounding from when Clint hit her, making her dizzy, but she fought to keep a hold of the paddle. She had to. But Benson was stronger, and he won.

He backhanded her, and she fell to the ground.

Benson touched the side of his face where she'd grazed him. He saw the blood on his fingers and glared down at her. "You fucking cunt!"

He readied his thick arm to swing the paddle at her head. She shielded herself as she tried to crawl backward from him, but no hit came. A loud thud echoed in the large room, followed by an even louder thud as Benson fell next to Rae, his body completely still. She looked up and saw Lily holding a long, thick wooden paddle, her eyes wild and red from crying.

"Mom!"

"I'm okay, honey. You did so good." Rae forced herself to stand up and gave Lily a quick, tight hug before facing Pearson again. She saw that Dayton had taken down the other man, but he didn't look good. His normal olive complexion was gray, and he was leaning against one of the intricately carved wooden pillars in the room.

"You're out of men, Pearson." She tried to grin, but her face hurt too much. "And I hear sirens."

Everyone noticed the blaring sirens then, and the few audience members left were already scattering. Pearson shot her one hard look before trying to hightail it from the hall as well, but there was no way in hell she was letting him escape like a cockroach under bright lights.

Just as she seized the long whip from the floor, the end of it covered in blood, she looked up to see Dayton throwing himself at Pearson, slamming him to the ground. Dayton pulled back his bound arms and punched Pearson's face, instantly breaking the man's nose with the force. When he punched him again, Pearson was already unconscious, but Dayton kept punching him until he collapsed across the older man's body.

Rae took Lily's hand, and they rushed over to Dayton, who had rolled off Pearson and was nearly unconscious on the floor.

"Dayton?" She touched his skin, which was cold and clammy. "Try to stay awake, okay?"

He was trying to tell her something, but his words were dribbling out in incoherent gibberish as he fell in and out of consciousness.

"Don't talk. Help is coming." She put pressure on his thigh wound and directed Lily to untie his bindings.

Dayton's police chief must've come through because officers and paramedics were now swarming the great hall.

"Over here! Please hurry!" she called to them. "And there are people locked in the basement—one is badly injured!"

She looked back at Dayton, at his shallow breathing and the blood soaked through his pants, and she knew he didn't have long. She pressed down on his leg wound harder, trying to stanch the bleeding.

"Just hang on, okay, Dayton? Please. Hang on for Carli." She couldn't lose him now, not after everything. "Hang on for me."

CHAPTER 63

RAE

2024—Two Months Later

When you want something bad enough, you need to pay the consequence.
Rae didn't want to hear her mother's words as she thought over the last
two months—the rush to the hospital, the blood on her hands and
clothes. Dayton's blood. All the fear of possibly losing everything. She
wanted to be in this moment, surrounded by people she cared about,
people who had been worth any consequence to save.

The July evening was hot, but it didn't prevent people from coming
to the Paseo District's First Friday Art Walk event. Rae watched Lily
and Klo strolling ahead of her and Angel on the sidewalk, their musical
laughter mingling with the sounds of the various street musicians playing at every corner of the historic stretch of over twenty art galleries.

Even with the excitement buzzing around her and the Oklahoma
sunset flaunting its dazzling hues, it wasn't easy for Rae to forget how
close her daughter had come to dying only several weeks before. She
tried not to relive that night and the unbearable pain of watching
Dayton slipping away from her.

She didn't like to think about what might've happened if Dayton hadn't called his police chief for backup after he'd killed the man who attacked him outside the Coulters' mansion. The truth was Pearson and Bobby probably had more men they could've called on to help them if it weren't for the arrival of the police. Instead, they were now sitting in jail, awaiting trial, along with many others being indicted every day as the police gathered more and more evidence of the money laundering and sex trafficking. There were dozens involved, and she hoped each one would rot in prison.

And Clint, he would rot too. Only, his right-eye blindness would make his confinement feel that much smaller. Anytime Rae thought she might feel a tiny bit of remorse for permanently blinding his eye, she thought about Beth or Maria . . . or her younger self—all the people he had destroyed.

Although they came through in the end, Rae still blamed the police for allowing Cierra Martin and Thomas Highsmith to die and for the countless other women who were still missing. She was thankful the other missing submissive, Ashley Jennings, survived, although she had been badly beaten and had suffered multiple sexual assaults. Devon was recovering from her abuse too. She'd told Rae she was getting out of dominatrix work as soon as she finished her master's degree to become a therapist, and Rae didn't blame her. Once the media frenzy cooled down, Rae planned to apply to a couple of schools so she could get her associate's degree. Maybe someday she'd be like Devon and try a different path. But her business with Angel was doing surprisingly well after everything. And she truly loved her work, even more so after almost losing it.

For now, she wanted to focus on making sure Lily was okay. Thankfully, Lily hadn't been assaulted while she was being held at the mansion, but she had witnessed a lot in the short time. They had started family counseling, and so far, it was helping. They were learning how to talk about it and process it all.

There was no easy way to talk about Clint, though, and what he could've done to Lily. Many nights, Lily would climb into bed with Rae, like she used to do when she was little after having a nightmare. During those times, all Rae could do was hold her baby girl and let her know she was safe.

They both had a lot of healing to do to be whole again. Rae was trying to process her abandonment issues through her work with the therapist, but she had no intentions of reaching out to her mother. Maybe someday she would, if only to have resolution. She already had the family she wanted and needed in her life, and she wasn't about to open herself to more pain and loss.

She held her silver watch up to her ear and listened for the soft, persistent ticking. *I miss you. Every day.*

Angel noticed and took her hand. "You okay, Rae-Rae?"

She nodded and squeezed Angel's hand.

"There they are, Mom!" Lily said, pointing down the sidewalk toward Planet Dorshak, Rae's favorite gallery.

Rae smiled, her heart lifting to see Dayton with Carli waiting to join them. The gunshot wound to his thigh was still healing, so he had a slight limp as he made his way over to her, his daughter close behind. Even though Carli was technically his first cousin once removed, Rae saw a lot of Dayton in her. Her skin was a darker shade, but she had his height, and her long dark hair had the same wave to it. And Carli was as beautiful as the photo of her mother, Tula, which Dayton had shown Rae.

They both knew it could be a long shot to pin Pearson to Tula's murder, and it was something Dayton was struggling to accept. But there was hope. Some of the sex worker witnesses interviewed when his cousin was murdered were still alive, and Rae was helping him track them down to see if they could confirm Pearson as the man who'd picked up Tula.

She met Dayton halfway on the sidewalk, and he embraced her and gave Lily a side hug. He looked a bit nervous as he introduced Carli to Rae and then to Lily, Angel, and Klo. She knew this was a big step for him, for them both.

"Is it okay if I hug you?" Rae asked Carli.

Carli smiled. "Sure."

Rae held her and whispered in her ear, "You know your dad is a hero."

Carli pulled back from her, a shy grin on her face. "He said the same thing about you."

"Can Carli come with us to watch Sam play?" Lily asked Dayton and turned to Carli. "Sam Kahre is an amazing cellist."

"Sure, of course."

Carli didn't waste any time and ran the opposite way with Lily and Klo to see the young, attractive musician.

Angel touched Rae's arm. "I'm going to go visit with my friend at Literati, okay?" She looked over at Dayton. "We're going to have to get you a cool cane to go with that pimp walk you've got going on."

"I know, right?" Dayton said at Angel's joke. He had worked hard to get off crutches and was too stubborn to use a cane.

Dayton turned to Rae, a smile playing in his dark eyes. "I think this is going well. Carli said I was being stupid for being nervous about it. As usual, she was right."

Rae cocked her head. "Is it going well enough that you've changed your mind about me doing sounding on you once you're all healed?"

He laughed. "Sounding is still a big hell no times infinity. Metal rods shouldn't be anywhere near cocks, much less inside them. Have you really done that to someone?"

"Not a client, but yes. I did a lot of training for it with a Domme from LA who was a former nurse, but I've never been with someone brave enough to try it."

"Well, I'm fine with not being brave."

"Okay, so no sounding. Flogging?"

"We'll see."

She playfully tugged his arm. "It's like a massage. I promise."

"In that case . . ."

They kissed, gently at first and then deeper, and she felt it through every part of her body, the need to be near him after she came so close to losing him. Whatever this was they were becoming, she welcomed it. He knew every hidden part of her now, just as Lily and Angel did. He was becoming her family.

She was ready to be with an open partner who knew all her secrets and still loved her and accepted the damaged, dark parts. She trusted him with her heart as he trusted her with his. It was all so new to her, but she was ready to shed her old skin and the shame and fear secreted away inside it.

She was ready to live with a new version of herself.

ACKNOWLEDGMENTS

It's impossible to fully express how much it means to have the support of readers. You are the reason why I write in between working a day job and caring for kids and a household. You are the reason why I strive to always be better at shaping stories that matter to me and, I hope, to you. Writing about BDSM is obviously nothing new, but my wish is to normalize kink and consensual sex work. Seeing the constant attacks on women's bodily autonomy and sexuality pushed me to write this book and give a voice to a strong woman who had been through fire and came out a phoenix. In many ways, we're all going through fire, but we can fight our way through and be stronger for it, together. Thank you for reading Rae's story and keeping an open mind.

Huge thanks to my wonderful agent, Sandy Lu. During most of the pandemic, I struggled to find motivation to do anything beyond getting through each day. I know many of us felt this way, and having Sandy's patient support as I found joy in writing again got me through the storm.

An immense thank-you to my developmental editor, Charlotte Herscher, for truly understanding Rae's story and what I was trying to accomplish. She pressed me to dig deeper, and Rae's story is so much better for it. Thank you to Alison Dasho, my acquiring editor at Montlake, for giving me the opportunity to share Rae's story with the world. I'm so thankful for her and everyone at Amazon Publishing for helping to make this book become a reality. You all are fantastic!

Thank you to my beautiful writer friends, who are too numerous to mention all here, so I apologize. My writing brothers, S. A. Cosby and Mer Whinery, thank you for always believing in me and making me feel like I can really reach for the stars. Some others who kept me sane through the process: Layne Fargo, Halley Sutton, Suzanne Miller, Cina Pelayo, Amina Akhtar, Paulette Kennedy, Samantha Bailey, and James Queally. I would not be the writer I am without the feedback, support, humor, and love from my fellow writers. A special thank-you to the writers who took the time to blurb this book—I can't say how much I appreciate and admire you all.

This book is dedicated to the kink community and to my favorite kinkster, writer extraordinaire Christa Faust, who read the first (horrible) draft of this book and gave me a much-needed writerly flogging. As someone who worked as a professional dominatrix, Christa forced me to get into Rae's head and her dominant sexuality, something that was foreign to my own masochism. And, boy, did I enjoy inhabiting Rae's head!

There are many others within the kink community who helped shape this book, namely those who can't be publicly named due to prejudice that still surrounds BDSM. However, I can and would like to thank Mistress Montana and her attorney, Gary Krupkin, who answered all my legal questions surrounding sex work as it pertains to my state of Oklahoma.

To my gorgeous babies, thank you for being so patient with me as I juggled writing and being a mom. I'm so proud of you both and of your kindness, intelligence, humor, and talent. And to my daughter, who's now on the verge of becoming an adult as I write this, I know you may never read this book, but if you do, you'll know I wrote Lily for you.

Last but never least, thank you to Kyle, my Bambi. You are my biggest support and most brutal first editor. To say I love you is never adequate, so I'll say that being with you is like being in perpetual subspace.

ABOUT THE AUTHOR

Photo © 2021 David Bricquet

Heather Levy is a born and bred Oklahoman and graduate of Oklahoma City University's Red Earth MFA program for creative writing. Her work has appeared in numerous journals and publications, including *CrimeReads* and *NAILED Magazine*. The *New York Times* called her Anthony-nominated debut, *Walking through Needles*, "a spellbinding novel at the nexus of power, desire, and abuse that portends a bright future," and the *Los Angeles Times* called it "a standout for its frank but sensitive exploration of trauma and desire." Levy lives in Oklahoma with her husband, two kids, and three murderous cats. Readers can follow her on Twitter and IG @heatherllevy.